MORE PRAISE FOR DEBRA DIER!

DEVIL'S HONOR
"Debra Dier will keep you turning the pages in this entertaining, fast-paced tale. . . . It both charms and delights with a little mystery, passion and even a bit of humor."

—*Romantic Times*

LORD SAVAGE
"Exhilarating and fascinating!"

—*Affaire de Coeur*

MACLAREN'S BRIDE
"The talented Ms. Dier captures the English/Scottish animosity to perfection and weaves an exhilarating tale that will touch your heart and fire the emotions. Great reading!"

—*Rendezvous*

DECEPTIONS & DREAMS
"An exciting and action-packed adventure. . . . Once again, Debra Dier proves that she is a sparkling jewel in the romantic adventure world of books."

—*Affaire de Coeur*

"*Deceptions & Dreams* is tightly plotted with plenty of well-developed characters. . . . Ms. Dier's writing is skillful and sure, painting with words a story filled with passion, adventure, and emotion."

—*Rendezvous*

A QUEST OF DREAMS
"Captivating from beginning to end . . . a stunningly beautiful and evocative love story brimming with action, adventure, and a touch of fantasy. Steamy and lush as the Amazon jungle, *A Quest of Dreams* will grab your heart and won't let go."

—Kathleen Morgan, author of *Firestar*

"A steamy romantic romp with just the right touch of fantasy. A treat for Debra Dier fans!"

—*New York Times* bestselling author Bobbi Smith

THE WAYS OF A SCOUNDREL

"I am not frightened of you."

"You should be frightened, Miss Wakefield. You need to realize just how reckless you have been. If you were facing a true scoundrel, he would not content himself with a mere kiss. Imagine what he would do." He unfastened the top button of her nightgown, slowly sliding the small pearl nub through the soft white cotton, allowing her to imagine what would follow. The second button fell beneath his deft fingers, while he held her in a steady gaze. He parted the cloth, revealing the hollow of her neck, the skin beneath. "A scoundrel would not stop, Miss Wakefield."

She lay beneath him, trembling with more than fear. Potent anticipation gripped her. She had never realized how intoxicating the complete obliteration of choice could be.

"A scoundrel would take you, Miss Wakefield."

Other books by Debra Dier:
MACKENZIE'S MAGIC
BEYOND FOREVER
SAINT'S TEMPTATION
DEVIL'S HONOR
LORD SAVAGE
MACLAREN'S BRIDE
SCOUNDREL
THE SORCERER'S LADY
DECEPTIONS & DREAMS
A QUEST OF DREAMS
SHADOW OF THE STORM
SURRENDER THE DREAM

Dangerous

DEBRA DIER

LEISURE BOOKS NEW YORK CITY

A LEISURE BOOK®

August 2002

Published by

Dorchester Publishing Co., Inc.
276 Fifth Avenue
New York, NY 10001

ISBN 0-8439-5038-2

Visit us on the web at www.dorchesterpub.com.

For Diane,
who has proven that a friendship forged by two teenage
girls can last through all the myriad changes that touch
a life. We share a friendship that has spanned distance
and time, flourishing today as warmly as it did so
many years ago. A friendship I treasure.

Dangerous

Chapter One

Charlotte awoke with a start. She sat bolt upright in bed, heart pounding, breath frozen in her throat. Icy foreboding crept over her skin, as though she had come too close to something wicked. What was it? What had awakened her? A sound perhaps. A creak of the floorboards. A whisper of something not quite right.

She had been dreaming of the Marquess of Andover's ball. Although it was not until next week, she could not contain her excitement about attending. She still could not quite believe she was truly in London, attending all the glittering parties of the Season. It was even more difficult to believe she was actually a success. At one time, she had thought she would never have a London Season, but Emma had made certain she would have her debut, her chance to make a dream come true. It was like a fairy tale, and she the

1

poor country mouse who had been turned into a princess at the touch of a fairy's wand.

She rubbed her arms, trying to chase away the chill. What had penetrated her dreams? Moonlight poured through the windows of her bedchamber, casting silvery squares across the flowers and wreaths in the carpet. She was not alone in the house. Her mother was sleeping across the hall. Her two sisters and her cousin Emma were nearby. The servants slept two floors below. Although it was London, the house was secure, she assured herself. There was no reason to feel such panic, such unrelenting fear. Yet she could not dismiss the prickling sensation moving along her spine.

A floorboard creaked. Charlotte jumped at the soft groan of wood. She turned toward the sound just as a figure emerged from the shadows near the bed. Her panic-stricken mind had time to register the shape of a man in a black greatcoat before he lunged at her. Her scream was cut off by the hand he slammed against her mouth. He pushed her back into the soft eiderdown mattress. A spicy scent of strong cologne stabbed her senses.

"Be a good girl, or I shall have to hurt you."

His harsh whisper ripped through her. Charlotte struggled in his grasp, panic squeezing her with each quick beat of her pulse. She clawed at him, her fingers digging into the black scarf tied across the lower half of his face. Moonlight slanted across his countenance, revealing the features of a man she knew. A man who could not possibly be here attacking her in this fashion. Yet reality stared at her from a pair of familiar eyes.

"I had no idea you would be such a little hellcat," he said, his soft voice filled with a terrifying measure of amusement. It was a cultured voice, a voice that often entertained ladies in the best drawing rooms and ballrooms of London. The voice of a man confident in his power over her.

She bucked beneath him, trying to free herself. He lifted his hand from her mouth. She sucked in air for her scream, but the cloth he shoved into her mouth gagged the sound. "Do try to be still. I would not wish to harm your mother should you happen to awaken her."

Charlotte froze at the thought of her mother entering the room and discovering this monster. He flipped her to her stomach and pushed her down into the mattress. A sharp pain lanced along her nerves as he slammed her wrists together.

Fear clawed at her vitals, a living thing, as tangible as the pillow pressed against her face. The scent of linen dried in the sunlight and stored with lavender seemed suffocating as she attempted to draw air into her lungs. Blood pounding in her temples, she struggled like a wild bird captured in a hunter's net.

After he bound her feet together, he fixed the gag in her mouth with a scarf. He grabbed her shoulder and rolled her to her back. She caught a glimpse of his smile before he dragged her off the bed and slung her over his shoulder. Her braid bobbed in and out of her line of vision as he carried her from the room. One question pounded through the fear clouding her brain: What did he mean to do with her?

"I certainly understand why Andover murdered her."

The words cut through the low din of music and conversation drifting from the ballroom, slamming into Sebastian St. Clair, Marquess of Andover, like a well-thrown fist to the jaw. He froze on the terrace near an open French door leading into the ballroom of his home. Inside, two women stood near the door, their attention fixed on the crowded room, their voices slicing through the shadows. He recognized one as Martha Hendrickson, the other as Judith Whately.

"If you ask me, he has always looked dangerous," Judith said. "Very mysterious."

His reputation had not prevented Judith from swooning into his arms at the Trevelyan ball last week. Although she had claimed the heat had taken her breath away, he suspected the pretty brunette's sudden swoon was an attempt to catch his attention. A few days before that, Martha had stepped in front of his coach in Hyde Park. When he had halted to ensure she was unharmed, she had insisted upon a ride to her home, during which she had made every effort to coax him into flirtation.

"I wonder if the truth about him will frighten any of the girls who are on that little list of his." Martha flicked her fan below her chin, like a cat swishing her tail, her reddish-blond curls fluttering about her face. "I should think it would."

"Yes." Judith laughed, the shrill sound grating along his spine. "I should think it would frighten more than a few of the girls looking to win that coronet."

"Oh look, there's Hannah Marsdale near the refreshment table. Mama said she thinks Hannah might be on Andover's list." Martha took Judith's arm. "I wonder if she has had a chance to read *The Wicked Duke*."

Judith giggled. "I think we should tell her all about it."

Sebastian remained on the terrace for a long moment after the girls had drifted away from the door. Like a ghost from his past, the rumors had risen again to haunt him. Rumors that questioned his honesty and his honor. Rumors that had been buried for six years. He drew air into his lungs, easing the constriction of his chest before he entered his ballroom.

He paused near a potted palm and surveyed the

crowded room. As much as he wanted to dismiss the rumors tossed about by Judith and Martha, he could not shake the feeling that he had been stripped naked and put upon a stage. Still, those who knew him would not believe the rumors today any more than they had six years ago. Those who believed the ugly rumors about him were not worth his consideration.

On the surface, it might have been any of the countless nights he had spent in London. Nothing in this place and time distinguished this gathering from other parties in his memory. He knew he ought to continue his search this evening, narrow the choices of the decision he must make. Yet he could not find the inspiration to do so.

"You are headed for disaster. Your mama agrees with me."

Sebastian glanced at the woman who strolled toward him. She was looking up at him, a glint of humor in her blue eyes. Aunt Dora was his father's only sister. Although she had raised four sons and two daughters, she felt compelled to direct the activities of her brother's family as well as her own. For as long as he could remember, Dora and his mother had been close friends as well as allies, particularly when it came to Sebastian. "Mama has been fond of lectures these days. Among other things, she is convinced I need a grand adventure."

"Your mama wants the best for you. As do I." Dora tapped his cheek with her fan. "I have taken a good look at the women you are considering, my dear young man, and I must say that your mama is quite right when she says they do not suit you."

"And did you have someone else in mind?"

"I have it under consideration. Sometimes it takes a while to put together precisely the right match. And I admit to being a little distracted. You are well aware that I am still contemplating the prefect match for Arabella."

Until his death a little more than a year ago, Dora's husband, Viscount Rodenhurst, had enjoyed most of the more popular vices and some that were more obscure. Opium had finally ended his life. Since her own marriage had proved a less than perfect match, Dora took the business of finding spouses for her children, as well as her nieces and nephews, with the same serious consideration to strategy that Wellington did with his campaigns.

Dora tapped her fan against her gloved hand, the gilt trim glittering in the candlelight. "What do you think of Earl Worth?"

The question caught him by surprise. "For Arabella?"

"Well, certainly not for you."

"Worth is one of my closest friends. I think very highly of him. But I also think he has no intention of marrying anyone. He places respectable women in the same category as he does the measles. Something to avoid if at all possible."

Dora tilted her head, yellow plumes fluttering in her dark hair. "He may change his mind when he gets to know Arabella better."

Sebastian had seen his aunt play matchmaker before. She went after her prey like a cat with the scent of a mouse in her nostrils. "I believe I saw cousin Arabella head for the gardens with Edward D'Orsy."

"D'Orsy?" Dora rolled her eyes toward heaven. "That will not do."

Yellow satin twitched around her plump hips as Dora hurried toward a French door that led to the terrace and the gardens beyond. As he recalled, she had been equally vigilant with his cousin Honoria. Only this time, she had her sights set on a confirmed bachelor. Montgomery Trent had no intention of marrying anyone. He was content to allow his younger brother to provide the next Earl of Worth.

Sebastian directed his attention toward the dance floor, where couples in several sets moved sedately through the steps of a cotillion. He, too, felt as though he were moving through the steps of a dance, each movement in his life carefully calculated and planned. It was as it should be, he assured himself. He was Marquess of Andover. He had responsibilities. He certainly could not rely upon something as ethereal as emotion to make his decisions. Still, he could not shake the odd feeling of restlessness churning deep within him.

The lively strains of the orchestra drifted from the musicians' gallery at the far end of the room, rising above the low din of conversation and laughter. The scents of various sweet waters mingled with the vials of lavender water warmed in the four chandeliers above them. The room was perhaps more elegant than many in London. The soft glow of candles behind crystal flickered against white and gold paneled walls. Delicate white and gilt-trimmed chairs and settees stood along the walls. Yet the room was filled with the same people one found at every party.

What he could say with conviction was that each London Season was much the same as the last. Each year he met the new crop of girls transported from the country. Each girl was much the same as the next. Conversation never varied. Thoughts and actions never held a hint of surprise. In truth, except for one youthful folly, he had never once been moved to strong emotion by any woman. And looking back upon that unfortunate episode, he realized he had mistaken lust for love. The only passion he knew was of a purely physical nature. The kind that did not linger beyond the bed curtains.

Someone touched his sleeve. He turned and looked at the woman standing before him. With one glance he knew he had never seen her before. Candlelight from the wall sconce nearby cast a golden glow upon her features; it slipped fingers of gold into the dark brown hair piled atop her head. The flickering light spilled down her long neck and spread in a loving caress over her bare shoulders, the soft swells of her breasts. The silver threads in her white gown shimmered beneath the light. She seemed descended from another realm, a place where starlight ruled supreme.

Their gazes locked. An unexpected sensation gripped him. Heat sluiced through him, from the top of his head to the tip of his toes, a tingling, swirling excitement that turned the air in his lungs to steam. The noise in the room became a distant buzz in his ears. The world faded into a hazy blur. He felt oddly suspended, as though time itself had taken notice of this particular moment and allowed it to stretch into an eternity. His own reaction startled him, but seeing the same confusion in her eyes stunned him even more.

He wasn't certain how long they stood this way. It seemed a lifetime, even though his intellect told him it must be only a few heartbeats. All the nonsense his mother had preached to him of destiny and love and passion whirled in his brain. It was nonsense, he assured himself. Still, he could not dismiss the sensation stabbing him just below his diaphragm, even though its meaning escaped him.

He lived his life ruled by logic and reason. The startling emotions this woman evoked could be explained. Perhaps not now. No, his brain was having a bit of trouble reasoning at the moment. Later, when his blood had cooled, he would look at this encounter in the light of reality and realize this strange, swift attraction could be explained. At the moment he was painfully aware he was staring at this woman like a demented schoolboy. With an effort of will, he grabbed hold of his wits.

"Odd. I thought I knew everyone who was invited tonight." He sounded like a man still in possession of his faculties, he assured himself. "Yet I know we have never met."

"No. We have never met." She glanced at the floor, and stared at the tips of her silvery white slippers for a long moment before she lifted her chin. When she met his gaze, all the confusion he had glimpsed in her blue eyes had vanished, replaced by a glimmer of determination. "But I have seen you from a distance on several occasions."

He resisted the urge to ask her where and when. "From a distance?"

"Yes." She tilted her head and regarded him, as though he were a painting and she wasn't quite certain she liked the style in which it was painted. "Although on close inspection, you are not at all what I expected."

He could say the same of her. Candlelight flickered upon skin as pale and smooth as ivory silk. Her nose was slim and straight. Her lips full and pink and moist looking. She was taller than average and very slender, not at all the petite, softly rounded ideal of beauty. Yet he could not shake the impression she was the most exquisite woman he had ever gazed upon. Oh yes, he would have to examine these sensations when his head was clear. "Dare I ask what you expected?"

She did not respond immediately. Instead she allowed him to stew while she regarded him in a cool, measuring way that made him want to glance in a mirror. "I thought you would look much harsher."

9

Sebastian stared at her, far too aware of a sudden pang near his lungs. This was not the polite conversation he had expected, the quiet murmuring of how lovely the room looked and how delightful the company. He knew outwardly he remained composed. Yet this slip of a female, with her huge blue eyes, had managed to surprise him. "Why is it we have not met until now?"

"I had no reason to meet you until now," she said, her gaze remaining steady.

"Reason?" All the horrible possibilities conjured by that simple statement fluttered through the mire she had made of his mind. "And what might your reason be tonight?"

She glanced behind her, as though she wanted to make certain no one was near. "I have something of great importance I need to discuss with you. But we cannot speak here. I wonder if you would accompany me back to my home."

Although he was quite certain his composure did not waver, inside he felt he was on the deck of his yacht in a storm. "You wish me to leave my own ball and accompany you to your home?"

"Yes. I really must speak with you. Alone."

"Who are you?"

"I shall tell you only if you come away with me." A faint smile curved her lips. "Will you?"

What adventure awaited him in the depths of her eyes? On the heels of that thought came another: Had his mother arranged the arrival of this blue-eyed angel? Of course, it would be like her. It must be a game, his mother's idea of demonstrating his need for romance. It was a game he had no intention of playing. He would proceed as he always proceeded, according to his own will. He was the master of his life. No one would interfere, not even his well-intentioned, terribly romantic mother. It was his party. He certainly could not leave.

Yet somehow he could not look away from her eyes. She had such large, beautiful eyes—the pale blue irises surrounded by an outer ring of darker blue. He saw apprehension in those eyes, mingled with a steely determination. Looking into those eyes he had a distinct impression that she was in some kind of trouble. Perhaps she had nothing at all to do with his mother. Perhaps fate had simply led her to him this night.

Without truly understanding his own mind, he took her arm and strode toward the entrance. Running away from his own party with a strange female certainly was not practical. Yet he could not remember the last time he had felt this exhilarated. What did she want from him?

Sebastian leaned back against the black velvet squabs of a town coach he suspected had been hired. He studied the woman sitting across from him, trying to put together the pieces of this particular enigma. He had been raised with five sisters, and had some measure of understanding feminine nature. Still, she managed to elude his every attempt at slipping her into a nice orderly category.

The light from the interior coach lamp flickered upon her right cheek, leaving the other in shadow. Although she was trying to look composed, the slight lift of her shoulders beneath her white cashmere shawl, the tightness at the corner of her lips, the implacable grip she held upon her reticule, all betrayed her tension. If she was an actress, she was uncomfortable with this role she was playing. Although his mother might have sent her to him, he could not dismiss the possibility she was truly in some difficulty. "Should I have packed my toothbrush?"

She looked startled by his question; her eyes grew wide, her lips parted. "Your toothbrush? Why would you think you might need a toothbrush?"

He hadn't expected the question to spark anything but a smile. Instead he saw a glimmer of fear in her eyes. What the devil was she about? "Is your home in London, or are we in for an extended trip?"

"It is in London." She slid the silver cord of her reticule through her gloved fingers while she responded. "We shall be there soon."

He set his teeth against the strange urge to ask her what dragons plagued her. He certainly was not a knight errant. As his mother and sisters liked to point out, he did not have a drop of romance in his veins. Still, something about this woman urged him to grab a sword and shield and dash about on a quest at her bidding.

He judged her age to be somewhere in the vicinity of four and twenty. Although there was nothing to suggest she was anything but gently bred, she had the look of a woman accustomed to taking care of her own affairs. He could see independence in the tilt of her chin, the determined look in her eyes.

What did she want from him? Without conscious thought, he realized what he wanted from her. Images flooded his brain, rising unexpectedly, hitting with the force of a clenched fist. His body reacted, growing heated and bothered, as though he had slipped naked between cool silk sheets and taken this woman close against his body. It was lust, of course. He was familiar with the emotion, but it had never struck with such force. He definitely needed to know more about this strange female.

"You have me curious, Miss . . ." He paused, expecting her to provide her name. Yet her only response was a twitch of a muscle at the corner of her lips. He tried not to notice the plump curve of her lower lip and the way he wanted to test its softness beneath his tongue. "Very well, since you will not provide your name, I shall think of one that suits you. Pandora will do."

"Pandora." She considered his invention a moment, studying him with eyes that were at once beautiful and disconcertingly critical. A keen intelligence lurked behind those stunning eyes. An intelligence that most women would try to hide. Not this woman. "You see me as a woman who will unleash all manners of plague upon man?"

She surprised him more with each passing moment. He was accustomed to women trying their best to please him. Although he was not a handsome man, his wealth and title had placed him in the path of every ambitious female in England. In fact, in all his years, he had never seen quite this look in another woman's eyes. "I see you as a mystery. Someone who will bring surprises into my life."

She directed her attention toward her reticule as she said, "You shall know all you need to know when we reach my home."

Something in her tone made the skin prickle at the nape of his neck. "Since you needed privacy to discuss this matter of some importance, I should think your coach would suffice."

"No. I am afraid I need to show you something as well." She fiddled with the silver cords of her reticule while she looked out the window of the coach. "We shall be at my home directly."

What type of female was she? Her gown was elegant, costly. Sebastian glanced to where her feet peeked out from beneath her silvery white gown. Silver threads were woven into the white satin of her slim slippers. She had very pretty ankles. Under his regard, she shifted her feet, drawing them back into the shadows. A maidenly gesture. One he hadn't expected from a female bold enough to invite him back to her home. It would appear Pandora was not only a mystery but a contradiction.

He was accustomed to women of experience. He had never in his life had a romantic liaison with any female who was not well experienced in the world. He had enjoyed the company of sophisticated widows, several actresses, and most recently a particularly skilled opera dancer. Yet he had an uneasy feeling this woman defied his experience. Perhaps it was part of the reason he was so attracted to her. It was only a matter of time before he dissected this odd attraction, and with the revelation would come the decline.

The coach rocked to a halt. He glanced out and discovered they had stopped in a lane behind one of several town houses that lined the street. "Am I to be smuggled into the house?"

She gripped her reticule with both hands. "I would prefer not to stir up any gossip."

He did not like the look in her wide eyes. Excitement, fear, and a glint of steely determination, all mingled uneasily in those huge intelligent eyes. Perhaps accompanying her to this place was not the most practical choice he could have made. He knew absolutely nothing about her. Still, he was a man capable of taking care of himself. He certainly could handle any hand the lady might deal him.

When the coachman opened the door, Sebastian descended, then turned and offered Pandora his hand. She hesitated a moment before placing her hand in his. Although they both wore gloves, the barriers did not hide the fine trembling of the slender hand in his grasp. Her fragrance spilled around him with her descent, a misty scent of roses in the rain that made him want to find all the places she had dabbed the perfume. She descended the step, then yanked her hand from his, as though she could not abide his touch. She looked up at him, moonlight illuminating her face before she swept past him. The utter contempt in her eyes stunned him. What the devil was she about?

A small rational voice whispered for him to leave. Yet, how could he leave without finding out what enigma lay behind her beautiful eyes?

He contemplated the mystery of Pandora while he followed her through the gate and into a garden behind a modest stone town house. Although it was a small space, it was filled with flowers. In fact, it looked as though someone had planted nearly every available inch of ground. Moonbeams sprinkled a silvery light over beds of pale blossoms. The fragrance wrapped around him as he walked beside his silent companion. Tension radiated from her. As much as he cudgeled his brain, he could not determine what possible reason this woman might have for her odd behavior. What could he have done to earn the contempt he had glimpsed in her eyes?

Light flowed into the garden through three sashed windows on the ground floor. She headed for that light, leading him through a door that opened into a small library. The scent of old leather mingled warmly with the fragrance of spring blossoms that sat in vases on the desk and an urn near the door. The wall sconces cast a flickering glow over the bookcases and furniture. He noticed the carpet was well worn; in places the roses stitched into the backing had dissolved into pale threads. The furniture was good solid wood, heavily carved and crafted along ample lines, the upholstery a dark floral brocade. Although out of fashion, the room was scrupulously clean, except for the large, claw-footed desk. Papers were scattered across the desktop, along with two open books. He suspected it was a place the maid was not permitted to touch.

Pandora crossed the room. She paused by an oak fireplace and looked into the lifeless hearth. "I want you to know, I will do anything to take care of my family."

Sebastian stared at her slender back. Her shawl had slid from one shoulder, exposing the pale curve of her neck. Once more he contemplated his reckless decision to run off with this beautiful, strange creature. Impulse and passion could lead a man straight to disaster. He had learned the truth of this a long time ago. Yet, contrary to every logical and practical fiber in his body, he could not find the will to leave this place and this woman. "What is it you need from me, Pandora? Why have you brought me here?"

"I thought it would be much more difficult to lure you back here. But then I suppose I underestimated how much of a libertine you are."

Libertine? He had been called many things in his life, but he certainly was not a libertine. Did her scheme have anything to do with the rumors that were circulating about him tonight? "I think it is time you told me exactly why you brought me here."

"Yes. It is time." She slipped her hand into her reticule. When she turned, the light from the wall sconce behind her glinted on the barrel of the pistol she held.

Sebastian stared at the gun, his mind grappling with the dichotomy of a deadly weapon in the hands of an angel. Impulse and passion. Only a fool followed his emotion. At the moment he felt the biggest fool in town, because as much as he wanted to deny it, he could not crush the humiliating sting of loss. For some ludicrous reason, he felt betrayed. By this beautiful stranger. By his own wayward need. He swallowed hard, forcing back the fury rising within him. He would not give her the satisfaction of seeing how deeply she had wounded him with this treachery.

"If robbery is your aim," he said, forcing his voice to remain soft and steady. "I am afraid I have very little of value upon my person."

Chapter Two

Emma Wakefield glared at the man, her anger surging at the insult. "I certainly did not bring you here to rob you. I am not some common footpad."

Andover inclined his head, his expression revealing nothing of his emotion. He might have been facing her from the opposite side of a chessboard. "Pardon me for insulting you. It was the pistol that threw me off. Since you have no plans to rob me, why not put it away and tell me the real reason you brought me here."

She kept the pistol pointed directly at his broad chest. Emma had never hated anyone as she hated this man. Yet in spite of that hatred, she could not ignore another emotion coiling through her. How on earth could she feel an attraction for the monster? As much as she wanted to deny it, she could not dismiss the excitement she had felt upon meeting him. It plagued her still, an odd tingling sensation that rippled in a heated current through the river of hatred coursing through her. That swirling heat curled around her vitals and drizzled into her belly, collecting there in a molten pool. What the devil was wrong with her? "I want you to tell me what you did with my cousin."

He hesitated a moment, his black brows lifting slightly in mild curiosity. "Your cousin?"

"Charlotte Usherwood."

"Miss Usherwood. Has something happened to her?"

Emma had expected to see fear in his eyes. Only a coward preyed upon the defenseless. Yet she could detect no fright in his dark brown gaze. Instead he appeared surprised. "Do not offend me with your feeble attempts to appear innocent. I have all the evidence I need to know you are the monster responsible for what happened."

"If something has happened to your cousin, I assure you I had nothing to do with it."

"I know better than that." She carefully kept the pistol trained upon him while she slipped her free hand into her reticule. After a moment of searching the contents of the silvery bag, she felt the cool surface of the button. She withdrew her hand and held the button up for his inspection. "I found this beside her bed the morning after she disappeared from her bedchamber."

"A button?"

"It is not an ordinary button, as I am certain you know. It is solid gold and engraved with a sword plunged into a stone. I have done a little investigating. Buttons such as this are worn by members of a very exclusive club. A small group of extremely wealthy, obscenely privileged men who feel they can do what they want, when they want, with whom they want. A club to which you belong."

"How the devil . . ." He took a step toward her.

19

"Do not move."

He paused, a frown digging twin furrows between his thick black brows. "At this distance, I can only take your word for the engraving."

She tossed the button to him. "Take a look."

He examined the button a moment, then looked at her. "You say you found this in Miss Usherwood's bedchamber?"

"The morning after you abducted her from her bed."

"I cannot imagine how this button came to be where you say it was." He closed the button in his palm. The concern in his eyes burned so brightly, it startled her. "When did this happen?"

"Six days ago. The day after you visited my aunt. That day, you seemed to think it was important for Charlotte not to encourage your nephew. Apparently you decided to take matters into your own hands. To save your blasted nephew from a possible match with a dear, sweet girl. A girl who never in her life harmed a living soul."

"It is true, I did hope to discourage Miss Usherwood from thinking of any alliance with my nephew. But believe me, I had only your cousin's best interests at heart."

She squeezed the wooden handle of her pistol. "What have you done with her?"

He held her gaze, as though he had nothing at all to hide. "Upon my honor, I did not have anything to do with her disappearance."

No scoundrel had the right to possess such beautiful eyes, so dark they were nearly black. How did a monster manage to look at her with such sincerity? "Men such as you enjoy speaking of honor. Unfortunately, you enjoy doing what suits you even more."

He held her gaze without flinching. "I do not know how that button came to be in your cousin's bedchamber. But I know it did not come from my coat."

She gripped the pistol with both hands. "You are guilty, Andover."

"Although you are mistaken, I can understand how you came to believe me guilty of this crime. Still, I am surprised you would take matters into your own hands in such a reckless manner."

Emma stiffened at his assessment of her behavior. Her aunt had described it in much the same manner. "It is not reckless. And even if it were, I will do what I must to find Charlotte. Do not imagine I will not."

He stood as unmoving as a statue; only the look in his eyes betrayed his humanity. That look was bereft of fear or guilt. Instead she saw a glimmer of compassion, an emotion that should not have been in those darker-than-midnight eyes. "Was there no gentleman to confront me? No one to help you face the danger you must imagine I represent?"

"I am quite capable of handling the situation." Emma had been taking care of her family without the benefit of a man since the death of her uncle five years earlier. "I do not intend to allow you to walk out of this house until you have told me how my cousin may be restored to her family."

"I understand how desperate you must be. But I did not have anything to do with Miss Usherwood's disappearance."

"For days I have wondered where she is, what she must be thinking. How frightened she must feel. I keep wondering what kind of man would kidnap and terrorize a nineteen-year-old girl." She smoothed her finger back and forth over the trigger. "Now I see he is a monster who can lie while looking me straight in the eye."

"Yes, it would take a monster to do something so vile." He held her gaze, a curious look entering his eyes, a look of disappointment. "And you honestly imagine I am that kind of man?"

Andover was not at all what she had expected. He did not look or behave as she'd thought he would. Still, she had analyzed the clues, investigated the possibilities, and found Andover at the end of her search. "I have the evidence that convicts you. There is no one else, no other reason for her abduction."

"The reason does seem a mystery." He was quiet a moment, as though he were mulling over everything she had said. "I intend to discover what truly happened to Miss Usherwood. But I cannot do that while I am your prisoner."

"Stay where you are." She wagged the pistol when he took a step toward the door. "I warn you, I can pop the cork from a bottle of wine at twenty paces."

"A useful skill, I am certain." He lowered his gaze to the pistol, then looked straight into her eyes. "Still, it is not the same as putting a bullet into a man."

He was testing her resolve. Although she cringed inwardly at the thought of shooting him, she would not show this monster her weakness. "I consider you less than an animal. I assure you, I will have no qualms about shooting a beast such as you."

"Murdering me will bring you no closer to finding your cousin," he said, his voice deadly soft and utterly composed.

Emma forced her lips into a smile, hoping she looked far calmer than she felt. "I need not murder you, Andover. I need only put a bullet through some less than vital portion of your anatomy."

"Less than vital?" He lifted his brows. "That is a matter of opinion. And I suspect our opinions in this matter differ greatly."

"Make no mistake. I will shoot you if I must."

"I was raised in a household with five sisters. I

22

learned at an early age not to doubt a female when she gets a particular look in her eyes." He smiled at her, a slight curving of his lips that seemed in perfect harmony with the glint of mischief in his gaze. "You have that look."

Where was the fear? The guilt? This was not going as she had planned. At a distance she had noticed Andover was a tall man, that his hair was black, his eyes dark, his face molded with strong lines and curves. Distance had provided a certain immunity to the man. A protection annihilated upon closer proximity. Distance had not revealed the true power of his blatant masculinity.

"It occurs to me I do not even know your name. I think an introduction is fair, under the circumstances."

She hesitated a moment, withholding her name as though anonymity might maintain a safe distance between them. "My name is Wakefield. Emma Wakefield."

"Wakefield." He considered this a moment, while she considered the odd sensations he evoked within her. "Are you connected to Earl Halisham?"

"Only by blood."

Andover held her gaze a long moment, then nodded, as though he had come to an understanding. "I see."

He looked at her in a way that made her feel as though he could see through every defense she might raise against him, straight into the dark places in her soul, the hidden, secret places where she kept all the horrible longing and pain of her youth. For some inexplicable reason, she had the irrational thought that he truly could understand her. He was far more dangerous than she had anticipated.

Lord Andover was not handsome, at least not in the poetic, delicately etched fashion so admired these days. His cheekbones were too sharply defined, his nose too chiseled, his lips too full, far too sensual to allow him the tame epithet of handsome. Yet there was a beauty in this man—bold, untamed, the same beauty of a hawk in flight, of a wolf beneath a full moon. Any woman who became embroiled with this man would soon find herself in a great deal of trouble.

"What have you done with Charlotte? Tell me the truth."

He held her gaze. "I have told you the truth."

This was not going the way she had planned. Still, there was no turning back from the course she had set. She could not allow him to leave. Not until she had the truth from him. "All I want is Charlotte returned safely. I assure you, we do not want a scandal. We will not bring in the magistrate. We simply want Charlotte returned to us, safe and sound."

He drew in his breath, his expression revealing far more compassion than any scoundrel had the right to feign. "I give you my word, Miss Wakefield, I will do everything in my power to help restore Miss Usherwood to her family."

Could he possibly be telling her the truth? It could not be, she assured herself. There was far too much evidence against him. And yet, she could not look at this man and see the monster lurking beneath the solid wall of respectability. "It would seem you leave me no choice."

"No choice? On the contrary, Miss Wakefield. You can either proceed with this reckless scheme to force an innocent man to confess, or you can release me and allow me to help you."

She had not planned for their confrontation to go this far. Indeed, she had envisioned the scoundrel on his knees begging for his life by this time. "Even if you were innocent, which you are not, why would you help me?"

He looked mildly surprised by the question. "I cannot think of a reason why I would not help you."

If she did not know better, she would take this man for a true gentleman, the kind who rushed to the aid of strangers in need. A knight cast here from another time and place. Yet she had suffered enough at the hands of arrogant aristocratic males to learn that a wise woman could not rely upon any of his species. "Step out into the hall."

He glanced toward the door, then back at her. "May I ask what you are planning to do?"

"I am planning to make your life as uncomfortable as possible, Andover. Of course, you can save yourself the inconvenience by simply telling me the truth."

"I see you are as stubborn as you are beautiful."

Beautiful? She knew better than to believe false flattery. Particularly from this man. "Start walking."

He inclined his head in a small bow. "It would seem I am at your disposal, Pandora."

Chapter Three

"He did not confess." Marjorie Usherwood paced the length of her bedchamber. She pivoted at the door leading to the hall, then paced the opposite direction until she reached the chair in which Emma was seated. She fixed Emma with a steady glare. "You said he would confess."

"Yes. I did." Only a coward would prey upon the defenseless as he had upon Charlotte. Yet, instead of dissolving into a pool of cowardice, instead of begging for his life, he had met her every accusation with icy composure. "I suppose he was too arrogant to believe I would truly shoot him."

"Possibly. Of course, there could be another reason."

"What?"

Marjorie folded her hands at her waist. "I watched most of your confrontation from the hall. And I must say, he was very convincing in his insistence on his innocence."

Emma shook her head, trying to dismiss her own doubts along with her aunt's words. "He is not innocent."

"If what you believe is true, then he is indeed a monster."

A monster with eyes so dark and beautiful they could buckle her knees. How could a monster possess such a direct gaze? Yet it must be Andover. "We have all the evidence I need to be certain he is the man who abducted Charlotte."

Marjorie rubbed her arms, as if she were chilled. "I keep wondering why a man such as he, a man with everything—power, position, wealth—why would he do something so vile?"

"Arrogance. He did it because it suited him. He wanted to make certain destiny flowed as he dictated."

"Yes, I suppose it could be as you say. He was quite insistent that Charlotte do as he wished. Still, I would never have supposed he would do anything so monstrous. He had such a direct manner. And there was a look in his eyes, something I cannot explain. It was the look of a man who stood by his word." Marjorie released her breath on a long sigh. "He was really quite charming."

"I am certain he uses his charm to gain an advantage." Andover was the type of man who took what he wanted and told the whole world to go to blazes. The type of man who could set her pulse racing with nothing more than a glance. The type of man who placed all manner of reckless, wanton thoughts into a woman's head. "He is dangerous. Definitely dangerous."

"You cannot be certain he is the man responsible for . . . that he did . . ." Marjorie clasped her hands together beneath her chin. "Dear Lord in heaven, where

27

can she be? What do you suppose has happened to her?"

Emma stood and took her aunt's arms in a firm grasp, as much to give strength as to take it. Since the day her cousin had been abducted from her bedchamber, Emma had felt as though a steel band had been cinched around her chest. With each passing day, it grew tighter and tighter, until she could scarcely breathe for the fear and anxiety crowding her chest.

Candlelight reflected upon the tears that shimmered in Marjorie's blue eyes. Emma understood the tears. Yet she had learned long ago that tears could not improve a tragedy, they could not wash away pain, they could not make things right. "We shall find her, Aunt Marjorie. I promise you. I shall not allow Andover to get away with this crime."

"You have always been so strong. If not for you, I do not know what we would have done to manage after dear Henry died. I know you feel you must take matters into your own hands. Still, I wish you had not taken this path."

"There was no other way."

"What if you are mistaken, Emma? What if Andover had nothing to do with this?"

Emma quickly crushed the doubts rising inside her. It was difficult to reconcile the man she had met this night with the image of a criminal. Yet she could not ignore the evidence. "If not Andover, then who could have done it?"

Marjorie shook her head. "I do not know. It does not make sense to me. Nothing makes sense. To think the Marquess of Andover may have entered my home and abducted my daughter is nearly beyond belief."

"It is not the first time he has committed a crime against an innocent female." In her mind Emma dredged up all the old gossip concerning the Marquess. It helped to fix the man as the villain in this horrible tragedy. "If you have forgotten, just take a look through *The Wicked Duke*."

Marjorie shook her head. "This is not a novel, Emma. This is real."

"The circumstances in that novel are every bit as real as this. He may have escaped the hangman before. He will not escape me now."

"Emma, I never truly believed he murdered that girl." Marjorie's eyes grew wide. "Dear Lord, you do not imagine he . . . my poor little girl. Would he have . . . Murder!"

Emma would not allow herself to consider that possibility. "If he had wanted to murder her, he would have done it in her bed. I feel he must have taken her somewhere."

"Yes. I must believe she is still alive. I must believe I shall see her lovely face again."

Emma's chest constricted at the desperation etched upon Marjorie's delicate features. Although Marjorie was eighteen years her senior, in ways Emma felt years older than her sweet-natured aunt. For the past five years, Emma had been making all the major decisions for her family. She was not about to weaken now. "We shall find her. I will not allow him to leave this house until he tells us where we can find her."

"I want to believe you, dear." Marjorie threw her arms around Emma and held her close "I keep wondering where she is. Is she cold? Hungry? Is she unharmed?"

Memories stirred within Emma as the sweet lavender scent Marjorie had always worn drifted through her senses, memories of a frightened little girl who had lost everything in the world. This woman had taken her into her home, given her the warmth of family. "We will find her."

Marjorie squeezed her tightly, then pulled away and met her gaze. "And if you are mistaken about Andover?"

"I am not mistaken."

"He is not a man to be taken lightly, my girl."

"I see no other path to take. I feel deep within my heart that the longer we wait for some other means of finding Charlotte, the less chance we have of ever seeing her again."

Marjorie pressed her hand over her heart. "Dear Lord, if only my dear Henry were alive. If only there were someone to help us."

"We shall manage as we have always managed."

Marjorie lifted her brows. "We have the Marquess of Andover locked in our cellar. Forgive me, but I cannot see how we are managing very well."

"A man such as Andover will not long tolerate the inconveniences of a cellar. He will soon tell us the truth."

"Did you leave him a lantern?"

"No."

"A blanket?"

Guilt prickled the nape of Emma's neck. "He can sit on a crate for all I care."

"The cellar is quite damp. And Matthews told me he saw a rat in it the other day."

Emma shivered at the thought of encountering a rat. "The man who abducted Charlotte deserves far worse than a night in the cellar."

"If he did it."

"He did." Still, Emma could not quite crush the doubts that stirred within her.

"Oh dear." Marjorie pressed her fingers to her lips. "I just had a horrible thought."

Emma curled her hands into tight balls at her sides to keep them from shaking. "What?"

"Do you think anyone from the party will realize he left with you?"

"I doubt anyone at the Andover ball knew me. It is not as if I have ever attended a London party." Emma turned away from her aunt, afraid she might betray some measure of regret for what she had lost so many years ago. She caught movement in the corner of her eye and glanced in that direction. Her image stared back at her from the mirror above her aunt's dressing table. The woman looking back seemed a stranger. "And if I did know anyone there, I doubt they would have recognized me. I scarcely recognize myself. I feel like Miss Sarah Kenrick, from *The Country Miss*. It is the way she must have felt when she approached Lord Worthington at her first London ball."

"In that book, did not Miss Kenrick shoot Lord Worthington?"

"By accident. She had intended only to keep him from running off with her sister."

Marjorie tapped her chin. "I believe I do see a similarity between you and Miss Kenrick."

Emma frowned at her aunt. "I would never be so clumsy with a pistol."

"No, of course not, dear. I am certain no one suspected that you had a pistol in your reticule. You look like an angel."

The gown of white gauze over a white satin petticoat was hardly the type of garment she would normally wear. Silver threads were woven through the gauze, making the dress shimmer like starlight when she moved. She had never owned anything so elegant. It had cost more than she usually paid for a dozen dresses. Although it was the height of fashion, she could not help feeling horribly exposed by the low, square-cut neckline. Still, the display of her bosom and shoulders had been necessary for her plan to succeed.

"I wonder if any practical use can be made of this gown. It is far too daring for Charlotte."

"If things had been different, you would have had your share of gowns such as this one and attended a hundred balls. You would have sparkled like a perfect, glimmering diamond."

Any chance she might have had for balls and parties and all the silly dreams of youth had long since passed. Emma quickly smothered the regrets swelling within her. Dwelling on what might have been—on all the possibilities that would never come to be—was useless. She did not wish Marjorie to realize how much she still longed for all the ordinary things that came with marriage and children and a life she would never know. Her past could not be altered. She could only make the most of each day she was given. She glanced down at her gown. "I feel a little foolish dressed like this."

"I do not believe I have ever seen you look more lovely. You are as beautiful as your mother."

Emma cast a critical glance at her image in the mirror. She was not the great beauty her mother had been. Still, in the elegant gown, with her hair swept up on her head in the Roman style, her image was no longer the ordinary woman who usually looked back at her from a mirror. And the look she had glimpsed in Andover's eyes had been far from ordinary.

At the ball, when he had looked at her, she had felt the world contract. The way he had looked at her made her feel she was not merely the most beautiful woman in the world, but the only woman who mattered to him. "I had thought it would be difficult to lure Andover back here. I suppose he assumed I intended to allow him liberties."

"Did you lead him to believe that might be the case?"

"I simply told him I wished to speak to him on a matter of grave importance." Emma looked at her aunt, feeling the need to defend her actions. In spite of the evidence she had to convict this man, a part of her could not understand how the man she had met this evening, the man who could set her pulse racing with a glance, could possibly be the beast who had abducted Charlotte. Although he had looked at her with such heated appreciation the air had actually grown warm upon her cheek, he had not attempted to so much as touch her. He had, in fact, given her the distinct impression that he wanted to help her. Somehow, she could not help feeling she had betrayed him. "I did not lie to him."

Marjorie held her gaze for such a long time, and with such a look of doom, that the fine hairs at the nape of Emma's neck prickled. "Have you given any thought to what we will do if Andover does not confess?"

Emma had not allowed herself to contemplate failure in a long time. Life had cast many obstacles in her path, and she had always managed to find a way around each of them. The Marquess of Andover was simply the next challenge she must face. "He will confess."

Marjorie did not blink. "And if he doesn't? How long do you expect to keep him a prisoner?"

Emma had enough experience with arrogant male aristocrats to know they would not long tolerate the conditions one would find in a cellar. "When he realizes the only way he will ever again see the light of day is if he tells us how we may retrieve Charlotte, he will confess."

Marjorie shook her head. "I do not know how I allowed you to talk me into this scheme of yours. It is far too reckless."

"It is not reckless. I have carefully considered my approach to this situation."

"Carefully? You are every bit as headstrong as your mother. I still recall the night I tried to convince Sophia not to run off to London."

"Mama was young and filled with notions of romance. I am quite old and not so filled with fancy."

Marjorie lifted her brows. "Yes, dear, at six and twenty you are certainly a step away from the grave. And considering your gifted imagination, I think we can safely say you are as practical as a Methodist."

Emma resisted the urge to stamp her foot. "I *am* practical. And I have explored all the possibilities. This is our best course of action."

Marjorie rubbed the skin between her light brown brows. "My dear girl, you have lived your life through books. This is not a novel by E. W. Austen."

"No. If it were, Charlotte would be back with us and the blackguard in our cellar would be punished as he deserves."

Marjorie sighed. "I suppose there is no point in regretting our actions now. But I must tell you, I am still not convinced of that man's guilt. And the thought of him in our cellar fills me with a horrible dread."

"He *is* guilty." Emma squeezed Marjorie's arm. "Now you must not worry about this another moment. I shall deal with Andover. You try to get some rest."

Emma left her aunt's room with every intention of putting the Marquess of Andover out of her thoughts. But she found she could not push the image of him sitting in that damp, dark cellar out of her mind.

What if she were wrong about him? The thought filled her veins like a stream of ice water. She wasn't wrong about him, she assured herself. She could not be wrong about him. For if she were wrong her chances of finding Charlotte were far from good.

He would confess, she assured herself. In the morning, he would be more than willing to trade information about Charlotte for his freedom.

After preparing for bed, she slipped between cool cotton sheets and hugged her pillow. The calming scent of lavender wrapped around her, yet it could not ease her anxiety. Although she tried not to think of him, she could not strip the images of Andover from her mind. She supposed she should have left him a blanket. Perhaps a lantern. The truth was she should not care about the man's comfort, yet she could not completely crush an odd concern for him. If he had done this horrible thing, he deserved far worse than a night in the cellar.

He would confess. One night in the cellar and the arrogant aristocrat would tell her what she needed to know. And if he didn't? Emma hugged her pillow close against her chest. Tomorrow. She would deal with that possibility tomorrow.

Chapter Four

Emma awoke with a start. She sat bolt upright in bed, disoriented by the dream she had escaped, the same dream that had plagued her since the day Charlotte had disappeared. Yet the nightmare had never awakened her before tonight. An overwhelming sense of urgency gripped her, an instinct that told her something other than the nightmare had disturbed her sleep.

Fog-tinged moonlight swirled against the windowpanes. The faint light lent a strange glow to the room, as though she still dwelled in the realm of dreams. Yet the soft groan of a floorboard nearby screamed of reality. Someone was in the room with her. Without another thought she reached for the pistol on the bedside table. Her fingers grazed the wooden handle. Before she could grip the pistol, a large hand clamped around her wrist. She lashed out with her free hand. Pain flashed along her nerves at the collision of her fist with bone.

"Confound it." In the next heartbeat, the intruder had pinned her back against the bed, covering her with his big body, forcing her down into the soft mattress. She bucked beneath him, twisting, thrashing her legs beneath the covers. He shifted above her, containing her struggles beneath the long length of his legs, pressing her wrists into the soft eiderdown on either side of her shoulders.

"I am not going to harm you."

The soft voice rippled through her. The identity of the man holding her stunned her so completely, she forgot her panic. "What are you doing here?"

The pale moonlight allowed no more than a hint of his features. Still, she could see him smile. "I was afraid you might bolt when you discovered I had managed to escape your cellar."

"You thought I would run away when I discovered you had escaped?"

"Do not misunderstand me, Miss Wakefield. I was quite certain you would retreat only until you could hatch another hen-witted plan to make me confess."

"Hen witted!"

"Since I did not wish to find myself embroiled in another of your reckless adventures, I thought we ought to clear up this matter before I left."

She glared at him. "It was a sound plan."

"No, Miss Wakefield. Plans born of desperation are seldom sound. The position in which you find yourself at the moment is testament to that fact." He cocked one black brow. "You never really thought of what you might do if I failed to confess, did you? The cellar was not originally part of your plan."

When he looked at her, she had the uncomfortable

feeling he could read every secret in her soul. From the moment she had met him she had felt off balance, as unsure of herself as a child straight out of the school room. Fluttery and jittery, heated and restless. All of which she did not appreciate in the least. "I underestimated your arrogance."

"I agree, you certainly did misjudge my character. But arrogance had little to do with it."

Although she wanted desperately to hide from those perceptive dark eyes, she forced herself to maintain his gaze. "How did you escape?"

"Fortunately the hinges were on my side of the door."

"I suspect we have a different perspective on what is fortunate."

He laughed softly, the sound a low rumble in her ear, a soft vibration against her breasts. He still held her so close she could not breathe without inhaling his scent. A warm, smoldering scent that acted like a drug upon her system, simmering through her veins, transforming anger and fear into a much more potent blend.

The sheer power of the attraction this man held for her struck her like a clenched fist. It defied logic, muddled reason, mocked justice. She lay still beneath him, afraid of any movement, far too aware of every place his body pressed against hers, powerful, blatantly male. Never in her life had she been more aware of her femininity. "What do you want from me?"

He looked straight into her eyes, as though he had nothing in the world to hide. "I want you to believe me when I say I had nothing at all to do with your cousin's disappearance."

She twisted her wrists in his grasp, trying to break free. Yet he held her, his grasp at once firm and oddly gentle. "And I suppose that is the only reason you

38

barged into my bedchamber, to convince me of your innocence?"

He studied her a moment, a look of understanding dawning in his eyes. "And now you are wondering what a monster such as I will do next?"

He might have taken her off guard, but she refused to play the role of the besotted spinster, no matter how attractive she found the scoundrel. She would face him as Sarah Kenrick faced the arrogant Lord Worthington in *The Country Miss*, without fear. "Take your hands off me."

"I am not the monster you seek."

She dismissed the instincts clamoring to believe him. He was the personification of Sylvester from *The Wicked Duke*, she reminded herself. Lust had a way of blinding a human, even a practical-minded female such as herself. "I prefer to believe the evidence, not the scoundrel."

He released his breath in a soft sigh, the damp heat brushing her cheek with a scent that reminded her of a woodland after rain. "And what would a scoundrel do in my position, Miss Wakefield? What would a scoundrel do with you?"

The dark current in his voice swirled around her, pricking her fear and another far more disquieting emotion. She stared into his eyes, looking for the truth in those dark depths. "I shall . . ."

"What, Miss Wakefield? What will you do?" He slid her wrists upward, gliding the back of her hands over the cotton pillowcase, conquering her resistance with a quiet display of power. "You will not scream. Because if you scream you will introduce your aunt to danger. And you would not want to risk her injury."

The truth of his words shivered through her. Emma gasped as he pressed her wrists together.

"What would a scoundrel do now?" He leaned

closer while he transferred his grasp, gripping both of her wrists in one large hand, so close his breath warmed her lips with each word he spoke. "Can you imagine what he might do with a beautiful, vulnerable woman?"

In spite of her best efforts, images rose in her mind, images that would never appear in an E. W. Austen novel, images that shocked her to the core. Unfortunately, she could imagine far too well what this man might do with her. With the pictures crowding her brain, fear trickled through her, a stream of ice threading the treacherous heat he conjured within her.

She acknowledged the fear, recognized it as sane. Yet the other emotions, the startling sensations that gripped her, were undeniable and anything but sane. She had never suspected the perverse nature of her own being. Yet it confronted her now, this strange attraction for a man who held her prisoner, this odd excitement coiling through her. "Take your hands off of me," she hissed through clenched teeth.

"Do you truly imagine a scoundrel would obey your command?" He brushed his lips over hers, no more than the touch of a butterfly skimming the petals of a rose. Yet the contact ripped through her like lightning across the midnight sky. "You really have no idea how dangerous your hen-witted actions have been."

She stiffened beneath him. "I did what needed to be done, in the most reasonable way possible."

"Reasonable?" He lifted his brows. "Confronting the man you believe to be responsible for this horrible crime was not a reasonable course of action."

He knew nothing of her. Nothing of the responsibilities she bore. Yet he had the arrogance to judge her. The audacity to try to cow her. "I am not frightened of you."

"You should be frightened, Miss Wakefield. You

need to realize just how reckless you have been. A true scoundrel would not content himself with a mere kiss. Imagine what he would do." He unfastened the top button of her nightgown, slowly sliding the pearl nub through the soft white cotton, allowing her to imagine what would follow. The second button fell beneath his deft fingers, while he held her in a steady gaze. He parted the cloth, revealing the hollow of her neck, the skin beneath. "A scoundrel would not stop, Miss Wakefield."

She lay beneath him, trembling with more than fear. Potent anticipation gripped her. She had never realized how intoxicating the complete obliteration of choice could be.

"A scoundrel would take you, Miss Wakefield." He slid his fingertip down her neck, spreading a simmering warmth beneath the soft touch. He glided his hand down the center of her gown, his fingertips grazing the tops of her buttons. Although he did not touch her, she felt a tingling heat all the same. The sensation spread across her skin, warming her as though he had brushed his hands over her breasts. The look in his eyes startled her. Hunger simmered there, the pure undiluted hunger of a man for a woman.

"You have lovely skin, Miss Wakefield. A scoundrel would enjoy devouring every luscious part of you."

No man had ever looked at her that way, as though she were not only the most beautiful woman in the world, but the only woman he wanted. She felt a temptress beneath the heat of his gaze, powerful in spite of his dominance of her body. She glared up into his eyes, hoping he saw disdain in her look and not the other, more disturbing, emotions she could not crush.

"A scoundrel would not pause at your slaying looks. Shall I show you what he would do?"

She tried to moisten her lips and discovered her mouth had turned to parchment. She sought some withering remark. Searched her mind for something a heroine in one of E. W. Austen's novels might say. Yet beneath his gaze, words evaded her.

He lowered his head, taking her imagination with him. She clenched her teeth at the soft brush of his lips against her neck, his breath warm and moist upon her skin, his lips soft and sure. As much as she wanted to declare her disgust at his touch, she could not banish the desire seeping into her veins, the heat spilling through her. Her heart pounded so loudly she was certain he could hear it.

"Such courage." He smoothed the back of his fingers over her cheek. The gentleness in his touch eased the tautly held breath from her lungs. "It will get you into trouble."

She stared into his eyes, trapped in his gaze. It must be a trick of moonlight, for it seemed she saw her own longing in his eyes, longing and the same horrible loneliness that crept upon her in unguarded moments. Never had she felt this powerful attraction; it pounded through her with each heartbeat, sinking straight into her very bones.

He was her enemy. He was a monster. She could not possibly feel what she was feeling at the moment. This strange connection could not be real, it could not be trusted, it must be as false as this man's declaration of innocence. Yet she could not deny the strange fluttering sensations gripping her. She felt as though she had been waiting all her life, holding her breath in anticipation of this moment, this man. Impossible. It could not be. It must be fear, it must be anger, it must be anything but this unwarranted attraction.

She watched his eyes, and in those dark depths she saw a flicker of recognition, a change that acknowl-

edged all that raged within her. In that look she felt
he could read each reckless thought that flickered
through her brain, as though he knew and shared each
tumultuous emotion pounding through her. The look
in his eyes both beguiled and terrified her. How could
a monster look straight into her soul?

She turned her head, trying to avoid his kiss. She
was struck by the completely irrational thought that
he was not a man at all, but a sorcerer who could steal
her will with one kiss. He checked her move, cradling
her head with his long fingers, holding her prisoner.

He lowered his head. Warm breath spilled across
her cheek. She sealed her lips, determined to resist him
and her own startling need. Soft lips touched her, sliding over the tight line of her mouth, taking gentle possession. A sigh shivered through her at the need in his
kiss. She fought her own need, the unexpected desire
for a scoundrel. She would be a stone beneath him,
unmovable, cold. Yet desire was there, deep within
her, shimmering, rising like mist in the moonlight.

She must not surrender to this monster, yet her body
refused to accept what her mind believed. Doubts of
his wickedness rose from the secret places where she
had tried to bury them. Her body responded, as
though she had been trapped in the dead of winter all
of her life, and he was the heat and light of the spring
sun. He moved his lips upon her, gently stroking,
coaxing her to open to him. She felt like mist, swirling
upward from her frozen bonds, lifting toward the heat
of this man, this conjurer of light and warmth.

She curled her hands upon his wrist, wishing for the
freedom to touch him. She wanted to feel the texture
of his hair, to know the slide of that black silk against
her fingers. And she wanted more. She wanted to test
the breadth of his shoulders beneath her palms, the
sleek curve of his chest. Heaven help her, she had to
stop this.

Chapter Five

Sebastian felt the tension in her, the anger that tightened each sleek limb. If she had been in possession of her pistol, she would have shot him. Still, it was his duty to teach her a lesson. She could not go about in this hen-witted fashion. This kiss had nothing to do with his desire to taste her lips since the very first time his gaze fell upon her. Her fragrance spilled through his senses, warm and womanly, the sweetness of rose water mingled with a spice that was hers alone. The scent dragged his thoughts to places he should not dwell. He caught himself wanting to explore her skin, to discover all the places she had dabbed the sweet water upon her silken flesh.

A voice shouted in his head, a sane voice that spoke of retreat. Honor and propriety must be upheld. Still, to retreat now would mark his own weakness. There was no true danger, he assured himself. He could control the baser instincts that plagued him. He was not a barbarian, ruled by emotion. Intellect was his sovereign. *A man who can keep his head in any situation is a man who can command any situation.* His father had often shared that bit of wisdom with him.

It was not lust or need that drove him. He was too practical to allow such emotions to grip him. Only a true scoundrel would take advantage of this situation. Only a monster would take a woman against her will. Although he wished her to believe the contrary, she was safe enough in his embrace. He was simply going to demonstrate the danger she might face if she tried anything so reckless again. It was the only method that would drive home his point.

She moved her legs against his, impressing the reality of long limbs upon his notice. Images arose in his mind, of her shapely body naked upon white silk sheets, soft skin brushing his thighs. Images of pale skin veiled in nothing more than moonlight. She bucked beneath him in an effort to throw him. He imposed his will upon her. Yet he could not prevent the images from creeping into his mind, the need from pounding through his body. He imagined kissing that pale skin, exploring her, tasting every luscious curve and valley of her. Heat stabbed him low and hard, a fist pounded in his loins, striking with each harsh beat of his heart.

He concentrated on the conjugation of Latin verbs, intent on maintaining his control. A man who kept his head was a man in control of the situation. And he had no intention of losing control. She was a high-spirited filly without the benefit of a strong hand on the ribbons. She needed his guidance. He would show her the danger. This was what happened when a foolish female tried to trap a dangerous male.

Without warning, her lips parted beneath his. Against reason, she kissed him, moving her lips on his with an unexpected ardor that ripped through him like the crack of a whip over a leader's head. The heat simmering in his veins flared, like flame tossed upon spilled brandy. This was not going as he had planned. Still, a part of him wondered whether this was what he had truly sought from the beginning. He wanted her to see him as the man he was, not the monster she believed him to be. He wanted to wreak the same havoc upon her senses that she roused with nothing more than a glance from those beautiful eyes.

He slid his lips upon hers, knowing a kiss would not be enough to quench the fires she had ignited within him. Still, this had to stop. Of course it had to stop. He had not come to this room to seduce her or to be seduced. He had come merely to put an end to her reckless campaign against him. He had meant only to frighten her into thinking clearly. Somewhere in the back of his mind he acknowledged the danger in remaining here. He should pull away from her. Now. While he still had the strength to resist the temptation of this unusual female.

Lord, she felt good beneath him. He had held more women than he could remember, kissed them, sampled all they had to offer. Yet nothing in his experience had prepared him for the intensity of this simple kiss. Never in his life had he tasted such need in a woman. With this kiss she made him feel as though he were the only man who had ever ignited passion within her. The only man she had ever wanted. She kissed him as though it was not his wealth and title that beguiled and tempted her. She kissed him as though kissing him was the last thing in the world she wanted, yet she could not stop herself. She kissed him as though he were the only thing in the world she could not resist. And he devoured the need in her kiss, reveled in her loss of her control.

He spread kisses over her cheek. She quivered beneath him as he slid his tongue down her neck. The scent of roses after rain filled his senses while the taste of her spilled over his tongue. He slid his hand between their bodies, felt the swift pulse of her heart before he closed his hand over her breast. A strangled sound escaped her lips, a sound of wonder and surprise. The firm globe filled his palm. Through the soft cotton of her nightgown he felt her nipple grow hard and tight beneath his touch, betraying her excitement. She turned her head back and forth upon the pillow, flexed her fingers against his wrist, reminding him of how helpless she lay in his grasp.

He looked into her eyes, saw the innocence there, and with it his own damnation. Lord Almighty, what was he doing? She lay staring up at him, trembling like a dove trapped in the talons of a hawk. Self loathing streamed through him, etching an icy path through the fires she had ignited within him. He lifted himself away from her, and got to his feet. He stood when he wanted to run. He remained, determined to salvage some measure of dignity from the wreckage she had made of his composure. "Have you finally realized what it must be like to find yourself at the mercy of a scoundrel?"

She flinched as though he had slapped her. Although he suspected she wanted dearly to hide from him and the truth of what had passed between them, she held his gaze. "Am I now to believe you are innocent?"

"Beautiful and stubborn." He held her gaze, hoping the years of training would not fail him now. Ever since he had assumed his father's title, he had learned the fine art of disguising his emotions. Calm and composed, that was what his mother had needed him to be after his father's death. A cool head, a sturdy shoulder, that was what his sisters had required of him. Duty and responsibility could not be handled properly without discipline. And so he stood before her, as still as a statue, while inside he fought to quell the emotions that threatened to betray him. It seemed there was only one path left to take. He lifted the pistol from the bedside table, while silently he contemplated the risk of what he was about to do.

Emma sat up, her lips parted, her eyes wide. "What do you intend to do with that?"

He tried not to notice the way her nightgown gapped at the neck, revealing the smooth skin he had so recently tasted. Yet the swift surge of blood though his veins would not allow him the luxury of denial. "I cannot make you believe me. You must do what you think is right, Miss Wakefield."

When he turned the pistol and offered the handle to her, she hesitated to take it. She glanced down at the pistol, then back into his eyes, with the wariness of a wild creature facing a predator. "What manner of trick is this?"

"It is a simple declaration, Miss Wakefield." He laid the pistol on the bed beside her, an odd mixture of emotions churning in his chest. After his behavior he would not blame her if she should decide to shoot him. Still, in spite of his brutish conduct, he hoped she might trust him. He wanted her trust more than he cared to admit. "You must decide what to believe."

She rested her hand on the handle of the pistol. He watched her, waiting, his breath hitched in his throat. He could see the battle rage in her eyes. Although he had been the object of speculation in the past, his honor tarnished with lies, his reputation injured, he still hoped beyond hope that this woman of all women might look into his eyes and see the truth of his soul.

"If not you, then who did this?" she asked, her voice raw with tension.

"I assure you, I do not know the monster who is responsible for Miss Usherwood's disappearance." He drew in his breath; she believed him. "But I intend to find out."

He inclined his head in a small bow, then turned and walked toward the door, eager to be away from this place and this confusing female.

"We do not need your help."

Her voice whipped against him. He paused at the door, and drew in his breath, uncertain what he might see should he turn to look at her. Still, he was not a coward. Moonlight carved her image from the shadows, an angel illuminated by a soft silvery glow. An angel who looked as though she wished she could send him straight to the devil. Still, she had not raised the pistol against him. "I can see by your success this evening how very little you need my help."

Emma clenched her hands into tight balls on her lap. "It was a sound plan."

"A sound plan?" She had learned nothing from their encounter. He could see she still retained the same defiance, the same misbegotten courage, that had led her into this desperate act. Something told him this woman might prove the death of him. "Sleep well, Miss Wakefield. And please, do not attempt to hatch any more of your hen-witted schemes. I shall handle the matter."

He did not give her a chance to reply, but closed the door softly behind himself. He marched down the hall, uncertain whether she might follow into the hall and shoot him. At the moment, he wasn't particularly concerned with his physical well-being. He needed to analyze the turbulent emotions she evoked within him. The sensations plaguing him could not possibly be what they seemed.

It was lust, he assured himself, more virulent than any he had suffered in the past, yet lust all the same. When he neared the top of the stairs, he heard a door open behind him. He did not hesitate. He did not glance in her direction. Let her shoot him if she wanted. He had the uncomfortable feeling that a bullet in the back now might be the lesser of the evils awaiting him.

Emma stared at the door leading to the hall, her anger rising with each furious beat of her heart. Apparently Andover had emerged from their encounter unscathed, while she could not deny the tremors gripping her, the heat, the ragged rhythm of her heart. His lovemaking had been nothing more than an attempt to teach her a lesson. Her fingers trembled as she fastened the buttons he had so deftly opened.

Of course he would not be moved by a kiss. He was a man of the world. A man who could claim a thousand conquests. The mysterious Marquess of Andover had his choice of women, women far more beautiful than she. "Of all the arrogant . . ."

She thumped her fist into the mattress. Perhaps he had not kidnapped Charlotte, and perhaps she had been hasty in convicting him. Still, that did not give him the right to barge into her bedchamber and toy with her, to treat her like some silly child.

She threw aside the covers and scrambled from bed. The pistol thumped on the floor. She didn't bother to retrieve it. Trust was something she did not give lightly. There was every reason to believe in his guilt. Yet she had not found the will to lift the pistol against him. In spite of the evidence that screamed his guilt, she could no longer place her entire faith in it. Still, if

Andover thought for one moment she intended to allow him to dictate to her, he was mistaken. She hurried across the room, intent on telling him precisely what she thought of him. She opened the door, dashed out into the hall, and nearly collided with Marjorie.

"Aunt Marjorie, what are you doing up?" Emma glanced past Marjorie while she spoke. The hall was empty.

Marjorie twisted the lace of her dressing gown, bunching the material beneath her chin. "The most dreadful thing has happened."

Emma's chest tightened. "What is it?"

"I knew this was a . . ." Marjorie moistened her lips. "I never should have . . . Oh my goodness, what will happen now?"

Emma took Marjorie's arm and led her into the room. "Aunt Marjorie, what is it?"

Marjorie gripped Emma's arms. "It is Andover. He has escaped. I saw him in the hall moments ago."

Emma nearly collapsed with relief. "Yes. I know. I thought something horrible had befallen us."

"You know he has escaped?"

"Yes. He was here."

Marjorie stared at her. "He was here? With you? Is that what he was doing up here?"

"Yes. He came to see me after removing the hinges from the cellar door."

Marjorie's eyes grew so wide, white showed all around the blue irises. "What did he want?"

"He wanted to assure me he had nothing to do with Charlotte's disappearance."

"Oh my goodness." Marjorie pressed her hand to the base of her neck. "I was afraid of this. To think you threw that poor man into the cellar. I suppose we can only hope he believes you are insane. Oh dear, if he does, he may very well move to see you placed in

51

Bedlam. Still, that would be better than the alternative."

"He does not believe I am insane."

Marjorie nodded, her expression revealing every bit of her despair. "I was afraid of that. He will have us transported. Quietly, of course. He will not want to stir up a scandal."

"He will not have us transported."

"No? Then I suppose he will find some other means to punish us for what we have done." Marjorie gripped Emma's arm and led her to the armoire. "Quickly, we must pack and remove ourselves from London. If he cannot find us, perhaps he will give up hope of obtaining his justice."

"Aunt Marjorie, I do not believe he will attempt to harm us. But I do think it would be best if you join the girls in Hempstead. I should have insisted you leave with them last week."

"I am not leaving you alone to face this." Marjorie threw her arm around Emma's shoulders. "Perhaps we can convince him you are not well. I think it would take very little to persuade him that you are indeed quite mad."

"You must not worry." Emma patted Marjorie's arm. "Only leave this matter to me."

Marjorie lowered her head, a soft moan escaping her lips. "We are doomed."

"I assure you, he does not have vengeance on his mind. I must admit, I believe I misjudged him. He may be arrogant, indeed I know this to be true, but he is not at all a monster."

"He is a very powerful man. A man you kidnapped and tossed into our cellar." Marjorie pressed her hand to her brow. "Oh dear, I fear I may faint."

"You are not going to faint." Emma gripped Marjorie's arm and helped her into the chair near the bed.

"Andover does not wish vengeance. He wants to help us."

Marjorie looked up at her like a child in need of assurance. "He wants to help us? He said he would help us?"

"Yes. He did."

"Oh, I knew he was a good man. I could see it in his eyes. To think he would actually help us after you tossed him into a cellar." Marjorie clasped her hands together. "This is almost beyond belief. The man is a saint."

"Aunt Marjorie, I was thinking . . ."

A look of horror crossed Marjorie's face. "Please, child, you make me very nervous when you do that."

Emma knelt by her chair. "I am quite certain we can handle this without help from Andover."

Marjorie gripped Emma's arm. "What did you say to him? You did not tell him to fly straight to the devil, did you?"

Emma cringed at the condemnation in her aunt's eyes. "I simply told him we did not need his help."

"You told him . . ." Marjorie stared at her for a full ten seconds before she continued. "Good heavens child, I begin to believe you truly are ill. The strain has been too much for you."

"Aunt Marjorie, I am fine."

Marjorie shook her head. "You cannot possibly be fine. Not if you told the Marquess of Andover that we do not need his help in finding Charlotte."

Emma sat back on her heels. "Aunt Marjorie, perhaps he had nothing to do with Charlotte's kidnapping, and I am willing to say he probably did not. Still, he may know the kidnapper. He may, in fact, know the monster well enough to want to protect him."

Marjorie clasped her hands in her lap, as though she

were trying desperately to maintain her composure. "What makes you believe such a thing?"

"The button."

"The button?"

"The button I found in Charlotte's room the morning after she disappeared." Emma stood and crossed the room. She retrieved the button from the top drawer of her dressing table, then returned to Marjorie's side. She opened her palm. Moonlight glowed upon the solid piece of gold.

"Perhaps it has nothing to do with Andover." Marjorie looked up from the button, desperation etched upon her features. "It could be that he has no acquaintance with the owner of that button. None at all."

"The button belongs to someone who is part of a very exclusive club. From the information I was able to gather, the Excalibur Club was started by Andover and several of his close friends when they were boys at Eton. Only a few other men have been admitted as members since that time. Andover must know the man responsible for kidnapping Charlotte, even if he isn't certain which of his friends did it."

"Perhaps he does. It does not mean he will not help us find her."

Emma rested her hand on Marjorie's shoulder. "Do you imagine he would betray the friendship of a man he has known for years to help us?"

"If he is a man of honor, he will do what he can to help find Charlotte." Marjorie held her gaze. "I think we must accept his help."

"A man of honor? Does a man of honor murder his fiancée?"

"I know you enjoyed the story of *The Wicked Duke*." Marjorie released her breath on a shaky sigh. "But I must be honest. I never believed the rumors about Andover."

Emma closed her hand around the button, the gold biting into her palm. In spite of her resolve, she found she could no longer believe the rumors of his guilt either. That fact alone would make her uneasy at the thought of becoming better acquainted with the man. When she thought of the other reasons for keeping her distance, she was decided. "Still, I do not believe we can trust him. We are far better off without his help."

Marjorie shook her head. "I hope you know what you are doing, Emma. Charlotte's life may well be at stake."

Emma knew very well what was at stake. She had no intention of putting her faith in a man with a jaded past. A man who could befuddle her with no more than a glance. She would not be under an obligation to him. The price might be far too high. "Trust me, Aunt Marjorie. I shall handle the arrogant marquess."

Chapter Six

"I wondered where you had disappeared to." With the tip of his polished boot, Montgomery Trent poked the footstool sitting before his chair. His voice was colored with the same amusement that filled his blue eyes. "She actually tossed you into a cellar? At gunpoint?"

"Yes." Sebastian sat on the edge of the claw-footed desk in his library. "I have no doubt at all that she would have shot me. She is a most determined young woman."

"She sounds intriguing," Jourdan Beauchamp said. "She must be quite extraordinary, if she lured you away from your own party."

Sebastian glanced at the tall, dark-haired man standing near the fireplace. Sebastian had been raised the only son in a family of five sisters. His cousin Jourdan was the closest he had come to having a brother. Aside from the bloodline they shared, Jourdan was one of his closest friends, had been since the day he and his mother had arrived at his father's door more than six and twenty years ago, survivors of the bloody revolution. Despite the intervening years, Jourdan had never lost the trace of France in his accent. It was one of the reasons women were entranced by him. He was just the type of man who could turn the head of a virago such as Miss Wakefield. Why that should rankle Sebastian, he did not know, but he could not deny the sharp stab of annoyance in his chest.

"She is reckless. A creature ruled by emotion. I doubt she knows the meaning of logic or reason."

"Even more intriguing." Jourdan smoothed his fingertips over the white marble mantle. "It is difficult to find a woman with fire in her soul."

Sebastian clenched his jaw. "I doubt you would be interested in her."

"No?" Jourdan studied his cousin a moment, a glint of humor entering his dark eyes. "And is this because she interests you, cousin?"

"Interests me?" Sebastian managed a laugh, although the sound did not have the cynical tone he would have liked. "She is hardly the type of female well suited to me. A man would not have a moment's peace with that virago. She is an incendiary device, waiting to go off at any moment."

"Clever. Brave. And unpredictable. I find I like all of those qualities in a woman. It is good to know she does not interest you, cousin." Jourdan inclined his head, a smile curving his lips. "I look forward to meeting her."

Sebastian restrained from commenting on his cousin's interest in Emma, just as he refrained from acknowledging the odd sensation in his chest. It could not be jealousy, he assured himself. He had met the woman once. It was enough to assure him they would not suit. No matter how virulent the physical attraction. It would pass. Lust always burned itself into ashes.

"You say someone entered the house and took the cousin from her bedchamber while the rest of the family slept." Montgomery drummed his fingers on the leather-clad arm of his chair. "That demonstrates a great deal of arrogance."

Before Sebastian could respond, the door opened and his Aunt Dora swept into the room. She fluttered toward Sebastian, looking like a plump parrot in dark green muslin. Arabella followed at a more sedate pace. Each time he saw his lovely cousin, he marveled that this tall, slender young woman with her golden hair and large blue eyes could have anything in common with the woman who had given her birth. "We have called for our carriage, Sebastian, but I could not possibly leave until I had a chance to say good afternoon to my favorite nephew."

Sebastian had little doubt Montgomery was the main reason for the sudden swooping down of his aunt. Violet water spilled around him when she kissed his cheek. She immediately turned to the other men in the room. After greeting them she presented Arabella to both gentlemen. The speculative glint in her eyes could not be missed as Dora watched Montgomery take Arabella's hand.

Sebastian's first inclination was to inform his aunt of Montgomery's vow never to marry. His friend preferred the company of whores over ladies. Sebastian attributed his aversion to marriage to the volatile relationship his parents had shared. Their fights were legendary and often held in full view of their eldest son. It had been enough to sour Montgomery on the entire idea of marriage. Still, Sebastian knew nothing could pry a bone from his aunt's mouth once she had her mind set on it.

Once she had established Arabella in conversation with Montgomery and Jourdan, Dora once again directed her attention toward Sebastian. "I understand you had a grand adventure last night."

Sebastian had little doubt his mother had supplied his aunt with all the details of the previous evening. "I spent a short while in a cellar."

"I wonder what type of woman could lure the very proper Lord Andover from his own party." Dora smiled like a cat who had fallen into the cream. "She must be quite extraordinary."

Emma Wakefield was unlike any woman he had ever met. "She is simply desperate, I believe. You know of the circumstances that brought about my abduction?"

The smile faded from her lips. "Do you truly imagine Bernard had something to do with it?"

"I hope not."

"That boy has been nothing but trouble. It is a wonder he has not sent his poor mama to an early grave." Dora glanced to where Arabella stood near the fireplace, in conversation with Jourdan. Montgomery remained in his chair, content to allow his friend to entertain the lovely girl in their midst. "French," she whispered, her tone disapproving. "I do believe it is time we took our leave of you."

Sebastian watched as Dora deftly removed her daughter from Jourdan's company. Dora lingered a moment in her farewell to Montgomery, before ushering Arabella from the room.

"Beautiful girl," Jourdan said.

"Beauty is but another weapon in the feminine arsenal," Montgomery said. "A respectable woman wants only one thing from a man—everything he possesses."

"And do you count Georgianna and Harriet in that league?" Jourdan asked.

"Sisters are not the same species. At least not to the family." Montgomery tapped his fingers upon the arm of his chair. "It is when they get their sights set on a man that they turn deadly."

Jourdan shrugged. "I, for one, enjoy women."

Montgomery grinned. "I never said I did not enjoy women. I simply prefer the ones who are honest about their price. A respectable female waits until she has a man's leg shackled before cutting open his purse and his veins."

Jourdan nodded. "I confess that I often find the not-so-respectable females far more interesting."

"They are all hen wits. My sisters included. Take this Miss Wakefield. She kidnaps a man, then tosses him into a blasted cellar. A man would never do anything so ridiculous."

Jourdan looked at Sebastian. "I cannot imagine she could actually think you could have done this horrible crime. You are a man of honor. Anyone who knows you knows that. Only a coward would abduct a woman."

"Miss Wakefield does not know me." Sebastian thought of the evidence Miss Wakefield had gathered against him. He had yet to share all of it with Jourdan and Montgomery. "And I am afraid she had her reasons for thinking I was guilty."

"This might be one of the reasons she was willing to believe the worst of you." Montgomery lifted a book from the floor by his chair and carried it to Sebastian.

It was a novel beautifully bound in dark blue leather with the title and name of the author tooled in gold. Sebastian glanced from the title of the book to his friend. "I did not realize you frequented the circulating library these days, Worth."

"Georgianna devours everything by this particular author. When she read this novel, she said I might be interested in the story." Montgomery tapped the binding of the book. "Take a look at the page I have marked."

Sebastian hesitated a moment, an uneasy feeling gripping the pit of his stomach. Still, he had learned from experience one could not avoid unpleasant surprises in life, just as one could not avoid facing tragedy. He flicked open the book and glanced at the page Montgomery had indicated.

He murdered her without the usual passion one might expect in such an act. No, there was little passion in the duke. Where his heart should dwell, a ragged piece of ice resided. Yet she had made the fatal mistake of inflicting a small wound in his enormous pride. No one insulted the duke and walked away unscathed. In her case, she had dared to love another man.

Sebastian stared at the words, certain his expression would not reveal any of the turmoil raging within him. He had learned to control any outward sign of emotion at a young age. The art of composure was essential for a man in his position.

Still, as hard as he tried, he could not crush the memories rising within him, memories that had taken six years to properly bury. "I see the unfortunate coincidence that might have made Georgianna see some resemblance to me, but it is no more than one of those dreadful novels meant to occupy the minds of silly females who frequent the circulating libraries. I understand a great many of these books feature the exploits of wicked aristocrats."

"I am afraid it is a bit more than that. E. W. Austen

is one of the most popular writers of this type of novel. From what Georgianna tells me, *The Wicked Duke* is a sensation. And one thing you can say about my sisters, they are always aware of what is in fashion."

"Apparently there are a great many ladies who have nothing better to do than to waste their time reading such nonsense." Sebastian could not help wondering if Miss Wakefield had read this dreadful novel. He suspected it was the type she would enjoy, filled with romantic nonsense.

Montgomery plucked the leather-bound book from Sebastian's hands. "Georgianna pointed out one of the reasons this particular book is being read in every house in London. Read even by those who do not frequent the circulating library."

The skin at the nape of his neck prickled. Sebastian didn't like that look in his friend's eyes. Trouble always followed that look. As he recalled, that same glint had been in Montgomery's eyes the day he had suggested leading a dancing bear into a certain *don*'s bedchamber. Sebastian had spent the rest of the term rusticating.

"Here is the description of the Wicked Duke." Montgomery cleared his voice in preparation for his oratory. " 'He was not a handsome man, the bones of his face were too sharply carved, his expression too fierce to be considered the poetic ideal of fashion. Yet he was a man who commanded attention. He was tall, and made in the fashion of an athlete, a superb member of the Corinthian set. His hair and eyes were as black as the devil's lost soul. A scar slashed through the far corner of one of his thick black brows, a reminder of a sword duel he had once fought over a beautiful widow.' "

Sebastian smoothed his fingertip over the scar at the corner of his brow. Had that blasted book colored Miss

Wakefield's opinion of him? "I suppose it would not be nearly so romantic to say I cut my brow in a fall from a tree. Still, at least E.W. Austen has elevated me in the peerage."

"Georgianna said this was a sensation?" Jourdan asked.

"I am afraid it is." Montgomery sat on the edge of the desk beside Sebastian. "I checked with two bookshops after I read this. Apparently they cannot keep enough copies on the shelves to satisfy the gossip-hungry masses."

Sebastian resisted the urge to stand and pace the room. Instead he sat like a man who had been turned to stone, while inwardly he dealt with all the emotions that churned within him. His stomach clenched and his heart pounded at the thought of all the rumors that would circulate once people read this book. "The *ton* does love gossip."

"Perhaps this is a blessing, cousin."

Sebastian glanced at Jourdan. "A blessing?"

"This course you have set for yourself, with this idea of how you will choose a wife—I think you are heading straight for disaster."

Few people would have the courage to speak so candidly to him. Jourdan and Montgomery were among a small circle of friends who were not kept at a distance by his title. "It is, in fact, an excellent plan. I see no reason why it should be doomed to disaster."

Jourdan lifted his black brows, just a bit, enough to make the skin at the base of Sebastian's neck prickle with apprehension. No one could say more with so little a gesture. Sebastian suspected he had not hidden much of his thoughts from his cousin. Jourdan had an uncanny way of sensing the truth behind the defenses people tried to raise against him.

In spite of his insistence on the sound nature of his

plan, the very thought of marrying one of the women from that list left Sebastian with a strange restlessness this morning. A restlessness that could not possibly have anything to do with the demented female who had thrown him into her cellar. As much as he tried to dismiss his attraction to the woman, he could not banish her from his thoughts. Even in dreams he was not safe from the tempting Bedlamite. He had awakened this morning as heated and restless as he had been when he had left her the night before.

"I am not certain Sebastian will have anything to concern him." Montgomery tapped his finger against the dark blue leather cover of the book. "Once the ladies on his list read *The Wicked Duke*, they won't go near him."

"You underestimate the English Huntress. A little scandal such as murder will certainly not keep the more ambitious chits from fighting to become a marchioness," Jourdan said.

"It certainly did not keep them at a distance six years ago, when the scandal was fresh." Sebastian lifted his coffee cup from the desk. "I doubt it will discourage any of the females I have chosen as possible brides. Each of them is much too practical."

"And have you no thought of love, cousin?"

The question elicited a chuckle from Montgomery. "Love is an illusion, old man, a spell to blind a man to the truth. And pity any man who falls under that spell."

"What is life without love? Or at least the pursuit of love."

Sebastian inclined his head toward his cousin. "Spoken like a true Frenchman."

Jourdan held his gaze, quiet meaning clear in the dark depths of his eyes. "Your mother, as I recall, is French."

"Yes. And she is filled with the same romantic nonsense as you."

Jourdan shrugged. "Perhaps. Yet I cannot imagine living with a woman I did not love."

"I am afraid I do not share your enthusiasm for chasing that particular fable." Sebastian took a sip of coffee. "It is better to enter into marriage with a clear head."

"A lesson learned from experience." Montgomery released his breath in a long sigh. "For my part, I choose to avoid the entire mess."

Sebastian wished he had the same freedom as his friend. "If you did not have Peter to provide an heir, and Andrew should Peter fail, you might see things in a different light."

Montgomery waved aside his words. "Leave it to the cadet branch, I say."

"I made a promise to my father."

"And yet I wonder whether he would approve of your method of finding a wife." Jourdan rubbed his chin. "I think he would not."

Sebastian tapped his fingers against his thigh. "There is nothing wrong with my method."

"He may be right. Look what happened the first time he was engaged. Beatrice is still making a nuisance of herself after all of these years." Montgomery rubbed his fingertip over the title of the book he held. "This blasted book will dredge up the whole story."

Sebastian thought of all he had endured six years before, the whispers behind his back, the curious stares. The people who knew him well had never given credit to the rumors. Still, it was humbling to realize so many were willing to believe he was a man capable of murder. Although he could tolerate the gossip and speculation, he did not care to have his mother and sisters subjected to the unpleasantness once again.

"Yes. I suspect it will. I overheard some nonsense about this last night from Martha Hendrickson and Judith Whately. I have no doubt they devour this type of book."

"You should sue the author for libel," Montgomery said. "Teach him what happens when he comes at a man from behind."

"My name is not used."

"Your name may not be used, but there is no doubt you are the devil described in the novel." Montgomery tapped his knuckle against the book. "I doubt it would take a great deal to make the publisher reveal just where to find this E. W. Austen."

"I suspect I could find a way to persuade the publisher." Sebastian settled his cup on the saucer upon the desk. If E. W. Austen were in the room, it would take a great deal of will to keep from slamming his fist into the blackguard's jaw. Perhaps a few discreet inquiries were in order. He knew precisely whom to hire for the job. Roger Tunnicliffe was quite good at uncovering information. E. W. Austen had exploited a tragedy in Sebastian's life for personal gain. He intended to make certain the author paid for that privilege. "I would like to meet the man and see what he has to say to me when we are face to face."

"If it is a man," Jourdan said. "E. W. could be a woman."

"A woman." Sebastian had not considered the possibility before now.

"A woman." Montgomery contemplated this a moment. "Yes. It would suit a woman to stab a man from behind. They seldom have the courage to face the opposite sex toe to toe. I suppose your Miss Wakefield is an exception to that. Even if she is a perfect hen wit."

Sebastian thought of the woman who had confronted him the night before and found himself wanting to defend her. "She had reason to believe I was the scoundrel who kidnapped Miss Usherwood."

"You said she imagined you would kidnap the girl just to protect that worthless nephew of yours." Montgomery held his gaze. "Was there more?"

"She found a button near the girl's bed the morning after she disappeared. It was solid gold." Sebastian glanced from Montgomery to Jourdan, then back again. "And it bore the insignia of the Excalibur Club."

"What the devil!" Montgomery shot to his feet. "It cannot be."

"I saw the button."

"We are a small group, cousin. I cannot believe any of our friends would have done this."

"By God." Montgomery paced a few feet, then turned and pinned Sebastian in a steady glare. "There has to have been some foul trick here."

"Yes. I am certain there was." Sebastian rubbed the taut muscles at the nape of his neck. "A button is missing from one of my riding coats. Apparently someone left it in Miss Usherwood's bedchamber."

"It would seem someone was in your house as well," Jourdan noted.

"Someone who would like to implicate you in the girl's disappearance." Montgomery paced to the windows, then turned to face Sebastian. "And why the devil did someone kidnap her in the first place? You said she has no money. What other reason could there be for a kidnapping?"

Sebastian's chest tightened when he contemplated that question. It had haunted him most of the night. The answers that kept ringing in his ears were not easy to accept. "Someone with personal reasons for wanting to take her."

"What could the blackguard possibly want with . . ." Montgomery stared at Sebastian, understanding dawning in his blue eyes. "Bloody hell. If that is true, then we are dealing with the devil himself."

"What can we do to help, cousin?" Jourdan asked.

"I think we should start with a list of men who were paying their addresses to Miss Usherwood." Sebastian rubbed a crease in the knee of his buff-colored pantaloons. "I intend to speak with Mrs. Usherwood this afternoon."

"And what about your nephew?" Montgomery tapped his clenched fist against his side. "There was that incident with Miss Fitzdowny. And he has never held you in much esteem."

Sebastian did not like to admit it, but the truth could no longer be denied. "I have sent for him. I intend to see if I might cause him to betray anything." As he spoke, someone rapped on the door. "I suspect that is Foster announcing the arrival of my nephew."

At his command the butler opened the door and announced the arrival of a visitor awaiting his lordship in the blue drawing room. Yet it was not the visitor Sebastian had been expecting. To his horror, a swift heat swept over him, as though someone had poured a bucket of hot water over his head. He was acutely aware of Jourdan and Montgomery watching his every reaction.

"Tell Miss Wakefield I shall be with her directly, Foster," Sebastian said, satisfied with the composed quality of his voice. After Foster left, he looked at his friends, certain he divulged none of his misbegotten excitement. "It seems I have an unexpected visitor."

"I wonder what the lady wishes with you today, cousin." Jourdan headed for the door.

"And I thought I would have to wait to meet her," Montgomery said, as he followed Jourdan across the room.

Sebastian rose from the desk. "I do not think this is

a good time to introduce you to the lady."

Jourdan turned at the door. "You would not have any personal reasons for keeping her all to yourself, would you, cousin?"

Montgomery grinned. "Has the chit got her claws in you, old man?"

Proprietary notions over a woman he had just met? A woman who had tossed him into her cellar? Ridiculous. "One woman is much the same as the next to me."

Jourdan lifted one black brow. "I am glad to hear it, cousin."

Emma stood near one of the long windows in the drawing room, steeling herself for the meeting that would follow. The unfortunate attraction she'd felt the night before certainly would not trouble her today. She would be as Isabel had been in *The Valiant Viscount*, completely aloof to the wicked advances of the evil Lord Stanwyck. The attraction last night had been an aberration, she assured herself. A reaction to the excitement of the unusual circumstances.

The fact he had stolen into her dreams was nothing to concern her. The shocking manner in which he had behaved—the kiss, the way he had touched her—had simply caused her imagination to take flight. That was all. She certainly was not attracted to the arrogant Marquess of Andover.

The door opened. Her heart thumped against the wall of her chest. She turned, and her breath snagged in her throat. Yet instead of the tall, dark form of Andover, a small woman with black hair entered the room. She smiled when she saw Emma, a look of amusement entering her dark eyes. Although Emma supposed she was somewhere between fifty and sixty, she was beautiful, one of those women who retained the attention of men all of their lives.

"I am Lady Andover," she said, walking toward Emma. "And you are the young woman who tossed my son into a cellar last night."

"Lady Andover, I realize my actions may seem a bit . . . peculiar. But I assure you I had excellent cause, or at least I thought I had an excellent reason for forcing your son into our cellar."

Lady Andover laughed softly. "I only wish I could have seen his face. Yet I suppose he did not betray much of his thoughts. He rarely does. I imagine he simply stepped inside your dark cellar and bid you a good evening."

Emma stared at her, stunned by the friendly tone of her voice. "As I recall, he said he wished I had pleasant dreams."

"At times I wonder how he could have a drop of French blood. I cannot recall him ever having lost control of his anger." Lady Andover waved her delicate-looking hand slowly, as though to dismiss her own words. "I apologize for his lack of passion, Miss Wakefield. I am afraid he had too much responsibility too early."

Lack of passion? The man who had held her last night had burned with hidden fire. Or had she only imagined his passion? Had she attributed to him the emotions he conjured within her? "I had expected him to be angrier at my treatment of him."

"Anger is an emotion. My son does not believe in indulging in emotion. Although I know he has a good heart." Lady Andover pressed her fingertip to her lips as though she were about to tell a secret. "There are more than twenty dogs at his home in Hampshire. I have lost count of them all. Every one has come from the London streets."

70

"He collects strays?"

Lady Andover rolled her eyes. "You should have seen the condition of some of those animals when he brought them home. At times his heart is far too tender."

"I would never have suspected he would allow a mongrel into his home."

"There is much that cannot be known from looking at his face. He guards his thoughts well. As I am certain you have already seen. Although he did not show it, I am certain you surprised him last night. And that is something that does not happen often."

"I realize my actions must seem a little . . . reckless." Emma folded her hands at her waist. "But I could see no other means to get to the truth."

"There is no need to explain. I understand completely." Lady Andover touched Emma's arm. "I am sorry to hear of Miss Usherwood's disappearance. It must be quite difficult for you, and for Mrs. Usherwood."

There was something about this woman, a warmth of spirit, that put Emma at ease. She saw understanding in the dark depths of her eyes, and a genuine compassion. "Thank you for your understanding."

Lady Andover squeezed her arm. "I have five daughters, Miss Wakefield. I can only imagine the horror of what you are going through. I would confront the devil himself if I thought it would help to bring back one of my girls. I can certainly understand why you tossed my son into a cellar. Although if you knew him better, you would know he is the most honorable of men."

Emma thought of the way he had touched her the night before. Obviously there was a great deal this woman did not know about her son. "I realize I might

71

have been a little hasty to have thought him guilty of this crime."

"Do not think of it again." Lady Andover took her arm and led her toward an armchair near the fireplace. "But you are still wearing your bonnet and pelisse. Can you not visit for a while?"

"No. I had only something I must discuss with . . ."

Just then the door opened and Lord Andover entered the room. Any hope Emma might have cherished of finishing her thought evaporated with the sudden heat that swept over her. A tingling sensation slid from the top of her head to the tips of her toes, leaving everything in between simmering with something she could not begin to label.

Andover strode toward her, as though he was completely sure of his legs and the floor beneath his feet, while she stood in fear of dissolving into a quivering bowl of aspic. She tried to think of what Isabel would do when confronted by the wicked Stanwyck, only to discover her brain was not fully functioning.

Andover paused before her, maintaining a polite distance, but her body remembered the press of his hardened frame. She had convinced herself it was merely the quality of candlelight and moonlight that had made this man so attractive the previous evening. Yet sunlight flooded the room this early afternoon, bathing his features, washing away every trace of her conviction. The pure golden light revealed every detail of his face, the faint lines at the corners of his incredible eyes, the black pinpoints of beard slumbering beneath the shaven surface of his lean cheeks. If someone had asked her to define masculinity, she could do so now, by simply thinking of Andover.

"Miss Wakefield, this is an unexpected pleasure." He took her hand, a smile curving his lips.

"Lord Andover," she said, trying to gather her wits.

Dangerous

"Are you going to introduce us, cousin? Or must I ask Aunt Jacqueline for the honor?"

It was then Emma noticed two men standing just behind Andover. She had never been the object of gallantry. Her life had not provided any opportunity to indulge in flirtation. Yet she did not need experience to identify the glint of male interest when she saw it. And much to her surprise both men regarded her with more than mild curiosity. She supposed in another place and time both of these men would not have taken any notice of her. Although she could not honestly say the reverse. She doubted any woman would fail to notice either of these men. They were what E. W. Austen would describe as "the type of men who had stepped out of a woman's dream." Although she acknowledged the male beauty of each man, neither raised the tingles Andover could muster with a single glance. That realization did nothing to improve her sense of calm. After a short while, the gentlemen left. Lady Andover soon followed, leaving Emma alone with Andover.

Emma sat on the edge of an armchair. Although Andover stood several feet away, he was still far too close to allow her heart to resume a normal rhythm. Despite the muddle he made of her brain, she recognized the problem with her strategy. Each time she tried to think of him as a villain in an E. W. Austen novel, he kept turning into the hero of the piece. It wreaked havoc on her attempts to smother the attraction she held for him.

He rested his arm on the mantel, his hand dangling over the edge. It was a powerful-looking hand, with long, elegantly tapered fingers. Her mouth grew dry when she thought of how he had touched her with that strong hand last night.

"Would you like a glass of wine, Miss Wakefield?

You are suddenly looking a little flushed."

"No. I am fine."

"Are you certain?"

"Yes. I am quite fine." At least she would be fine if she could manage to crush her impossible attraction to this man. "Lord Andover, I came here to tell you that, although I appreciate your offer to help find Charlotte, we do not need your aid."

Andover held her gaze, and she had the horrible feeling he knew everything she was thinking. "You may not want my help, Miss Wakefield, but I suspect Miss Usherwood needs it."

She held his gaze, wishing she could see beyond the beauty of his eyes into his mind. Yet his thoughts were well guarded. "I wonder at your reason for wanting to help us, Lord Andover."

"From what I was given to understand, you have no one else to help you find your cousin."

"And that is your reason? You have nothing else in mind? No hope to gain an advantage over me?"

He held her gaze, a curious look entering his eyes. "You imagine I am offering to help find a lady who has been kidnapped because I wish to have some hold over you? Is that truly what you believe?"

"You would have me think you are doing this simply out of the goodness of your heart. That you are some knight errant come to our rescue." Emma held his gaze when she wanted very much to turn and run from the room. Still, she would not surrender to the weakness. "I find it difficult to believe, Lord Andover."

He drew in his breath, as though he were trying to quell the anger she could see flickering in his eyes. When he spoke, his voice was low and tightly controlled. "I see that it is far easier to believe I am a scoundrel, a blackguard who would use this unfortunate situation to put you under some obligation to me. Do you imagine I intend to offer you a carte blanche?"

It suddenly sounded outrageous and far too filled with conceit. Perhaps it was ridiculous to imagine this man would actually want to force her into his bed. Heat prickled the base of her neck. Still, there were other, more logical reasons not to accept his help. "Not precisely. But it is a matter of . . ."

"Do you truly imagine I must coerce women into my bed, Miss Wakefield?" He stalked her, his eyes fierce with emotion. "Do you truly believe I have no other means to find my pleasure?"

Chapter Seven

Emma rose as he drew near. Lady Andover's words rang in her brain. Yet this was not a man devoid of emotion. This was a man with fury blazing in his dark eyes. Every instinct shouted *Run!* Still, no heroine worth her salt would flee. "Perhaps I was ..."

"Do you imagine I must pay a woman to lie with me?" Andover advanced, stalking her like a lion annoyed by a particularly vexing mouse.

Emma backed away. "My lord, I certainly ..."

"Do you imagine I must use my title, my wealth, my power, to gain an advantage over a woman? Do you imagine a woman could not possibly find anything attractive in me?"

She did not wish to contemplate his wiles. Last night she had crashed headlong into his beguiling masculinity. She knew all too well how potent this man could be when he applied his charm. He approached. She stepped back and bumped into an armchair. "I can see now that I . . ."

He closed the distance between them, trapping her between the chair and his powerful frame. "Am I so unappealling, Miss Wakefield?"

She stared up into his eyes, stunned by the emotions flaming in the dark depths. The anger was clear. Yet there was more, much less easy to perceive, longing and need, and . . . loneliness. She recognized the latter most of all. Too often it gazed back at her from her own mirror. She had wounded his pride, and she did not wish to contemplate the retribution for such a transgression. "Lord Andover, I . . ."

He gripped her arms when she tried to sidle away from him. Slowly he drew her toward him, until her breasts pressed against the hard wall of his chest. Sensation swirled through her, warm and tingling. It occurred to her then that this was what she had wanted since he had walked into the room.

"Does my touch fill you with revulsion, Miss Wakefield?" he asked, his voice low and oddly strained.

She only wished it did. Last night he had given her a taste of passion, a mere glimpse of what might come to pass between a man and woman. He had haunted her dreams, holding her, kissing her, touching her in all the ways she imagined a man touching the woman he adored. All her life she had imagined finding a man who could set her pulse racing, her hopes soaring. Only it could not be this man. It was foolish to think of him romantically. They did not belong to the same world. He did not adore her. She could not trust him. What was worse, she could not trust the treacherous feelings he evoked. They were not destined for a happy ending.

"Do you intend to teach me another lesson, my lord?"

"A lesson?" He lowered his gaze to her lips. Although he did not touch her, she felt a strange sensation spread across her lips, as though they had been caressed by his. "How deceitful conceit can be."

Andover was so close, his mouth a whisper from hers. Emma caught herself lifting upward, seeking the warm brush of his lips upon hers. "Conceit is often bred by power, my lord."

"Experience should have taught me long ago. A strong-willed woman will not be led in anything."

She clenched her teeth when he slipped his hands from her arms. It took all her will to keep from reaching for him as he stepped away from her. The air felt chilly against her where his warmth had bathed her skin. She smothered the longing that screamed within her. There was no future with this man. None of her wishful imagining could alter circumstances. Even E. W. Austen could not write a proper ending for her.

He drew in his breath. She could see him rebuilding his composure. Still, she had glimpsed the volatile male beneath his cool facade. Primitive. Passionate. At once frightening and beguiling. She suspected only the strength of his will kept the beast within at bay.

"Miss Wakefield, I am not offering my help in finding your cousin in the hope of forcing you to become my mistress."

Of course he would not wish her to be his mistress. She was hardly the type of woman he would keep as one of his lady birds. From what she had gathered in her research on him, he chose only the most beautiful women to warm his bed. "I should not have assumed so much, my lord."

He inclined his head in a small bow. "You have my

word, I have only the most honorable intentions in this matter."

Emma thought of the button and the motives he might have behind his offer to help her. "Still, my lord, I find it strange that you would offer to help us, unless, of course, you had another motive."

He stared at her, his dark eyes narrowed, the muscles in his jaw tense. "Is it truly so hard to imagine I might offer my help for no other reason than that it is needed?"

Emma lifted her chin. "Yes, my lord, it is."

"Tell me, Miss Wakefield, do you distrust all men, or me in particular?"

"Experience is an excellent tutor."

Andover frowned, twin furrows digging between his black brows. He was quiet, and in the silence she heard a hundred questions, none of which she wanted to answer. "I cannot speak for the men you have known. I can only give you my word that I intend to find Miss Usherwood."

Before she could respond, someone knocked on the door. At Andover's command, the door opened and his gray-haired butler announced the arrival of Mr. Bernard Radbyrne.

"Tell him I will be with him directly." When the butler had gone, Andover turned to Emma. "I need to speak with my nephew."

"Do you suspect he knows something about Charlotte?"

He did not respond. She had the feeling he was judging her, determining how much to tell her.

"I will not be kept in the dark, my lord. If you wanted Charlotte to stay away from your nephew, I must assume you believe him to be something less than honorable."

"I cannot say for certain if Bernard had anything to

do with Charlotte's disappearance. But I cannot say for certain he did not."

"I want to be there when you speak with him."

Andover smiled. "I doubt he would be any more forthcoming if you were present."

Emma looked him straight in the eye. "You would not intend to protect him, would you, my lord?"

"It would seem you are a long way from trusting me, Miss Wakefield." He took her arm and headed for the door.

Emma twisted free of his grasp. "If you imagine you can simply usher me out of the house . . ."

He pressed his fingertip to her lips, the gentle touch scattering her words into a gasp. "You may wait in the hall outside the library gallery. I shall leave the door open. If you remain in the hall, he will not be able to see you, but you should be able to hear everything that is said. Will that make you more comfortable?"

Emma could not imagine ever feeling comfortable around this man. He had the most unfortunate way of making her blood pound through her veins. A way of making her think of things she ought not to imagine. "How do you intend to make him confess?"

Andover lifted his brows. "Are you always so quick to convict?"

"Just in case he is guilty, how do you intend to make him confess?"

"I doubt tossing him into a cellar will get us what we want, if that is what you are thinking. I intend to speak with him." Andover took her arm. "Come along, Miss Wakefield. And above all, resist the urge to barge into the room."

Emma hesitated a moment when he offered her his arm. Although she knew it was nothing more than a polite gesture, the idea of taking his arm seemed terribly intimate. She clenched her teeth. She was not a foolish spinster who dissolved into hot pudding at the simple touch of a man's arm, she assured herself. She placed her hand on his arm, grateful that she had not removed her gloves. Still, her glove did not permit ignorance of what lay beneath her palm, the strength of muscle and bone.

She looked at a landscape hanging upon one of the wainscoted panels in the hall, stared at each wall sconce they passed, listened to the soft sound of footsteps upon the polished floorboards, all in an attempt to dismiss the man walking beside her from her thoughts. Yet Andover was there in her periphery, tall and powerful, impossible to ignore.

The scent of him filled her every breath, a smoldering blend of herbs and leather and man. The warm scent swirled through her head, teasing memories from their carefully guarded tombs. How could she hope to ease the horrible pounding of her heart, when Andover was so near? When every brush of her gown against his leg reminded her of the press of those long legs on hers? When each shift of muscle beneath her palm teased her with the thoughts of his arms closing about her? She really must get a rein upon these terribly wayward thoughts. They were foolish. Worse, they were dangerous.

Sebastian glanced at the woman walking beside him. A bonnet covered her hair, allowing only a few wisps to frame her face. Her apple green over-garment was buttoned to her neck. The pale green muslin of her dress peeked out from the front edges of the pelisse with each step she took. Although he did not consider himself an oracle of fashion, as Brummell did, he was familiar enough with women to recognize fashionable attire when he saw it. And he could definitely say Miss Wakefield was not at all fashionable. In fact, she was in danger of being called a dowd. There was certainly no reason why he should think she looked beautiful this afternoon. And therein lay his problem.

This morning, before she had come to his house, he had convinced himself it was the alchemy of candlelight, the magic of moonlight that had made her so attractive to him the night before. Yet the moon was far from rising. Not a single candle burned in the wall sconces they passed. And still his blood ran hot. It had taken every scrap of his will to keep from kissing her. His chest still burned from the memory of her breasts snuggled close against him. A fist pounded in his loins, striking with every quick beat of his heart.

The soft rustle of her gown conjured images of long pale limbs sliding upon white silk sheets. He tried to remember the last time a woman had bothered him in this fashion. Yet the answer was nearly as disturbing as the unsettling emotions she evoked in him. Never. Never had a woman managed to overset his composure in quite this way. Quick and scalding, the need for her had hit him as soon as his gaze had fallen upon her. Worse was this emotion that he could not quite label, a powerful force that gripped his vitals and threatened to crush his intellect in its vise.

It would pass, he assured himself. This affliction named Emma would fade in time. Yet even as the thought formed, doubts surfaced to nibble away at that comforting hope. He was not a barbarian. He lived his life based on logic, not on the unreliable shifting of emotion. Yet he could not cool his blood, not with all the power of his considerable intellect. Not while Emma was so near. Not while her fragrance— the faint perfume of roses after rain—spilled through his senses, coaxing him to press his lips against her neck. Not while her hand rested upon his arm, warming him through the layers of cloth, teasing him with all the ways he wanted to feel her hands upon his skin. Not while her gown brushed against his leg, sparking thoughts of her limbs entwined with his own.

She walked beside him, without glancing at him, her chin lifted with pride and defiance. What had happened to destroy her trust in men? Although he told himself it was none of his concern, he could not help wondering if her heart had been shattered by a lover in the past. With that thought came other, more disturbing ones. He had only met her yesterday. The thought of another man touching her should not stab him like the thin blade of a rapier, but it did. He really had to analyze these emotions. They could not be what they seemed.

When they arrived at the hall outside the library gallery, she took her hand from his arm. Still, he felt the brand of her touch. "Remember, stay here. No matter what you hear," he whispered. "Do you think you can manage to keep your temper in check?"

Anger flared in her eyes. "I am quite coolheaded, my lord," she whispered.

"Of course you are, Miss Wakefield." Without another word, he left Emma in the hall, then entered the library gallery. The mellow scent of leather wrapped around him, washing the fragrance of roses after rain from his nostrils. Still, he could not shake the restless feeling that had gripped him upon first glance of Emma.

He paused at the baluster and looked into the library. Below him, Radbyrne stood beside the liquor cabinet, as though the house were his. He turned when he noticed Sebastian descending the narrow circular stairs leading from the gallery to the room below. He held a decanter of brandy in one hand, a snifter in the other. "I have always admired the quality of your cellars, uncle."

"I have noticed." Radbyrne had a habit of confusing what was his and what belonged to Sebastian. More than once the young man had signed his uncle's name in place of his own on various bills. Sebastian had managed to curb that particular practice, earning his nephew's contempt.

Sebastian's sister Aveline blamed her son's tendencies toward larceny on the fact of her husband's death twelve years before, when Radbyrne was fourteen. Since Sebastian's own father had died when he was twelve, he had a different view of this particular proclivity.

A loud *ping* rang in the room when Radbyrne dropped the stopper back into the decanter. "I heard an interesting rumor last night, uncle."

Sebastian crossed the room, causing Radbyrne to turn away from the gallery to keep him in view. "One of the things you can rely upon in London is the abundance of interesting rumors."

Radbyrne sipped his brandy, the look in his eyes that of a boy eager to play a trick on an unsuspecting elder. He was a tall man, more slender than his padded coat would suggest. With golden locks carefully shaped into disheveled waves and the sculpted features and large blue eyes that turned feminine heads, Radbyrne had quickly discovered the power he held over the females in his midst. Unfortunately, he had his own ideas of what constituted the meaning of honor. "This was particularly disturbing."

The back of Sebastian's neck prickled. "I suspect the more disturbing the rumor, the more opportunity for it to circulate."

"Yes. And one can so seldom believe rumors. Can one, uncle? People are quick to spread their malicious little *on dits*, even though there is not a shred of truth in them." Radbyrne tapped his fingertip against the side of his glass. "Particularly if the rumor concerns someone from a prominent family."

Sebastian sat on the arm of a leather chair near the fireplace. He had an idea of what would follow. Radbyrne's strategy was not difficult to decipher. "Are you referring to the rumor about you and Madeline Fitzdowny, Bernard?" he said, checking his nephew's move.

"I would have thought those rumors had died weeks ago." One corner of Radbyrne's mouth tightened, his smile growing pinched. He drifted to one of the long windows and directed his attention to the gardens. "You cannot still imagine I had anything to do with that unfortunate incident."

There was a coldness about his nephew, an icy disdain for anything and anyone who threatened to spoil his sport. It came from thinking himself above everyone. "I have yet to uncover the truth of what happened that night," Sebastian responded.

Radbyrne tugged at the hem of his waistcoat. "You sound as though you are still looking into the matter. I cannot imagine a more prodigious waste of time."

"Shall we say, I do not care to allow the mystery to go unsolved."

"It is your time, uncle. If you choose to spend it chasing after moonbeams, it is your choice. Still, I would think you had more important things to concern you." Radbyrne turned and faced Sebastian. "Did you summon me this afternoon to discuss that piece of ancient history?"

"No." Sebastian fixed his nephew in a steady gaze, allowing the moment to stretch. If he took no humor in Radbyrne himself, he did at least find his costume amusing. Apparently his nephew had abandoned his attempt to join the Corinthian set to ally himself with those gentlemen less prone to sport and more to the excesses of fashion. The points of his collar nearly obscured his ears while the cherry red striped waistcoat screamed for attention. "I wanted to speak to you about Miss Charlotte Usherwood."

Radbyrne brushed his fingers over the leather binding of one of the books lining the mahogany and brass bookcase beside him. "Miss Usherwood? I do not know why you would want to speak to me about her."

"You have been paying your addresses to the young lady."

"That does not mean I had anything to do with her disappearance."

Sebastian's chest tightened. He would like to believe in his nephew's innocence, if for no other reason than for his sister Aveline's sake. Yet he could not dismiss the possibility of his guilt. "And how did you know of her disappearance?"

Radbyrne fiddled with the diamond stickpin in the folds of his neck cloth, sending shards of colored light over his hand. "Why would I not hear of it?"

He noticed the way Radbyrne glanced past him as he spoke, his gaze lifting to the gallery. Sebastian glanced in the same direction, hoping he would not find a beautiful virago glaring down at them. Fortunately, he did not see anyone standing beyond the brass railing of the gallery. "I did not suppose anyone knew of Miss Usherwood's disappearance."

"I believe I heard it from my valet. And he heard it from one of the maids." Radbyrne cleared his throat. "You know London. Nothing is a secret for long. Servants have a way of spreading news more effectively than the *Times* or the *Post*. Apparently the chit has run off with a lover."

It was a reasonable story. One he might have believed if he were not dealing with Radbyrne. "Since you spent much of your time in her company, have you any idea who may have won her affections?"

"I have no idea." Radbyrne glanced down into his glass. "Someone fool enough to allow his head to be turned by a pretty face and an empty purse."

Sebastian silently willed Emma to remain in the hall. Outwardly, he knew his composure did not falter. He had conquered his emotions long ago. At least, in most cases he could rely upon his self control. Emma Wakefield was the exception, he assured himself. In spite of the anger that simmered within him, his voice remained steady when he said, "You spent a great deal of time in her company. Yet I take it you never had any intention of offering for the girl?"

Radbyrne glanced up from his contemplation of the brandy in his glass. He fixed his uncle with a cool glare. "I enjoyed her company. What man could not enjoy the company of a pretty female? But it will take more than a pretty face to shackle me. She was but one of countless girls who come up each year from the country. Prettier than most, perhaps. But you know what they are like. You must know how dreadfully cunning ambitious chits can be. They will do anything to trap a man into marriage."

Sebastian knew precisely how ambitious women could be in their hunt for prey. He had the scars to prove it. He also knew the rules of engagement in battle. Seducing innocent females was not the done thing. Unfortunately, Radbyrne did not abide by those rules. It was the reason he had warned Mrs. Usherwood to keep her daughter from the company of his nephew.

"Why the devil are you interested in the Usherwood chit? You certainly were not considering her as a possible bride? Is she on your list?"

"List?"

"Come now, uncle, everyone knows you have a list of women you are considering for the post of Marchioness of Andover." He paced a few steps, then paused beneath a stained-glass window depicting St. George slaying the dragon. Sunlight slanted through the colored glass, slashing a line of red across Radbyrne's cheek. "It never ceases to amaze me how quickly news travels in this town. I suppose you did not even realize that most of London is making wagers on which lady you will choose as your marchioness."

Sebastian had learned a few days ago that the subject of his bride quest had become popular knowledge. The realization had come the night he had seen his name in a betting book at White's. Still, he had no intention of allowing Radbyrne to divert him. "I had an interesting conversation with Miss Usherwood's cousin last night. Miss Wakefield seemed to think her cousin had been kidnapped."

"Kidnapped?" Radbyrne laughed, as though he had not a care in the world. "From what I have seen of that cousin of Charlotte's, she is a supercilious bluestocking. An ape leader who would run screaming into the night should a man wink at her. You certainly cannot abide by what she might say."

"Perhaps." Sebastian fought the inexplicable urge to plant his fist in his nephew's jaw. "Still, I would appreciate it if you would let me know whether you hear anything more about the girl. I am certain her family would like very much to know with whom she has eloped."

Radbyrne rolled his glass between his palms. "I take it then that you will be looking into the matter?"

Sebastian molded his lips into a smile. "As I have said, I do not like to leave a mystery unsolved. You will let me know if you hear anything?"

"Of course. I shall be alert to any information." Radbyrne drained his brandy, then walked toward the door. He set his glass on a small commode near the door, then turned back to face his uncle. "I do not suppose you have heard of a book entitled *The Wicked Duke*?"

Sebastian had suspected this was the rumor that had delighted his nephew. "Interesting choice of reading, Bernard. It sounds like a book bored ladies would enjoy."

Radbyrne's nostrils flared. "From what I understand it is all the crack this Season. It is about an arrogant aristocrat who murders his fiancée because she wants to marry another man. And the really disturbing thing is, the description of the aristocrat is like a well-painted portrait of you."

Sebastian held Radbyrne's triumphant gaze, well aware that his nephew was searching for a reaction. He did not give him the satisfaction of seeing his annoyance. "It is obvious there is little else to amuse the *ton* this Season."

One corner of Radbyrne's mouth twitched. "It is terrible really. It seems the book is stirring up all the old rumors about how you murdered Beatrice. You will not be able to go anywhere without people gossiping behind your back."

"People do not need my back to gossip."

Radbyrne's lips tightened into a flat line. "I should think you would be much more comfortable in Hampshire, until the rumors die out. Given the circumstances, I doubt any of the ladies on your list will be eager to accept your suit, so it will gain you nothing to remain in London."

Sebastian lifted his brow. "Strange you would recommend that course of action. It seems the cowardly thing to do. You would not be questioning my honor, would you, nephew?"

"No, of course not." Radbyrne tugged the hem of his waistcoat. "I only thought of your comfort, uncle."

"Not to worry, Bernard, I shall take your suggestion in the spirit it was given."

"Excellent. Well, I shall bid you good day then." With that Radbyrne opened the door and left the room.

A moment after the door closed, Emma stormed onto the gallery. She gripped the balustrade and glared down at him. Sunlight slanted through the windows, glinting on the brass beneath her hands, casting a soft glow upon her face. The picture she presented brought to mind a portrait of an avenging angel, beautiful in her wrath. Although he tried to prevent it, he could not stem the swift tide of heat washing over him.

He watched her descend the circular staircase, curious about the reason for her anger. He did not begin to understand the triggers that lead to her explosions. She was obviously a creature of grand passion. The type of female he usually avoided with the same care he would avoid a rabid dog. Yet for some reason he did not want to avoid her. For some unfathomable reason he wanted to catch her up in his arms, lay her down upon the nearest piece of furniture, and make love to her until he could no longer remember what day it was.

She marched to where Sebastian was sitting and glared at him. "You allowed him to leave."

Her anger had deepened the pink of her cheeks. He tried not to think of how very pretty she looked. Yet he could not shake the urge to touch her, to feel that blush beneath his lips. "What precisely did you imagine I would do with him, Miss Wakefield?"

"He did it." She gestured broadly with her hands. "Did you not hear him? He knew of the abduction. He all but confessed to kidnapping her."

"Is there any possibility that one of your servants

may have spread the story of Miss Usherwood's elopement?"

"No."

"Servants do like to gossip."

"We have a small establishment, my lord. Our housekeeper and butler have been with us since I was a child. Mr. and Mrs. Carruthers were the only ones who knew what happened. I assure you, no one spread any story about Charlotte's elopement. He lied to you. He can tell us where Charlotte is. And you allowed him to walk out of here."

"Miss Wakefield, allowing your emotions to get the better of you will not improve matters."

She turned away from him, marched a few steps, then pivoted to face him. "You are trying to protect him."

The accusation struck with the force of a blow. Anger welled up inside him, stunning in its intensity. Still, he managed to keep his voice steady when he said, "I assure you, Miss Wakefield, that is not the case."

Her eyes narrowed. "Why did you let him leave?"

He could not say why her anger and distrust bothered him so violently. He told himself she was an emotional creature. He assured himself it was circumstance that led her to believe he was a blackguard without honor. Yet all his attempts were no more than a drizzle upon a blazing fire. "We cannot be certain he is responsible for her disappearance. I have no evidence against him. No means to make him divulge the whereabouts of Miss Usherwood."

"He did it."

"I suspect he did have a hand in it, or at least he knows what happened. Our best chance of finding out precisely what he knows is to keep an eye on his

91

movements and hope he betrays himself or his accomplice."

She stared at him. "You intend to do nothing."

"On the contrary, Miss Wakefield. I intend to find out exactly what part he played in your cousin's disappearance."

She held his gaze, as though she were trying to look into his soul. "And did you ever discover what part he played in Madeline Fitzdowny's death?"

"What do you know of that?"

"Only what I read in the newspapers. And heard through rumors. A few weeks ago she was found floating in the Thames. As I recall, she had been at Vauxhall. It was believed she had fallen in while taking a stroll." Emma clasped her hands at her waist, as though trying to contain all the emotion he could see blazing in her eyes. "From what I heard today, I surmise you believe your nephew had a hand in her drowning."

"I have not been able to prove anything, Miss Wakefield." Sebastian turned away from her, hoping some distance might clear his head. The confounded woman had a disturbing way of muddling his brain. "But under the circumstances, there are a few things you should know."

Chapter Eight

Emma watched him cross the room. Although he was a large man, he moved with surprising grace. Unfortunately almost everything about him took her by surprise. Each time she saw him she realized more and more just how wrong E. W. Austen had been in describing this man. Here was not a man of ice. She told herself the trembling in her limbs was caused by anger. Yet the emotion shivering through her refused to settle under that nice, comfortable label. It refused to settle at all.

Instead it coiled through her, swirling, slithering, setting her pulse racing, simmering low in her belly. It mocked reason. It laughed at logic. It defied her every attempt to crush it. A practical woman would not entertain the thoughts whirling through her brain. A reasonable woman would look at everything she knew of this man and keep her distance.

The problem was that when he was near, her brain

stopped functioning properly. Her emotions took control. Emotions she had only imagined in the past. Emotions she should not feel for this man. Yet here she stood, staring at his broad back, with visions of Italian statuary flickering in her mind. Bold. Bare. Man idealized in cold white marble.

What would he say if he knew how much she wanted to touch him again? As much as she wanted to deny it, she could not. She wanted to rip open his shirt and slide her hands over the sleek muscles of his chest. She wanted to feel the heat of his skin, find all the places he was rough, everywhere he was smooth. She wanted to press her lips against his neck and feel the pulse of his blood. She had never explored the exotic terrain of a man's body. Before Andover she had never met a man who conjured such wanton thoughts in her.

He opened a cabinet across from her. "I hope I can trust you to keep a confidence, Miss Wakefield. I do not wish to subject my family to needless gossip."

Emma forced air past her tight throat, ignoring a sudden prickle of guilt. "I have my own reasons to keep this matter private, my lord."

"I understand." Andover lifted a decanter from the cabinet and poured what she assumed to be wine into two glasses.

When he turned to face her, he did something completely unexpected. He smiled. Not one of those tight grins she had often see him employ, but a genuine smile. One that lit the depths of his dark eyes. Her knees quivered. Oh no, E. W. Austen did not do this man justice in creating *The Wicked Duke*. Emma forced starch into her back as he approached her. She would not be swayed by Andover's brand of masculinity. No matter how potent it might be.

He offered her a glass. "Would you care to remove your coat?"

She gripped the fluted glass. "No."

He gestured toward a large leather sofa. "Would you care to sit?"

"I prefer to stand. I do not plan to be here any longer than necessary."

He lifted his brows, just slightly. If she had not been so aware of every detail of his face, she would have missed the change in his expression. "You are very direct, Miss Wakefield. Other women might actually have allowed me to believe they could tolerate my company."

Emma imagined most women would more than tolerate his company. "Ours is not a social connection, Lord Andover. Under other circumstances we would never have met."

"True." His long thick lashes lowered, shielding the expression in his eyes. "Our situation reminds us that we are all subject to the whims of destiny."

Destiny? She could not entertain thoughts of destiny in connection to this man. "What part do you believe your nephew played in Miss Fitzdowny's drowning?"

He looked at her, his eyes narrowed, his lips tipped into a crooked grin. "You are very eager to make certain this conversation does not delve into the personal, are you not?"

She set her wineglass on a pedestal table near one of the sofas. If she held on to it much longer, she was certain to spill. Her hands were trembling too much. "There is nothing personal where you and I are concerned."

He grimaced. "Delivered with all the precision of a right hook to the jaw, Miss Wakefield."

A thrill careened through Emma. It came from the suggestion that this man might want more from her than a mere acquaintance. A sane voice chased that thrill, a voice that spoke of arrogant aristocrats and what they might offer a woman in her position. "I do not mean to insult you. I am afraid I am not adept at casual flirtation. I have never been in the position to practice my skills as a coquette."

"And did you imagine I was flirting with you, Miss Wakefield?"

Although she did not have experience in these matters, she was not a green girl. She knew something of men, enough to recognize some measure of interest in him. "Yes. Were you flirting with me, Lord Andover?"

He looked surprised, as though she truly had slammed her fist into his jaw. "I believe I was."

"I suspect a man in your position is so accustomed to flirtation that it becomes as natural as breathing. I am not. And, as you can see, I am also not very good at it."

He rubbed the tip of his forefinger over his bottom lip, his expression that of a man who was carefully considering what she had said. "A beautiful woman who has not perfected her skills at flirtation. I did not think such a creature existed."

Beautiful? Her heart missed a beat. Did he truly imagine she was beautiful? Even as her heart fluttered foolishly, her mind corrected her course. She glanced away from him, her gaze resting on the stained-glass window across from her. "Another bit of flirtation. It is quite wasted on me, I assure you."

"Because you find me so disagreeable."

She moistened her lips. "Because I am quite beyond the age when one engages in such foolish games."

"And when does flirtation become foolish?"

"I am six and twenty, Lord Andover. Hardly a girl straight out of the school room."

"I do not find girls straight out of the school room

particularly interesting." He sipped his wine. "Yet you, Miss Wakefield, intrigue me."

She suddenly wished she had taken a seat on the sofa. Her legs were trembling so violently, she feared they might give way. "I suppose you do not meet many women who toss you into a cellar."

He laughed, the sound of a man comfortable with laughter. That surprised her as well. "Why have I never met you until now? Where have you been hiding all my life?"

He was very good at this game. He knew precisely how to make her feel pretty and desirable. And that was the essence of flirtation, was it not? Her every attempt to quell the quick pace of her pulse ended in failure. She was feeling every bit as green as Miss Kenrick in *The Country Miss*. The few country parties she had attended before Uncle Henry's death had not prepared her for a man like Andover. If fate had been kinder, Emma would have been able to cross swords with him in this game. As it was, he had the advantage.

Still, Emma knew questioning fate was pointless. Time and time again she had wondered what her life would have been like if her parents had not died at such an early age. If her Uncle Henry had not taken ill and died so unexpectedly. Yet the past could not be altered. All one could do was make the most of the present and work toward a better future. She was a quick study in most things. Was flirtation truly any different? "Are you so sure we have never met?"

His eyes narrowed, a look of uncertainty filling the dark depths. "I would have remembered."

She wanted to believe him. It was a pleasant fantasy, to imagine what might have happened if she had walked into his ballroom at the tender age of eighteen. She would have worn a white dress and pearls and her hair in ringlets. And of course she would have noticed him. Every girl in the room would have noticed Andover.

It was pleasant to imagine that he would have taken one look and fallen desperately in love with her. They would have married. By now they would have had three children. Yes, it was pleasant. And it was a fantasy. "I wonder if you would have noticed me. I imagine you meet a great many girls every Season. All of them fresh and eager. I might have been but one of them, a face in a sea of faces."

He touched her cheek, a soft brush of his bare fingers across her skin. Yet that gentle touch squeezed the air from her lungs. Although sunlight revealed every detail of his face, she knew she must be imagining what she saw. It must be her own need reflected in his eyes. Her own longing. Her own loneliness. "You have a very memorable face, Miss Wakefield. I would have noticed you. I would have remembered you."

The room grew dim, a mere collection of colors without shape and form. Only he had substance. He filled her vision, blocking out the rest of the world. It seemed the sunlight was spinning golden threads around them, binding one to the other. In this instant she could almost believe the past had altered, space and time had shifted. All the possibilities of her wishful imagination fluttered in her mind. All her longing and need. In that instant the dream seemed so real, she could touch it. Yet it was as ethereal as mist.

She stepped back, breaking the soft contact of his hand upon her face. "We never met, Lord Andover, because I never had a London Season. I have lived most of my life in Hempstead."

Although she stared at a blue and white porcelain bowl that sat on a small table near one of the windows, she could still see him from the corner of her eye. He stood watching her, as though he were trying to fit together the pieces of a puzzle. She knew the questions flitting through his head without hearing them. The answers to which were none of his concern.

She turned to face him. "Do you believe your nephew murdered Madeline Fitzdowny?"

He did not reply at once, and in the silence that stretched between them she held his gaze and hoped he would not press her for more than she was willing to give. Finally he said, "I have found from experience, even an innocent man may be suspected of something as vile as murder."

Emma thought of his history and of the rumors that haunted him. Strange, she had never truly considered the impact those rumors must have had upon his life. Now she realized it was something better not contemplated. "What connection did he have to her?"

"Three days before she died, her mother paid a visit to my sister Aveline, Bernard's mother." Andover drifted to the fireplace. He rested his arm on the mantel and stared down at the polished andirons. "It seems Miss Fitzdowny was with child. And according to the lady, Bernard was to blame."

Emma's chest tightened. "Murder was his way of taking care of a problem."

"Possibly." He glanced at her. "It is also possible that they met that night, argued, and Miss Fitzdowny accidentally ended up in the river. All I can say for certain is that Bernard was seen at Vauxhall that night. Although I have found no one who saw him with Miss Fitzdowny."

"You investigated what happened that night?"

"My sister is a widow." Andover set his wine glass on the mantel. "She came to me after Miss Fitzdowny's death. She wanted me to find out what had happened that night. I am afraid I have not been able to solve that particular mystery."

Emma held his gaze, a chill creeping over her skin. "Do you truly believe he is innocent?"

"My nephew lives his life by a different set of rules than most of us do. He does what he likes and the rest of the world can go straight to the devil." A muscle flickered in his cheek with the clenching of his jaw. "No. I do not believe in his innocence."

"Charlotte may be in his hands. The man is capable of murder. What would he do to her?" The strength withered in her legs. She took two steps and sank to the edge of the sofa. Light from the stained-glass window streamed across her lap, casting a tangled pattern of red and blue and yellow. "We have to find her."

"Yes." He crossed the distance and sat on the sofa beside her. "I shall do everything in my power to find her, Miss Wakefield."

Although he did not touch her, she felt as though he had slid his arm around her shoulders. His presence was so powerful, his manner so confident, she had the feeling he could fight dragons should they get in his way. She looked at him, saw the sincerity in his eyes, the compassion for her plight. Yet she wondered if she could trust what she saw. "Is that the reason you intend to help me find Charlotte? Because you believe your nephew may have had a hand in her kidnapping? Do you hope to quell any scandal?"

He studied her a long moment, and although she could not say for certain how she knew it, she could say with certainty that he wanted something from her. Something that began with trust. "I do not wish to contemplate your opinion of me, Miss Wakefield. I can only say that a man who would do nothing after learning of Miss Usherwood's disappearance is hardly fit to be called a gentleman."

Had she misjudged him so completely? Experience had taught her not to put a great deal of faith in the honor of arrogant aristocrats. They tended to do what suited them, not what was most honorable. Yet the more she saw of this man, the less she believed in the rumors that followed him. He was either an honorable man who had simply been caught in a tragic web, or he was a scoundrel capable of murder. In either case, she would have to be very careful.

Sebastian stood near a window in the blue drawing room, watching for Miss Wakefield to leave his house. She had refused his offer to escort her home. She had refused the use of his coach. Instead she chose to walk home. He could not remember the last time he had met a woman with a fiercer streak of independence. Headstrong. Temperamental. Unreasonable. Termagant!

"Miss Wakefield is a very interesting young lady, is she not?"

Sebastian turned at the sound of his mother's voice. Jacqueline drifted toward him in the slow elegant stroll he had always associated with her. Although she was smiling, the glint in her dark eyes warned of dangerous currents lurking beneath the innocuous facade. "She is one of the most infuriating females I have ever met."

Jacqueline paused beside him. "She needs your help."

"And she will have my help. Whether she likes it or not."

"You have always been so dependable. You have always taken your responsibilities seriously." Jacqueline patted his arm. "I believe that is why you are intent on making such a horrible debacle of your life."

"If you intend to discuss . . ."

101

Jacqueline lifted her hand to silence him. "I must say once again this list you have made is a terrible mistake."

"On the contrary, Mama. My plan is logical and quite practical."

"Logical. Practical." She waved aside his words. "And you think to make a success of marriage when you look upon it with such cold eyes. Disaster. Nothing can come of this but utter disaster. I wish you would reconsider your decision."

"It is a perfectly sound decision."

"Have you no thought of love?"

"Love?"

Jacqueline's eyes narrowed. "Why do you look as though I speak of a myth? Do you truly have no faith in the most profound of all emotions?"

"It is not that I dispute the existence of love. Yet I believe it is rare. And I have no wish to succumb to such a violent emotion."

"When you meet your match, you will have no choice but to surrender to the passion that builds within you. *C'est destin.* And it will find you one day." Jacqueline sighed softly. "I only pray it is before you have destroyed any chance you may have at living your life with your one and only love."

Sebastian could not help smiling. His mother and father had shared a wondrous affection, the kind poets celebrated and authors sprawled across the pages of sweetly written romances. Even now, nearly twenty years after his father's death, Jacqueline still grieved. Although on the shady side of sixty, she still retained the beauty that had beguiled his father, a beauty and vivacity that could enthrall any man in her company. She could have her pick of a hundred men; she chose instead to remain a widow.

Somewhere deep within, he acknowledged a certain

longing for the same glorious experience his parents had known. Yet he knew he was not the type of man who was meant to live such a heated and passionate life. He was far too practical to allow his emotions to dictate his life. He had imagined himself in love once. And that truly had been a disaster. "I have outgrown the tendency to allow my heart to rule my head."

Jacqueline studied him a moment; she had always possessed an uncanny way of peering into his thoughts. "Beatrice was as beautiful as she was treacherous. That she caught you in her web was unfortunate. Yet if you allow her to destroy any chance you have to find your true love, then you have allowed her to manipulate you once again."

"I assure you, Mama, I am long over that particular illness. My decisions have nothing at all to do with Beatrice."

Jacqueline studied him a long moment, her dark eyes narrowed. "I do not understand how you could think to marry without passion."

Sebastian laughed softly. "Spoken like a true French woman."

"At times I wonder how you could have been born without a drop of French blood." Jacqueline looked up toward heaven. "To choose a wife in this fashion, as though she were a brood mare, this is not as it should be. You are mistaken if you imagine you can use pure intellect to make a decision that should come from your heart."

"But I am not a man ruled by my heart, Mama. A clear head rules the day. A man who can keep his head in any given situation is a man who can control any situation. Impulse and passion lead to grave errors in judgment."

She stared at him, her eyes wide. "We are speaking of love, not a chess match."

He felt like a boy of ten who had managed to disappoint his mother in the most profound way possible. "I made a promise to Papa."

"You had too much responsibility at too early an age. Duty, honor, responsibility. You wear them like armor."

"Would you have me break my promise?"

Jacqueline glanced out the window. "You were a child when you made that promise to your papa. Your father did not intend you to marry a woman you did not love. He did not wish you to lead an unhappy life. He wanted you to marry, this is true. But he would expect you to wait until you met your match."

"My match." Sebastian lifted his mother's hand and pressed his lips to the back of her fingers. "And who is to say there is a match for each of us, my dear Mama? Perhaps destiny has not accounted for me."

Jacqueline pursed her lips. "You need a grand adventure. Something to stir your blood."

"I do not need a grand adventure."

"You do. More than you realize." She squeezed his arm, a fierce look entering her eyes. "I wish you would meet a woman who would turn your world upside down, a woman who would shake you so you could not see straight, a woman who would make your French blood boil so furiously, it would melt all that English ice in your veins."

"Papa was English." He winked at her. "As I recall, you liked him."

"I adored him." Jacqueline glanced toward the portrait hanging on the wall across the room. A man with thick black hair and blue eyes regarded her from the confines of an ornately carved rosewood frame. There was laughter in those eyes, humor in the tilt of his lips. Simon St. Clair had been happy until the day he had taken his last breath. And Sebastian knew a great part of that happiness had stemmed from his life with this woman. "And true, he was English, but I was the woman who melted his English ice. I doubt any of the females on your list could conjure enough heat to do the same for you."

Sebastian had little doubt his mother was right. He knew everything there was to know of the six women who graced his list of prospective brides. Their bloodlines reached back into English history as far as his own. None of the women on his list placed a high regard on the ethereal emotion of love. They did not expect what he could not give. There would be no hypocrisy in his marriage. Any of the women on his list would make an excellent choice for his marchioness. Yet each time it came to choose, he found he could not decide.

Indecision was new to him. He prided himself on his rapier-sharp intellect. Still, when it came to this choice, he was at a loss. He supposed he might drop their names into a bowl and draw his future bride. Would it make any difference in the end? Time and time again he had questioned himself on this regard. What was he hoping to find? Why could he not make up his mind? Unbidden, an image of Emma Wakefield rose in his mind. The implication careened through him like a runaway horse. Quickly he dismissed the notion. Emma was certainly not his match.

"Promise me you will not rush into a marriage you will soon regret." Jacqueline's long fingers bit into his arm. "Promise me you will give yourself a chance to find true happiness."

Sebastian pressed his lips to her smooth cheek, and the scent of lilies flooded his senses. "I promise you, I will take my time in deciding upon my future marchioness."

Jacqueline cupped his cheek in her warm palm.

"Open yourself up to the possibilities, my darling. Allow yourself to enjoy life. It is far too short to be unhappy."

Life could be short. That was a certainty. His father had died in a shipwreck when he was only five and forty. Sebastian would be thirty in three months. It was time to fulfill his promise to his father. Still, he acknowledged the truth in his mother's sentiments. Was it possible for a man such as he, a man who did not live by strong emotions, to find a love passionate enough to take away the chill deep within him?

He looked out the window in time to see Miss Wakefield descend the three steps leading from his front door. A lock of hair had escaped her pins to tumble down her back. The breeze toyed with it, lifting it upward, spreading the silken strands to the sunlight. An image crept through his mind of all that soft-looking hair spilled across his bare chest. With the image came a tightening low in his belly. Confounded female!

"Miss Wakefield is very odd, is she not? But then one could only expect her to be, given her mama."

Sebastian dragged his gaze from Emma and found his mother watching him. Jacqueline was smiling as though she had a particularly interesting secret she was eager to share. "You knew her mama?"

"I knew of her. All London knew of the scandal." Jacqueline drifted away from him, allowing him to stew while she paused to examine an arrangement of flowers that stood in a large crystal vase on a round table nearby. She shifted a long white lily as she said, "I heard her sing once. She had a remarkable voice, so clear and pure. It was truly a pity she could not continue as she wished. But then, society has a way of crushing the hopes of any woman who wishes to do something out of the ordinary with her life. And when the eldest daughter of the Earl of Carrick runs away to become an opera singer, it is considered out of the ordinary."

"An opera singer? She actually went on stage?"

"Ah, I knew it would shock you." Jacqueline wagged her finger at him. "And tell me, why should a woman not go on stage, when she has a wonderful gift to share? And Sophia had a gift. When she sang, no one in the theater spoke. We sat as if afraid to breathe. It was as if an angel had descended from heaven to beguile the mortal world with her voice and her beauty. Miss Wakefield looks a great deal like her mama, I think."

"Her mother ran off to become an opera singer." Sebastian rested his shoulder against the window frame, both astonished and at the same time completely unsurprised. "Apparently Miss Wakefield gets her impetuous nature honestly."

"And her beauty. Of course, you did notice her beauty. It is also not in the usual fashion."

Sebastian laughed softly. "There is little about Miss Wakefield in the ordinary fashion. Did you know that she is related to Earl Halisham?"

"Her father was the earl's eldest son. The old tyrant all but disowned him after he married Sophia." Jacqueline shifted another lily in the vase. "From what I heard, he refused to have anything to do with the poor little girl after his son and daughter-in-law were killed."

Sebastian glanced out the window. He watched Emma walk down the street. She did not saunter, as so many women did. Her stride was quick and sure, as though she had somewhere to go and something to do, an oddity in itself for a gentlewoman. He thought of Emma's reaction to her grandfather when he had asked about the relationship. Perhaps it was one of the reasons she had little faith in men. He suspected the man who had been her uncle's heir was another. "What about her uncle's heir? Would he not help Mrs. Usherwood and her family after her husband's death?"

"From what I heard, the property was entailed. The widow and her daughters were left nearly destitute. And the blackguard offered her nothing more than five hundred pounds a year to help them survive." Jacqueline gave a delicate shudder. "When I think of how easily a woman can be turned out of her house, it makes me cold inside."

"The laws are not fair, Mama." Sebastian knew his father had intended his only son to secure the title and all that came with it. His father and his uncle had not gotten along. Once he secured a wife, Sebastian's duty would be to produce an heir. And for some reason that brought his mind back to Emma Wakefield. "Five hundred a year does not allow for a London Season."

Jacqueline made a soft sound in her throat. "Five hundred would scarcely buy gloves for a Season."

Sebastian knew his mother had a tendency to be extravagant. Yet he knew, even with the strictest economy, five hundred a year would scarcely put food on the table and a roof overhead. It certainly would not provide for a gown such as Emma had worn last night. For that matter, it would not have clothed Miss Usherwood for her debut into Society. What was the family's source of income? The possibilities ripped through him, tearing at his vitals like the talons of an angry hawk. "Do you imagine Halisham has repented? Could he have heard of his granddaughter's situation and decided to provide her with a suitable income?"

"I suppose it is possible." Jacqueline glanced past the flowers to Sebastian. "Yet this is a man who turned his back on a little girl who had just lost her parents.

Does that type of man suddenly see how cruel and petty he is?"

Sebastian wanted to believe Halisham had suddenly found some compassion for his only granddaughter. Still, he knew the man. And his knowledge of Earl Halisham gave him little hope that the old man had provided Emma with so much as a farthing. Emma turned the corner, disappearing from his sight but not his thoughts. "There must have been another source. A small inheritance from her mother's side of the family. Otherwise, how would Mrs. Usherwood have managed to give her daughter a Season?"

"I had not thought of it. I suppose there must be something. How else would they have been able to come to London? A woman does not have many opportunities for making her own way."

Sebastian knew the paths available to a woman. She could become a governess or a companion to a wealthy woman, which Emma obviously had not. Or she could become a companion to a gentleman, a man who would provide a home and clothes and spending money. That had not been her course, he assured himself. It was a mystery. And Sebastian had never been able to allow a mystery to go unchallenged.

Still, he had other concerns at the moment. "I think I shall pay a call upon Mrs. Usherwood this afternoon. I want to reassure her that I will do everything I can to restore her daughter to her."

"Do you truly imagine Bernard had a hand in Miss Usherwood's disappearance?"

Sebastian met his mother's worried gaze. "I think there is a very good chance he did."

Jacqueline crossed the distance between them. "I do not feel we should tell Aveline of this. I think we should allow her to enjoy her visit with Marguerite and the baby."

Aveline was in Hampshire, enjoying a visit with her daughter and Marguerite's three-week-old son. "I see no reason to worry her with what we suspect. There will be time enough when we know for certain what role Bernard played."

"What will you do if you find he is guilty?"

Sebastian set his jaw. "I shall make certain he does not have the opportunity to harm another girl."

"I trust in your judgment, son." Jacqueline squeezed his arm. "Aveline is fortunate to have you to help deal with that boy. I only hope he has not harmed the poor Usherwood girl. I can well imagine the torment that her mother is going through."

Sebastian needed answers, and he needed them quickly. The longer Charlotte was missing, the less chance they had of ever finding her alive. He had an idea of where to begin his search for those answers. It was dangerous, but he had no choice. Tonight he would see what he could uncover about his nephew.

"I do not like it in the least that Andover has taken an interest in finding this girl."

Radbyrne stared out the window, watching a curricle pulled by a pair of grays rattle past the house. "I can handle Andover."

"Can you?"

The back of his neck prickled. He knew Gaetan's eyes were fixed upon him in a steady glare. Still, he did not turn and face his partner in this endeavor. It was far better to keep his expression hidden. Doubts were not easily masked, and this was hardly a time to betray any weakness. "He has only his suspicions. Nothing more."

"If you had not left that button in the girl's chamber, Andover would not have been drawn into this situation."

Thinking back on it, Radbyrne supposed leaving his uncle's button was not a wise idea. Still, it had seemed devilishly clever at the time. "In case anyone was suspicious of me, I thought only to cast the shadow of blame upon him. With that book coming out this Season, I could not resist adding to his legendary reputation."

"It was foolish. You must have known he would be compelled to lend his considerable support to Mrs. Usherwood. The man belongs in another age. Something like this would have him donning his armor and setting out to slay the dragon before you could say 'St. George.' "

Radbyrne clenched his hands so tightly, his nails bit into his palms. "He shall learn that a dragon sometimes turns a knight errant into a charred piece of rubble."

"You should have discussed this with me before you did anything. I never would have given you leave to kidnap that girl."

Radbyrne ground his teeth together. He did not appreciate the lecture. He had helped establish this enterprise. If not for an unfortunate string of events, his current partner would never even have known of this business. "I had every right to . . ."

"You had no right to kidnap that girl."

"There must be fifty girls like Charlotte Usherwood every Season. Girls of a good family with no fortune and no one to protect them. Beautiful, innocent. They are literally worth their weight in gold."

"It is far safer to rely upon the women who answer the advertisements. And I must say, far more acceptable."

Radbyrne knew the entire business was scarcely acceptable to his partner. Yet circumstances demanded that Gaetan continue. "This is much more profitable."

"I would not take it kindly if your greed put me at risk. Where is the girl?"

Radbyrne watched the breeze bend the branches of the elm growing in front of the large town house. He had no intention of divulging the truth to his partner. It could lead to disaster. "I have no idea what has become of her."

"Andover shall not . . ."

"You need not worry. I would rather see my uncle floating in the Thames than allow him to destroy our business venture."

"It would not be the first time you helped someone to an early grave, would it?"

Radbyrne had not intended to murder the Fitzdowny girl. He also had not expected to feel the rush of excitement that had washed over him when he had felt her take her last breath. Killing his uncle would be far more enjoyable. "There is no need to worry. I will see to it that Andover does not disturb your peace."

"I do not care for murder, Bernard. You will manage to handle this situation without staining your hands with Andover's blood. Or you will have to deal with me. Do you understand?"

A chill gripped him, as though Gaetan had suddenly spilled ice water over his skin. "Of course."

It would require subtlety, Radbyrne decided. A murder that looked like an accident. He smiled at his reflection in the glass. Yes, he would enjoy taking care of his annoying uncle.

Chapter Nine

"I have a very bad feeling about this." Marjorie paced back and forth behind Emma, her reflection drifting in and out of the mirror above the dressing table, like an indecisive ghost. "It is far too dangerous."

"I will be careful, dearest." Emma sat at her dressing table, fumbling with the ties of the white cap she wore. She only hoped Aunt Marjorie would not notice the way her hands trembled, complicating the simple task. "There is really no reason to worry."

"What of Andover?" Marjorie paused, her reflection trapped in one corner of the oval mirror. "You ought to wait to see what he thinks of this plan. I doubt very much he would approve."

Emma clenched her teeth. "Aunt Marjorie, I certainly do not need Andover's approval."

"He said he would handle everything, Emma. And he seems quite capable."

"Yes. I have no doubt that he is." Emma studied the

image reflected in the mirror above her dressing table. From what she had seen this afternoon, her costume would make her blend in with the rest of the household. As long as no one took notice of her, she should do well. "Unfortunately, I wonder whether he has Charlotte's best interests at heart. If his nephew is guilty, I cannot truly imagine he would choose to help us at the expense of his sister's eldest son."

Marjorie folded her hands at her waist. She met Emma's eyes in the mirror. "When he came to speak with me this afternoon, he seemed quite genuine in his concern. I believe he wants to help us."

Emma stared at the gold button that lay atop a painted porcelain tray on the top of her dressing table. "I understand why you would want to trust him. He has a powerful presence. Yet I cannot feel comfortable placing Charlotte's well-being in his care."

Marjorie rested her hands on Emma's shoulders. "You have relied upon your own resources far too long, my dear girl. I understand why it is difficult for you to trust him. But I have to believe he will help us."

"I hope you are right. I hope he is honorable." Emma patted her aunt's hand, wishing she could be as comfortable with Lord Andover as Marjorie was. "Yet I cannot wait to be certain of the man. Charlotte needs my help."

"I cannot allow you to do this. It is far too dangerous."

Emma turned to face her aunt. "What do you imagine would have become of me if you had not taken me into your home after Mama and Papa were killed? That man who sired my father would sooner have seen me dead on the streets of London than have raised a finger to help me. You gave me a home, a family. Charlotte is like my own sister. I must do everything in my power to help her."

Marjorie smoothed her fingers over Emma's cheek. "Dear child, you do not owe me a debt. You are my sister's daughter, as dear to me as my own girls. I cannot let you risk everything in this reckless manner."

"It is not reckless." She was quite certain this was precisely what Isabel would have done in *The Valiant Viscount*, should the need have arisen. Isabel was one of E. W. Austen's most resourceful heroines. Emma liked to think she was every bit as courageous and resourceful. "I have carefully considered my approach to this situation."

Marjorie groaned. "As I recall, you said the same about your scheme to make Andover confess."

"This is different. It is not nearly as filled with risk."

"I do hope you are right. Still, I can see there is no hope of stopping you." Marjorie gripped Emma's arm. "Take care, my girl. Take great care."

"I will." After kissing her aunt's cheek, Emma turned and walked toward the door. It was not dangerous, she assured herself. Well, perhaps there was some measure of danger in the venture. But she had to take the risk. Charlotte could very well be a prisoner in Radbyrne's house. And she could think of only one way to discover the truth. She drew a breath past the constriction in her throat, gathered her courage, and left to search the lair of a monster.

A floorboard creaked under Emma's foot, the low groan shuddering along her spine. She paused in the hall outside a bedchamber in Bernard Radbyrne's house, her pulse pounding in her ears. She had watched Radbyrne leave the house several hours earlier. The servants were all in bed. It was her own tread that had caused the noise. There was no reason to panic. Still, she could not suppress an uneasy prickle at the base of her spine, the instincts that whispered she was not alone.

She forced air past her tight throat. There was no time to stand around coddling her fear. Isabel certainly would not be frightened. Although she suspected Radbyrne would not return until the last glow of moonlight had faded beneath the first rays of dawn, she did not care to take a chance that he might return early. She must finish her search.

Her plan had worked as she had expected. Radbyrne's was a large establishment. No one had taken notice of a woman dressed as a chambermaid entering the house. After she had gained entrance, she had hidden in a hall closet until she was certain the master was gone and the servants had retired for the evening. Everything had gone as she had planned, except she had found no trace of Charlotte in the cellar, the upper story, or anywhere else.

An uncomfortably sweet scent closed around her when she stepped into the room, an aroma of cloves soaked in honey. The light of her candle fell upon the faces of a pair of carved wooden dragons standing guard on each side of the door. A faint glow of moonlight spilled through the windows, mingling with the light from her candle. Her attention was drawn first to the bed. It was large and made shiny by black lacquer. Gold dragon heads sat atop each of the thick four posts. More gold dragons swirled across the dark red canopy and swags. The light of her candle flickered upon the gold dragons that prowled the dark red wall covering, lending life to the beasts. She had little doubt she had found Radbyrne's chamber.

She paused beside a shiny black dressing table. The light of her candle revealed dragons carved into the wood here as well. Gold and gems glittered upon fobs and seals and stickpins in a tray. She wasn't certain what she was looking for. Perhaps some clue that might lead her to her cousin.

"I see you have decided to try your hand at house-breaking."

Emma's heart slammed against the wall of her chest at the sound of that soft voice. She pivoted and found the Marquess of Andover standing a few feet away. The glow of her candle sought him in the shadows. Dressed entirely in black, he looked like a phantom of the night. Excitement swirled through her, sparking her imagination. He seemed a dark, romantic figure who prowled by candlelight, a thief who slipped into the bedchambers of ladies and stole more than their jewels, a character fit for the next E. W. Austen novel. Although he was smiling, the candlelight betrayed a hard glitter in his dark eyes. "What are you doing here?"

"I am looking for answers." Andover moved toward her, closing the distance like a lion slowly stalking prey. "The question remains, what the devil are you doing here?"

He stood so close she could feel the heat of his body radiate against her. His scent infiltrated her breath, darkly masculine. She wanted to press her lips against his neck and breathe his essence deep into her lungs. Shocked by the turn of her thoughts, she stepped back, and bumped into the dressing table. "I have as much right to be here as you do."

One black brow lifted. "It may surprise you, Miss Wakefield, but neither of us has a right to be here."

"I had to find out if Charlotte was here."

"I told you I would handle this."

"I could not sit idly by and allow that. . . ."

He pressed his fingertip to her lips, snuffing her words as though she were the flame of a candle. Yet the soft touch ignited flame deep within her. She was about to demand an explanation for his action when she heard voices coming from the hall. She glanced toward the door. Other than the window, it was the only exit. And from the sound of Radbyrne's voice, he was too close to allow a safe escape. They were trapped. She turned toward the armoire, wondering if they might hide in it.

Andover snatched the candle from her hand and snuffed the flame between his fingertips. A thin trail of smoke coiled from it. He then grabbed her hand and hurried toward the bed.

"What are you doing?" she demanded, her voice a harsh whisper.

"Get under the bed."

She pointed toward the tall armoire. "I think we should . . ."

"Get under the blasted bed."

Although his voice did not rise above a whisper, the command in that low tone made her jump. "Of all the arrogant, high-handed . . ."

"I cannot imagine why I never noticed you before," Radbyrne said, his voice sounding as though he was just outside of the room.

Andover got down on his knees, then pulled her down beside him. "You can argue with me later."

She glared at him before scrambling under the bed skirt, shoving gold dragons out of her way. She scooted on her back, with Andover moving close beside her. When she stopped, he nudged her with his elbow, coaxing her to move farther under the bed. She slid a short distance then halted, the sound of the door closing freezing her where she lay. Andover halted as well, inches from her.

"I do prefer my own bed. One can never be certain of the sheets at Gaetan's," Radbyrne said.

The bed skirt sealed out most of the moonlight that had invaded the chamber. Without the benefit of sight, her other senses rushed to grasp the details of her surroundings. She was acutely conscious of Andover beside her. Although he did not touch her, the heat of his body bathed her from her shoulder all the way down to her ankle.

"Do you like the gown?" Radbyrne was saying. "I thought it was much more attractive on you than that dark red you were wearing."

He had brought a woman with him into his bedchamber. The implication of what would follow was nearly enough to make Emma run from the room.

"It is lovely."

Glass pinged against metal. "I suppose I should take a more active role in choosing the costumes for the girls. Woolgrove has such awful taste."

The scent of sulfur spilled through Emma's senses. A moment later light shone below the bed skirt. The yellow glow of a candle reflected on the shiny black shoes Radbyrne wore. She eased away from that light and those shoes, the movement bringing her flush against Andover. Through the thick gray cotton of her gown, she could feel the press of his long limbs against hers. She realized she should move away from him. Yet he was so solid, so warm, so very powerful, she could not break the contact. Let him pay heed to propriety if he wished.

Instead of pulling away from her, he rested his hand on her arm, a gesture she knew was meant to provide some measure of comfort. It certainly should not have made her even more fluttery than she already felt, but it did. Somehow he managed to make her feel protected and threatened all in the same beat of her heart. She knew the turmoil of a heroine attracted to the wrong man.

"I am curious, what did you imagine you were applying for when you answered the advertisement? Did you expect to find a position as governess or as personal companion to a distinguished lady?"

"It doesn't matter."

The advertisement? Through her turmoil, Emma recognized something strange about this conversation.

"No, I suppose it does not." Radbyrne moved away from the bed. She followed his progress from under the bed skirt, seeing his shoes, and then the lower half of his legs. He walked straight to the armoire. "Still, I am curious."

"A governess."

"I doubt you would have found employment in that profession, my dear. You are far too young and much too pretty to suit most mamas."

Emma bit her lower lip when she realized how exposed she would be at the moment if she had taken refuge in the armoire.

"You are obviously a gently bred young woman. How did you come to answer an advertisement for a position as governess?"

"My father thought the way out of his financial troubles was to place a pistol to his head. And I had far too much pride to live with one of my relatives."

The woman had sought a position as a governess? How in the world had she ended up in this man's bedchamber?

Radbyrne laughed as though he were enjoying a joke. He moved toward the woman while he continued.

"I wonder what your papa would say if he could see you now."

She made no reply. Emma could not shake the feeling this woman was not here by choice. Still, she suspected the woman was a prostitute, and she doubted prostitutes were often eager to bed their clients.

"Take off your clothes, Ariel," Radbyrne ordered.

The tone of his voice was that of a master to a slave. A few moments after the command, pale blue cloth fell around Ariel's ankles. A white cotton shift followed. Emma clenched her hands into fists, hoping for some reprieve from what would come.

"Very nice," Radbyrne murmured. "On your knees."

Emma squeezed her eyes shut, wishing she could close all her other senses. Yet she could not block the sounds of the couple just beyond the bed skirt. Neither could she ignore the man lying beside her. Andover lay as still as stone. Except stone had never felt so warm and vibrant. The bed slats creaked above her. Emma clenched her teeth so tightly her jaw ached.

"If you had become a governess you would never have felt this," Radbyrne said before issuing a deep guttural sound. The bed above her flinched. "Tell me you like it."

"I like it," Ariel said, her voice sounding as though she were reading the words from a book.

The bed creaked with each quick violent movement above her. Guttural noises assaulted her ears. Emma pressed her hand to her mouth, afraid the scream rising within her might escape. Andover squeezed her arm, silently giving comfort, while above them Radbyrne pounded into Ariel.

Each sharp flinch of the bed made Emma's mind wander to thoughts better not explored. In spite of her every effort, memories conspired against her. She could recall the feel of Andover's hand upon her breast, his lips upon her mouth, the long length of him pressed against her. As much as she reminded herself that the coupling above her was primitive and ugly, she could not keep from wondering what it might be like to feel Andover's hands upon her bare skin. Heaven above, was she truly so depraved to think of such things?

Fortunately it ended quickly. After a few excruciating minutes, Radbyrne released one low groan and the bed ceased moving. Emma lay tense beside Andover, her skin tingling as though she stood naked in the midday sun. She was aware of his every movement, each soft rise and fall of his chest against her side.

"A beautiful woman such as you should not be wasted on a lot of screaming brats. You are far better suited for this position."

"I used to imagine someone might help me. Now I know there is no longer a place for me in the polite world."

Help her? Emma's blood chilled at the possibilities those words conjured in her brain.

"As a governess you would have spent your days with spoiled brats, your evenings mending or doing some other menial task. And you would never have known the pleasure of my company."

"Instead, I would still know the pleasure of making choices about my life."

Radbyrne laughed, as though he were Lucifer amused by a recently arrived sinner. "So many of you women are all the same. You lament what you imagine to be the loss of freedom. When in reality you never truly had the luxury of choice. Only wealth and position allow you that, my dear. Without it, you are merely a pawn in this game we live."

Emma lay frozen beneath the bed while a suspicion slithered through her veins, cold and evil. She heard Radbyrne tell the woman to get out of bed and get dressed. In a short time the light was extinguished and the two of them left. The door closed, leaving her alone with Andover and the specter of her fear. They waited a few moments, silent in the darkness before Andover left her to make certain it was safe to escape Lucifer's lair. Although he was gone only a moment, it seemed an age before he returned to assure her it was safe to leave.

He took her arm when she emerged from beneath the bed. Emma expected a lecture. It would certainly suit the man to point out precisely how foolish and reckless she had been this night. Instead he held her arm and led her quickly out of the house, as though he knew the turmoil raging within her. Fog had begun to roll across the city, yellow in the light of the street-lamp in front of Radbyrne's house. The chilly mist brushed her face with the scent of burning coal, a scent that forever plagued the city. Tonight it seemed worse. Tonight it seemed the scent came from the fires of hell itself.

A large coach stood waiting near the corner. As they drew near, a footman materialized from the fog to open the door and lower the step. Andover ushered her into the conveyance, then climbed in behind her. It would come now, she thought as he settled upon the black leather squabs across from her. Andover would certainly not miss a chance to lecture her. Light from the interior coach lamp fell golden upon his face, illuminating every nuance of his expression. He was studying her, a look that could not possibly be admiration in his eyes, no matter how much it seemed so.

"A maid. It was a clever way to enter the house without being noticed."

Clever? She stared at him, looking for the sarcasm that must lurk behind the words. Yet there was not a trace of mockery in his eyes. Instead she saw sincerity and something more, a heated look that whispered to the desire lingering deep within her. "Is this not the time to tell me how foolish I was to enter Radbyrne's house?"

He drew in his breath, the inhalation lifting his broad shoulders. "You are accustomed to dealing with problems on your own, Miss Wakefield. Perhaps I should have told you my intent. Although I doubt it would have swayed your course, since you do not trust me."

The coach swayed, the movement brushing his long legs against hers. The contact sizzled along her nerves, confirming the power he held over her senses. The knowledge of how easily he could set her pulse racing chafed her. The more she wanted to deny the attraction, the deeper it sank its talons in her. She could not prevent the insidious thoughts from swirling through her brain. She wanted to slide her arms around his neck, and capture that little half grin beneath her lips. And that was only the beginning of what she wanted to do with this man.

Heat crackled through her when she thought of the ways she wanted to touch him. And those thoughts were merely kindling compared to the bonfire of images that rose in her head when she thought of the ways she wanted to feel his hands upon her. What would he do if she slipped off her seat and crawled onto his lap? For one horrible moment she was afraid she might do it, the attraction was that intense. "Did you find anything that would tell us where Charlotte is?"

Andover glanced down, shielding the expression in his eyes. "I found a few things that require further investigation."

Had he been struck by the same horrible suspicion as she had? "The girl, Ariel. I had the feeling she was not there by choice."

"I had thought at first she was a prostitute." He

tapped his fingertips upon his knee. "Yet there was something not right about the encounter."

"Do you know of this place, Gaetan's?"

"I suspect it is a brothel." He glanced up at her, his lips tipping into a lopsided smile. "And it may surprise you, but I do not have an intimate familiarity with all the brothels in London."

It did not surprise her. From what she had been able to uncover about the Marquess of Andover, he did not need to frequent a brothel to find women interested in warming his bed. His last mistress had been Lady Phoebe Langdon, the widow of the Earl of Carlton. A pretty opera dancer had preceded the beautiful Lady Carlton. He had a long line of former mistresses, each having one thing in common: beauty. It seemed he did not indulge in more than one mistress at a time, but he seldom kept the same woman for more than a few months. "Radbyrne asked her about an advertisement. He wanted to know if she had applied for the position of lady's companion or governess. How would he know such a thing?"

A muscle bunched in his jaw at the clenching of his teeth. "It is difficult to say."

He was holding something back from her; she could see it. "Unless the advertisement was used to lure young women into a snare."

He regarded her a moment, his expression revealing nothing of what was going on behind those dark eyes. "It is possible."

Emma's chest tightened with a possibility she could not ignore. "In all the time since Charlotte disappeared, I have asked myself one question over and over again. Why did someone kidnap her? Tonight, listening to Ariel, I had a horrible suspicion. What if she was taken because of her beauty. What if she was taken to a place like Gaetan's?"

One corner of his lips tightened. "Miss Wakefield, you will only cause yourself a great deal more sorrow if you allow your imagination to take you down that path."

Emma clenched her hands in her lap, trying to rein in her emotions. She would not dissolve into a watering pot in front of this man. "How do we find Gaetan's?"

"I will find Gaetan's."

"I will not sit idly by while Charlotte may be in a place such as that."

"I will keep you informed, Miss Wakefield. I promise you. Do not concoct some foolhardy plan as you did this evening."

He might have slapped her. She stiffened against the cushioned seat. "Foolhardy? There was nothing foolhardy about my plan."

"Venturing into a man's house, alone, unprotected, a man who could very well be a murderer. You do not call that foolhardy?"

"And I suppose placing my trust in a man who may very well have murdered his fiancée is far more intelligent?"

Chapter Ten

As soon as the words escaped, Emma regretted them. She regretted the look that entered his eyes, cold and heated at the same time. She held her breath, waiting for the blow of his anger.

"Is that what you believe, Miss Wakefield?" Andover asked, his voice low and controlled. "Do you truly believe I murdered my fiancée?"

There was a time when she had believed in his guilt. Now it was far more difficult to imagine this man could have done anything so vile. E. W. Austen had been wrong about him, mistaken in a variety of ways. "Anger is a powerful force."

"And so is rumor, Miss Wakefield." He held her gaze, as though daring her to look away from him. "I suppose you have read *The Wicked Duke*. From what I understand, it is the fashionable thing to do this Season."

Emma held his gaze in spite of her desire to look

away, suddenly uneasy with the depth of her knowledge of each of the novels by E. W. Austen. "Have you read it?"

He rubbed his eyebrow, the one that had a narrow white scar slashed through the far corner. "Enough of it to know that it will once again plunge my family into a mire of speculation. Apparently E. W. Austen has no scruples when it comes to circulating unsubstantiated rumors."

Emma squeezed her hands together in her lap. "Your name is never used."

"True. Perhaps it is merely a coincidence that the Wicked Duke, a man who murdered his fiancée, as rumor would say I did, bears a remarkable physical resemblance to me."

"According to the book, your fiancée was being forced into marriage with you, though she was in love with another man. Is that also true?"

He laughed softly, the dark sound filled with bitterness. "Her parents did wish for her to marry me, but no one wanted to be a marchioness more than Beatrice. Unfortunately she did not want the man who came with the coronet."

She could not imagine a woman wanting another man, not while she had this one. "She must have made you very angry."

"Angry?" He considered her suggestion a moment. "I suppose I was angry, but not because she had decided she was in love with another man. By the time I had discovered the truth about her, I had come to realize we would not truly suit one another. No, it was not her infidelity that angered me, so much as that she had succeeded in deceiving me, even for a moment. You see, Miss Wakefield, I value honesty above all else."

Heat prickled the base of her neck. "You had nothing at all to do with her death?"

"I was visiting a friend in Scotland when she died. Apparently she fell from her horse and hit her head. She was in Kent at the time. The distance between us did not prevent people from assuming I had murdered her." He rubbed his chin, regarding her as though he were facing her across a chessboard. "And here you have judged me again, based on little or no fact."

He made her sound like a perfect idiot, a female who ran about jumping at conclusions without a shred of fact. "Passion causes people to do things they normally would not. It is not so difficult to believe a betrayed lover may strike out in a fit of rage."

"I am not a passionate man. Love had nothing to do with my engagement to Beatrice. I doubt I am capable of succumbing to that elusive emotion. I am certainly not a man ruled by passion."

Not a passionate man? How could he say such nonsense when he burned with hidden fire? It was not merely her imagination, she assured herself. It was not merely a trick of the light that betrayed the anger flickering in his dark eyes. Still, she pursued a subject any reasonable female would skirt. She wanted to know the truth about him. More, she needed to understand him. "You intended to marry her, yet you were not in love with her?"

"I was three and twenty. And Beatrice was one of the most beautiful creatures I had ever seen." He tapped the pads of his fingertips together. "I was infatuated with her."

"You felt lust for her, but nothing more?"

"It is a primitive emotion, but a powerful one, particularly to a man of that age. Still, it cooled quickly enough, as infatuations always do."

It was as if he had set himself apart, at a distance

from the very emotion she had always sought. It should not bother her. The man meant nothing to her. Although she couldn't identify the reason, she could not deny the way his words pricked her anger. "And the women on your list? Your prospective brides? Is it infatuation you feel toward each of them?"

"More rumors."

"Does that mean you do not have a list of prospective brides?"

His lips flattened into a tight line. "Not precisely. I am considering marriage this year. And I have several women in mind."

The thought of him married to another woman jabbed her like the sharp end of a knitting needle. It should not matter, she assured herself. Yet for some reason, it did. "Since you are such a practical man, I suppose you have carefully listed each lady's accomplishments and qualifications."

He tilted his head. The lamplight touched his thick black lashes and illuminated the glimmer of annoyance in his eyes. "It would not be practical to consider marriage to a woman without certain assurances that she would make a suitable wife."

"Suitable? You make it sound as exciting as choosing a new sofa for your drawing room. Or a mare for one of your prize stallions."

His eyes narrowed. "I suppose you would not understand a practical approach to marriage."

"No." A hero in an E. W. Austen novel would never marry for anything but love. True, he might have to be taught how to love by the heroine, but he would never settle for less. "I cannot imagine marriage without love."

"You are a creature of passion, Miss Wakefield. Ruled by emotion and whim."

"And what rules you, Lord Andover? Intellect? Icy reason?"

"I prefer to live my life in an orderly fashion. It is reasonable to select a wife based on similarity of temperament and common interests. Still, I doubt you would understand, since you are the type of woman who would marry a penniless poet if you fancied yourself in love with him."

Her temper flared, less from his brutal assessment of her than from his icy attitude toward marriage. Was he really ready to settle for an imitation of what should be warm and genuine? "And you are the type of man who would choose a woman who cares nothing for you, simply because her blood is blue enough and she is every bit as cold as you are. Or do you intend to marry some poor unfortunate female who has made the mistake of falling in love with you?"

He held her gaze, his expression betraying nothing. Yet his eyes revealed the anger flashing within him. At the moment there was nothing cold about the look in his eyes. "I was not aware falling in love with me would be a tragedy, Miss Wakefield."

"When love is one sided, my lord, it can bring a great deal of heartache."

"My wife would have a great deal to compensate her for my lack of affection."

"What good is wealth if it means living each day with a man who does not truly care whether he sees your face or that of any other women? I am not certain which is worse. What good is awakening each morning to a face you do not love? If I loved a man, I would live in a garret if it meant being with him."

"Ah, but what disillusion awaits you when you realize the excitement you felt in the beginning has faded. When you realize you have deceived yourself into believing in the most deceptive of human emotions. What tragedy awaits when you discover the face you once loved no longer fills your heart with sunshine and roses?"

"Even if I falter, at least I have tried to make a real marriage." Emma scooted forward on the seat. She wanted to grab his broad shoulders and shake him until his teeth rattled. "Will you truly be satisfied, living your nice calculated life? Without love? Without passion?"

He leaned toward her. "Respect and common interests provide a far more stable foundation than moonbeams and lust."

He was so close, she had only to lean forward to press her lips against his hard mouth. Was he really so cold inside? She could not believe it. "I cannot imagine for one moment living that type of farce."

"Farce?"

"Yes. A marriage where you will take your mistresses and your wife will take her lovers. Do you deny you will take mistresses?"

He tapped his fingertips upon his thigh. "I do not deny the possibility."

"That, sir, is a farce."

"And I suppose you would be happy in your garret, eating bread and water and living on love."

"I can imagine nothing more fulfilling than to love and to be loved. To feel that each sunrise is brighter because you are sharing it with the man you love. To be able to share all that makes life worth living. The little things like a caring touch, a warm embrace. The ultimate joy of bringing children into this world, of watching them grow. To share your life with someone, truly share each day and every night with a man who loves you as much as you love him, that, sir, is more precious than all your wealth and power."

He stared at her as though she had just dropped into

his coach from the far side of the moon. "And is that why you have never married, Miss Wakefield? Have you never found the paragon who meets your ideals?"

Looking into his dark eyes, she had the strangest sensation, as though she had lived her entire life searching for this man. It was as though she had always known him. In spite of everything she knew of him, she could not prevent the need from rising within her.

She wanted to throw her arms around him, to hold him until he realized there was more to this life than he was willing to accept. She wanted to kiss his hard, cynical mouth until he opened to her, truly opened, until all the defenses he had built lay shattered between them. She wanted to shout at him, to prod and poke until she broke through the shell and found the man she sensed hiding deep in his soul. "He need not be a paragon, my lord. He need only be willing to open his heart."

He held her gaze, the anger in his eyes fading, replaced by something more heated, something that whispered of hope and possibilities. Her heart pounded so wildly she thought he must hear it and know the power he held over her senses. Yet if he knew, he did not betray any arrogance in that knowledge. He looked at her as though he were trying to find the pieces to a puzzle without knowing precisely what it was he was trying to solve. After what seemed an eternity he touched her cheek, his bare fingers warm upon her skin. "He must also be able to win your heart, Miss Wakefield."

With his hand on her cheek, she could scarcely draw enough breath to form words. She settled instead for a simple "Yes."

His thick black lashes lowered with his gaze. He looked at her lips as he said, "How will you know if it is real, Miss Wakefield? How will you know that what you are feeling is not merely an infatuation?"

"I suppose all anyone can do is have faith in one's instincts." Yet, at the moment, she wasn't certain she could trust any of her instincts. Not with this man.

"It is far wiser to live by one's intellect than by one's instincts."

"Perhaps." She eased back, breaking the gentle contact of his hand upon her cheek. "Yet is it truly living, or merely existing? What is life without emotion?"

He leaned back against the seat. "Orderly."

She held his cool gaze. "Boring."

A muscle flickered in his cheek with the clenching of his jaw. "Perhaps you are not satisfied unless something explodes in your face every day, but I assure you, Miss Wakefield, I am quite content with my life."

She felt as though he had hit her in the stomach. Of course he was satisfied with his life. He was wealthy and powerful and he had his choice of the best of everything. She was certain he must regard her as a silly woman, a creature who flitted about on the current of her emotions, a woman who lived her life through the pages of popular novels. At the moment she was inclined to agree. What could be more silly or foolish than for her to imagine this man in the same context as romance? The only connection they had was one of a tragic nature. She must keep focused on Charlotte and not her unfortunate attraction to Lord Andover. "Your nephew must know where Charlotte is being kept."

One corner of his mouth tightened. "I suspect he does."

"What will you do to make him tell you?"

"Miss Wakefield, if I force my nephew's hand at this moment, I am afraid we may lose our chance to find

Charlotte. If she is at Gaetan's, and I press Radbyrne, he may well have her disappear."

The implication slammed into her with enough force to ram the breath from her lungs. "If you or someone else were to threaten his life, it might make him . . ."

"He knows I have no proof. At this point it is better if we allow him the opportunity to lead us to Gaetan's."

"And that is it? You simply intend to follow him and hope he leads us to Gaetan's?"

"I intend to follow him. But I also intend to try another path." He cast his gaze into the fog-shrouded street. Lamplight fell upon a profile so rigid, he seemed carved from bronze. "I am hoping someone who shares Gaetan's trade may know of the establishment."

It was a logical assumption. She expected nothing less than logic from the practical Lord Andover. He appeared to honestly want to help. Still, trust was not something she gave easily. There was too much at stake to place all her trust in this man. He might be as honorable as he claimed. He might actually be willing to help her find Charlotte. He certainly intended to insinuate himself into the middle of their troubles, giving her little choice but to accept some measure of help. Still, she knew one thing for certain—no self-respecting heroine would sit back and do nothing while her loved one was in danger. She intended to do everything in her power to find Gaetan's and Charlotte.

After seeing Miss Wakefield to her door, Sebastian sent his coach ahead to wait for him at an address in St. James's Square. He felt too restless to remain in the confines of the vehicle. His blood was pounding furiously through his vessels. He felt edgy and restless, as though he wanted to slam his fist into a wall. Worse, he wanted to follow Miss Wakefield into her little house, grab her by her slender shoulders, and kiss her until she could not see straight. And that was only the beginning of what he wanted to do with her. The images blossoming in his brain had nothing to do with a comfortable bed and soft silk sheets. He had wanted her right there in the coach. In truth, he could not remember seeing her and not wanting her. Hell and damnation, he didn't need to see her to want her. And she thought his wife would be a poor, unfortunate creature.

Fog licked his face, cold, wet, bitter with the smells of smoke and horse dung. A stark contrast to the scent of roses after rain that filled his senses when Emma was near. He turned his collar up against the chilly night. Yet he could not ease the chill deep within him. Her words kept spinning around and around in his brain, like leaves caught in an autumn storm.

It was a lot of nonsense, he told himself. There was nothing wrong with his life. His plan for finding a wife was much more practical and would yield far better results than relying on the whims of animal attraction. Lust burned hot and hard and burned itself out in an instant. A marriage based on common temperaments and interests would certainly be much more stable. Still, the more he argued the point, the more cold-blooded it seemed.

The sound of a cotillion drifted on the fog. Lights glowed from one of the large town houses he was passing, the drapes thrown open to the night, boasting of the gaiety inside. He had been attending balls and parties for what seemed his entire life. His was a life of privilege. He had everything a man could want, including his choice of beautiful women. There was no reason to feel as though an anvil sat upon his chest when he thought of his future. Yet he could not shake the feeling that he was trapped in a large, plush cage.

Confounded woman. He knew his place in society. He had responsibilities. From the time he was twelve, he had known there would be no more children born to his mother and father. No more chance for someone who might share the burden of producing an heir. No, he must marry and he must choose his wife carefully. He certainly could not marry a woman like Emma Wakefield. A man would never know what to expect with her. She was an incendiary device. He could forever expect her to blow up in his face.

Order was not a word in her vocabulary. His house would forever be in turmoil. Their children would never obey rules. He would never know what to expect from one moment to the next. And she had the temerity to suggest he was a fool for living his life in a sane, practical manner.

What had she said about awakening to see the same face every morning? Strange, when he thought of awakening to the sight of her face, some of the tension lifted from his chest. She was fresh and honest. A man would never grow tired of her.

He paused near a lamppost, the pale gas jet producing a yellow halo in the fog. Marry Emma Wakefield? He must be mad. He could not possibly marry a woman like Emma. Insanity obviously ran in her bloodline. Her mother had run off to become an opera singer. Emma ran around with a pistol, abducting innocent men and tossing them into cellars. No, he most certainly could not marry Emma Wakefield. And since he could not marry her, he could not seduce her. He could not strip away all the barriers and feel the slide of her bare skin against his. He could not plunge into her, could not feel her sleek sheath close around him. Even if he wanted her more than he had wanted anything in his life. Seducing innocent females was not a sport in which he indulged.

The attraction he felt for her would pass. It was like any ailment. It need only run its course. He would get over Emma Wakefield the way he got over measles when he was a boy.

By the time he reached the town house of Orlina Vachel in St. James's Square, he had managed to pull his emotions under tight rein. He intended to keep his focus on Charlotte Usherwood instead of her maddening cousin. It was close to two in the morning when he entered, but the drawing room was still crowded with gentlemen who had come to enjoy the evening. On any day of the week, except the Sabbath, a gentleman could partake of an excellent dinner, prepared by Vachel's French chef, engage in play at one of the gaming tables set up in the music room, and be entertained by one of the elegantly attired women who lounged about the house. As long as he had enough gold in his pockets.

Sebastian smiled at the beautiful dark-haired woman moving toward him. Orlina was a survivor in every sense of the word. The daughter of a French count, she had escaped the revolution with her life and little else. Beautiful and shrewd, she had chosen only wealthy and generous men as her lovers. One of them, the Marquess of Wansford, had unwittingly financed her current establishment several years ago, thus eliminating her dependence on anyone. Her selection of only the loveliest, most genteel Cyprians had ensured her success with the men of the *ton*. The six burly footmen who stood about in emerald and gold livery ensured the men behaved. Although most of the residents of St. James's Square were aware of their neighbor's profession, no one spoke of Orlina's drawing room. Perhaps because most of the gentlemen were very happy she was there.

"When I saw you walk in, I thought at first I was dreaming," Orlina said, slipping her arm through Sebastian's. She smiled up at him, mischief glinting in her dark eyes. "It has been an age since you have graced us with your company. Your search for a bride takes up too much of your time."

Sebastian frowned. "Does the whole bloody town know about my intentions?"

She laughed, the sound husky. "Dare I hope you have come for more than supper?"

"I have come for something other than supper, Orlina. I was hoping for a few moments of your company."

Orlina lifted her dark brows, a look of surprise entering her eyes. "It has taken you a long time to finally accept an invitation I issued two years ago. From what I have heard from several of my girls, you shall be more than worth the wait."

Chapter Eleven

Although he knew Orlina was accomplished at flattery, Sebastian smiled at the compliment. After Emma's bitter scorn, a little of Orlina's honey was welcome. "Another time perhaps. Tonight I was hoping to speak to you on a matter of some importance."

"You have come here to speak with me?" Orlina patted his arm. "Now you have done something no man has done in a long time. You have surprised me."

Without another word, she ushered him out of the room, down a wide hallway and into an elegant salon. After closing the door, she turned to face him. "Would you like something to drink? Cognac perhaps?"

"Cognac would be nice." He rested his hand on the mantel and turned his face toward the fire burning on the hearth.

She opened a cabinet near the door and poured two glasses of cognac, then joined him near the fireplace. "Your hair is curling with the dampness, your cheeks

140

are reddened with the chill. Did you walk here?"

He sipped his cognac, the mellow liquor warming his throat and chest. "I needed a little exertion."

"One can always find that here." She gave him a wicked grin. "Instead you wish to talk."

The invitation in her eyes was unmistakable. If bedding her could take his mind off Emma, he would do it. Right here on one of the emerald velvet sofas. Yet he had an uncomfortable feeling coupling with Orlina would only make his absorption with Emma all the worse. "What do you know of a place called Gaetan's?"

"Gaetan's." All the humor faded from her eyes. "I have heard rumors of the place, nothing more. And from what I have heard, it is not a place for a man such as you."

"I believe a young woman may be in this place against her will."

"And of course, you wish to rescue her, as you came to my rescue that night at Vauxhall. It is like you to do something so noble without thought of the danger."

"I merely persuaded Hastings to keep his hands off you."

"As I recall, he was about to strangle me." Orlina smoothed her hand down his arm, a smile curving her lips. "Several other gentlemen saw what was happening that night and turned away. But you came charging at him like a knight of legend. I shall never forget the look on his face when you hoisted him up by his neckcloth. You never even raised your voice."

"He heard the message."

She brushed her fingertip over his lower lip. "How is it you and I were never lovers?"

"I did not wish to take advantage of you."

Orlina studied him a long moment, taking his measure in the way of a woman well experienced with men. "You are a rare gentleman, Lord Andover."

A pity Miss Emma Wakefield did not share the same appreciation of his worth. "What have you heard of this place called Gaetan's?"

Orlina rolled her crystal glass between her palms. "A few weeks ago a man became very ugly with one of my girls. If a girl is willing, I have no objection to any service she may provide one of our guests. But in this case, the man did not take no for an answer. I had one of my footmen escort him from the premises. Before he left, he said he did not need my cows, he could find anything he wanted at Gaetan's. There the whores are not allowed to deny their masters anything."

A chill crept along Sebastian's spine. "Their masters?"

"From what I have heard of Gaetan's, the women have no choice in anything." Orlina drew in her breath. "I have heard the girls are brought to Gaetan's against their will. Kept as slaves. Girls are kidnapped or tricked into Gaetan's web. And once they are taken to that place, they have no chance to escape."

Sebastian squeezed his glass. "If people know of this, why has no one closed the place?"

"The girls at Gaetan's are prostitutes, whether they chose the profession or not." Orlina glanced down into her glass. "And no one cares about a whore."

Sebastian suspected the monster preyed on girls who had no family or at any rate no one to protect them. Girls such as Charlotte Usherwood and Ariel. And what role did Radbyrne play in this horrible game? "Do you know where this place is?"

"No. And if I did, I would not wish to tell you. You should not become involved in this. Men such as these will do anything to protect what they see as their property."

Dangerous

I used to imagine someone might help me. Now I know there is no longer a place for me in the polite world. Ariel's words echoed in his memory. At the time it had taken all his will to keep from betraying his presence in Radbyrne's bedchamber. He knew he could not expose Emma, and he could not take a chance of hurting their chances of finding Charlotte. Although he had sensed something was amiss about the encounter, he had not realized she was in need of help until he had heard her speak those words. Even then, he had not surmised the true extent of the situation. "It is difficult to believe that men know these women are there against their will yet do nothing about it."

"It is possible that the girls are too frightened for their lives to tell any of the men who use them." Orlina looked up at him. "It is also possible they have given up hope of help."

"If the girls in Gaetan's do not believe anyone will help them, I think it is time to show them they are mistaken. I need to find this place."

"I wish you would reconsider, but I know you will not." Orlina drew in her breath. "I shall do what I can."

"You said one of your guests knew about Gaetan's. Who was it?"

Orlina pursed her lips. She hesitated a moment before she replied. "Sir Percy Fennigold."

From what Sebastian knew of the man, he was not surprised to find him connected to a place such as Gaetan's. "Thank you."

Orlina rested her hand upon his chest. "If there is anything else you need, anything at all, please do not hesitate to come to me."

Sebastian lifted her hand and kissed the back of her fingers. "I shall keep your kind offer in mind."

Orlina patted his chest. "Take care, *mon cher*. You

are dealing with the most ruthless of men."

Sebastian contemplated all Orlina had said as he walked with her back into the drawing room. He was so deep in thought, he might have missed a certain young woman sitting in the drawing room if she hadn't risen like a pheasant spooked by a hound upon seeing him. He froze when he saw Emma, surprise slamming into him like a well-thrown right to the jaw. It took him only a moment to gain his wits, and in that moment his anger soared like a hawk taking flight. He marched toward her, aware of the eyes upon him, the other men and women standing about the room. The audience was all that kept him from grabbing her by the shoulders and shaking her until all that rich dark hair fell from her pins. She took a step back as he drew near, then froze. Her chin lifted like that of a fighter about to meet an opponent in the ring.

He took her arm. "Come with me."

She resisted the gentle pressure on her arm. "I did not come here to speak with you."

"I am certain you did not." He kept his voice low, for her ears alone, even though he wanted to shout loud enough to be heard in Kensington. "Unless you want all London to know a certain young lady visited a well-known brothel, you will come with me now."

She cast a quick glance toward a group of four gentlemen sitting playing cards at a nearby table. Two other gentlemen stood near the fireplace with a couple of women. They had all turned in the direction of Sebastian and Emma. Although he saw mutiny in her eyes, she chose to allow him to lead her back toward the salon that he and Orlina had recently vacated. Although Orlina cast him a curious glance, she made no move to stop him. He ushered Emma into the room and closed the door.

"I had wondered how you and your aunt managed

144

to finance a London Season on your modest income. Now I see."

Emma stared at him blankly for a moment. Yet it took only a few quick beats of his racing heart before her beautiful eyes registered his meaning. "How dare you imply . . ."

"What the devil are you doing here?"

"I might ask the same of you." She planted her hands on her hips. "I thought you said you did not frequent such establishments."

He leaned toward her. "I believe I also mentioned making inquiries about your cousin at such establishments."

"And obviously that is why I am here. To discover if Madame Vachel has ever heard of Gaetan's."

"How did you even know about this place?"

"Vachel's is hardly a secret."

"To the gentlemen of the *ton*."

"I see you are one of those men who believe women are all deaf and blind." She released her breath in a strangled laugh. "I doubt there are many women of the *ton* who are not aware of the most elegant brothel in London."

"Miss Wakefield, I was reared with five sisters. I do not think women are deaf and blind except when they choose to be. In most cases that is when they wish to keep men in their proper place, which to most women is in the dark." He leaned toward her, so close his nose nearly touched hers. "What does amaze me is a certain young woman's propensity for putting herself in danger."

"I am quite capable of taking care of myself. I have been taking care of myself and my family for a long time."

Her breath brushed his face, threaded with a faint scent of cinnamon. It took all of his will to keep from clasping his mouth over hers, from plunging his tongue past her lips to taste her mouth. Did she have no idea how dangerous it was for her to wander about unprotected? "I told you I would handle this matter."

"Did you find out where Gaetan's is?"

"I suppose if I told you where Gaetan's was, I could expect you to waltz into his establishment and demand the release of your cousin."

"I do not need to have my actions approved by you."

He could see it then, the determination in her eyes. If she knew where Gaetan's was located, she would do precisely what he had suggested. She would waltz into the drawing room, withdraw her pistol, and demand the release of her cousin. And in the process get herself killed or worse. "You would do it, would you not?"

Her eyes narrowed. "I would face the devil himself if it was the only way to save Charlotte."

"And what would you do if the devil took one look at you and decided you would make an excellent addition to his establishment?"

She lifted her chin. "I would shoot him."

Sebastian stared at her, a legion of emotions warring within him. He wanted to throw her over his knee and spank her for the foolish child she was. He wanted to sweep her into his arms and hold her, protect her from all the ugliness in the world. And through all of the turmoil raging within him, a hot current streamed— lust. Pure and undiluted, potent with need, it surged through his every vessel, heating his blood and gathering in a simmering pool low in his belly. "You are very brave. And very foolish."

"And you are very arrogant." She turned away from him. She put several feet between them before she pivoted to face him. If she had meant to compose herself, she had failed. Her eyes flashed blue fire. A blush rode high on her cheeks. She looked furious and flustered and so beautiful his chest ached. "Charlotte is young and beautiful and filled with promise. She has her whole life ahead of her, a chance to marry and have a home and children. I shall not stand idly by while some monster steals that from her."

She revealed more than she realized in those heartfelt words. He heard her need beneath the words, the need for all she wanted and hoped and dreamed for Charlotte. "You cannot go running about, challenging men who have so little conscience they would do such horrible things to any human being. You put yourself at too much risk. You put Charlotte and the other women at risk as well."

"I have to do what I can to help her."

"What you can do is allow me to find her without worrying about the next ill-conceived thing you shall do."

"Ill-conceived!"

"At the moment Gaetan does not know we are trying to close his establishment. Surprise gives us an advantage we shall lose if you continue in this reckless fashion."

She planted her hands on her hips.

"If you go running about like a perfect ninny, you shall manage to get yourself into trouble and spoil our chances of rescuing Miss Usherwood and the other girls who may have fallen victim to the monster."

"A perfect ninny." She marched toward him, pausing so close the scent of roses in the rain swirled in each breath he took. "If I were a man, I doubt you would question my methods, would you?"

Sebastian recognized the truth in her words and at the same time the folly of them. "The last time I looked, you were not a man, Miss Wakefield."

Her eyes narrowed, her nostrils flared. "I am every bit as capable as any man."

Somewhere in the back of his mind a sane voice spoke calmly, of maintaining his composure, of dealing with her as though she were an irrational child. A man who remained in control was a man who controlled the situation. Yet when she was near, all the rational thoughts sank below the emotion raging within him. "You are certainly capable of getting yourself into a great deal of trouble."

"I will do what I think is necessary to get Charlotte safely back home." She tapped her finger against his chest, punctuating each word.

"You will stay out of the way and allow me to find your cousin. I have the resources to rescue her without anyone getting hurt."

A sound escaped her lips, a strangled scream. "You will not dictate to me. I will do what I think needs to be done. If I want to march into Gaetan's and shoot the monster, I will shoot him."

"No. You will not," he said, managing to keep his voice low and composed, while every emotion within him threatened to explode.

"Oh, you . . ." She stamped her foot on the floor. "You have no authority over me. You have no say in anything I should decide. . . ."

Her words ended in a gasp as he wrapped his hands around her waist. He lifted her straight off the floor until her beautiful, furious eyes were level with his. He acted without thought, without logic, without reason. He only knew she was in danger and he must keep her safe, even if it meant she would kill him in the process. And he had little doubt he was doomed. All he had to do was look at the flames in her eyes to know his world would never again be the same.

She planted her hands on his shoulders, her eyes

wide, so wide he could see the flicker of something far more heated than anger in their depths. "I demand you put me down," she said, her voice a breathless whisper. "Immediately!"

"You are the most infuriating female on the face of the earth."

"And you are the most odious male I have ever had the displeasure to meet."

"Confounded woman!" he whispered, before tossing her over his shoulder. Her reticule smacked against his hip, betraying the pistol hidden in the dark green cloth. He supposed he should count himself fortunate the termagant had not shot him. She shrieked and grabbed his coat, as though she were afraid he might drop her on her head. Which, when he thought of it, might actually be a good idea. It might knock some sense into her.

"What are you doing?" she demanded.

He marched toward the door. What the devil was he doing? He must be mad, but he could see no other way to take care of this particular problem. There was only one way to deal with Emma. "I am taking care of a problem."

"I am not your problem!"

"Unfortunately, you are." From the moment he had glimpsed her, she had become his problem, his torment, his salvation. She had managed to wiggle her way past his defenses. No, she had blown them straight to perdition. Now she would learn the consequences of shattering his carefully composed world. He grabbed the handle and pulled open the door.

"Let go of me!"

He ignored her, as best a man can ignore a wiggling female pounding his back. He found Orlina waiting for him in the hall. Although a glimmer of surprise filled her expression, she did not turn a hair at the sight of Sebastian with a struggling woman over his shoulder. "I am in need of a bedchamber."

"What did you say?" Emma demanded.

Sebastian ignored her. "Do you have one available for the entire night?"

Orlina laughed softly. "My guests do not usually bring their own girls."

"Put me down!"

Sebastian flinched when one of Emma's small fists connected with his ribs. "I suspect one of your girls would be a great deal more accommodating. Still, I seem to be plagued with this one."

"He is kidnapping me! Help me."

Orlina shrugged. "Good fortune is wasted upon some women. Now I would know precisely what to do should I be so fortunate as to be kidnapped by Lord Andover."

Emma bucked upon his shoulder. "I will make you regret the day you were born, Andover."

"No doubt of that." He lifted his brows and grinned at Orlina. "I wonder if you might grab her reticule before she withdraws her pistol and shoots someone."

Orlina did not hesitate. She quickly wrestled the bag from Emma and handed it to Sebastian. "You certainly do select your women with an eye for the dramatic, *mon cher.*"

"I am not his woman!" Emma shouted.

Orlina shrugged. "Then you are a far more foolish woman than you appear at the moment."

Sebastian laughed in spite of the small fist that Emma planted against his waist. Emma released a frustrated growl. "Let go of me, you big brute!"

Sebastian winked at Orlina. "Of course, I shall hire the bedchamber."

Orlina raised her hands. "You shall do no such thing. My house is your house, *mon cher*. If you need anything, and I do mean anything at all, remember I am here for you."

Chapter Twelve

The meaning in Orlina's voice was unmistakable, as unmistakable as the emotion rising within Emma. The sharp claws sinking into her belly could be only one thing—jealousy. It was absurd. She could not possibly be jealous over this man, Emma assured herself. Yet the emotion was there, cold and sharp, mocking her every attempt to deny the feelings she had for Andover.

"Thank you, Orlina," Andover said.

The soft sound of his dark voice grated on her nerves. She did not have to see his face to imagine the smile he was giving the beautiful French woman. Emma pounded her fist against his back.

"*Bon chance, mon cher*," Orlina said. "I think you will need it with that one."

What did he plan to do with her? Did he plan to strip away her clothes, touch her and kiss her and make love to her the way he had in her dreams? The thought shivered through her, sparking an odd expectancy where fear and revulsion should have risen.

"I am afraid Miss Wakefield is in need of a keeper. Since her family is far too soft-hearted to have her sent to Bedlam . . ."

"Bedlam!" Emma nearly choked on her anger.

". . . it appears I am the poor misbegotten fool who has the responsibility of taking care of her," Andover continued, as though Emma were not even there.

It was obvious that he wanted to teach her a lesson. Arrogant men were forever thinking they needed to teach women a lesson. Memories from his last lesson rose like sparks from a fire; they swirled through Emma, threatening to melt her anger in the inferno they made. He held her with one powerful arm cinched around her thighs, as though he had the right to touch her as he pleased. Was that what he planned?

"You may take the large chamber at the back of the house," Orlina said. "It is your favorite, I believe."

"It should do nicely. If you do not mind, I shall take the back staircase. I think we should disturb your guests as little as possible."

"An excellent idea. I shall make certain no one believes the lady is in danger."

"The man is a blackguard," Emma shouted.

"Enjoy yourself," Orlina said.

Andover turned, swinging Emma like a sack of linen. She clenched her teeth. She did not wish to think of how often Andover came to this place, or how familiar he was with the proprietress of the most elegant brothel in London. He started walking down the hall, obviously familiar enough with the place to find his way without help. She would not imagine what he did here when he came. It certainly was not her concern.

Yet she could not prevent the images from unfurling in her mind, of Andover and a bevy of beautiful cour-

153

tesans. She had seen erotic engravings before. She had
viewed statuary of perfectly formed male bodies de-
picted in all their glory. Her imagination managed to
fill in all the details her inexperience might have omit-
ted. Desire coiled and slithered through her, a treacherous snake. Oh she could scream!

Pins tumbled from her hair, spilling the heavy mass
over her face and down the back of his legs, as though
surrendering to his power. Well, he would soon discover she would not surrender to her misbegotten
need any more than she would surrender to him. "Put
me down!"

"You may shout as loudly as you can. Perhaps it
will cause a mild curiosity among the gentlemen in the
drawing room." He squeezed her thigh, his hand
warming her skin through her gown. "Of course, if
someone were to stop us, I would be obliged to tell
him precisely why I am escorting you out of a
brothel."

Emma bit her lower lip. The blackguard had her in
check. The last thing she wanted was to stir up any
scandal that might harm her aunt and cousins.
Through the dark, swaying curtain of her hair, she saw
the crimson and gold carpet lining the hallway. She
did not wish to contemplate what activities were taking place in the chambers above them. Yet her imagination would not obey her commands. She fought the
scream of frustration rising within her. "Oh, I shall
make you regret this."

He started up a narrow staircase. "You will have to
win the battle first, Miss Wakefield."

Blood pounded in her temples. Each step he took
drove his broad shoulder into her middle. With each
long stride, her fury grew, equalled only by an expectation she could not crush. As much as she wanted to
strangle him, she also wanted to throw her arms

around his neck and kiss him until all the ice around his heart melted, until every idea of marriage for the sake of practicality withered beneath the heat of her passion. A part of her realized this was what she had been craving ever since he had first touched her. "If you think you have won this battle, think again, Andover."

"Oh, I think this battle is just beginning, Miss Wakefield." He left the stairs and stepped into a wide hall.

Through the pounding of blood in her head, she heard feminine laughter followed by the husky voice of a woman who said, "You can carry me away any time you like, my lord."

"Perhaps another time," Andover said, without pausing in his stride.

Heat flooded Emma's cheeks when she thought of the spectacle she made, tossed over his shoulder like some hapless, defenseless female in a Viking raid. She thumped her fist against his back. "You will pay for this."

"I am trembling, Miss Wakefield."

He was laughing at her. The beast. He paused long enough to open a door, then carried her across the threshold of what could only be one of the bedchambers. He had used this chamber before. That realization hit her like a clenched fist in her belly. If he thought she would tumble into his arms without a fight in the chamber where he had bedded some nameless tart, he would soon learn he was mistaken. "Put me down."

"I have every intention of putting you down." In spite of his words, he carried her across the room, treading over wreaths and flowers stitched in blue and rose and ivory, all the while ignoring the constant beat of her fists upon his back. It made her feel like a butterfly attacking an elephant.

He shifted her in his grasp. The next instant she was falling. Ivory silk billowed up around her. Soft eiderdown wrapped around her as she sank into the mattress. She braced herself, expecting the weight of his body to press down against her. Her heart thumped wildly in her chest. Her skin tingled. Her mind prepared for war, her body for something far different. Yet he did not pounce upon her. In fact, he was walking away from the bed.

Emma struggled up from the thick cushion of eiderdown and silk. "What are you doing?"

Andover turned at the door. "I am making certain you do not get yourself hurt."

"You intend to leave me here? Alone?"

A smile curved his lips, a little grin filled with the same mischief that lit his dark eyes. "Is that disappointment I hear in your voice?"

"Of all the . . ." She scrambled off the high four-poster and marched toward the door. "If you imagine I am going to remain here . . ."

"Good night." Andover closed the door before she could reach him.

She rushed to the door. A soft click whispered of the lock sliding into place. She grabbed the brass handle and tried to open the door. It would not budge. "Andover, you cannot leave me in this place."

"I cannot allow you to run around London like a perfect hen wit."

"Arrogant buffoon!" She rattled the handle. "Let me out of here!"

"I want you to think about how easily I overpowered you, Miss Wakefield. Think about what might have happened if I were a man such as Gaetan."

Emma rattled the door handle. "I thought you had given up trying to teach me a lesson?"

"It is a fool's errand, I agree. Still, someone must try

to keep you from getting yourself injured. The task has fallen to me."

"I am not your responsibility."

"Have a pleasant evening."

"Wait!" Emma's mind raced. "What about my aunt? She will be ill with worry."

"I shall inform Mrs. Usherwood that you are spending the evening with friends."

Laughter floated from the chamber next to hers, soft and feminine, followed by the robust laughter of a man. "I cannot possibly spend a night in a place such as this."

"Rest assured, Miss Wakefield. You are safe enough. Orlina would never risk injury to one of her guests by allowing him to come near you."

She glared at the oak-paneled door. "I shall make you regret this, Lord Andover."

The dark rumble of his laughter penetrated the door to prick her anger. "I look forward to the next battle, Miss Wakefield. Have a pleasant evening."

"What are you going to do about Gaetan? Are you going there?"

"I have yet to uncover the location of Gaetan's. When I do, you may be certain I will do everything in my power to bring your cousin safely home."

She pressed her hands against the door. "You have no right to lock me in here. Charlotte is my responsibility. Do you understand?"

He was so quiet, for a moment she thought he had walked away. When he finally spoke, his voice was low and gentle. "Although I understand why you wish to put yourself at risk, I cannot allow you to continue in this fashion."

She wanted to scream. "You do not have authority over me."

"It would appear I do."

"I am not a child, Andover. I have every right to—."

"Have a pleasant evening, Miss Wakefield."

"Do not walk away from me while I—"

"Until tomorrow, Miss Wakefield."

"Blackguard!" She pressed her forehead against the cool wood. Although she could not hear his footsteps, she knew he was walking away, leaving her to spend the night in a brothel. Oh, she would strangle the man. She was not a child to be sent to her room at the whim of an unreasonable adult. Worse than anything was the truth she had to face, a truth that sat like a lump of ice in her belly. She had expected him to try to make love to her. Instead he had simply wanted to be rid of a nuisance.

Heat flooded her cheeks when she realized the true extent of her foolishness. Not only had she expected him to kiss her and touch her and try to seduce her, but she could not extinguish the disappointment within her, a disappointment that led directly to ruin. Experience was a wonderful tutor. She would not make the same mistake twice. Apparently he was immune to the fever that had gripped her, this horrible attraction that had infected her every fiber. She would make the man regret the day he was born. If he thought he had won, she would show him he was wrong.

She took a deep breath before she turned to face her prison. Aside from the door that led to the hall, there was another across the room. She hurried to it, hoping it might provide some method of escape. It led to a small dressing room that contained a chamber pot and a wash stand. She walked back into the bedchamber and threw back the drapes. The window overlooked a walled garden. Unless she could sprout wings and fly, there was no escape by that access. She was trapped.

At least for the moment. Trapped in a very elegant prison.

The chamber was not what she had expected. The sweet scent of lavender wafted from porcelain bowls set atop the round commode near the door, on the dressing table, and the bedside table. A delicate floral pattern covered the ivory silk that streamed from the plastered ceiling to the oak wainscoting covering the lower half of the walls. The same pattern graced the ivory silk drapes, the swags and the canopy above the large four-poster bed, and the delicate gilt-trimmed furniture. She stood by the bed trying not to contemplate all the activity this particular piece of furniture had seen. Yet it was not something she could ignore.

She pulled back the ivory counterpane and the covers beneath. The sheets looked clean. They smelled of lavender, nothing more. She did not know how many women had serviced countless men in this bed. She did not care. There was only one man who mattered. In spite of her attempts to prevent them, images flooded her mind, unfurling like banners caught by the wind. Andover with beautiful courtesans, their bodies entwined in positions she was not even certain were possible.

She sat on the edge of the bed and silently vowed she would not allow the man to get the better of her. She was not a foolish child straight out of the school room. She could control her emotions. True, she did not have much experience controlling her emotions, but in this case she would learn. Quickly.

She would not allow anyone to prevent her from doing all she could to find Charlotte. A soft moaning sound filtered through the wall from the room next door. She clasped her hands over her ears and tried not to imagine what was happening in that room. Oh, she would strangle the brute.

* * *

Gunshot pierced the morning air. The thick scent of gunpowder burned Sebastian's nostrils. He stared through the blue-gray smoke to the target and frowned. His shot had missed the mark by the width of a finger. He had always been better with a sword than with a pistol.

"What of Radbyrne?" Montgomery Trent lifted his pistol from the low wooden wall that separated the shooters from the target area. Taking little time to aim, he fired. The bullet slammed into paper and wood, piercing the heart of the target. "Do you think you can persuade him to tell you where this Gaetan's is located?"

"I am not sure how deeply my nephew is involved with Gaetan." Sebastian handed his spent pistol to his footman. He lifted a freshly loaded weapon from the shelf in front of him. "If he kidnapped Charlotte Usherwood, then it is safe to assume he may do more than simply patronize the place. And if that is true, the only way to protect himself is to protect Gaetan."

"Do you really believe Radbryne kidnapped her and took her to a brothel?" Montgomery glanced at the target and fired. The shot pierced the paper a hairsbreadth from the first. "What point would there be in doing something so vile?"

Sebastian frowned at his friend's target, then made a mental note to practice at Manton's more often. "Radbyrne has always worshipped at the altar of greed. He has expensive tastes and a modest income. I have often wondered how he manages to afford his extravagances. I never suspected it might be in this particular trade."

"A beautiful lady of quality. Untouched." Jourdan lifted his pistol and fired. The shot pierced the heart of his target. "There are men who would pay a great deal to destroy such innocence."

Sebastian's stomach clenched when he thought of Charlotte in a place such as Gaetan's. He could only pray they would reach her before she came to such harm. "I think it would be wise to see what Fennigold can tell us."

"That addlepate Fennigold has been sniffing about my sister's skirts. Claudette does not want him, but she likes to keep him and a pack of others dangling after her the way a cat likes to play with a mouse before she kills it." Jourdan handed his weapon to his footman. "Fennigold would love to find a way into my good graces. I might let him know I am looking for some particularly interesting sport."

Sebastian aimed his weapon and fired. The bullet slammed into the target just left of the mark. "We need to find this place as soon as possible."

"I think I will spend the evening at White's. I know of several members who might enjoy a place such as Gaetan's." Montgomery lifted his pistol and fired, hitting the heart of the target once again. "Perhaps I can learn something that will be helpful."

"I will keep an eye on my nephew. Perhaps he will lead us straight to Gaetan's." Sebastian looked at his friend's target, his mind turning once more to the woman he had imprisoned at Orlina's. How well did Emma handle a pistol? *I am every bit as capable as any man.* It would not surprise him to learn she could shoot as well as he could, if not better.

Sebastian had experienced more than a few twinges of guilt when it came to the beautiful Bedlamite. Perhaps he had been a bit high-handed with her. She was right in saying he did not have any authority over her. Yet for some reason he did not wish to understand, he could not deny the need to protect her. Of course,

Emma would not see it as protection. No. She thought he was an arrogant male who simply enjoyed lording his power over her.

When Sebastian left Manton's, he headed for Orlina's. He had kept the termagant stewing long enough. It was time to face her . . . and her wrath.

He should be dreading this encounter. He knew she would be furious. Yet he could not crush the excitement simmering in his veins at the thought of seeing her again. She was reckless, impractical, a creature who thrived on emotion. A man would never know what to expect with her. He leaned back against the black velvet squabs of his coach and smiled. She certainly would never bore him. He shook his head, trying to clear away the ridiculous notions flitting through his mind. Emma was certainly not the type of wife he needed. She would make a shambles of his life. No, he could not under any circumstances marry Miss Emma Wakefield. His coach rocked to a halt in front of Orlina's town house. He took a deep breath and prepared to face the furious Miss Wakefield.

One of the footmen showed him into Orlina's sitting room. A scent of spices and flowers wrapped around him when he entered the room. Orlina lay upon a Grecian chaise longue sipping a cup of chocolate. The ivory silk of her dressing gown spilled artfully over the dark blue velvet upholstery, exposing one shapely leg from her knee to the ivory silk mule she wore. The first few pearl buttons of the garment were open, blonde lace parted to reveal the hollow at the base of her neck and nothing more. It was a pose meant to tempt a man with just a glimpse of the charms hidden beneath lace and silk.

A small greyhound left its place at the foot of Orlina's chaise longue to investigate him. The little dog sniffed at his boots, then gazed up at him, its rear swinging with the swish of its tail. Sebastian bent to stroke the dog's sleek head. The dog promptly lay down and presented its belly for him to scratch. Sebastian obliged while he softly praised it for being a good dog.

"I see my Marguerite has fallen victim to your charm. She always did have excellent taste in men. She bit Lord Ashwell once. Jumped up and got him right in the . . ." Orlina winked at him. "Shall we say, the gentleman was in no mood to enjoy any of my girls the rest of the evening."

Sebastian looked at the dog with an entirely new respect. He gave her one last pat, then strolled to Orlina. "Did it take a while to train her to do that particular trick?"

Orlina shrugged, allowing the dressing gown to slip a bit from her bare shoulder. "It was her own idea."

Sebastian took Orlina's outstretched hand and kissed her fingertips, her spicy sweet perfume flooding his senses. "I hope Miss Wakefield did not cause much trouble."

"None at all." Orlina patted the cushion beside her, inviting Sebastian to sit. Her thigh brushed his hip when he accepted the invitation. She sipped her chocolate, her dark eyes filled with humor. "But I think you should know, Antoine informed me a knife was missing when he took away her breakfast tray."

"A knife?" The back of Sebastian's neck prickled. "And did he retrieve it?"

"I thought it was too dangerous for him to try."

Sebastian wondered whether he should allow Miss Wakefield to stay another day, then decided against it for more than a few reasons. She was far too dangerous to foster upon anyone else. "You were probably right. He might have walked away with it sticking in his skull."

"I suspect she would have aimed much lower." Orlina patted the cushion beside her, inviting the dog to join her. The small greyhound leaped up beside her mistress and settled upon the blue velvet pillow. "I think you will be able to disarm her without any harm coming to either of you."

Sebastian rolled his eyes. "At the moment, Miss Wakefield would like nothing better than to see me drawn and quartered. I suspect she is angry enough to do it herself, with a butter knife."

Orlina laughed softly, the sound of a woman accustomed to employing laughter to win a man's answering smile. "This girl, she means a great deal to you."

"I am trying to help her find her cousin. It is possible she may have been taken to Gaetan's."

Orlina's eyes grew wide with understanding. "And this cousin is the girl you are trying to rescue."

"Unfortunately, Miss Wakefield prefers to take matters into her own hands. If someone does not stop her, she will very likely get herself into a great deal of trouble."

Orlina sipped her chocolate, regarding him with her dark eyes in a way that left no doubt about her experience with the male of the species. "You intend to protect her from her own reckless nature. It is your only interest in her?"

Sebastian glanced away from Orlina's perceptive eyes. His gaze fell upon a porcelain figurine of a woman upon the white marble mantel. The figurine was nude, her long black hair swirling over one shapely hip and down her pale thigh. It bore an astonishing likeness to Orlina. "I wish only to help find her cousin. And to make certain this Gaetan does not have the opportunity to harm other girls."

Orlina leaned forward and rested her hand upon his arm. When he looked at her, she smiled. "Did you know a man gets a certain look in his eyes when he sees a woman he wants? I know this look. I have seen it many times. Including last night, when you looked at your Miss Wakefield."

Sebastian lifted his brows. "I am a sensible man, Orlina, far too practical to wish to spend my life with a powder keg. I can think of nothing less comfortable."

Orlina patted his arm. "I, for one, will take passion over comfort on any given day. It is the way of the French. You should know this."

"Fortunately, I have not been plagued by the passion of my French ancestors." He rose and straightened the cuff of his dark gray coat. "I think it is time I faced the little virago."

Orlina lifted her dark brows. *"Mais oui, mon cher."*

Chapter Thirteen

Emma had a knife. That thought repeated itself over and over in his mind as Sebastian made his way down the hall to the chamber where he had left Emma the night before. What defense could a man employ against a lady? Only one came to mind. A man could only hope to disarm her before she could do much damage. And of course he must do it without inflicting any harm upon her, no matter how much he wanted to grab her by the shoulders and shake her until her teeth rattled.

Good sense told him to open the door to her bedchamber without warning. Good manners demanded he knock. He hesitated just a moment before rapping upon the oak door. "Miss Wakefield, it is Andover."

No reply. As the seconds ticked by, apprehension scraped along his nape, like the sharp claws of a hawk. What the devil was she doing?

Sebastian gripped the door handle. "Miss Wakefield."

He received no reply. He waited another few moments while he imagined the ways she would attack. He took a deep breath, then opened the door, prepared to dodge a missile. Nothing came hurling at him. His nemesis sat near one of the windows, reading a book. Emma did not so much as glance up at him when he drew near. Instead she stared at the page, as though this book were the most enthralling epic ever written.

Sunlight streamed through the lace curtains at the window, casting a tangled pattern across her face. Dark smudges marred the skin beneath her glorious eyes. Her hair was pulled back and kept in place by a piece of satin ribbon he suspected had once adorned the curtains. Sunlight wended through the thick shining mass, mining gold in the dark brown tresses. In place of the modest dress she had worn the night before, she wore a gown of sea-green muslin that had obviously been supplied by Orlina. Although it was far from indecent, the square-cut neckline dipped low enough to reveal the pale swells of her breasts.

He became aware of the blood pounding through his veins. He felt as though he stood on the edge of a precipice; if he took one step forward, he would fall. What bothered him more than anything was the fact that for some reason beyond logic, he wanted to take that fatal step.

He wasn't certain how long he stood looking at her, as though he had come upon a painting by da Vinci, a masterpiece that had long ago been lost. When he realized he could go on standing like this for hours, he prodded his wits. "I see you have found a way to amuse yourself."

"I would wager you were not even aware that Orlina had a library." She kept her gaze on the page, as though his presence did not disturb her in the least. "Books are not precisely the entertainment that brings you here."

The accusation hit with the force of an open palm across his cheek. It should not bother him that this woman held him in such low esteem, but it did bother him. "I have never pretended to be a saint, Miss Wakefield."

"It seems Orlina has quite a diverse library. She likes to give the girls a chance to improve their minds when they are not servicing the base instincts of the London male." Emma looked up from her book; the ice in her eyes would have been clear at a distance. Since he was standing within five feet of her, he felt the chill sink into his bones. "Do you even regard the girls who warm your bed as people? Or are they simply vessels in which to deposit your lust?"

"I regard the women who work here as I would any servant who performs a service for a fee."

"What makes this place any better than Gaetan's? Or the men who come here any better than those who use the women there."

It was a direct slap to his honor. He did not care to be placed in the same club with men who would use a woman against her will. Anger flickered inside him. Intellectually he knew it was a useless emotion, one that might cause trouble, one that he had always been able to keep under close rein, until Emma stormed into his life. Still, he had decided she would not destroy his composure. He was not a creature of whim. Intellect could always rise above emotion. "The women who work in this establishment have chosen this profession for various reasons. If they are not happy, they leave. Choice, Miss Wakefield, makes a great difference."

"I cannot imagine any of them are happy being used as they are."

"On the contrary. Susannah, for instance, could not abide working as a dressmaker's apprentice another day. She likes to wear pretty gowns much more than she likes making them. Clarice was a kitchen maid before coming here. Nancy labored in a scullery. She told me making money lying on her back on clean sheets was far better than washing them. Millie was a . . ."

She snapped her book shut. "Is there no one in the house you have not bedded?"

What did he see in her eyes? Something more interesting than anger. Something that should not be there. Jealousy? Was she truly possessive about him? The notion did something odd to his insides. It made him want to jump up on the nearest chair and shout. Since the nearest chair was a delicate piece of fluff trimmed in gilt and he was a practical man, he chose instead to remain standing where he was, with the blood pounding through his veins. "Orlina has new girls starting every month or so. She helps each of them invest a portion of their earnings with an eye to retirement."

"You make it sound as though Orlina is providing a wonderful opportunity for these girls."

"When they come to her, Orlina teaches them to walk and talk and dress properly. If they do not know how to read or write, she teaches them. She provides an opportunity for the type of life they could not have had without an establishment such as this."

"As much as I hate to say this, you are right."

He did not like the look in her eyes. "I am?"

Emma stood and walked toward him, slowly, in a way that made the hair at his nape rise. "You said choice makes a difference. Still, I wonder what real choice women have. There are so few opportunities for women in this world, that employment in an elegant

169

brothel is all some poor girls can hope to achieve. Of course, even that is only available for pretty girls."

He could not help wondering once again how she had managed to finance a London Season for her cousin. "There are few opportunities for women, I agree. Which makes me wonder—"

"A girl of quality aspires to marriage and hopes her life is not made miserable by the man who has taken control of her, since she gives up most of her rights as a human being the day she speaks her vows."

"I would imagine many women—"

She wagged her finger at him. "And if she does not have a fortune, or beauty, then her chances of marriage are slim. Which leaves her other possibilities."

Other possibilities. He found those possibilities more than a little disturbing in the case of one young woman. "It would seem you have—"

"She could become a governess, if she wishes to give up her family and become a servant who must deal with unreasonable brats and equally unreasonable parents."

He watched her pace to the fireplace and back to where he stood near the bed. "I can see why a woman would not choose to become a governess. Of course, it does—"

"Or she could become a paid companion to some ill-tempered crone who regards her with less considera-tion than her pug." Emma turned and paced to the window, then turned back to Sebastian. She halted in front of him and pinned him in a cold glare. "And do you know why a woman has so few options, my Lord Andover?"

Oh no, he certainly did not like the look in her eyes. By nature, most women were unpredictable at best. Creatures ruled by emotion could seldom be de-pended upon to do anything logical. With this woman, all bets were off. Where the devil was the knife? "I have a feeling you are about to tell me, Miss Wakefield."

"Because of men such as you, Lord Andover. Arrogant males who swagger about the—"

"Swagger! I never swagger."

She tapped his chest with the tip of her forefinger. "Who *swagger* about the world, trampling people beneath their heels simply because it suits them."

Sebastian clenched his hands into tight fists at his sides, fighting the anger rising inside him. It was merely the crest of a wave of emotion threatening to swamp his self control. "I do not go about trampling people, Miss Wakefield."

"And what would you call kidnapping me?"

"Doing my best to help you."

"Help me! You wanted to teach me a lesson. If that is not the height of arrogance and conceit, I do not know what is."

"I had thought it might show you just how dangerous your actions could be. Obviously my efforts were wasted upon you."

"You had no right to lock me in this place. You have no business meddling in my life."

She was right, of course. He had no authority over her, no right to constrain her, no rights of any kind when it came to her. Yet he could not seem to help himself when it came to this blue-eyed virago. "If I saw a woman about to throw herself off London Bridge, I would stop her. The same way I stopped you from running about London last night as though you were a madwoman."

"Oh, you . . ." She thumped his chest with her book. "I am not insane."

"Pardon me, Miss Wakefield, but if you are not insane, you are certainly running about pretending to be."

"Brute!"

"Reckless. Foolish. Completely unreasonable. You give the word termagant new meaning. I am amazed you have managed to survive this long without a keeper."

"Arrogant, contemptible . . ." She whacked him again and again, all the while ranting about her own sanity and how a woman could go insane listening to bestial grunts and groans all night, and it was all his fault. She wailed about her own right to look after her family, the arrogance of men in general, and of him in particular. She delved into the depths of how she could and would take care of herself without his help.

If she had been wielding a dictionary, her beating might have done some damage. As it was, a slim volume wielded by a slip of a female, each thump was no more than a nuisance. Since he had lived with five sisters, he knew better than to do anything but allow the storm to pass. When he made no response, she dropped the book and glared up at him.

Her cheeks were deepened to a dusky pink, her eyes alight with fury, her lips parted, her breath ragged as though she had run a race. At some time in her tirade, the ribbon had slipped from her hair, allowing the heavy mass to tumble about her shoulders. A thick lock fell upon the bodice of her gown, drawing his attention to the curve of her breast. His fingers twitched.

She was looking up at him, as though she were expecting him to say something. In the back of his mind, half hidden beneath the rubble she had made of his thoughts, he realized he should respond, make some intelligent observation about her behavior. Yet somewhere in the tirade he had become far too distracted to make an intelligent observation about anything. All he could think about was how much he wanted to take this woman into his arms. Before he could analyze this odd drive, he found himself moving. He slipped his hand into her thick hair. His fingers slid through cool silk that grew warm near her nape.

She pressed her hands against his chest. Her eyes grew wide as he lowered his head. "What are you doing?" she asked, her voice barely more than a whisper.

"This." Against all reason, defying every piece of logic by which he lived his life, he slid his mouth over hers. He expected her to push him away. Yet her fingertips curled against his shirt, her nails scraping him through the soft white cambric cloth.

He had thought of those few moments when he had held her that first night over and over again, like a foolish boy with his first infatuation. Intellect told him he was making too much of the episode. No woman could captivate so completely with merely a kiss. The circumstances had beguiled him. Yet his considerable intellect could not explain the reaction of his body to this woman now. Logic could not make sense of the need swelling within him.

The fragrance of roses in the rain swirled through his senses, penetrating his blood like a drug that made him want to fall to his knees before her. One soft touch of his lips upon hers should not heat his blood this way. The simple pressure of her mouth beneath his should not make him ache this way, want this way, need this way. Yet here he stood, like a callow youth, blood pounding, heart racing, intellect fading.

He was a man of logic and reason, completely devoid of passion and flare. This attraction was completely beyond his experience. One look at her kindled flames within him.

He wanted her more than he wanted his next breath.

He wanted to taste her, to explore the warm terrain of her skin, to discover every lush valley and mound with his hands and his lips and his tongue. Need pounded like a fist in his loins. Heat sluiced through his vessels, carried in waves of fire with each furious beat of his heart. Still, he might have saved himself from the fall if she had not parted her lips beneath his. Even then logic might have survived the inferno she ignited within him if he had not tasted her own need in the kiss. Need surged within him.

Logic and reason crumbled beneath the heat rising within him. Emotion rose from wells locked deep within, surging upward in ever increasing waves of longing and need. He slid his arms around her, held her close against his body and surrendered.

What had she ever done to deserve this fate? A sane woman would have gone running from the room at the first opportunity. She knew he would not stop her, not if she broke away from his embrace. He had far too much pride to chase after her for that purpose. Yet she could not find the will to leave him.

She must be insane. Insane and wicked. For she had wanted him from the first moment she had glimpsed him. Wanted him even when she had thought him a monster. Against reason and logic and sense, she wanted him. She had never felt the power of her femininity until she felt his touch. He was maleness personified, power and grace barely leashed. And now, she realized she had never wanted anything more than this man, his lips upon hers, his hands sliding up and down her back, his big warm body wrapped around her.

She could not resist the need to touch him, to slide her hands over the warm wool covering his wide shoulders, to delve into the black silk of his hair, to hold him as she returned his kiss. Where experience lagged behind, instinct surged ahead. She opened her lips beneath his, feminine ardor rising to guide her in this ancient dance. She leaned into him, snuggling her breasts against the hard plane of his chest. Sensation scattered within her, like sparks tossed from a fire.

She slipped her hands inside his coat, following a desperate need to feel him. The wool of his coat trapped the warmth of his body. The heat bathed her skin while she sought the man beneath the layers. Through the soft cambric of his shirt, sleek muscles flexed against her palms, as though reacting to her touch. She shivered with excitement. The deep growl that rose from low in his chest vibrated against her hands before the husky sound brushed her ears. The primitive groan did something wicked to her insides.

He slid his hands down her back, cupped her hips and lifted her into the heat of his body. Through the layers of muslin, cotton, and wool, she could feel the hard thrust of aroused male flesh against her belly, thick and heavy. It should have shocked her. It should not have excited her. Yet she could not deny the feeling spreading through her. She was water tossed into a kettle, and he was the fire beneath, heating her until she felt as restless as bubbles roiling to a boil.

Wicked. Wanton. Foolish. Heaven above, she could not allow this to happen. Yet she could not prevent the need from rising inside her, a need that was far more powerful than sense. She had dreamed of a moment like this, of pure passion and pleasure. How could she deny those dreams?

"Emma," he whispered, her name a prayer upon his breath. He kissed her as though he had been waiting for her all his life. And in that instant, she felt as though he wanted her more than he had ever wanted anything else.

It was magic, the way he made her feel, as though she were beautiful and desirable. He kissed her cheek, her jaw, her neck, warm lips moving softly against her skin, as though he wanted to memorize her taste and texture. He slipped his hand between their bodies and cupped her breast. At the slow slide of his thumb over the sensitive peak, sensation skittered over her nerves.

She felt quick, urgent tugs upon the ties of her bodice, and realized things were escalating quickly. If she did not stop him now, there would be no stopping him. Yet she could not halt her own need, much less his. Before meeting this man she had imagined what it must mean to feel desire. She had thought it primitive, a tug upon one's senses. She supposed those who were not of a strong will could be coaxed into foolishness by desire. Now she saw the error in her judgment. Desire hit with the force of a hurricane. It did not ask, it did not plead, it did not coax, it grabbed hold and sucked her straight into the storm.

The warmth of his hands slid across her shoulders as he peeled down the gown and shift. Sunlight streamed across her breasts, as though illuminating a gift offered up to this dark pagan god. She felt beyond herself, transformed by a look from this man. The plain, ordinary woman melted in the heat of his gaze, like wax beneath a flame. In her place a temptress rose, molded from desire. She reveled in the soft touch of his hand upon her naked flesh. She tipped back her head, a wanton sound sliding from her lips at the first brush of his mouth upon her.

She understood now how thrones had toppled for passion. She knew now the frailty of will, the fragility of reason. Nothing mattered in this instant, but him. He touched her with the exquisite care with which an artist applies his brush to canvas. She held him against her while he lavished attention upon first one then the other breast, suckling her, flicking his tongue upon her, driving her mad with need.

He swept her into his arms. "Do you have any idea how much I want you?"

He gave her no chance to answer. Instead he covered her lips with his own. Cambric and wool, warm from his body, brushed against her breasts with the sensual shift of powerful muscles. She snuggled against him, pressing her aching breasts into his hard chest. Cool ivory silk caressed her back as he laid her down upon the bed.

She felt as though she were coming awake from an endless sleep, as though she were experiencing her senses for the first time. His scent swirled through her as he covered her, pushing her down into the silk and the soft eiderdown. This was what she had hungered for since the first time she had met him.

He moved against her. She felt a fine trembling in his hands as he slipped the gown lower, baring her belly to his warm gaze and the warmer brush of his lips, the brand of his tongue. She tipped back her head, arching upward, surrendering herself to this man and the magic he conjured with his touch.

His hand stiffened upon her bare hip. She opened her eyes and found him half reclined on the bed, his powerful thighs straddling her legs, one sun-darkened hand upon her pale hip, the other clenching her gown. Her gown slanted across her body, baring her from her neck all the way to below her belly. But he was not looking at her. His attention was suddenly riveted on something across the room.

Chapter Fourteen

It was then Emma heard it. The soft sound of feminine laughter drifting from the room next door. It was followed by a low, masculine rumble.

Andover grimaced at the sound, as though someone had hit him. He looked at her then. The fire in his dark eyes faded, cooling into a look of sheer disgust. He yanked her gown over her body, trying to cover her. Since part of the muslin was stuck under her hips, he managed to cover her belly and nothing more. He scrambled off the bed and turned his back, as though he could not abide the sight of her. He plowed a hand through his hair, smoothing the black waves she had ruffled with her restless fingers. "I must be mad."

She flinched, reality hitting with the force of a fist. Apparently madness ran rampant in this room. Sunlight flowing through the windows left no dark corners in which to hide. She lay on a bed in the most elegant brothel in London, half naked, partially seduced, and entirely foolish. Worse than foolish, because part of her could not help wishing he had ruined her. She would have preferred total ruin to this icy rejection. It was as if, having taken a look at the goods, he had decided she was not worth the bother.

Humiliation flooded her cheeks with a sharp stinging heat. She sat up and struggled with her clothes. The molten desire that had coursed through her blood pooled in her belly, cooling into a solid chunk of regret. She glared at his broad back and thought of the knife she had stolen at breakfast. Perhaps it had been a good decision to put it safely in a drawer. Because if she had had it at the moment, she might very well have plunged it into that broad back.

He shifted his shoulders, lifting them up and back as though her murderous thoughts had caused him some discomfort. "Miss Wakefield." He rubbed the back of his neck. His dark voice sounded husky when he continued. "When you are dressed, come downstairs. My coach will be waiting to take you home."

Emma sat staring at him, watching him march across the room, each step trampling her pride. He left without so much as a glance at her, as though she were nothing more than one of Orlina's girls. It occurred to her that was precisely his intent. He had wanted to teach her a lesson. When a night in Orlina's had not done the trick, he had seduced her. She could almost hear him saying, "this is what happens when a hen-witted female marches into battle with a man." She closed her eyes against the sting of tears. Yet she could not prevent the tears from leaking beneath her lashes. Never in her life had she felt more foolish. She had actually believed he had wanted her with the same reckless passion that had overwhelmed her. She had believed for one incredible moment that he might care for her.

She thumped her fist into the rumpled counterpane. Well, if he had meant to teach a lesson, he had done a marvelous job. If he had wanted to make her feel used and foolish and completely miserable, he had succeeded. Yet if he thought for one moment the war was over, he was mistaken. It was a battle fought and lost. The next one would not end in the same fashion. Oh no, she would be prepared for his tactics next time. She slipped off the bed and contemplated her next move. Yet nothing that came to mind would do the scoundrel justice. The man deserved to be shot for what he had done to her.

He should be shot. Sebastian stood near an elm tree in the square across from Orlina's, watching Emma climb into his coach. He could not remember the last time he had felt so foolish. They shot rabid dogs to put them out of their misery. Perhaps a bullet in the heart was the only cure for this insanity he was experiencing. When he was certain she was safely on her way home, he began walking. He only hoped exercise would untangle the tight knot Emma had tied in his belly. Clouds gathered above him, strangling the sun.

Lightning flashed in the distance, followed by a soft rumble. A fat drop of rain struck his face. He scarcely noticed. He was a man who faced facts. And there were certain facts that could not be avoided in this case. No matter how much he tried.

First, he had seduced a lady of quality in the most elegant brothel in London. A lady he had placed under his protection. It was an offense that could not go unchallenged. Yet even in his muddled state, he realized a duel with himself was out of the question.

Second, if he had not been reminded of his whereabouts, he would have finished the deed. He actually would have made love to Emma on a bed where he had coupled with numerous whores.

Third, if he had stayed a moment longer in that bedchamber, with her scent teasing his nostrils and the feel of her fresh in his memory, he would not have given a farthing for where he was. He would have taken her and let the consequences be damned. Taken her as though she meant nothing more to him than one of Orlina's tarts.

Fourth, she did mean more to him than one of Orlina's tarts. The breath turned to lead in his lungs. He paused near a lamppost and gripped the wet wrought-iron post while a wave of dizziness washed over him.

The woman was a termagant. She strewed turmoil about her the way his collie shed hair in June. Any man who became involved with the beautiful virago was a man destined to have his life ruled by chaos.

He glared at a fellow in a yellow and red waistcoat who had paused to stare at him. The dandy turned on his heel and scampered away, high heels clicking on the sidewalk, black umbrella bobbing with each step. Sebastian drew in his breath and forced his feet to move.

He and Emma did not suit. Not in the least. He was a quiet man. He admired logic and reason, practicality. He expected his life to proceed in an orderly manner.

A man could not have a nice orderly life with a whirlwind in the house. Although his actions today dictated he set matters right, he must believe marriage to Emma would only result in the early deaths of them both. She would shoot him and thus hang for her crime. It was as simple as that. Yet there was nothing simple when it came to Emma. Something must be done. He could not leave matters in this disreputable manner.

He swiped the rain from his eyes. There must be an

alternative. Marriage was completely out of the question. She must go her way. He must go his. And for the sake of sanity, they must not go in the same direction.

At the thought of allowing Emma to walk out of his life, a sharp pain stabbed close to his heart. He halted on the sidewalk, appalled by the thoughts careening through his head. Marriage to Emma. It was the most insane notion that had ever occurred to him. No, he could not and would not offer marriage. Yet something must be done. He had compromised her.

At the moment, he could see no way clear of the mess. The only thing that was clear to him was the odd sense of regret he felt. He realized part of him regretted having left her. If he had taken her, the matter would be settled. He would have no choice but to marry the beautiful Bedlamite.

He had the uncomfortable feeling she would be the death of him. He released his breath in a long sigh. The soft sound caught the attention of a dog who stood in a nearby alley, sniffing at a pile of refuse that had been left against the building. The dog tilted his head and regarded Sebastian in that way canines have of seemingly reading a human's mind.

Sebastian extended his hand palm up and waited for the dog to decide whether he was friend or foe. After a moment the animal came forward, his head lowered, his gaze fixed on the human. He was tall and lanky, with a trace of spaniel visible in his face and long ears. He sniffed Sebastian's hand, then plopped his bottom on the sidewalk and looked up at him, his expression expectant, as if he were asking what this man might require of him. The animal was a mongrel, one of hundreds that roamed the city. Resilient animals, they survived in a hostile world when they were meant to share the companionship of humans.

Sebastian smoothed his hand over the dog's wet head, the scent of dirty wet canine cutting through the rainy air. The animal was soaked, his thick hair plastered to his sides, revealing the sharp definition of his ribs beneath his black and white coat. "You look as though you could do with a good meal."

The dog plopped his paw on Sebastian's thigh. He cocked his head, his ears pricking forward as though he had understood every word.

"Come along with me and we shall see what Cook has for you." Sebastian straightened and shoved the wet hair back from his brow. At the moment, he probably looked as much like a stray as the mongrel.

Sebastian started walking again, without truly noticing or caring about his direction. The dog trotted at his side as though they had been friends for years. Strange thing about dogs, they could usually make you feel better about the world. Usually. This afternoon, nothing could drag Sebastian's thoughts from one infuriating female.

He lifted his wet collar in a futile attempt to quell the chills gripping him. It was raining so hard, the street sweepers had abandoned their stations. Rain streamed down his face. His shirt clung to him beneath the layers of his sodden clothes, chilling him to the bone. The sound of rain striking the ground kept harmony with the patter of rain upon his head.

He reached a corner and paused, waiting for a curricle to rattle past before he stepped into the street. He had gone no more than a few feet when the dog began barking, loud and urgent. He glanced down just as the animal leapt at him, planting his paws in the center of his chest. Caught off guard, Sebastian staggered back, fighting to keep his balance. His feet slipped out from under him. Pain slammed through his shoulder as he hit the pavement. Through the confusion he heard a rumble of horse hooves, a clatter of steel wheels. In the next instant a town coach thundered past, splashing water in all directions.

Sebastian lay stunned against the paving stones, staring after the coach. When he caught his breath, he struggled to his feet. He shifted his arm back and forth, grimacing at the pain. Although it felt as though a smoldering coal were pressed against his shoulder, nothing appeared to be broken. Odd, the driver had not so much as paused to see if he had been hurt. If the dog hadn't knocked him down, the coach would have rammed straight into him. He had come very close to death. As the thought formed another surfaced in his mind. Had the near collision been an accident?

A soft poke against his hand brought his attention to the dog standing beside him. He stroked the creature's head. "I will tell Cook that I believe you would enjoy a nice thick beef steak this evening."

For the first time in a long while Sebastian took note of his surroundings. He should have been near Berkeley Square by now if he had taken the proper path to his house. Obviously he had not. The houses that lined both sides of the street were far too narrow to be those that graced the square. He glanced across the street, staring through the rain at a familiar front door. "I must be insane."

She must be insane. Emma held her hands out to the warmth of the burning coals on the hearth in her drawing room. She had spent the last half hour telling her aunt about everything that had happened last night and this morning. Hearing herself describe the events of the past few hours made it all seem unreal, as though she were relating something she had read in a book. Certainly such things did not happen to ordinary females such as herself. Yet of late her life had been far from ordinary. Insanity was the only explanation for the way she had behaved with that blackguard. "And then he left, without so much as an apology for his arrogant behavior."

"You went to that place, that brothel, alone. What were you thinking?"

Emma cringed at the horror in Marjorie's voice. It was the fourth time Marjorie had asked the same question. "I thought Madame Vachel could help me locate Gaetan's."

"And if she had told you where this horrible place might be, I can only imagine what you would have done. Emma, you really must stop trying to rescue Charlotte. Or I am afraid someone will have to rescue you. Thank goodness Andover was there to make certain you did not get into any more trouble."

"He was more interested in making certain I felt defeated than he was in my well-being." Emma stared down at the glowing red coals, her anger smoldering with the same intensity. She could not decide if she was angrier with herself, for allowing the scoundrel to toy with her, or with him, for the lesson he had taught her. "I was doing fine without his interference."

"I, for one, am quite grateful for his interference. If you were not so determined to manage things yourself, you would also be thankful. Of course, there is the other matter; that is a bit disturbing. He kissed you, rather violently, and then left you there without a word about what had happened between you?"

Emma clenched her teeth, regretting the fact she had discussed that part of the morning at all. Still, Marjorie had been so intent on placing Andover on a white charger and dressing him in shiny armor that Emma had not been able to contain all her anger. With the flow had come a few of the more humiliating details. "He left me as though I were one of Orlina's tarts."

"I cannot imagine why he left without mentioning an offer of marriage. Are you certain, at sometime during the course of events, he did not offer for you?"

Emma's chest tightened. "I am certain."

"I suppose you may have been too distracted to hear him."

"I would have heard something of that nature."

"Odd. Very odd."

Emma glanced over her shoulder at her aunt. Marjorie was sitting upon the sofa, watching her with a distinct look of expectation in her eyes. "Aunt Marjorie, I certainly do not expect an offer of marriage from Lord Andover."

"No?"

"The man was simply trying to teach me a lesson. Lord Arrogance is not content unless everyone does as he sees fit."

"A lesson." Marjorie smoothed her hand over the green velvet cushion beside her. "Whatever the reason for his behavior, when a gentleman such as Andover seduces a lady of good family such as you, an offer of marriage is the only honorable thing for him to do. And from all you have said, and even more from all that you did not say, it is clear he certainly did a very good job of seducing you."

"Aunt Marjorie, I assure you that I am not some silly schoolgirl who can be seduced so easily."

"Then I suppose he did not hold you close against his body." Marjorie rested her hand over her breast. "And I suppose he did not touch you in a most intimate manner."

Emma's skin tingled with the memory of Andover's hands upon her. "It was not seduction. It was . . . it was . . ."

Marjorie clasped her hands in her lap. "Yes, dear, do explain what it was."

"It was an unfortunate lapse in judgment. And I do not have any intention of forcing him into a proposal of marriage because of what happened. I am not some pitiful spinster who must go about setting traps in hope of bagging a husband. And I certainly would not have chosen Andover to bag if I were. He is not what I consider husband material."

Marjorie regarded her a moment, a curious look in her eyes. "You do not consider Lord Andover husband material?"

"Not at all." Emma marched to the chair across from her aunt and plopped down upon the hard velvet-covered cushion. "I would not dream of marrying him."

"Andover is wealthy, young, and from what you have told me, very healthy. If he is not husband material, I am at a loss to think of another unmarried man in London who is. And you obviously find him attractive or you would not have behaved as you did."

Heat crept upward along Emma's neck. "He does not believe in marriage for the sake of love. In fact, he told me he does not even believe he is capable of powerful emotion."

"Not capable of strong emotion?" Marjorie shook her head, a small smile curving her lips. "My dear girl, a man who is not capable of strong emotion does not allow emotion to overcome him. Particularly a man who takes pride in his intellect and his self control. From what I can surmise, Andover's brain had very little to do with what happened between you and him."

"It was all calculated." Emma rubbed her aching temples. "He intended to show me just how dangerous the consequences of my actions might be. He certainly was not carried away by emotion. If he had been, I doubt he would have stopped, since I was foolish enough to have allowed my emotions to get the better of me."

Marjorie stared at her, eyes wide with curiosity. "He did more than kiss you. Did you allow him to make love to you?"

"No." Emma glanced at a small landscape painting hanging near the door. "Aunt Marjorie, what happened between us this morning does not signify in the least. It was a lesson. And I have learned my lesson well. I shall never again allow that man to get the better of me. The next battle will end quite differently."

"A wise young lady would see to it that Andover set things right. You have him on your hook. Reel him in."

"I do not wish to reel him in. I wish I had never met him. He is arrogant and high-handed and insolent and proud and . . . and . . . arrogant."

"You are repeating yourself dreadfully, my girl."

Emma groaned. "I cannot think when it comes to him. He is like a fever that permeates my entire body, destroying reason, drowning intellect, encouraging all of my weaknesses. I cannot explain this power he has over me. But I do know I have found the cure for this particular ailment. I shall never again be fooled by the scoundrel."

"And I have always thought you were such an intelligent girl." Marjorie tilted her head and smiled. "It is really quite obvious what ails you. Love. You are in love with him."

"No." Emma raised her hands as if to ward off a blow. "I am not in love with him. I cannot be in love with him. I do not even like him."

"Really? Strange, for I like him a great deal. I believe you can take all the qualities of a man and roll them together to determine whether he is a rock or a sponge."

Emma stared at her aunt, wondering for a moment if insanity ran in their family. "A rock or a sponge?"

"Yes. The finer, more admirable qualities, such as honor, loyalty, courage are heavier, more dense. You see, a rock will be there when things are difficult. A rock can save you when the water rises all around and nothing else will prevent you from drowning. A woman can stand upon a rock. She can rely upon a rock." Marjorie held her gaze, a wistful look entering her blue eyes. "A woman is fortunate if she finds a man who is a rock. Andover is that kind of man."

"Unfortunately there is a rock where his heart should be."

"A challenge indeed." Marjorie tapped her fingertip against her chin. "If he is as attracted to you as you are to him—and from all you have said it certainly appears as though he is—you just might be able to take that fire and direct it straight at his heart. Even a rock will melt if the fire is hot enough. One need only look at a volcano for proof of that."

Emma was not certain if rocks dissolved in molten lava, although she supposed it was possible. "I suspect lava would have an easier time with rocks than I would with Andover, if I took it into my head to force him into marriage, which I have not and will not."

"I have never known you to back away from a challenge when you wanted something. And my dear girl, your behavior tells me how much you want him."

"Even if I pressed the issue and some misguided sense of honor compelled him to offer for me, it would certainly not be fair of me to accept. I am not the type of woman he wants for his wife."

Marjorie raised her hand. "He did seduce you."

"It was a lesson. Nothing more. If I so much as mentioned marriage, he would laugh. I can hear him now." Emma deepened her voice and tried to sound as pompous as possible when she continued. "Any female who behaves in such a reckless manner certainly must take the consequences of her actions."

Marjorie shook her head. "I cannot imagine he would treat you in such a poor fashion."

"He did not do what he did this morning out of any desire for me. He did it out of a desire to put me in my place. I want nothing to do with that man. If I never see him again it shall be too soon."

Marjorie smoothed her hand over the cushioning at her side. "Emma, I understand you are a bit angry with Lord Andover at the moment, but . . ."

"If I were a man I would call the blackguard out. I would put a bullet between those thick black brows of his. I would run a sword through his heart."

"I believe gentlemen are only allowed one choice of weapon in duels, my dear. Still, if you were a man, we would not be in this situation."

Emma stiffened. "I can take care of us as well as any man."

Marjorie took a moment before she replied. "In most circumstances that is true. But I think we must keep Charlotte in mind. Although you would like to manage her rescue all by yourself, I feel it is best if we allow Andover to help us."

Heat crept into Emma's cheeks when she realized how little thought she had given Charlotte in the past few hours. "You truly believe we can trust him?"

"My dear child, you have been taking care of me and the girls for such a long time with little help from anyone. I know how difficult it is for you to rely upon someone else, particularly a man such as Andover, but I feel we must."

Emma accepted the truth of her aunt's words, even though she wanted to disavow them. She knew in this case she was in deep water. "Yes, as much as I would

like to deny it, I suspect we will need his help. I only
hope we can trust him."

"I feel we really must trust him. He is our best hope
for finding my little girl."

As much as she wanted to deny the truth, it was
staring her straight in the eyes. They needed Andover.
Somehow she must learn to keep her heart from racing, her pulse from surging, her mind from clouding
each time he was near. She could do it, she assured
herself. Now that she truly realized how cold his blood
ran, she could be near him and not want him. Was
there ever an end to the difficult lessons one must
learn in life?

"I suppose we must place some faith in the man.
Still, it does not mean I must like him. And I certainly . . ." Emma hesitated at a soft rap upon the door.
At Majorie's command Hoskin entered and announced
the arrival of Lord Andover. In spite of her best intentions, Emma's heart plunged into a headlong gallop.

"Show him in, Hoskin, and ask Mrs. Barrow to pre-
pare some tea," Marjorie said.

"Madame, I am afraid His Lordship does not wish
to come in."

Marjorie looked as surprised as Emma felt. "He does
not wish to come in?"

Emma tried to swallow, but all the moisture had
evaporated from her mouth. What the devil did Andover want?

Chapter Fifteen

"No, Madame," Hoskin said. "He has a companion with him whom he does not wish to leave outside alone."

"A companion?" Emma asked, her mind racing with the possibilities.

"Well, show this companion in as well," Marjorie said.

Hoskin folded his hands at his waist. "The companion is a dog, madame. And His Lordship thinks it would be best if they both remain outside. He has gone around to the garden and hopes Miss Wakefield will come to the door of the library."

"He is in the garden." Emma rose from her chair. "But it is raining."

"I believe His Lordship is aware of that, miss. He asks only that you come to the door."

"Thank you, Hoskin," Marjorie said.

When Hoskin left the room, Emma turned to face

her aunt. "What do you think he wants?"

"I think you shall soon know." Marjorie rose from the sofa and hurried to one of the windows that overlooked the garden. "I see him. He is walking along the path. And he is not so much as wearing a hat. Very odd. The dog with him is certainly a strange-looking animal. I suppose it must be some foreign breed."

Emma joined her aunt. Rain poured down the glass in quivering sheets, distorting the world outside. A large, black and white dog trotted beside Andover, as though he had been with the man all of his life. "It is probably a stray. His mother told me Andover collects strays."

"Really. How very unexpected of him. Of course I would not have expected him to be running about London without a hat on either. An umbrella would have been a good idea."

"Yes. I cannot imagine Andover going out unprepared." As he drew near the house, she noticed a thick lock of hair lay plastered against his brow. His coat clung to his hips. Even from a distance she could see the way his breeches molded his long legs.

Marjorie released a sigh. "My goodness, he certainly has fine legs."

"Aunt Marjorie!"

Marjorie shrugged. "When a man has a physique such as his, I challange any healthy female not to notice. I would wager the breadth of those shoulders has nothing at all to do with the skill of his tailor. He really is handsomely proportioned."

Emma did not need a reminder of his splendid physique. The memory of his body pressed against hers was seared into her soul. "What do you suppose he wants?"

"You will not know if you remain up here. Now hurry along." Marjorie flapped her hands as if to shoo away a fly. "The weather is dreadful. He must be chilled to the bone. Make certain you invite him to come inside."

Emma crossed her arms at her waist. "He can drown for all I care."

"I have never heard of anyone who has drowned in the rain. Of course there was Mr. Henderson back in Devonshire. He fell into a rain barrel and drowned, but that was after he had spent far too much time in the Red Lion. And I do not believe it was raining at the time."

Andover paused near the terrace and glanced up, catching them at the window, as if he could sense them staring at him. He looked straight into Emma's eyes. The distance did not protect her from the impact. The world contracted around her, dissolving like a chalk picture in the rain, until only Andover existed.

"He is going to catch a lung fever if he stays out in this. You are not too embarrassed to face him after this morning, are you?"

"Of course not." Emma rubbed her arms, feeling chilled just looking at him. "Perhaps I should see what he wants."

"Yes. Invite him in. We cannot allow him to remain in the rain. My goodness, he must be terribly uncomfortable."

Marjorie's words scarcely registered in the mire Andover had made of Emma's mind. What the devil was he doing here? That question kept repeating over and over in her mind as she hurried to the library. The mingled scents of leather and flowers filled her senses as she crossed the room. She forced her steps to slow, hoping to appear completely unconcerned by the presence of the most infuriating man in the world in her garden. Although a narrow roof protected this part of the small terrace, the wind cast a fine mist against her face.

Andover was leaning back against the wall, taking some shelter from the storm. The dog was curled up under a wrought-iron bench that sat nearby. Although the dog lifted his head to get a better look at her, Andover did not move. He did not speak. He simply remained where he was, staring into the garden. Even though water dripped from his clothes and she knew he must be cold, he still managed to radiate power. Sheer masculine power. The kind that pulsed with the same intensity as the storm raging around them.

The sound of rain striking the brick-lined path filled the silence stretching between them until she could take it no longer. "There are those who would claim a man who walks about London in the rain without a hat or an umbrella is a mutton-headed dolt."

One corner of his lips tightened. It was all that betrayed his annoyance. "I had a coach when I left home. In it was an umbrella. I seem to have misplaced both along with my wits."

Emma stiffened. "Have you come here to teach me another lesson, my lord?"

He closed his eyes and muttered something under his breath. When he looked at her she could see his struggle for control. "I have been standing here thinking that I might have been better off if you had shot me that first night we met. At least I would have died with my intellect intact."

The damp breeze sent a chill whispering across her skin. She noticed the way he hunched up his shoulders. In spite of her best effort, she could not suppress the insidious need to tend to this man. She wanted to usher him inside and to wrap him in a warm blanket. "My aunt has told me I should invite you in. She is afraid you will catch a lung fever. I suppose I should obey her wishes. Your friend looks as though he would like to sit by the fire."

Andover glanced down at the dog. The animal had curled himself into the tightest ball an animal his size could manage. Sheltered by the roof and the bench, he had found the snuggest spot in the garden. "You do not mind if he comes inside?"

She molded her lips into a smile. "I would rather have him by the fire than you."

He grimaced. "A well-directed blow, Miss Wakefield."

She inclined her head. "Do come in. I have no intention of catching a chill simply because you choose to stand there like a dolt."

"What I have to say will not take long, Miss Wakefield. There is no reason for me to drip all over your carpet. I will simply say what needs to be said and then be on my way."

A chill gripped her that had nothing to do with the storm. He intended to wash his hands of her. More importantly he intended to wash his hands of Charlotte. She tried to convince herself it did not matter, that she could find her cousin without his help. Yet not until this moment had she truly realized how much she had come to rely upon him. "What is it you have to say?"

He pushed back the wet hair from his brow. "I doubt you will disagree when I say that you and I are as opposite as fire and water. And everyone knows what happens when you mix the two."

"You produce steam?"

He shot her a narrow look. "Perhaps it was a poor analogy."

She hugged her arms to her waist, trying to ward off the chill, in the damp air. "Since I do not know what point you are trying to make, I cannot say for certain."

"What I mean to say is that you and I do not suit. I am a quiet man. I prefer my life to go on in a predictable manner. I expect my house to be orderly." He looked at her as though she had just confessed she was one of Napoleon's agents. "You, Miss Wakefield, are a true menace to order and predictability. You are like Midas. Only instead of gold, everything you touch turns to chaos."

A gust of wind whipped rain across her face. She blinked the water from her eyes and fixed Lord Arrogance in a glare. "You came all this way in the rain to insult me?"

He hunched his shoulders against the cold. "I do not mean to insult you. I am simply stating facts. You have the most infuriating way of blotting out the light of logic."

"And you have the most infuriating way of placing logic above all else."

He gestured widely with his hand. "There, you see. This is precisely what I have been saying. You and I do not suit. Our marriage is doomed before we even speak the vows."

She stared at him, her brain grappling with the words he had just spoken. "Speak the vows? What are you saying?"

"I am saying, in light of the unfortunate incident this morning, an incident I deeply regret, there is no honorable alternative but for you and me to be married."

Although he kept his voice low, the words struck her with the force of a clenched fist. The world wobbled. Her vision darkened. She gripped the door handle for support. Unfortunate incident? Did he truly regard what had happened between them as merely an unfortunate incident? When the wave of dizziness

197

passed, she focused her attention on his face. He was staring at her, as though she were the gatekeeper to hell and he had just been summoned to stand before Lucifer. It was obvious that marriage to her was the last thing on earth he wanted. "It would seem Aunt Marjorie was right about you."

His black brows drew together. "And what does that mean?"

"She told me you would feel obliged to make an offer of marriage based on what happened between us. I told her she was mistaken."

A muscle flickered in his cheek with the clenching of his jaw. "I am certainly glad she, at least, had some faith in my honor."

Emma squeezed the door handle, the cold brass slick beneath her damp palm. It occurred to her that this was a man who truly did live by a code of honor. Seducing innocent women of quality hardly fit that code. Although she wanted to think him a blackguard, a scoundrel, a horrible libertine, she could not employ those epithets while looking into his troubled eyes. How did he manage to look so incredibly handsome while soaking wet? In spite of everything, she caught herself wishing she could throw her arms around him and hold him close. He wanted to marry her. Her heart pounded so furiously she could scarcely draw a breath. The man she wanted most in the entire world wanted to marry her. For all the wrong reasons.

Sebastian told himself it didn't matter what she said. He recognized all the reasons he should celebrate if she refused to do the sensible thing. Yet he could not crush the anxiety coiling in his stomach. And his heart was hammering against his ribs with all the fury of a racing stallion.

Emma glanced down at the brick-lined terrace. "I realize you are . . ."

At that moment, Marjorie brushed past Emma, cutting off her words. "Lord Andover, what a surprise to see you," she said, hurrying toward him.

Sebastian felt an odd urge to howl with frustration. Instead he inclined his head in a polite bow. "Mrs. Usherwood."

Marjorie took his arm. "You really must come inside and have some tea. You must be chilled to the bone. And nothing feels better than a hot cup of tea on a day like this."

Sebastian hesitated when Marjorie started to usher him into the house. "Thank you, but I am afraid I would drip all over the carpet."

"The carpet will dry." Marjorie patted his arm. "I hope you do not mind, but I have sent a boy to your house to fetch your coach and a fresh change of clothes. I really would feel horrible if I were to allow you to continue in this dreadful weather."

"I have a friend with me." Sebastian gestured toward the dog. "I would not wish to impose upon you."

"There is no imposition where you are concerned." Marjorie looked at the dog and snapped her fingers in a way that betrayed her familiarity with canines. The dog hopped to his feet, recognizing a command he must not disobey. "Come along. There is no need for either of you to remain out on this dreadful day."

If he had not been so wet and cold and sore, Sebastian might have found the finesse required to elude Marjorie's offer of hospitality. Yet he had unfinished business with Miss Wakefield, and his breeches were beginning to chafe. Besides, no gentleman could rightfully refuse such a dear lady. The matter settled, he allowed Marjorie to usher him into the house.

"I am certain you will feel much more comfortable when you get out of those wet clothes." Marjorie led him across the library and into the hall. "I am afraid there is no one of your size in the house. Our butler is a small man, and the footman but a slender lad. Still, I think if you bundle up in a warm quilt you will feel much better. And it will serve until your clothes arrive."

Marjorie maintained a steady flow of conversation as she ushered him upstairs. She spoke about the weather in London, the quality of the air, and how much she preferred the country. Since she did not pause for a response, Sebastian saw no reason to interrupt her. Her soft voice had a certain calming quality about it. Since Emma had his vitals tied into tight knots, he found Marjorie a delightful distraction.

"You can stay here while you wait for your coach to arrive," she said, leading the way into a small bedchamber. "The coals were lit a short time ago, but it should soon be nice and warm. You will find a stack of towels and a thick quilt on the bed. Tea will be ready soon."

Sebastian glanced around the little room. Tiny pink flowers coiled upward along ivory-colored walls. The same pattern covered the two lyre-back chairs that sat near the fireplace. Four delicately carved posts lifted a lacy white canopy above the bed. It was a room obviously meant to please feminine eyes. He suspected it had been a long time since a man had held any influence in this house.

Marjorie turned toward the door, then turned back to face him. "I do not care to think what might have happened if you had not taken care of Emma last night."

Sebastian looked for some trace of sarcasm in Marjorie, but found none. "Your niece assures me she is quite capable of taking care of herself. I am afraid she is not at all happy with what she sees as my interference."

"I realize Emma may appear a bit managing. Perhaps even a bit reckless in her devotion to my daughter." Marjorie folded her hands at her waist. "But there is reason for her actions. She does not place a great deal of trust in men."

"She certainly places no trust in me."

"Emma lost her parents when she was very young. Her grandfather is Earl Halisham. Soon after her parents died, I took Emma to see him. I thought seeing his granddaughter might be comforting. And by all rights, she was his ward, although he had never before met her. I do not believe he had ever even seen her before that day."

Sebastian knew Earl Halisham. They both belonged to White's. "Halisham had never seen his granddaughter?"

"No. He all but disowned Neil when he married my sister. You see, the earl did not approve of the match. It was not that my sister did not come from a good family. Our father was the Earl of Carrick." Marjorie glanced down at the needlepoint carpet. "But Sophia was a bit headstrong. She ran away from home to . . . well, first let me say that she had a beautiful voice. She loved to sing. She went to London and for a while she sang in the opera. For a very short time. That is where Neil saw her and fell in love with her. He married her even though his father disapproved of the match."

"He must have been a man of strong conviction."

"Neil was a wonderful man. They were very happy together. Unfortunately, his father never accepted my sister. It was three weeks after the accident that I took Emma to meet her grandfather. You can imagine how tender she was from the blow of losing her parents.

We were shown into a very pleasant drawing room. I remember Halisham walked into the room and looked at this beautiful little girl as though she were some foul-smelling animal. He said . . ." Marjorie paused, as if she were composing herself. "He said, 'You look like your mother. She was a whore. The worst thing that could have happened to my son. I will have nothing to do with her demon seed.' And he said it with such venom. I remember hugging Emma against me, trying to protect her."

Sebastian clenched his teeth. "Any man who abuses the innocent cannot regard himself as a gentleman."

"Many little girls would have been frightened. They might have cried. Emma looked him straight in the eye and said, 'My mama was a fine lady. I think perhaps you were the worst thing that ever happened to my papa.' I remember thinking she was braver than I was."

"She is far too brave for her own good, I am afraid."

"Since my husband died, we have had to rely upon our own resources to survive. I am afraid she has seen little to give her faith in men. I tell you this only so that you may understand why she is so intent on finding Charlotte without depending upon anyone."

"I understand. She is fiercely independent. Yet if she continues in this reckless manner I am afraid she will be hurt. We are dealing with dangerous men."

"I shall do what I can to contain her." She rested her hand on his wet sleeve. "I know you will do your best to keep her safe."

"She does not feel an obligation to listen to reason."

"I know." Marjorie released her breath in a slow sigh. "Now I shall allow you some privacy. I have kept you standing in those wet clothes long enough."

Sebastian remained where he was a long moment after Majorie left. Thoughts spun around and around in his brain. What could he do to keep the headstrong little termagant safe? Marriage would not change her, even if she did accept his offer. Would she accept his offer? He rubbed the stiff muscles at the nape of his neck. Any reasonable woman would. From the time he came of age, he had been the target of every matchmaking mama in town. Women had used every trick in their arsenal to get him to the altar. And here he was waiting for the response of the most infuriating, irritating, maddening female he had ever met.

Which would be worse? Life with the termagant or life without her? When he thought of his future resting in her slender hands, he wanted to scream. Still, he had posed the question. It was her place to decide the issue. He had no intention of leaving this house without an answer.

Chapter Sixteen

Emma paused in the hall outside the bedchamber where Andover was staying. Only a coward ran from battle. No matter how much she would like to avoid the man, she could not. A moment after she knocked on the door, Andover's voice rumbled through the wood. She drew in her breath, then opened the door. He was sitting on a chair near the hearth, wrapped in a quilt, staring down at the dog that lay across his feet. The animal lifted his head when she entered. Andover did not even glance in her direction.

She started across the room, slowly pushing the cart over the thin carpet. "I have brought you some tea."

Andover looked at her then, straight into her eyes. Her heart plunged into a headlong gallop. She squeezed the handle of the tea cart to steady herself. It simply was not fair. Why must this man of all men be the one who could set her pulse racing with a glance?

Emma paused near him, determined to keep her emotions under close rein. He thought she was incapable of reasonable thought. She intended to show him she could be every bit as logical as he could. "Aunt Marjorie thought you might be hungry. There is plum cake, lemon tarts, scones, and strawberry jam. And a few sausages for your friend."

"Thank you." He took a sausage and handed it to the dog. The mongrel eased the meat out of Andover's hand, then proceeded to chomp the sausage in several quick bites, as though someone might take it from him before he had a chance to chew it well. Andover spoke softly to the dog while he handed him another sausage. "No need to worry, my friend, you will never have to fight for your supper again."

There was such gentleness in his voice and his manner, Emma caught herself wishing he might speak to her in that same reassuring tone. She watched while Andover fed the dog sausage after sausage. Never had she met a man more infuriating than this one. He made her feel safe and protected, vulnerable and threatened all at once. She wanted to curl up on his lap, feel his strong arms around her, shutting out the world. At the same time she wanted to take his broad shoulders and shake him until he felt what she felt, this same restlessness, this same horrible need.

Here he was, wrapped in a quilt, sitting on a delicate little chair as if nothing was amiss. She wished she had not noticed the pile of clothes sitting on the bricks of the hearth next to his boots. She tried not to think of the fact he was bare beneath that quilt. Yet she could not crush the images rising in her mind. He should by all rights look ridiculous. The quilt wrapped around his large shoulders had little pink rosebuds embroidered all over the white cotton background. Yet the feminine surroundings merely served to accentuate his stark masculinity, the sheer male power of the man. The quilt shaped a vee beneath his neck, revealing a dark wedge of black hair.

She had never in her life glimpsed a naked man. This morning she had allowed Andover to remove her clothes to touch her and kiss her, and she had not even so much as seen his bare chest. It wasn't fair. And it certainly was not wise to regret not having touched him in the ways he had touched her. Yet she could not crush that longing. A pulse fluttered to life in her nether region.

Think of something else! This path led straight to disaster. She directed her attention to the dog. "Does he have a name?"

"I think Ulysses might suit him. I suspect he has had many adventures. And I know he has a brave heart."

She tried her best to steady her hands while she poured tea into a cup. The conversation was going well, she assured herself. Nice and civil with no hint of the way he had her vitals twisted into tight knots. "Are you going to send him to Hampshire, to live with your other dogs?"

He looked up at her, his expression revealing his surprise. "What do you know of my dogs?"

"Your mother told me you collect strays." She handed him the cup, careful not to touch him. Odd things happened when she touched this man. Her mind stopped functioning. That would not happen this afternoon. She intended to proceed in an orderly fashion. Her emotions would not get the better of her this time. She would be every bit as cool as Lord Arrogance. "I thought it was an odd practice for a man who likes his life to be nice and neat and orderly."

He patted the dog's head. The animal looked up at him with adoration in his brown eyes. "Perhaps I am just trying to keep the streets of London nice and neat and orderly."

And perhaps he was simply a very generous-hearted man. She did not wish to think of him in that light. It was far wiser to think of him as an arrogant, overbearing, high-handed aristocrat. The more she knew of him, the more difficult it was to face the truth: He was nearly everything she had ever wanted in a man. All he lacked was a deep, abiding love for her. She could not settle for less than true, honest affection. A marriage could not succeed without it. Could it? No, of course it could not. She could not even think of marrying him. Yet since he had made his startling offer, she had caught herself weakening. The quicker she ended the temptation, the better.

"Lord Andover, I realize . . ."

"Miss Wakefield, I believe . . ."

They spoke as one, their words overlapping. Emma paused, expecting him to continue. He did the same. After a moment of silence, they tried once more, their words bumping into each other again. Finally, Andover lifted his hand in invitation for her to speak.

Emma drew air into her lungs, slowly, trying to regain her composure and with it some measure of dignity. "Earlier, when you offered to make things right, I realize you were acting out of a misguided sense of honor."

"Misguided sense of honor?"

"Yes. Misguided because the incident was certainly not entirely your fault." Emma squeezed her hands into tight balls at her sides, her nails biting into her palms. "I do not believe it would be wise to plunge both of us into what could only prove a disaster because of a fleeting error in judgment. On my part as well as yours."

"Disaster." He sipped his tea, then stared into the

cup for a long moment before he continued. "You cannot mean to take part of the blame for what happened? You were under my protection, Miss Wakefield. I should not have kissed you. I am entirely responsible for what happened."

"No, you are not." The truth was something she often disliked but never avoided. The fact was, she had wanted him from the moment he had stepped into that bedchamber at Orlina's this morning. No, the honest truth was that she had wanted him from the first moment she had looked into those blacker-than-midnight eyes. This morning, she had felt so frustrated by being near yet not near enough, that she had whacked him and ranted at him until she knew he must lose his composure, all with the hope he might take her into his arms and kiss her as he had that first night. Even now she recognized the need nibbling at her vitals, an insidious need to throw her arms around him and kiss him until he melted beneath her touch. She moved to the chair across from him and rested her hands on top of the smooth wooden back.

"I believe in taking responsibility for my actions. I am not a child. I should not have allowed you to kiss me. It is clear that we were both carried away by intense emotions. It was the place. The argument. The situation got the better of both of us."

He shook his head. "It is hardly an excuse for my actions."

It was not pleasant to realize the kiss and what had followed was merely the result of lust. Yet she was not a woman to turn away from the truth. He was a man. When presented with a woman who had all but demanded he kiss her, he certainly would not refuse. It was not in a male's nature to ignore an obvious invitation. She stared at the little pink rosebuds marching in neat rows along the seat of the chair. "Intense emotions can often precipitate even more intense emotions, my lord. I suspect that is what happened to us. I was very angry with you. You felt the same toward me. We were both swept away by that strong emotion and the situation became muddled. One is forever reading of such behavior in books. People being carried away by intense feelings. Perhaps it is true that passion and fury are closely related. It would seem so."

"You believe passion and fury are closely related?"

"One often reads of such things in novels. There is excellent example in *The Wayward Countess*. Lady Katherine could not help succumbing to the passion she felt for her husband's brother. He made her furious most of the time, but that fury was actually a facade for something far more dangerous."

"*The Wayward Countess?*" He released his breath in a long slow stream. "I should have known you would enjoy the circulating libraries."

She cast him a glance and found him studying her with a certain wariness in his eyes, as though he was not quite certain what to expect from her next. "There are a great many good books to be found in a circulating library."

"Books that fill a woman's head with stories of other women cavorting with their husband's brothers? It is the type of rubbish written by the likes of a jackanapes such as E. W. Austen."

Irritation poked her, threatening to free the anger she had carefully locked away in a tight little space inside her. Silently she reminded herself it was anger that got her into this tangle in the first place. "And have you ever read a book by E. W. Austen?"

"I have read enough to know the man, or woman, enjoys exploiting the lives of others for the sake of money. Hardly an admirable trait."

Heat prickled her neck. "Kidnapping women and

locking them in brothels is not precisely what I would call an admirable trait either."

His lips pulled into a tight line. "I scarcely think printing lies about someone for self gain can be compared to trying to keep a hen-witted female out of trouble."

She stiffened at the insult. "You had no right to lock me in that place."

"You understand and forgive me for trying to seduce you, in a brothel of all places. But you cannot comprehend why I might try to prevent you from running into trouble?"

She gripped the back of the chair, to remain anchored there. She would not approach the blackguard. If she did, she could not be responsible for what she might do. "You locked me in that room to prove your power over me, Andover. You wanted me to see just how vulnerable I could be. You wanted to teach me a lesson. That was high-handed and arrogant and mean spirited."

"Mean spirited!" He rose, took a step toward her, then halted as though he'd hit an invisible barrier. "What do you call kidnapping an innocent man and tossing him into a cellar?"

She lifted her chin. "It was the best approach to the situation."

"It was foolish and reckless and it could very well have resulted in getting both you and your aunt murdered. Just as running about London last night, searching brothels for a monster could have resulted in getting you murdered or worse."

Emma resisted the urge to stamp her foot. "I could not sit back and do nothing."

He raised his eyes to the heavens as though looking for divine intervention. "At some time in my life I must have done something very bad. I cannot think of what it was, but I know it must have been quite un-forgivable in the eyes of the Almighty for Him to have sent you into my life."

She flinched. "You may walk out of my life at any time, Lord Andover. I did not ask for your interference."

"No, Miss Wakefield, you have not asked me for anything." He stood and paced to the windows, then turned and marched toward her. He froze a few feet from her. "I nearly seduce you and do you have the common sense to demand I make reparation? No, you do not."

"Was I supposed to demand you offer marriage?"

"Any sensible woman would expect a decent offer of marriage. Did you?"

"I am not so . . ."

"No, you did not," he continued, rolling over her attempt to defend herself. "You, a young inexperienced female, start talking about responsibility. Your responsibility! When the responsibility is mine. Not yours."

"I am hardly young, Lord Andover. I am six and twenty. And I . . ."

"I do not give a farthing for your age. The fact remains, you are inexperienced. I knew that, or at least I suspected it was true. It was my responsi—"

"What do you mean you suspected I was inexperienced? Did you imagine for one moment I made a habit of consorting with men in such a wanton manner?"

"Not precisely. I have been curious about how you and your aunt managed to finance a Season for your cousin. It occurred to me that you might have . . ." He hesitated, and in the silence his eyes betrayed precisely what he had thought of her. "It really does not matter what I thought might be possible."

It took all her will to remain where she was. She wanted to lunge at him, to knock him to the floor for the insult. "What did you think? That I sold myself to some man? Bartered my services in bed for a few pieces of gold? Did you truly imagine I was some man's ladybird?"

He rubbed the skin between his brows with one hand, while he held the quilt in place with the other. "It is obvious you have never bedded a man before today."

Her cheeks burned. "And why is it so obvious? Was I so lacking? Did I fumble so terribly?"

He drew his lips into a tight line. His shoulders lifted beneath the quilt with the tightening of his muscles. She could see him clamping down hard on his composure. Composure was what they both needed. She knew it. Yet she could not crush the urge to shatter his composure into a thousand tiny pieces. "Miss Wakefield, most ladies would be insulted should a gentlemen suggest they acted in the same fashion as a woman of experience. Yet you are insulted because I recognized your innocence. Most ladies would have the good sense to place the blame precisely where it belongs. On my shoulders. If you had a modicum of sense, you would demand I marry you."

"I refuse to play the role of a simpering miss simply because you expect every female to have her heart set on marrying you." She squeezed the back of the chair, fighting the urge to close the distance between them. It was hard enough to be clear-headed at a distance. When she got close to this man, her brain stopped functioning completely. "I assure you, I am not so desperate to marry that I must go about trapping men into offering for me. And I certainly did not set a trap for you."

One corner of his mouth twitched. "I never said you

set a trap for me. Still, under the circumstances I see no other . . ."

Her chest felt so constricted, she could scarcely draw a breath. "It is best if we both forget what happened this morning."

He stared at her, his lips parted. "That is your solution? You choose to ignore what happened and refuse my offer of marriage?"

Marriage to this man. The freedom to touch him, to kiss him, to feel his arms around her. To share his life. To bear his children. Marriage to Andover. The thought teased her. How easy to say yes, to abandon herself to the dark promises she saw in his eyes. Yet lust did not have the same qualities as affection. It was not constant. It could not warm one's heart. She could not possibly be in love with this man. It was far too foolish. She knew if she ever truly gave her heart to him, she could expect nothing except a great deal of pain. "What happened between us was a mistake. We were both to blame, and that is the end of it. As you said, we do not suit in the least. Marriage to each other would only result in making both our lives miserable."

He stared at her as though she had just declared her intention of taking a walk to the moon. He glanced to the hearth, then back at her. After a long moment he finally said, "I suspect you are quite right, Miss Wakefield. Obviously what happened this morning was an aberration. I can only say I must have lost my wits along with my temper."

Her chest felt as though someone had just dropped a boulder on top of her. "Apparently madness was quite contagious in that room."

He held her gaze, his expression betraying nothing. "If you are willing to forgive me for my part in this debacle, I shall certainly not trouble you with my misguided sense of honor again. Shall we consider the matter closed?"

She tried to think of something clever to reply, something that a character in one of E. W. Austen's novels might say. Yet her brain was not fully functioning. She molded her lips into a smile. "Yes. I think we should."

"Fine." He drew in a deep breath. "So it appears we have avoided disaster."

Disaster? Did he actually consider marriage to her a disaster? Regret stabbed far too close to her heart as she stood there looking at him. Yet she could not afford regrets where this man was concerned. There would be far too many of them for her to survive under their weight. "Do you still intend to help us find Charlotte?"

He pulled his lips into a tight line. "I gave your aunt my word. I will do anything in my power to help bring Miss Usherwood home safely."

"Will you let me know when you find Gaetan's? I want to accompany you when you go there."

He looked at her, his eyes narrowed. "Do you still not trust me, Miss Wakefield?"

Trust was not something she gave easily. But in spite of all the reasons she should not trust him, she could not deny that he had somehow managed to make her believe in his honesty. Andover was arrogant and high-handed, perfectly infuriating. He was also brave and loyal, the type of man who felt comfortable with the weight of the world upon his broad shoulders. Perhaps if she had not had such strong feelings for him, she might have been able to accept marriage on his terms. "If Charlotte is in that horrible place, I want to be with you when you find her."

The look softened in his eyes. "I understand. If you give me your word to remain out of harm's way, I will make certain you have an opportunity to be there when I search Gaetan's."

Emma considered his words, crushing the urge to defend herself and her ability. As much as she wanted to deny the truth, she knew deep within that without this man's help, she had little chance of finding Charlotte.

"Do you think you can manage to do as I ask and stay out of trouble?"

If she did not cooperate with him, she might not have the chance to be there when they found Charlotte. "I think I can."

He smiled, warm and generous, a smile that might have added a beat to her heart. If her heart were not already racing. "When I find Gaetan's, I shall make certain you are there to comfort your cousin. Providing we find her there."

"Do you think there is a possibility she will not be there?"

"I think it is possible."

Emma's throat tightened. "If Radbyrne did not take her there, what would he do with her?"

Andover took a step toward her, then hesitated. She had the impression he had intended to touch her, to comfort her. Yet instead he kept his distance. "Please, do not torture yourself with possibilities, Miss Wakefield. It will only cause you more pain. Instead, have faith that we shall bring her home safely. No matter what it takes, I will find her."

"I believe you, Lord Andover."

Before he could respond, Emma turned and left the room. She could not remain another moment longer. Confessing her trust in him made her feel far too vulnerable. That must be the reason her eyes burned with unshed tears. It had to be the reason she felt like running to her room and hiding under her covers. It could not be the fact that she felt as though refusing his offer of marriage was the biggest mistake of her life. Still, her chest felt as though she had just been kicked by a wild horse.

Sebastian felt as though he had been hit by a swift blow to the chest. He stood in the bedchamber in Emma's home and watched her walk from the room. It had been a simple statement, just five short words. Yet she had managed to steal the breath from his lungs with them. Perhaps because he realized how difficult it had been for her to speak those words. Emma was not a woman who gave her trust lightly. In spite of all their disagreements, their differences, their quarrels, she had decided to trust him. It did not make sense. After his behavior this morning, she should not trust him within a mile of her. Yet that was Emma. She seldom made sense. At least not in the usual fashion. She did nothing in the usual fashion. Most women would leap at the chance to become a wealthy marchioness. Not Emma. Oh no, not Emma.

He flinched at the soft click of the door closing behind her. After a moment of staring at the door, he walked back to the little chair near the fireplace and sank onto the hard cushion. Ulysses looked up at him, as if to ask what was wrong. Sebastian slid his hand over the dog's head. "I should be relieved. Any reasonable man would be relieved to have escaped certain disaster. And marriage to Emma Wakefield would definitely be a disaster. We would no doubt have half a dozen arguments before breakfast every morning."

Still, the thought of breakfast with Emma every morning did something odd to his insides. It made him feel warm in a place that had always seemed cold. He shook his head. "She showed a great deal of sense

216

today. It is far better if we both forget the unfortunate incident this morning."

Yet memories kept haunting him. The texture of her skin, her scent, her . . . Good Lord, his blood stirred just at the thought of her. He shifted the quilt across his lap. What was it about the woman? Why did she linger in his thoughts as no one had before her? He had the uncomfortable feeling he would be thinking of her long after she had walked out of his life. Yet what could he do? He certainly had no intention of sniffing after her skirts like a besotted puppy. He had made his offer. She had refused him. The matter was ended. "I shall never again make a fool of myself over that little termagant."

Chapter Seventeen

"Their specialty is debauchery. Gambling, opium, and, of course, women." Jourdan stood near the fireplace in Sebastian's library. "They make it very clear there are no restrictions. For the right amount of money, a man can do anything he wants with one of the women."

Sebastian sat on the edge of his chair, eager to meet the monster face to face, and at the same time reluctant to discover Charlotte Usherwood's fate. He stroked his hand over Ulysses's head; the large dog was sitting beside him with his muzzle propped upon Sebastian's knee. "Orlina had said as much."

"It certainly did not take Fennigold long to take you to the place." Montgomery tapped his fingers against the leather-clad arm of his chair. "When no one at White's knew of the place, I had the impression this Gaetan's was a secret."

"It is a private club." Jourdan stared down into the

logs burning on the hearth. "The man who attended the front door was reluctant at first to allow me entrance. Fennigold convinced him I would cause no problem."

"Did you see Gaetan?" Sebastian asked.

"Yes. He was sitting in a large gilt-trimmed chair at one end of the main saloon. He has the looks of a man who wallows in his pleasures. One would think him fat and lazy if not for his eyes. There is the look of a predator in his eyes. He had a woman sitting on a stool beside his chair. She was naked, except for a gold collar around her neck. He was petting her, stroking her shoulder as though she were a dog."

Could a woman's spirit survive in a place such as that? If they found Charlotte, what would remain of her? Sebastian thought of Emma. She was right. It would be best if she were with them when they found her cousin.

"The woman I was given for the evening, her name was Susan. She was lovely, petite and blond," Jourdan said. "Her eyes would have been beautiful if they had not been so haunted. The look in her eyes reminded me of the look I saw in my mother's eyes for a long time after we left home. I remember Mama would awaken at night, screaming with visions of the guillotine. I can only imagine what demons haunted this girl's dreams."

Sebastian's hand stilled upon Ulysses's head. The dog cocked his ears, as though he sensed the growing tension within his master. "Did you find any trace of Charlotte Usherwood?"

"No." Jourdan sipped his coffee. "They keep most of the women locked in bedchambers. You describe what you want and they escort you to a chamber, unlock the door and leave you alone."

Sebastian smoothed his thumb over the rim of his

coffee cup. "Did the girl know Miss Usherwood?"

"It took a while to convince her I was there only to talk. She had been there just a week. And in that time she had not been allowed to leave the chamber." Jourdan kicked the stones on the raised hearth with the tip of his boot. "She had been innocent when they brought her to Gaetan's. The first night she was there, they took her to a room and forced her to stand on a raised platform. The room was filled with men sitting as though they were waiting for a concert. Only it was not a concert, it was an auction. A man slowly removed her clothes. When she was naked, the bidding began. She told me they bid upon her as though she were a mare at Tattersall's. The highest bidder took her upstairs and raped her."

Sebastian closed his eyes and whispered an oath. What part had his nephew played in that tragedy? "How was Susan brought there? Was she kidnapped?"

"No. She answered an advertisement in *The Gazette* for a lady's companion. She is the eldest of four sisters and three brothers. Her father is a vicar in Kent. She thought to help the family by supporting herself."

Montgomery rolled his coffee cup between his palms. "You said Ariel mentioned something about an advertisement, too."

"Yes." Sebastian sipped his coffee, but the warm liquid did nothing to melt the ice in the pit of his stomach. "Apparently that is how Gaetan manages to acquire some of the girls."

"We must get her out of there, cousin." Jourdan looked at Sebastian, his dark eyes betraying his anger. "And the others like her."

Sebastian placed his cup on the table near his chair and stood. "I think it is time we pay Gaetan a visit."

"This morning?" Montgomery asked.

"This morning we should not have many club members to bother us," Sebastian said.

"Just the men Gaetan has guarding the place." Montgomery set his coffee cup on the round table beside his chair. He looked at Jourdan. "How many guards do you think there are?"

Jourdan shrugged. "I would say six, perhaps seven."

"And here I thought we might need help." Montgomery rose from his chair. "Shall we go?"

Nothing about the place set it apart from the other buildings along this part of St. James's Street. Emma sat in Andover's coach, in front of Gaetan's. She had passed this building countless times. She never would have suspected the large stone building housed a living hell for the women trapped within its walls. Was Charlotte there?

It took all her will to remain seated in the coach. She wanted to run from it, throw open that dark green door, and tear the place apart looking for her cousin. A soft metallic click brought her attention to the man sitting beside her. Andover turned a pistol over in his hand, examining the weapon as though he wanted to make certain it was in order. Strange, she had not truly thought of their errand as being dangerous until this moment. Until now, she had only thought of Charlotte. Now she realized there existed another threat, to Andover. "Do you think you will need that?"

"I hope I do not need to use it." Andover slipped the pistol into the pocket of his charcoal gray coat. "But I suspect it may be necessary to convince Gaetan's minions to mind their manners."

Although she knew he must go, she had the sudden urge to throw her arms around him and hold him. In spite of her best efforts to purge the man from her thoughts, he remained, like the haunting refrain of a piano concerto one has heard and cannot forget. It had been three days since she had last seen him. Yet it seemed years had past. This morning when he had called for her, there had been a distance that had not existed before. He was polite, overly so. If he had ever harbored any feelings for her, they had died and were now carefully buried along with the thought of marriage to her.

She only wished she could bury the feelings she had for him. She only wished she could sit here beside him and not be so painfully aware of him.

Andover looked at the two men sitting across from him. "Ready?"

His friends both nodded. The excitement she sensed in them was so powerful, it could not be missed. They actually looked as though they were enjoying themselves. She supposed only men could understand the true enjoyment of a battle that could lead to bloodshed. Andover leaned across her and opened the door, his arm brushing her sleeve. The slight contact constricted her chest. The coach swayed as Jourdan and Montgomery left the vehicle. When Andover rose to leave, she touched his arm. He glanced at her, a question in his dark eyes.

She snatched her hand away from him, afraid she had already betrayed far too much. "Do you have a plan?"

"Yes. I intend to walk inside and take the girls out. I also intend to make certain Gaetan knows his little business is closed."

"And you think you can do that without getting yourself or anyone else injured?"

A look of surprise flitted across his features, followed by a slight smile. "Do not concern yourself, Miss Wakefield. If your cousin is in this place, I shall bring her out safely."

Emma drew the strings of her reticule through her gloved fingers. Through the soft cloth of the bag, her pistol rested with a comforting weight upon her thigh. "I would feel better if I were going in with you."

His eyes narrowed. "You gave me your word, Miss Wakefield. Do you have any plans to break your vow?"

She held his gaze, her anger rising to meet the emotion she saw there. "I do not see why I cannot accompany you. I assure you, I know how to use a pistol."

"Perhaps you do, Miss Wakefield. But there is no need for you to risk your life."

"I do not see any reason why I should sit here like some frightened mouse while you and your friends rush in to rescue my cousin."

"It is dangerous. We do not need to be concerned about watching over you while we are trying to find your cousin."

She squeezed her pistol through the cloth of her reticule. "I am not a child, Andover. You and your friends need not look after me as though I were in the nursery. I assure you, I can take care of myself."

He released his breath in a hiss between his clenched teeth. "Try to trust my ability. I realize this is difficult to believe, but I can manage without your hen-witted attempts to behave like a man."

"And I can manage without your arrogance."

Anger flashed in his eyes. Still, his voice was low and calm when he said, "Take heart. With any luck, we shall find your cousin and our connection will soon end."

His words struck her with the sting of an open hand across her cheek. She stared at him, trying to think of a suitable reply. Yet he was already climbing from the coach. She flinched at the sharp slam of the door. He was eager to be rid of her. Well that was fine with her.

"Arrogant, contemptible beast." She watched him cross the sidewalk and stroll through the wrought-iron gate, trying her best to maintain her anger. Yet other emotions kept getting in her way. Fear, hope, and anxiety all rippled beneath a sadness she could not shake. He was right. When they found Charlotte, their connection would end. He would return to his orderly life, and she would return to her less-than-orderly existence. He would soon forget all about her. She would forget about him, perhaps not as quickly. In time she would read of his marriage to a perfectly orderly woman and she would smile, thinking of how she had managed to avoid the trap of marrying the arrogant beast. And that night when she thought of another woman lying in his bed, she would cry until she finally fell into oblivion.

"I have to forget him," she whispered. There was no other alternative.

She watched the men climb the three wide stone steps leading to the large front door. Andover rang the bell. The other two men stood a little behind him. The door opened. Sunlight poured through the entrance, illuminating a very large man. Although the footman was not much taller than Andover, he looked at least four stone heavier. Even from a distance she could see he did not look happy. Of course she wondered if anyone with features such as his could indeed look pleasant. He looked as though he had once made his living with his fists, and had often dropped his right. It would not surprise her if he suddenly lashed out and knocked Andover to the ground.

Emma squeezed her pistol. She realized she had given him her word, but in spite of his assurance to the contrary, she knew she could help him. She could use a pistol as well as any man. After Andover spoke a few moments with the man, the giant shook his

head. He started to close the door. In the next instant
Andover surged forward, pushing the door open with
such force, the giant stumbled back. Before the man
with the crooked nose could react, Andover drove his
right fist into his jaw. He followed with a sharp left to
the footman's belly. The large man staggered back out
of sight. Andover and his friends surged into the
house and closed the door behind them.

It had been a primitive display. Blatant male power.
Emma squeezed her hands into tight fists on her lap,
her heart pounding as though she had been the one
doing battle. "My goodness, Andover certainly knows
how to use his fists."

It should not have excited her. Yet she could not
help comparing Andover to the hero of *The Adventurous Earl*. How in the world could she hope to forget
him, when he was the most intriguing man she had
ever met? And how in the world would she manage
to keep her word? Charlotte could be in there. Andover was definitely in danger. And she was supposed
to sit and wait like a meek little kitten? Isabel in *The
Valiant Viscount* certainly would not have remained in
the coach. She gripped the door handle. Still, she had
promised not to put herself in harm's way. What
would one of E. W. Austen's heroines do in this situation?

Sebastian gripped the lapels of the footman's claret-
colored coat and hauled him to his feet. The big man
glared at him, sheer murder in his eyes. "My friends
would like the keys to the chambers where the girls
are kept. Be a nice fellow and hand them over."

The big man wiped the back of his hand over the
blood seeping from a cut on his lower lip. He reached
into his pocket.

"In case that is a pistol you are about to withdraw—"

Sebastian pulled his own pistol from his pocket and aimed at the man's massive chest—"might I suggest you put it on the floor and shove it over to me."

The footman hesitated a moment, then eased the pistol from his pocket and did as Sebastian demanded, the heavy weapon scraping against the polished oak flooring. Keeping his pistol aimed at the footman, Sebastian kicked the confiscated weapon over to Jourdan. "As I said before, my friends would like the keys to the chambers where the girls are kept."

The big man licked his lips. "I don't have 'em. Billy, upstairs. He has 'em."

"We'd better take care of the guards before we try to take the girls out of here," Jourdan said. "One of them might get hurt if we do not."

"Good idea." Sebastian smiled at the footman, a smile he knew was cold enough to chill the other man's blood. "What is your name?"

The footman swallowed hard. "Mortie."

"You will show us where your friends are staying, Mortie. And remember, you can always find another line of work, if you live to see tomorrow. Do you understand?"

"Aye sir, I do. And I won't be making any more trouble, sir. I won't. I swear. I never did take much to this place. But a man's got to make a living, he does."

Sebastian gestured with the pistol. "Lead the way, Mortie."

"Most everyone is still abed. There's Billy and Denton in the hall upstairs. And Curtis and Davie with the boss."

Mortie was true to his word. He did not try to interfere while Sebastian and his friends gathered the other guards. When they were all safely locked in the cellar, Mortie led them into a dining room at the side of the house. There Gaetan sat at a table, surrounded by an enormous array of dishes. Two guards stood on opposite sides of him, like the hounds of hell guarding Lucifer himself. Jourdan and Montgomery took the guards away, while Sebastian remained with Gaetan.

Gaetan leaned back in his chair, wood groaning beneath his weight. "Lord Andover, to what do I owe the honor of your visit?"

Sebastian sat on the edge of the table and rested his pistol across his thigh, keeping the barrel pointed at Gaetan. "I was not aware that we had met."

Gaetan laughed, the loose skin beneath his chin quivering with the sound. "I make it a point to keep abreast of all the great personages of London. You, sir, are not a man who goes unnoticed. Particularly when there is such a delicious book about you out this Season. I wonder, have you read *The Wicked Duke*?"

A breeze swept through the open windows, carrying the scent of flowers from the gardens. "I am not surprised you enjoy such rubbish."

"Rubbish?" Gaetan pressed a white linen napkin to his lips. Sunlight flowing through the windows across from him caught the rings that adorned his pudgy fingers. Diamonds, rubies, emeralds glittered, sending shards of color in all directions. It was a wonder he could lift his hand under the weight of the gems. "Apparently you have been depriving yourself of the talents of E. W. Austen. Let me assure you, the books are quite entertaining. I have often wondered if E. W. is a peer. He writes with such insight when he describes the wickedness of the English aristocrat."

"You would be an expert on the subject of wickedness."

Gaetan shrugged, his thick shoulders lifting the red and white silk of his dressing gown. "We merely provide a service here at Gaetan's. I would think a man

227

who found a convenient way to dispose of his fiancée might appreciate our services."

Sebastian smiled as though he were not seething with anger inside. He had a great deal to learn from this man. Anger would only get in his way. "I have never found slavery very appealing."

Gaetan sipped from a large tankard of ale, all the while keeping his small dark eyes fixed on Sebastian. In those eyes Sebastian saw the cunning of a man adept at survival, a man capable of any trick to save his skin. "I have committed no crime."

"A magistrate might see kidnapping as a crime."

Gaetan blotted his lips with his napkin. "I would be careful about involving a magistrate. Unless of course you do not mind plunging your family into another scandal."

Sebastian allowed the moment to stretch between them, unwilling to appear too eager for information he already suspected. "What is it you think you know, Gaetan?"

"Although I find it amusing to allow people to call me by that name, I am not Gaetan." The large man smiled, wrinkles crinkling at the corners of his small eyes. "I am merely a manager here. Sidney Woolgrove at your service, my lord. And I must confess, I have absolutely no part in acquiring the merchandise. I simply make certain things here run smoothly."

Sebastian's heart pounded with a horrible certainty. Suspecting his nephew's involvement and proving it were two different things. "You may not have anything to do with acquiring the girls, but you do know who does."

He laughed, the sound dark and oily. "As well as you do. Your nephew and his partner. This is their establishment. I was only hired to run the place. They actually advertise for girls. Oh, not for their true purpose, mind you. But for girls seeking a position as governess or companion to a lady. The advertisement attracts only the most genteel of girls. When the little doves venture in for an interview, they are captured in a net and brought here."

Sebastian smoothed his thumb over the rosewood handle of his pistol. "Who is Radbyrne's partner?"

A glint entered Woolgrove's eyes, a look of sheer amusement. "Now that will surprise you. Gaetan is not a true name, but an identity the head of this endeavor uses to separate real life from business. My employer is very guarded, and for excellent reasons. I only found out by accident his true identity. I doubt you would ever suspect the person behind the name. And you are close enough to guess. You might say Gaetan is slumbering directly under your nose."

The implication trickled down his spine, like a stream of ice water. "Who is he?"

Woolgrove leaned back in his chair. "Lord Andover, I begin to suspect all the infamous rumors about you have been exaggerated. You are actually quite heroic. I am afraid it will prove your undoing."

Sebastian squeezed the handle of his pistol. "Who is my nephew's partner?"

"I am delighted to say that your nephew is working with . . ."

The crack of gunfire ripped through the room. A look of surprise crossed Woolgrove's features. He glanced down at his chest. Blood spread from a ragged hole in his dressing gown.

Sebastian glanced toward the door and found Montgomery standing on the threshold, smoke curling from the muzzle of the pistol he held. The scent of seared gunpowder spilled through the room.

"I had no choice," Montgomery said.

Sebastian did not take the time to question his

friend. Instead, he surged forward as Woolgrove slumped against the table. He grabbed the man's shoulders, his fingers sinking into soft flesh. He pushed Woolgrove back against the chair. The man's head lolled to one side, a trickle of blood sliding from one corner of his mouth.

Montgomery crossed the distance and paused beside Sebastian. "Is he dead?"

Sebastian pressed his fingertips against the pulse point in Woolgrove's neck. Beneath the soft pillow of his neck, the blood lay still in his veins. "I am afraid he is."

"It was fortunate I came in when I did."

Sebastian glanced at his friend. "He was just about to name Radbyrne's partner."

"That is not all he intended to do." Montgomery pulled Woolgrove's right arm out from beneath the table. Sunlight spilled across the polished barrel of a small pistol, still gripped tightly in the dead man's hand. "He was just about to shoot you."

Sebastian glanced down at the dead man. Bile rose in a burning stream upward along the back of his throat when he acknowledged that he might be the one lying with a hole in his chest if not for his friend's marksmanship. "Yes. It was fortunate you happened by." He looked at Montgomery. "I never realized how much I would appreciate your skill with a pistol."

Montgomery shrugged as if killing a would-be murderer was an everyday event. Still, Sebastian noticed the way his friend's hands trembled as he slipped the pistol back into his coat pocket. "If I had taken an extra moment, I might have been able to disarm him without killing him. But I am afraid I reacted rather quickly."

"You did what was best." Sebastian forced air into his tight lungs. "Miss Usherwood, did you find her?"

"Jourdan is freeing the women now. We found another guard in one of the bedchambers. I took him to the cellar. That is why I was down here. I cannot say if Jourdan has found her yet."

"Are we certain the place is secure?"

"Yes." Montgomery swiped his hand over the moisture beading on his upper lip. "After we found this last guard, Jourdan and I made one final tour of the place to make certain it was safe."

Sebastian thought of Emma and her concern for her cousin. Although he was reluctant to bring her inside, it was time. "I'd better . . ."

At that moment Emma dashed through the door. She halted a few feet into the room. She glanced from Sebastian to Woolgrove. There her gaze froze, her eyes growing wide with shock. "He looks as though he . . ." She swallowed hard. "Is he dead?"

Anger speared him, followed by a sharp stab of protectiveness. Sebastian marched across the room, then stood before her, blocking her view of the grisly scene. "What the devil are you doing here?"

"I heard a shot. I thought you might have been hurt." Emma touched his sleeve. Although he could scarcely feel her touch, it was enough to tighten the muscles in his chest. "You are all right?"

The confession caught him off guard. As much as he wanted to maintain his anger, he felt it deserting him, chased away by the concern shimmering in her eyes. "I am fine."

"That man." Emma looked past him. "Is he Gaetan?"

"Not exactly." He took her arm and ushered her toward the door. "You shouldn't be here."

"What do you mean by not exactly?" Emma halted when they reached the door.

"I will explain it later. At the moment . . ."

231

"Have you found Charlotte?"

"Not yet. Jourdan is looking for her now."

She resisted when he tried to escort her into the hall. "I am not going back to that coach. I intend to be here when we find her."

Until now he had not realized how much he admired her courage, her loyalty, and that streak of determination that made her eyes glitter. She stood in front of him, ready to do her best to knock him down should he try to keep him from her protecting her cousin. In spite of his desire to protect her, he realized the strength in this woman. He wished he had not. For the more he knew of her, the more difficult it became to keep his distance from her. "I gave you my word, Miss Wakefield. There is no need to shoot daggers at me. If your cousin is here, she will be in one of the bedchambers above us."

She released her breath on a quick exhalation. "Thank you."

Without waiting for him, she hurried into the hall. He hesitated a moment, then followed her. Independent. Impulsive. Infuriating. She was the antithesis of what he thought he wanted in a woman. He was a man devoid of strong emotion. Yet for some inconceivable reason his emotions always got the better of him when it came to her. Emma was going to rescue her cousin, without a care for her own welfare.

She froze near the end of the hall, her gaze riveted on the scene unfolding before her. Jourdan was descending, holding the arm of a small blond woman. Behind them, in a narrow procession, walked the other women two by two, arm in arm, as if lending support to one another. Each woman was dressed in a white cotton nightgown that covered her from chin to toes. The innocence of the costumes belied the haunted looks on their faces. Sebastian's chest hurt when he thought of what they might have endured.

Jourdan paused at the base of the stairs. The women halted behind him. Emma walked toward the stairs, moving slowly, as if she were not certain of the solidity of her legs. Sebastian followed her, wanting to protect her, knowing he could not. He could not shield her from the truth. When she reached the base of the stairs, Emma hesitated, her gaze roaming from one woman to the next.

Emma turned toward him, her eyes wide. "Charlotte? Where is she?"

Sebastian looked to Jourdan. "Is this everyone?"

Jourdan nodded. "I am afraid we did not find Miss Usherwood."

"I felt so certain." Emma turned back to the women. "Do any of you know her? Charlotte Usherwood. She is a tall girl, blond hair, blue eyes. Very pretty. Have you seen her? Do you know what happened to her?"

Several of the women shrank back at the sharp tone of Emma's voice, as if they were afraid a blow would follow. Several others stood where they were, staring at her, as though they had not understood a word she had uttered. One woman stepped forward. Although she was not above average in stature, there was a dignity about her that made her seem taller. Light brown curls framed her heart-shaped face. She was a woman a man would notice in a crowd. "No one named Charlotte has been here since I arrived three weeks ago."

Sebastian recognized her voice. This slender young woman with the large green eyes was Ariel. The memory of what he had overheard made him want to strangle his nephew.

Emma rubbed her arms, as if she were cold. "Where could she be? I thought we would find her here."

Sebastian slipped his arm around her shoulders. Although he feared she might pull away from him, she did not. Neither did she lean upon him. He could feel her trembling. He could sense the fragility of her composure.

She looked up at him, tears glittering in her eyes. "Where could she be?"

Only now, when she was so close to breaking, did he realize how hard she had fought always to appear strong. A single tear escaped her self-control. It spilled down her cheek and caught in a glittering droplet at the corner of her lips. In that moment it took all his will to keep from sweeping her up into his arms. "We will find her. I promise you."

She wiped her tear away with her fingertips. "I do not understand. I was certain Radbyrne had brought her here. If not here, then what has he done with her?"

"I intend to find out where she is."

She gripped her reticule. "Radbyrne knows where she is."

He squeezed her arm. "I will handle Radbyrne."

Emma pulled free of his grasp and glared at him. "You should have handled him days ago."

Her words struck with the same violence as the anger in her eyes. Although he had followed a logical course of action, Sebastian could not avoid the accusations he saw in her eyes; he could not ignore the doubts swelling within him. He had been so certain they would find Charlotte here. Perhaps he had been too cautious in dealing with his nephew. He had been afraid Charlotte might very well end up floating in the Thames if he pressed Radbyrne. Now, it seemed his careful plans had failed. "Believe me, Miss Wakefield, I intend to make my nephew regret the day he was born. Nothing will keep me from finding your cousin."

Chapter Eighteen

"In a strange way I am thankful she was not in that place." Marjorie sat on a sofa beside Emma in their drawing room. She stared down at her lace-trimmed handkerchief while she continued. "From what you said of the women you found there, the way they looked and acted, I fear Charlotte could not have survived."

Emma thought of all she had seen that day. She had never realized the true extent of cruelty until she had looked into the eyes of Ariel and the other women they had found in Gaetan's. Nine in all. "They looked so haunted. Frightened. When I reached out to touch Ariel, she shrank back, as if I was going to strike her. And she was one of the strong ones."

"You say Andover took them all to his home."

"Yes. He told each girl not to worry. He would make certain they always had a place to stay."

"He cannot mean to keep them all at his home. Not forever."

"When I asked what he planned to do with them, he told me it depended on what each girl wanted to do. They will remain at his country home until they decide." Emma squeezed her hands together on her lap. "After he left to deal with his nephew, his mother told me he intends to establish a trust for each woman. He told her that although he could not make amends for all the suffering his nephew had caused, he would make certain they have no more financial worries in the future."

"He is a very generous man."

"Yes, he is." Emma squeezed her hands so tightly her fingers ached. Still, she could not prevent the tears from stinging her eyes. "And kind. So very gentle. You should have seen him with those poor women. He knew precisely what to say and do. Before I left his house to come home, Ariel told me that for the first time since she was captured, she had hope again. And it was all because of Andover. He truly is a remarkable man."

"You have been through a great ordeal these past few days. You should lie down and rest. Put your mind at ease for a while. We are very fortunate to have Andover helping us. We should think of him and have faith he will bring Charlotte home to us."

Emma's cheeks grew warm with memory. "I am afraid I became very agitated when we did not find Charlotte at Gaetan's. I was very cross with Andover."

Marjorie patted her shoulder. "You have a tendency to be a bit emotional, my dear. And the situation itself was emotional."

Emma closed her eyes, trying to shut out the image of Andover's face and the pain she had inflicted with her careless words. Tears spilled from beneath her lashes to trickle hotly down her cheeks. "I am not proud of my behavior."

"When next you see him, I am certain you will apologize. And I am equally certain he will understand and accept your apology."

"I hope he will." Emma swiped the tears from her cheeks. "But I would not blame him if he thought me an ungrateful wretch."

"I cannot imagine he would do such a thing. He will make Radbyrne tell him the truth. He will find Charlotte. I have to place my faith in him." Marjorie's voice cracked with emotion.

Emma slipped her arm around her aunt's slender shoulders, ashamed at her own pitiful display of tears. This was not a time to indulge in self-pity. Not when Aunt Marjorie needed her. Marjorie leaned against her, as though all the strength had left her. "If anyone can find Charlotte, Andover can. He is a very capable man."

"He will find her. I know he will." After a long moment, Marjorie pulled back and blew her nose. "Still, I am surprised that you have finally decided to put your trust in him. What changed your mind?"

"He has this way about him. I keep thinking he would have been right at home in the days of knights and tournaments. I can see him atop a large black steed, wearing armor, of course, riding into battle against a vexing dragon." Emma stared at the coals smoldering on the hearth. "And I suspect the dragon would not stand a chance against him."

"You regret it, do you not?"

Emma glanced at her aunt and found Marjorie regarding her with a wistful smile upon her lips. "Regret what?"

"You know perfectly well what I mean." Marjorie clasped Emma's hand and squeezed gently. "You regret that you refused his offer of marriage."

The regrets were there, lingering like tiny trolls, each with a sharp stick and a nasty habit of jabbing her in the vitals each time she was near Andover. "I have regrets, yes. I regret that I am not the type of woman he truly wants as a wife. I regret that I would dearly love to change, but know I cannot. I regret that I cannot make him happy. If I could, I would be anything he wanted me to be. But I know my nature would reveal itself in time. I regret all these things and more, but I do not regret refusing his generous, misguided offer of marriage. I would never want to make him unhappy. Never."

"My poor girl." Marjorie cupped Emma's cheek in her warm palm, spilling the scent of lavender around her. "You love him."

Emma closed her eyes, shutting out the pity she saw in her aunt's gaze. "I keep hoping this horrible feeling will go away. Perhaps it is like the measles. It makes you feel terrible and you want to die, but then it goes away and you are stronger because you survived."

"And what if you are wrong, dear? What if you are precisely what he needs and wants?"

Hope fluttered with Marjorie's words. A terrible thing, hope. It made one think all things were possible. Emma rose and walked to the fireplace, feeling suddenly chilled. The sun had ducked behind thick clouds that afternoon, stealing the warmth from the day. She held her hands out to the heat rising from the small pile of coals on the hearth. "We cannot be together for more than ten minutes without arguing about something. And he dislikes arguments. He admires dignity. He worships at the altar of logic and practicality. He expects his life to be orderly and neat with no surprises. Do you really imagine I could possibly make that man happy?"

"He has a look in his eyes when you are near. It is the smoldering look a man has when he is interested in a woman. He is attracted to you."

Emma laughed, the sound pitifully sad to her own ears. "Lust. It is hardly a good basis for marriage."

"Marriages have been based on far less and succeeded. And where there is lust, there is the possibility something much deeper will grow."

Was there a chance for something deeper to grow? Could lust be altered, transfigured, the way an alchemist might hope to transform lead into gold? Once again she felt the stirring of hope within her. Each time it rose, it became harder and harder to crush. Emma drew in her breath, the scent of burning coal stinging her nostrils. "It does not matter now. I have refused him."

"Yes. Still, I wonder if you might not find a way to force the issue again. You never know when lust will get the better of a man."

Emma spun around to face her aunt. "You are not implying that I allow him to seduce me?"

"No. Of course not. It certainly would not be proper for me to suggest such a thing." Marjorie fiddled with the lace at the edge of her handkerchief. "I simply mean to say that a man does not always know what he wants until a woman shows him. You may be precisely what he needs and wants. He just has to realize it."

Emma shook her head, trying to deny her aunt as well as the hope blossoming within her. "When we find Charlotte, our connection ends. More than likely I shall never see him again."

"When we find Charlotte." Marjorie bowed her head and closed her eyes. "I hope he is able to convince his nephew to do the proper thing. I hope he brings back my girl."

"Andover will make Radbyrne tell the truth. You will see." Emma stared into the coals, their edges gray and spent, their hearts still glowing red with warmth. A few days ago she had not needed Andover in her life. She had been happy without him. She could be happy again. In time this horrible feeling of loss would pass, she assured herself. In time she would forget she ever knew him. She had to forget. There was no other way.

"I knew this would happen." Gaetan paced the length of Radbyrne's drawing room. "The moment you told me about the Usherwood chit, I knew it would lead to trouble. Andover is not a man to have as an enemy."

Bernard rubbed his palms together. "Woolgrove is dead?"

"Shot." Gaetan laughed, the sound harsh and bitter. "Andover has taken all the girls to his home. From what I understand, he intends to set up a trust for each of them. To help make amends for what his nephew has done."

"Bloody hell." Bernard rose from his chair, his legs shaking so badly he feared Gaetan might notice. "I will kill the bastard."

"No. You will not."

"But he . . ."

"You will leave town. Perhaps you must leave the country. I think you should give some thought to emigrating."

Bernard glanced toward the door, his heart pounding with a horrible fear. "What will we do about the business?"

"It is ended. I have been thinking of ending it for months. The profit is no longer worth the anxiety. Or the guilt." Gaetan stared down at the floor. "Today was the first time I had ever seen those girls. Until today they were merely names upon paper. I should never have continued the horrible place. But the debts were crushing me. And the profits from Gaetan's were so incredible. With that I justified the means. Fortunately, I am no longer in debt and I shall never again sell my soul to the devil."

"But I am. I need that money."

Gaetan looked him straight in the eyes. "You made a great deal of money in this ugly business, Bernard. You were in this business for two years before I took over the reins. If you have nothing left, it is because you are a fool. And if you stay here another few moments, you shall prove just how great a fool you are. Andover is no doubt on his way here as we speak. Do you want to face him?"

"This is not ended." Although Bernard wanted to stay and argue, he could not. He hurried from the room. There were things to do. He had no intention of being here when Andover came knocking upon his door. He also had no intention of allowing his arrogant uncle to walk away after what he had done. He did not need a partner. Once he got rid of his uncle, he would go into business for himself.

Sebastian poked at the coals smoldering on the hearth in Emma's drawing room. Sparks scattered beneath the pointed tip of the poker, gray ashes puffing out around the smoldering lumps of coal. A pungent scent scratched his nostrils and scrawled a bitter taste upon his tongue. He was a man who faced the truth eye to eye, no matter how unpleasant it might be. At the moment he had to face a particularly ugly demon. He had made a muddle of things.

His nephew had disappeared. Woolgrove was dead. And he had lost his best chance of finding Charlotte Usherwood. Sebastian would have understood if Mrs.

Usherwood had thrown him out of her house. Instead she had thanked him for his help before excusing herself for the evening. At the moment he suspected she was upstairs crying on Emma's shoulder. He could only imagine the choice words Emma would have for him when she returned. She had made it clear this afternoon what she had thought of his futile attempts to find her cousin. He did not blame her. He had failed her. He had failed her aunt. He had failed that poor lost girl.

The door opened and closed softly behind him. He did not need to look to know Emma had returned. The air changed when she was near, grew warmer upon his skin. He heard the soft swish of her gown and petticoat and knew she was moving toward him. She stepped into his line of vision, a slender figure dressed in soft blue muslin. It was time to face her disdain. He clenched his teeth and turned to face her. What he saw stole the breath from his lungs. He had expected one of her fiery stares, the kind that reduced his composure to ashes. He had anticipated her barbed comments. He had prepared himself to be struck by a flying vase. Still, she managed to surprise him.

"I thought you might like some hot chocolate." Emma offered him one of the white porcelain mugs she was holding. "It always makes me feel nice and warm on a night like this."

He hesitated a moment, half expecting her to toss the contents of the mug in his face. Yet she made no violent move. She simply stood there, holding the mugs, looking as unsure of herself as a girl at her first London ball. When he looked down at the mugs, he noticed the chocolate rippling beneath the soft trembling of her hand. Odd, he had never imagined Emma would feel unsure of herself at any occasion. Somehow her trembling made him feel less vulnerable.

He took the mug from her hand, his fingers touching the side of her hand. Although it was no more than a grazing of skin against skin, he felt a spark at the contact that darted along his nerves. Her eyes grew wide. The startled look in those gorgeous blue eyes told him she had felt it too—a spark that should not exist but did. A sweet scent swirled with the rising steam as he sipped the chocolate and sought the right words to say. "How is your aunt?"

"Better than you might expect. She is a strong lady. Although we have suffered a setback, Aunt Marjorie prefers to believe we shall find Charlotte."

Sebastian's chest ached. He wanted to think Emma believed in him, but knew better than to hope. "I assure you, Miss Wakefield, I will do whatever needs to be done to find her. I have already taken steps to cut off my nephew's funds. I have set several hounds upon his trail. I will find him. And I will find Miss Usherwood."

Emma moistened her lips and glanced down into her own mug. "Lord Andover, I wish to apologize to you for my behavior this afternoon. It was most unhandsome of me to imply you had not done your best to find Charlotte."

Once again she managed to tip him onto his head. Most women he knew could live a lifetime and not surprise him. Emma made it a daily practice. "There is no need to apologize. I did what I thought should be done, and I failed. You have every right to be angry with me."

"No, I do not." She looked up at him, a wealth of emotion in her eyes. "You have been more than generous with your time and your patience."

Generous? Did she have a fever?

"You have made every effort to find my cousin. And I have mistrusted your every attempt to help us. I convicted you without ever speaking to you. I threatened to shoot you. I threw you into a cellar. And still you have done your best to keep me from harm. You have, in fact, been a knight errant. And I do not know what we would have done without your help."

Knight errant? Perhaps he was the one with a fever. His legs suddenly felt shaky.

"I should have respected your abilities; I did not. When you deserved trust, all I gave you was an argument."

She looked so sincere, so uncomfortable, so earnest in her self rubuke. It was all he could do to keep from smiling. "Am I to believe you are now willing to trust me?"

"You risked your life this morning. You deserved praise, my lord, not the sharp words of a . . . a . . ."

"Termagant?"

She flinched as though he had slapped her. "A termagant?"

"A virago?"

Her brows lifted. "Virago?"

"You seemed to be at a loss for the proper word. I was only trying to help."

She gripped her mug with both hands. He stiffened and prepared to duck. A grim look flickered across her features followed by the barest hint of a smile. "You are roasting me, are you not?"

"If I say yes, will you toss that cup of chocolate at me?"

She glanced down at the chocolate, then up at him. "You must truly think I am contemptible."

He looked into her eyes and saw how unhappy she was. Her unhappiness spurred a surprising need within him. He wanted to chase away the sadness from those beautiful eyes. He wanted to take her into his arms and protect her from all of the ugliness in the world. The fierceness of his emotion startled him. "I think you are incredibly brave, fiercely loyal, and brutally honest. Those are not qualities I would ever call contemptible."

She glanced away from him, her gaze plunging into her mug. "I would prefer if you were not kind to me, Lord Andover."

"And do you imagine I am saying these things simply to make you feel better?"

"I know you are trying to make me feel better." When she looked up at him he found the tears in her eyes had hardened into glittering steel. "But I assure you, I do not need to be treated as though I were a wounded child."

He had never thought of this woman as a child. That was part of his dilemma. "I am not saying these things simply to make you feel better, Miss Wakefield."

She regarded him a moment, a glimmer of wariness in her eyes. "I thought you considered me a contemptible hen wit."

"I have thought you headstrong. Reckless. Impetuous. But certainly never contemptible."

She pursed her lips. "I am not reckless."

He gripped the reins of his rising agitation. Yet he could not keep from pointing out the obvious. "Chasing about London, searching for dangerous men is not exactly cautious behavior."

The unhappiness in her eyes faded, consumed by the anger rising in the blue depths. "The situation called for action, my lord, not caution. I should think you would understand my approach by now."

"And I should think you would see the folly of your behavior by now."

"I realize the danger. Still, given the circumstances, I believe I behaved appropriately."

"Appropriately." When he thought of how many

times she might have been murdered, he wanted to scream. "What is it about you, Miss Wakefield, that spurs me into an argument each time I am with you? I realize you may not believe this, but I am usually a calm man. I am not quick to anger. I seldom argue with anyone. Except you."

She tilted her head, her lips forming a pout. Not the kind most women used to flirt and tempt. But the kind that reflected frustration. "Perhaps you never argue with anyone because they are always too quick to agree with you."

"You certainly do not have that propensity, Miss Wakefield. If anything, you are too quick to oppose me."

"I did not intend to argue with you, Lord Andover. I intended to apologize. Yet I find there is something about you that stimulates my sensibilities. I find I cannot control my emotions around you. I want to strike you one moment and the very next I find myself wanting to . . ." She hesitated, an expression of pure horror crossing her features.

The unspoken words hovered between them, teasing him with the possibilities. He suddenly found it difficult to breathe. "What is it you find yourself wanting to do, Miss Wakefield?"

"Nothing. It does not signify."

It should not matter what she thought of him. She had settled things between them the day she had refused his offer of marriage. Yet it did matter to him. "When you are not contemplating hitting me over the head with the nearest blunt object, what are you thinking of doing with me?"

She moistened her lips. "At the moment I am thinking of how very pleasurable it would be to toss you into the cellar and throw away the key."

"I see." He placed his cup on a small pedestal table

near the hearth. Then he took her cup and placed it beside his. In the first place, a cup of warm chocolate was much too tempting a weapon in her hands. In the second, there was something he needed to know, and he did not want the cups in his way. "You once said passion and fury were closely related. I wonder how true that is."

She stepped back when he moved toward her. "I am not sure I like the way you are looking at me."

"No? And how am I looking at you?" He advanced toward her. She retreated.

"I imagine the same way a cat looks at a mouse he is about to pounce upon."

He laughed; he could not prevent it. She had read him perfectly. It occurred to him then that this was one of the things he liked about her, the blunt honesty with which she always confronted him. Too often his position interfered with honesty.

He moved toward her, slowly, the way he might stalk a deer he wanted to pet in his park. Although he did occasionally hunt for birds, he had never been able to take the life of a creature as beautiful as a deer. Any deer on his property was assured a long and peaceful life. He could not say the same for Emma Wakefield. Life would never be calm and peaceful with her. Still, a question kept haunting him. A few days ago he had abandoned the thought of any future with this woman. Now he wondered if what burned between them might not be worth a fight to possess.

"You are hardly a mouse, Miss Wakefield. A tigress is more like it. Any man who gets too close will certainly end up bloody and ragged from your claws."

"Strange." She stepped back and bumped into a large armchair near the fireplace. "You do not look the least bit frightened."

"It would seem we have at least one thing in common." He planted his hands on the hard back of the chair, on either side of her, his palms sliding upon soft green velvet. "At times we are both a bit reckless."

"Reckless?" She pressed her hands against his chest, as if to push him away from her. Instead her fingers curled into the soft cambric of his shirt. "Is that what this is, my lord? Reckless behavior?"

"What else could this be?" He lifted his hand, knowing he would be lost if he touched her. Still, all the sane reasons why he should not make love to Emma were slowly turning to ash beneath the heat of the desire she kindled within him. He smoothed his fingertips over her cheek, absorbing the warmth of her skin. "Becoming entangled with you is certainly not cautious or even sane, for that matter. You are unpredictable and undisciplined, impetuous and infuriating. The first night I met you, I had a feeling you would demolish my world. The name Pandora suits you."

Emma lifted her chin. "And you are arrogant and high-handed and insolent and proud and . . ."

"Do you know you get a crinkle between your brows when you are angry?" He touched the skin between her brows, smoothing away the crinkle. "It is not quite a frown, just a little crease."

She drew her hands into tight fists against his chest. "I do not appreciate being mocked, my lord."

"And I do not appreciate having my life tipped wrong side up. Yet you have been making a practice of it since the day I met you." He leaned against her, trapping her between his body and the chair. The scent of roses after rain swirled through his senses, coaxing him to press his lips against her neck and breathe her fragrance deep into his lungs.

She leaned back against the chair, trying to avoid contact with his body. "And you have been trying to dictate to me since the day we met."

"What is it about you? Why do I want to strangle you one moment and make love to you the next?"

Her eyes grew wide. He saw something intriguing in those blue eyes, something that eased the uncertainty in his chest. Something that could only be described as hope. "Passion and fury. They are closely related."

"Passion and fury." He brushed his lips over the curve of her jaw. She sucked in her breath. "Each a powerful emotion. Yet one is destructive and the other is not."

"Both can be destructive," she murmured. "Passion can lead to disaster. And when you touch me, I cannot think clearly. Please, keep that in mind, my lord. One of us must keep a clear head."

He understood her meaning. She would not stop him if he continued. If he were not careful, bridges would be burned. There would be no choice for either of them should he lay her back upon the sofa and plunge into the silken heat of her body. His blood surged with the images rising in his mind, of long slender legs wrapped around his waist, of her beautiful face filled with the wonder of passion's first ecstasy. "A clear head. How can you expect me to think when the scent of your skin is swirling through my brain, destroying my every attempt at rational thought? When memories of holding you keep taunting me? When all I can do is imagine what it will be like to make love to you?"

She closed her eyes, but not before he saw the answers to all of his questions burning like flame in her gaze. "You must not say such things, my lord."

"I want you."

A gentle tremor rippled through her. "Lust."

It must be lust. Yet it did not resemble the ailment he'd known in the past. Lust had always seemed a fairly tame emotion, one he could control should he wish to. This feeling defied his every attempt to crush it. "I never realized lust could sink its claws into me with such vengeance. I have never in my life wanted a woman the way I want you."

She flexed her fingers against his chest. When she looked at him, the pure need in her eyes whispered to his own longing.

"Well now. What have we here, uncle? Have I arrived just in time to spoil a little sport?"

A bolt of horror shot through Sebastian at the sound of his nephew's voice. He turned and found Radbyrne standing near the door leading to the hall.

"It would appear you are about to add Miss Wakefield to your long list of conquests." Radbyrne made a clicking sound with his tongue. "And here I thought you were helping her for purely altruistic purposes. Now I see you had something else in mind."

Emma straightened so quickly, she bumped his chin with her brow. Yet Sebastian scarcely noticed. His attention was riveted upon his nephew. Light from the wall sconces reflected reddish gold against the barrel of the small pistol Radbyrne held. Sebastian turned to place his body between the barrel and Emma. "Do you need a pistol to face me, nephew?"

Bernard laughed softly as he walked toward them. He paused a few feet away from Sebastian, the pistol aimed directly at his chest. "I need a pistol to make certain you do not cause any more trouble, uncle."

"I am curious, nephew, what made you decide to involve me in this drama?" Sebastian kept his gaze fixed on Radbyrne's face, while he calculated the space between them. He had to find a way to get past that pistol. "You must have known leaving one of my buttons behind in Miss Usherwood's chamber would plunge me into the thick of things."

"That tantalizing book by E. W. Austen had just become a rage, and I thought it would be amusing if I added to your celebrity."

The blasted book again. If he ever met E. W. Austen, he would dearly love to plant his fist in the blackguard's jaw. "Then it seems I have E. W. Austen to thank for this adventure."

"You left the button because of *The Wicked Duke*?" Emma asked, her voice betraying her astonishment.

"It was an error on my part." A muscle flickered in Radbyrne's cheek with the clenching of his jaw. "I had not calculated on your taking matters into your own hands, Miss Wakefield. I underestimated just how much of a hen wit you were."

"Why you . . ."

Sebastian grabbed Emma's arm when she stepped toward his nephew. "I am surprised you decided to return to town. I assume you heard that we closed Gaetan's today."

Radbyrne's delicate nostrils flared. "You had no right to barge into my place. You had no right to ruin everything."

"As usual, nephew, you have managed to twist circumstance to suit you." One shot. That was all his nephew would have. If he could draw Radbyrne's fire, he would keep Emma from getting hurt. "I believe most people would say you do not have the right to—"

"What have you done with my cousin?" Emma demanded.

Bernard's eyes narrowed. "What a great deal of trouble you have caused, Miss Wakefield. If not for your interference, my little club would still be open and I would not be in this uncomfortable situation."

"Your little club?" Emma glared at Radbyrne.

Sebastian recognized the look in her eyes. It usually

251

preceded a storm. In this case, she could get herself killed. He gripped her arm and tried to coax her back behind him.

Emma remained as she was, frozen in defiance. "You kidnap women and force them into the most unspeakable kind of slavery and you call it a little club."

Bernard tapped the pad of his thumb upon the handle of his pistol, his features revealing his annoyance. "The women at my club had no place in life. They were looking for positions as governesses or companions. Instead of brats or old women, I allowed them to serve a much more interesting purpose."

It took all his will to remain where he was when what he really wanted was to strangle his nephew. Sebastian knew that he needed to keep his head. If he did not approach this carefully, Emma might get hurt. "They might have preferred a choice."

Bernard shrugged. "I decided the matter for them. Most women need a man to make their choices in life."

"How dare you." Emma stepped forward. "You had no right . . ."

Sebastian hauled her back, holding her tightly when she tried to break free of his grasp. The little idiot would get herself killed if she wasn't careful. He returned her angry glare with a smile. "We would not like to awaken your aunt with a gunshot."

For a moment it looked as though she intended to argue with him. Instead she turned to face her true enemy. "What have you done with Charlotte?"

"The same thing I am about to do with you. And with my uncle." Radbyrne smiled, slowly, as if he were enjoying a particularly interesting secret. "I sold her."

"Sold her," Emma whispered, her voice betraying her horror.

"You've found a buyer for me?" Sebastian stepped

to the side, hoping to draw Radbyrne's attention away from Emma. As he hoped, Radbyrne turned, keeping the pistol aimed at him. "I am curious, is it a man or a woman?"

"Since you and Miss Wakefield seem to be rather fond of each other's company, you will be pleased to know that I sold you both to the same man. He has been one of my best customers. I have sold several girls to him. For some reason, they don't last long and he needs more. I believe you know him." Radbyrne looked pleased with himself. "Martin Hollington."

Sebastian resisted the urge to clench his teeth. He had met Hollington several years ago, when the man was pursuing one of his sisters. Genevieve had taken an interest in the handsome young man, which had prompted Sebastian to learn more about him. Hollington was intelligent, charming, and wealthy. The bulk of his earnings came from three plantations he owned in Jamaica. Sebastian might have approved of the match if Orlina had not enlightened him as to the peculiar requests he made of the women in her employ. It did not surprise him to learn Hollington had been involved with Radbyrne and Gaetan's.

Sebastian took another step to his left. "I certainly hope you were paid well. He has very deep pockets."

"Yes, indeed he does. I remembered you and he had a bit of a row a few years ago. Fortunately he is still in town. He had plans to set sail for Jamaica in a few days. I believe he now plans to sail tonight. He said something about enjoying the freedom of being in a place where no one cares if they hear a bit of screaming. I cannot say whether he was more excited about getting his hands on you, or the idea of plowing into your lady. I think he will allow you to watch when he takes her. After that, one can only speculate."

Sebastian's stomach clenched when he thought of

that man putting his hands on Emma. "I shall find a way to murder him with my bare hands before he ever touches her."

"Forever arrogant." One corner of Radbyrne's mouth twitched. "Perhaps Hollington will cure you of that flaw."

"Did you sell Charlotte to this monster as well?" Emma demanded.

"No." Radbyrne's gaze darted to something behind Sebastian. "I had a very special request for your cousin."

A floorboard creaked behind Sebastian. It was then he sensed the approach of someone near his back. He pivoted just as a large man reached for his arm. He grabbed the man's outstretched arm and yanked him forward, shoving him directly at Radbyrne. The big man stumbled a few steps.

"Careful!" Radbyrne shouted just before the big man rammed into him.

Sebastian surged forward as his nephew struggled to keep his balance. He slashed his clenched fist against Radbyrne's wrist, forcing the pistol from his grasp. The weapon fell with a thud to the carpet. In the next instant Sebastian snatched the pistol from the floor. Before he could raise the weapon, something hit him hard across the back of the head. Pain cracked through his skull. Distantly he was aware of his legs crumpling beneath him, but he never felt the collision of his body with the floor. The darkness that wrapped around him saved him that one last indignity.

Chapter Nineteen

The scent of stale onions and unwashed skin stabbed Emma's nostrils with each step her captor took. His footsteps slapped the oak planks of the deck beneath them. From what she could see it was a large ship. Yet she could not see a great deal in her position. Her captor carried her slung over his shoulder as though she were a sack of potatoes. Some of her pins had fallen from her hair, allowing long locks to tumble down over her face. His shoulder rammed into her middle with each step. A damp evening breeze penetrated her gown, chilling her skin. The blood pounded in her temples. Yet her mind was in such turmoil, she scarcely noticed the petty discomforts.

She twisted her head, trying to see Andover. He was being carried by the large, dark-haired man walking behind her, the same man who had cracked him over the head with the handle of a pistol. Although Andover had been unconscious, they had bound and gagged him, as they had her. He had remained unconscious during the long coach ride out of London to an isolated beach. He did not stir when they loaded him into a small boat and rowed to the ship. From what she could see, he still had not roused. How badly was he hurt?

Moonlight gave way to the light of a lamp when her captor carried her through a narrow doorway. He turned right, then set her on her feet. Blood swam before her eyes. She might have crumpled if it had not been for the powerful hand that gripped her arm. As the blood cleared from her vision she saw the man carrying Andover. He was marching in the opposite direction, carrying his burden down a narrow flight of stairs. They were being separated. At that moment fear crept from dark crevices deep within her. It rose, like a giant birdlike creature, dragging its claws along her vitals as it soared upward through her. Through the blood pounding in her temples she heard the distant sound of her captor rapping on an arched oak door and the command that came from within.

The man opened the door and gestured with his hand. "In there."

Emma could not tear her gaze from the empty space where Andover had disappeared. Even though he was bound and gagged and unconscious, his presence had made her feel safe. What would they do to him?

"Move," the brute said, tugging on her arm.

Emma twisted, trying to break free of the brute's grasp. The man squeezed her arm so tightly, she gasped.

"Careful, Dixen. I paid a great deal for this merchandise; I do not want it bruised."

The soft, silky quality of the voice startled her. Emma glanced past the short, squat brute who held her, to the tall, long-limbed man who had spoken.

Martin Hollington sat on the long cushioned seat that was built beneath a double row of windows at the far end of the cabin. At first she thought there must be a mistake. This could not possibly be the man who had bought her as though she were a slave on the block. How could a man who looked so divine possess a soul so damned?

Candles flickered behind the crystal globes of brass sconces affixed to the oak-paneled walls, filling the large cabin with a soft golden glow. Candlelight slipped yellow fingers into the dark brown waves that fell in artful disarray over his wide brow. He was one of the most beautiful creatures she had ever seen, male or female. His features were perfectly carved—his nose slim and straight, the bones of his cheeks precisely chiseled, the slant of his brows in exquisite harmony with the almond shape of his large, light blue eyes. He was a man who would never escape a woman's notice. He smiled at her, a slight curving of finely molded lips that said he knew exactly how startled she was by his appearance.

"Do come in, Miss Wakefield. I assure you, there is nothing to be gained by disobedience."

She glared at him while she resisted the insistent tug of her captor's grasp. He would soon discover he had not purchased a lamb to be slaughtered. She would fight him with every ounce of strength she possessed. When her captor tugged once more on her arm, she stomped as hard as she could on his foot. The man gasped with pain.

"Bitch!" He lifted his hand to strike her.

"No, Dixen."

The silky voice of Hollington froze Dixen. He lowered his hand and looked at Emma as though he would like nothing more than to strangle her.

"My dear Miss Wakefield." Hollington tapped the

pads of his fingertips together, while he regarded her with a measure of surprise in his eyes. "If you would like Andover to remain in one piece, I suggest you behave yourself."

The implication struck her with the force of a fist. If she defied this man, Andover would pay for her insolence.

Hollington smoothed his hand over the emerald velvet of the cushion beside him. "Now come over here like a good girl."

Although her legs felt like quivering aspic, she forced her feet to move. "Tell the captain it is time to leave."

Fear sank deeply into her stomach when Emma thought of what Radbyrne had said of this man. He wanted the freedom of being in a place where no one would care about a bit of screaming. She faced him, hoping he would see only her disgust.

Dixen closed the door behind her, leaving her alone with this fallen angel. She paused before him, her chin lifted with the determination to maintain her dignity, no matter what this man did to her.

Hollington studied her, his gaze traveling from her tumbled hair, over the blue muslin of her gown, down to the toes of her black shoes. Although he did not touch her, it felt as though he were slowly dragging his hands over her body. Bile rose in a scalding path along the back of her throat.

"Very nice. I can see why Andover took an interest." He looked straight into her eyes, the heat of arousal naked in his eyes. "Has he plucked the rose yet? A simple nod or shake of your head will do."

She hesitated a moment, unsure of her answer. If she lied and said Andover was her lover, Hollington might lose interest in taking her. He might also kill both of them.

"Come now, Miss Wakefield. Tell me, has Andover spoiled my sport? Have you bedded him?"

She shook her head.

A smile slowly spread across his lips. He rose and moved toward her. She was enveloped by the spicy scent of an expensive cologne when he paused in front of her. "Do you see the bell rope near the bed?"

Emma glanced toward the bed that was built into one of the oak-paneled walls. An emerald bell pull with a gold tassel hung beside it. Emerald velvet swags draped the alcove that sheltered the bed. Fear prickled her skin when she thought of what this man would do with her in that elegant space.

"If you are a good girl I will have no reason to use that bell pull to summon one of my men. If you do not do as I say, it will be most unpleasant for you as well as Andover." He gripped her chin and forced her to meet his gaze. "Do we have an understanding?"

The ice in his eyes could not be mistaken. This was a man who could kill and enjoy watching his victim take her last breath. She had to find a way to get away from him, or neither she nor Andover would survive. She nodded, allowing him to believe he had frightened her into submission.

He smoothed his hand over her rumpled hair, as gentle as a breeze over the petals of a rose, the touch a sharp contrast to the look in his eyes. "I always like women who know how to behave properly."

She glanced around the room, while he untied her hands and removed the gag from her mouth. If not for the sway of the floor beneath her, she might have thought she was in the bedchamber of an elegant London town house. The cabin measured the entire width of the ship and at least a quarter of the length. The emerald velvet that shrouded the bed and covered the chairs, as well as the long seat built beneath the windows, screamed of wealth and fashion.

The corners of her mouth were sore from the gag. Her wrists burned from the rub of the rope that had bound her. Still, she refused to show any sign of weakness to this man. Instead she looked him straight in the eye. "I suspect women come easily to you. I cannot imagine why you would lower yourself to something as vile as kidnapping."

"It is never amusing when it is easy." He lifted a lock of her hair and fiddled with the strands, sliding them between his long fingers. "And from the look in your eyes, I can see nothing is easy with you. If not for the fact I could have Andover brought in here and sliced to pieces before your eyes, you would fight me like a little she-cat. Instead you will resist without violence."

Emma hoped the fear pricking her insides did not reveal itself in her eyes. The sound of canvas snapping came through an open window. The ship swayed, as if suddenly yanked in one direction. "It is all a game to you, is it not? It is all about power. You like to control people."

He lifted his dark brows, a glimmer of surprise filling his eyes. "You are very perceptive, Miss Wakefield."

"You are not that difficult to read, Mr. Hollington." She turned away from him and strolled to the desk that was built into the wall across from the bed. As she hoped, a letter opener sat atop the desk top, beside a brass paperweight in the shape of a horse. The slender steel blade glittered in the candlelight.

"And do you find Andover so easy to read?"

"Most men are fairly easy to understand. They are not nearly as complicated as women." She turned and sat on the edge of the desktop, sliding her hands back, s though she were simply lounging there, while she eached for the letter opener. "For instance, I would uess you are interested in using me as a pawn to nflict some manner of revenge upon Andover."

"You really are very perceptive." He rubbed his hin. "I have very special plans for Andover."

"You are going to murder him."

Hollington laughed, the sound soft and velvety in he quiet room. "Not at all. One cannot enjoy tormenting a dead man."

"Do you dislike him simply because he opposed a natch between you and his sister? Or do you dislike im for another reason? Is it his blatant masculinity hat bothers you?"

Hollington stared at her a moment. "His blatant masculinity? And why would that bother me?"

"The comparison to yourself. He is so utterly male." Emma bumped the paperweight with her fingers. Does he make you feel . . . inferior?"

"Inferior?" Hollington moved toward her, his expression betraying his curiosity. "And who is playing game now, Miss Wakefield? What do you hope to lo, make me angry with you? Do you truly think it is vise to make me angry?"

He paused before her, so close his legs brushed the kirt of her dress. "I think you are angry," she said. You certainly are not satisfied with your life."

"Not satisfied?" He lifted the dark blue ribbon at the enter of her high square neckline. Slowly he tugged he ribbon, pulling apart the bow. "Perhaps I am not atisfied, at the moment. But I shall be."

"Forcing me to service you, that will be satisfying or you?" Her fingers brushed the cool silver handle f the letter opener. Her heart pounded with equal neasures of fear, hope, and dread. "I would think it ar more satisfying to bed a woman who wants you."

261

"You will want me." He cupped her breasts and slid the pads of his thumbs over the tips, the touch scattering chills across her skin. "That is part of the enjoyment. Watching you fight your own base instincts. You see, passion really has little to do with anything except physical manipulation. And I learned all about that from my stepmother at a very early age."

She squeezed the handle of the letter opener, gathering the courage to use it against him. "I will never want you."

He leaned forward and brushed his lips against the skin beneath her right ear. "You are mistaken."

Emma pressed the tip of the letter opener to the soft skin beneath his chin. In her fear she poked it so hard that she pierced the skin. Blood pooled around the tip of the blade. "Do as I say, Hollington, or I shall plunge this straight through your neck."

He stared down at her, his eyes wide with disbelief. "Why you little . . ."

Emma gasped as he grabbed her wrist and pulled the letter opener away from his neck. Before he could force the weapon from her grasp, she brought her knee up sharply and rammed his groin. He sucked in his breath and stumbled back, folding at the waist, grasping his injury with both hands. He turned his head and glared at her. "You . . . will . . . regret the . . ."

Emma lashed out with her foot. The toe of her shoe connected just beneath his chin. His head snapped back. A low groan escaped his lips. He crumpled onto his side, unconscious on the green and gold carpet. In the next instant the door to the cabin swung open.

Emma pivoted, lifting the letter opener like a sword. She expected one of Hollington's minions to cross the threshold. Instead, Andover rushed into the room holding a pistol. He glanced from Emma to Hollington and back again. "I thought you were the one who needed rescuing. Obviously I was mistaken."

Without a thought she ran to him and threw her arms around his neck. "Thank heavens, you are all right."

He hugged her close, then pulled back, far enough to look down into her face. "Did he hurt you?"

His concern for her was so tangible it wrapped around her, as snug as the embrace of his powerful arms. "I am fine."

"Thank God." In the next heartbeat he kissed her, fast and hard. It lasted a moment, no more. Yet it was enough to send a swift flood of hot desire sluicing through her veins. He pulled back and cupped her cheek in his hand, his palm warm upon her skin. "We'd better leave, before one of his men notices something is wrong."

It was then she noticed the charred remains of his cuff. She gripped his hand and examined the burns on his wrist, her chest tightening at the sight of the scorched and blistered flesh. "What happened?"

"I used a candle to burn the rope."

She stared up at him. "You burned yourself."

"Yes. Clumsy of me." He grabbed her hand and marched to the door. "I suggest we leave. I do not wish to be here when someone notices I am not where they put me."

Emma stared at him in complete confusion when he threw the bolt and locked the door. He turned and tugged her toward the windows.

Emma followed him, trying to divine his escape plan. He shoved the pistol into his coat pocket, then knelt on the cushioned seat below the windows, unfastened a latch and threw open the window. The opening was more than large enough for a man to crawl through, if that man were crazy enough to jump into the sea.

Emma froze when he tugged her toward him. "What are you doing?"

"The deck is swarming with his men. It is best if we jump from here."

Emma looked out the window. It must be fifteen feet to the rolling waves below. "Jump?"

He tugged on her hand. "Come on. They may notice my guard is missing at any moment."

"I cannot."

He pulled her down to the seat beside him. "There is no choice."

She looked at him, appalled at her own weakness. "I cannot swim."

"I see." He turned his attention out the window. "That makes it a little more complicated."

Moonlight illuminated the dark shapes of trees growing near the shore. They were not so very far away from land. Yet it might have been twenty miles for all the good it would do Emma.

Andover looked at her, a fierce expression in his eyes. "I will get you safely to shore. Jump with me. I will not allow you to drown."

He was asking for her trust. He wanted her to jump into the sea with only the assurance that he would save her. She glanced down at the water. Moonlight gathered on each rolling wave, shaping glittering mirrors that were shattered in the next instant. She turned her gaze to Andover and realized there was no one else in the world she trusted more than this man. "What do you want me to do?"

The fierce expression on his face softened with relief. He squeezed her hand. "Hold on to me. No matter what happens, hold on to me."

Shouts sounded in the hallway. Andover did not so much as glance at the door. Instead he swung his legs out of the window and sat on the wide sill. Then he reached for Emma. "Crawl onto my lap and sit astride my hips."

He helped her, guiding her onto his lap and drawing her legs around his hips. Her dress slid upward, exposing her thighs as she straddled him. A cool breeze licked across her skin, raising goose flesh. The hard thrust of masculinity pressed against her nether region. A current slashed through the fear that pounded in icy waves through her veins, crackling like hot oil poured into a pool of cold water. How could desire spark through her at a time when her life was in danger? Yet it was there, making her blood simmer. In his eyes, she saw an answering flame in the darker-than-midnight depths.

The look in his eyes obliterated everything else in her world. The roar of the sea slashing against the ship below dissolved into a distant swish of sound. The light from the cabin faded into a blur of color. Nothing mattered except this man.

He smoothed his fingertips over her cheek. "Hold on to me, sweetheart."

Sweetheart? The world wobbled. If she had been standing, her legs would have given out.

Someone pounded on the door. She threw her arms around his neck and hugged him close. She kept thinking of how many things she had left to do in this world. It was not a good time to die.

Andover cinched one arm around her waist. "Hold on."

She felt him push forward, and then they were falling. Air rushed through her hair and tugged at her clothes. Andover held her close against his body. The air rushed from her lungs at the sudden impact of her body with the cold sea. They sank, as if tied to a bolder. For one heart-pounding moment she feared they would both drown. She fought the terror screaming inside her, the fear that demanded she struggle against the powerful arm holding her. Only her will kept her from fighting him.

He stroked with his free arm, kicked with his legs, struggling against the downward pull of the sea. Soon they broke the surface of the water. Emma dragged great gasps of air into her lungs. Andover paused for a moment, keeping them afloat with the strong movement of his legs and arm. He glanced around, as if gaining his bearings, then struck out for shore. She clung to him with one arm, while she mimicked the motion of his free arm, hoping to be less of a burden to him. After what seemed an eternity, they reached water shallow enough to stand. Sand sucked at her feet as she staggered beside him, leaning against him, allowing his strength to pull her to safety. When they reached the shore, they both collapsed onto the sandy beach.

She lay beside him, staring up at the sky, where a scattering of stars peeked out from dark patches of cloud. The moon lay on the breast of one thick cloud, as though cushioned on a plump black pillow. She dragged air into her burning lungs, her breath coming in the same ragged gasps as his. He lay on his side next to her, his cheek resting upon her shoulder, his each quick exhalation warm upon her damp neck. Strange, she had an odd sense of contentment lying there on the sand, wet and exhausted. She supposed this was the feeling men experienced when they had done with battle and survived. If not for Andover, she would not have survived. Still, that was not the reason for the emotions unfurling inside her, the warmth suffusing her limbs in spite of her sodden clothes and the chill evening air.

Lightning flashed through a plump cloud, as if mimicking the sensation that careened through her when she thought of him. A moment later thunder rumbled. She turned her head and looked at the man lying beside her. Thick black lashes lay upon the crest of his cheek. A single lock of hair curled in an ebony wave above his ear. A truth burned inside her, one that could no longer be ignored. Andover was the most infuriating man she had ever known. He was also the most intriguing man she had ever known. Arrogant one moment, compassionate the next. Strong and confident, powerful and sure. And so very male. How could she ever have thought to guard her heart against him?

He lifted his head and caught her staring at him like a silly schoolgirl with her first infatuation. He stroked his fingertip over the curve of her jaw. "Are you all right?"

"Thanks to you I am fine."

He smiled, a warm and generous smile that tugged at her heart. "You were doing fine without me."

A chill gripped her when she thought of life without him. Yet what choice did she have?

He glanced at the gathering clouds, then back toward Hollington's ship. "We'd better find shelter."

She looked across the water at the dark shape of the ship. Moonlight spilled across the sails, lending a strange glow to the vessel. "Do you think Hollington will send someone after us?"

"I do not think he will be very happy with us when he awakens." He rose and helped her to her feet. "There is a storm coming. We need to find shelter."

Although he said no more, Emma knew what was going through his mind. It was the same thought that kept repeating in her own brain. They needed to find shelter before Hollington could find them.

Chapter Twenty

The Green Turtle Inn was a small establishment, with only eight rooms available for hire. Fortunately Mr. Tillison and his wife had no objections to accommodating a pair of travelers who arrived at their door wet to the skin and without a farthing. They believed Sebastian when he told them he was the Marquess of Andover; his signet ring helped. They accepted his story of an attempted kidnapping with a great deal of commiseration, and they were eager to make Sebastian and his companion comfortable. Unfortunately the storm that had hit soon after he and Emma had trudged off the beach prevented Mr. Tillison from sending a message to London that evening. It was far too dangerous to travel.

The scent of beeswax and lavender drifted past his senses as Sebastian followed Emma into one of the bedchambers. It was a small room. The beams were exposed against a white plaster ceiling. The furniture was large and sturdy. The chamber looked as neat and clean as any in his own home.

"I shall send up a tin of warm water and something for you to wear, my lady. I am afraid it will not fit properly, you being such a slip of a girl, but it will keep you nice and warm while you sleep."

Mrs. Tillison drew down the bed covers while she chattered merrily. She was barely five feet tall and nearly every bit as round. Her husband was only a few inches taller and from what Sebastian had seen of the man, he enjoyed his wife's cooking as well as she did. Yet both Tillison and his wife were amiable, the sort of people who managed to make one feel at home when far away from one's own bed. Or when one has just escaped a monster.

He watched Emma cross the room. She had said little since they had fled Hollington's ship. Although she had assured him the blackguard had not physically harmed her, he could only wonder at the impact the brute had made upon her in other ways. In her life she had seldom been able to place her trust in men. He wanted her trust, and more.

Mrs. Tillison fluttered toward him, like a plump sparrow. "I will bring up some of Tillison's clothes for you, my lord. Yet I am afraid they will not suit, you being such a tall man. And our boy is but a lad of twelve."

"I am certain they will suit me much better then these wet clothes, Mrs. Tillison."

Deep dimples sank into both of her plump cheeks when she smiled up at him. "If you and the lady leave your clothes in the hall outside your doors, I will make certain they are clean and dry for you in the morning."

"Thank you."

Brown curls bobbed about her face when she curtsied. "Oh, and Tillison will be up directly with a bottle of brandy. Now you mustn't worry a bit about anything. We will make certain no one will be bothering you tonight. You are safe here."

Sebastian took some small measure of comfort in her words. He suspected they would be safe enough here. Yet he had no intention of lowering his guard. After Mrs. Tillison left, he turned to face Emma. She stood near the window, staring through the rainswept glass. She looked lost and lonely, and somehow the loneliness he sensed in her seemed habitual.

"Would you feel more comfortable if I stayed here tonight?"

She turned and looked at him, her eyes wide, a question forming on her lips. Before she could say a word, he clarified his intent.

"I could sleep on the floor near the door."

She glanced at the rough planks of the floor. The sound of rain striking glass filled up the silence stretching between them. "That is very kind of you to offer, but I shall be fine."

He crushed the urge to argue with her. He suspected she wanted and needed privacy, especially after her encounter with Hollington. "I have left the pistol I took from the ship with Tillison. Once he has cleaned and reloaded it, I shall have him deliver it to you."

She shivered in her wet dress, and it was all he could do to keep from crossing the room and taking her into his arms. "You are going to give me the pistol?"

"I thought you would be more comfortable tonight if you had a weapon."

She held his gaze, a look of surprise in her eyes. "What about you?"

"I will manage."

She hugged her arms to her waist. "I would imagine

the rain will keep Hollington from searching for us tonight."

His first impulse was to assure her they were completely safe. Yet she was a woman who demanded honesty. It was one of her most endearing qualities. "It depends on how angry he is. If he is wise, he will continue home. If not, he will try to retrieve us."

"I had the impression I was just a pawn to strike at you." She scrunched her shoulders forward. "If he has a chance, he will murder you. Perhaps you should take the pistol."

"No. You keep it." He gripped the handle of the door, reluctant to leave her. "If you need anything, I will be in the room directly across the hall."

"How are your hands?" she asked, when he opened the door.

"A little sore. Nothing to be concerned about."

"They should be tended to."

An image rose in his mind, of Emma gently stroking his scorched flesh. With the image came a rush of heat. "I shall soak them in cool water. I will be fine."

He stood for a moment outside her door, fighting the urge to go back into her room. Lust could make a fool of a man.

He had offered marriage. She had refused. The matter should be closed, yet it was not. His life would be sane without her, orderly, dignified, as he wanted it. He thought of the days and weeks and months and years that stretched before him, each much the same as the last, without the excruciating excitement brought about by one infuriating woman. What was he going to do about Emma?

Emma stared at the door for several moments after he left her. What in the world was she going to do about Andover?

All her life she had dreamed of the man who would win her heart. He would be intelligent, kind, compassionate, and he would set her pulse racing with a glance. He, of course, would share the same deep affection she had for him as well as an unshakable passion. Somewhere along the way things had become a bit muddled. The damp of her dress conspired with the cool air to send a legion of shivers across her skin. She began unfastening her ties, while she contemplated her dilemma.

Clearly Andover was not the man destiny had meant her to meet. They wanted different things from life. She wanted and needed more than the momentary excitement that came from an attraction that was purely physical. And he was incapable of giving her more. Or was he? She froze, her dress partially off her shoulders, her mind grappling with an interesting possibility. Her aunt Marjorie's words echoed in her memory: *A man does not always know what he wants until a woman shows him. You may be precisely what he needs and wants. He just has to realize it.*

Was it possible? Could she wiggle her way into his icy heart? Could lust be twisted and shaped into something far more substantial? A woman could make a fool of herself thinking such thoughts.

She was not the type of woman he wanted as his wife, she reminded herself. Men enjoyed a challenge. At the moment she presented a challenge. After the conquest, he would lose interest. He'd admitted as much to her. He always lost interest in a woman. She knew herself well enough to know she would not accept his defection without a fight. She would spend her days and nights trying to win back some scrap of his attention. Far more beautiful women had tried the same feat. Women with far more experience than she had. They had all failed.

Andover definitely presented a challenge. Her life had been filled with challenges. She had never backed away from one before. Not when it was important. Not when she wanted something with all of her heart.

But how in the world did a woman make a man fall in love with her? She thought of all the heroines created by E. W. Austen. What would Isabel, Sarah, Katherine, Victoria, or Marisa do in this situation? Yet all of the books in the world could not answer her most daunting questions. Which was worse? Living with him after he had lost interest in her or living without him?

She peeled off her damp clothes and threw the quilt from the bed around her shoulders. Oh, she wanted to scream. Andover had her acting like a love-sick ninny. Somewhere along the way she had allowed the man to insinuate himself into her life. Men had a way of making a woman miserable. If a woman allowed it.

Her life had been just fine before she had met him. It would be fine after he was gone. She would not allow the Maddening Marquess to get the better of her. No man would make a fool of her.

When Mrs. Tillison arrived a short time later with a nightgown for her to wear, Emma inquired about ointment for Andover's burns. She had no intention of neglecting his wounds. A half hour later she knocked on Andover's door.

She straightened her shoulders and prepared to do battle with her own wayward emotions. She would not allow him to muddle her thoughts, she assured herself. She would simply make certain his hands were tended. Nothing more. After she had tended his hurts, she would return to her room, where she would lie in bed and force her mind to think of anything except Andover. She was not some silly spinster lost to a horrible infatuation for a man who would do nothing but make her life miserable. No, she was made of stronger stuff.

He opened the door. Her heart rammed into the wall of her chest. The faint light of the wall sconce behind her did not spare her the full impact of his appeal. His hair fell in undisciplined waves around his face, making him look younger and more approachable. The white cotton of his shirt was stretched tight over the breadth of his shoulders. He had left it unfastened, allowing the shirt to spill open halfway down his chest. She tried not to notice the dark shadow of hair and skin revealed by the cotton. Yet she could not block out the intriguing image, any more than she could ignore his male magnetism.

She glanced down at the bowl she held, hiding from his gaze. It would not do to allow the man to see just how easily he could overturn her composure. "Mrs. Tillison assures me this is a very fine ointment. She makes it herself and uses it on all manner of cuts and scrapes and burns. It should help the burns on your hands. And she provided some clean white linen for bandages as well."

"Are you certain it is not something she uses for the horses?"

She glanced up at him, and found him frowning at the greenish white salve in the small white bowl. "Actually she did mention something about it working very well upon a stone bruise her mare had last spring."

"My hands are feeling fine."

"From what I saw they were not fine at all. If something is not done, you could die. And it would be entirely your fault for not allowing me to take care of your hurts."

"Die? I doubt I would ..."

"I think you should sit over by the fire and allow

me to tend to those dreadful burns." She held his gaze
without trying to disguise the determination that
burned in her. She would not leave until she had
tended his hands. If she had to hit the man over the
head to make him see reason, then she would hit him
over the head. He needed her help.

Sebastian had seen this look in her eyes before. It always heralded an argument. Although he was not
keen on the idea of having horse ointment spread
across his sore hands, he did like the notion of having
her fingers upon him. That thought whispered
through him like the soft song of a siren, deciding the
matter. "Perhaps you are right."

She looked surprised and pleased—a fighter who
has just walked out of the ring and left his opponent
bleeding on the ground. "Sit and I shall spread on the
salve."

He refrained from asking her if she had ever tended
to hurts before. Her experience really did not matter.
Her concern for him did. And as long as she was with
him, he could protect her. He intended to protect her,
from his own lust as well as from any outside threat.

She crossed the threshold as though she had no
qualms at all about entering his room. Clearly she
trusted him. He closed the door, the soft click sounding unnaturally loud to his suddenly heightened
senses. He watched her cross the room, her bare feet
silent upon the thin carpet.

She wore a multicolored quilt slung over her shoulders, covering the white nightgown Tillison's wife had
provided for her. Her hair fell in a mass of wayward
dark waves around her shoulders. Her color was high,
emphasizing the paleness of her eyes. He had not lived
the life of a monk. He had taken his first mistress when
he was seventeen. He had seen countless negligees,

elegant, silky, filmy, each designed to tease and arouse. Yet he had never seen any woman look more beautiful than Emma in this bulky cotton quilt.

Although she was completely covered, he remembered the curves hidden beneath. Memories stirred within him, sparking life from the smoldering desire she had ignited long ago. Heat slithered through his body like a fiery serpent.

He reminded himself of the ordeal she had suffered this evening. The last thing she needed was another man panting and salivating after her. The last thing he needed was to injure the trust she had placed in him. He could keep his base instincts under rein. He was not a man ruled by emotion, he assured himself.

She set her bowl, linen, and her pistol on the table near the fireplace. "Sit," she commanded, pointing toward the chair near the table.

She watched him move toward her, a glint of humor entering her eyes. "I have heard young men strive to emulate the elegant fashion of the Marquess of Andover."

The breeches he wore were large enough in the waist to accommodate another person. Fortunately Tillison had provided a length of rope to cinch them. Unfortunately the breeches also fell several inches above his knees. Sebastian sat on the wooden armchair he had abandoned upon her arrival. "I can only say I am glad my valet cannot see me. He would fall into a fit of apoplexy."

She sat on the chair beside him. "With any luck we shall both be able to make ourselves more presentable tomorrow before we leave for London."

The quilt parted when Emma extended her hand toward him, revealing the pink flowers embroidered beneath the high neckline of the gown. The gown was made to fit the plump figure of Mrs. Tillison. On

Emma's slender frame, it sagged at her neckline, revealing the delicate bones at the hollow of her neck. "Give me your hand."

At her soft command, he rested his hand upon hers. Although it was a simple touch, the spark of contact flickered through him. The startled look in her eyes told him she felt it too. Were they both lost to the same attraction? He watched her turn her attention to the burns on his wrist. He felt the subtle trembling in her hand and recognized it for the same agitation that coiled through him.

He lived his life surrounded by friends and family, a life of wealth and privilege. Yet since he had met Emma he had felt an ever-increasing awareness of what was missing in his life. All the nonsense his mother had spoken of destiny and love and passion did not seem so foolish when he thought of Emma. No, it did not seem like nonsense at all. He drew air past his tight throat, dragging the scent of burning coal into his lungs, when he craved the fragrance of her skin.

He winced when she spread the ointment over the scorched skin at his wrist and the back of his hand. She looked at him. If he did not know better, he would say she had suffered a twinge of pain along with him.

"You have hurt yourself dreadfully," she scolded him, her sharp tone a direct contrast to her gentle touch. "I suppose you could not think of another way to escape."

The coals on the hearth cast a reddish-gold light upon her cheek, made shadows of her thick, dark lashes. He could not remember a moment when she looked more beautiful. "At the time I thought it imperative to reach you as soon as possible. I should have realized my help was not needed."

"You know very well I could not have managed to

escape if you had not come charging to my rescue."
She wound a piece of linen around his wrist, leaving
his fingers free. "If I neglected to thank you, I apologize."

"There is no need to apologize. And certainly no
need to thank me. My nephew is the reason you and
your family were dragged into this ugly business."

"And you could have ignored him and his business,
as many men would."

"You have a rather low opinion of men."

"Not all men." She looked up at him and smiled.
"Just most of them."

He would like to think he had fought his way out
of the pit where she placed most men. Although he
did not like to admit it, her opinion of him mattered.

After she bound the bandage, she took his other
hand and smoothed ointment upon his blistered skin.
"What are we going to do now? How are we going to
find Charlotte?"

Sebastian had been debating the same question since
they had left Gaetan's. "I either have to find my
nephew or Gaetan. They are the only two who know
where Charlotte has been taken."

She held her gaze down while she wound linen
around his hand, keeping her thoughts to herself.
When she finished binding the wound, she fastened
the bandage in place with another strip of linen. "Does
it feel any better?"

Although the burns felt much as they had before her
ministering, he was glad she'd come. Just knowing she
was concerned about him made him feel better. "Yes."

She sat back in her chair and pulled the quilt close
around her, as though she were cold. "You must see
a surgeon when you return to London."

He doubted a surgeon could do much for his
wounds, but he refrained from arguing with her. He

preferred to have her fuss over him rather than to have her arguing with him. "Would you like a glass of brandy? Tillison brought me two glasses. I suppose he thought you might join me. It has a way of warming you inside."

She considered his suggestion a moment before she replied. "Yes. I think a glass of brandy would be nice."

"I suspect Mr. Tillison has an acquaintance with a smuggler of two." Sebastian lifted the bottle and poured brandy into the extra glass Tillison had provided. "The quality of his brandy is unmistakably French."

"I would not know. I have never had brandy before." The quilt parted when she reached for the glass, revealing the smooth curve of her neck and the hollow below.

Sebastian tried not to notice the way the candlelight played upon her smooth skin. Still, he could not banish the image of brandy drizzled into the hollow of her neck. The images that followed twisted his vitals into a tight fist of need. He felt his will unraveling, as though she were a kitten who had snagged the ball of yarn that was his self control. When he was with her it was easy to forget everything except his need for her.

He sipped the brandy in his glass, while she took her first taste of the liquor, drinking it as though it were water. She sucked in her breath and looked up at him, tears welling in her eyes.

He laughed, he could not prevent it. "It is a bit potent at first."

She glared at him with watery eyes. "You might have warned me."

"I did not think of it. It really is excellent brandy. If you savor it."

She looked doubtful. "Savor this?"

"First you should inhale the fragrance, allow the aroma to tingle your senses." He demonstrated by lifting his glass and drawing in his breath. The heady fumes licked past his nostrils, filling his senses with the rich bouquet.

She hesitated a moment before following his lead. She lifted the glass and sniffed at the contents. Her brows lifted above a look of surprise. "I can see how it might help if one had a cold."

"Put the glass to your lips and take a sip, enough to drench your tongue, no more. Allow it to warm your tongue and then your throat. Feel the warmth spread into your chest. Let it embrace you, slowly."

A warmth kindled in her eyes at his soft words. She quickly glanced down into her glass. After a moment of contemplation, she lifted her glass and took a sip. A grimace quickly followed. "You say this is excellent brandy?"

"Yes. It could only have come from France." Sebastian sipped his liquor. "I wonder if Tillison might consider introducing me to his supplier."

"You would deal with a smuggler?"

He shrugged. "This is very fine brandy."

She shook her head, as if to dismiss his words. "I would never have suspected that the very proper Marquess of Andover might consider dealing with a smuggler."

"A smuggler is just a fellow out to make a living. And this has been a very long war."

"You surprise me." She tilted her head and studied him. "You are not at all the way I imagined you would be."

"Considering the fact you thought I was a monster when first we met, I would say it is good that I am not what you expected."

"A monster." She contemplated the brandy in her

glass. "In the past few days I have come face to face with true monsters. And I now know the difference."

His stomach clenched. "Did he hurt you?"

"No." She sipped her brandy. "This gets better with each sip."

He caught himself staring at her lips, where a sheen of brandy tempted him. He must think of something else. He certainly should not contemplate licking the brandy from her lips. "It should make you sleepy."

"Hollington said I would enjoy what he intended to do to me. That I would not have a choice, because pleasure came from mere physical manipulation." She swirled the brandy in her glass. "I wonder if that is true for some people. Obviously it was true for him. It must be true for men who frequent places like Gaetan's. Perhaps even for the men who frequent Vachel's. It would seem men do not need anything but the physical aspects of coupling with a female to find pleasure."

Sebastian rubbed the taut muscles at the nape of his neck. "I suspect men in particular are capable of reducing such things to a purely physical nature."

"Lust." She shivered as though she were cold. The movement dislodged the quilt from her shoulders.

Emma didn't seem to notice or care that she sat before him in nothing more than a nightgown. Yet he noticed. Even though the voluminous white cotton allowed him no more than a hint of the lush curves beneath, the sight was enough to kick his pulse into a gallop. He had the uncomfortable feeling this woman could stand before him in a grain bag and he would find her the most alluring creature he had ever seen.

He knew he should not touch her. His need for her lurked beneath the hard fist of his will, waiting to break free at any moment. Yet she looked so lonely, he could not resist a single touch. He leaned forward and slid his fingertips over the crest of her cheek, where candlelight flickered gold upon the pale ivory of skin that felt like warm satin beneath his touch.

He half expected her to pull away from him. He was prepared to face the sudden surge of her scorn. Yet her reaction struck with a much more potent blow. Her lips parted with a soft sigh that warmed his wrist. He drew back his hand, unwilling to risk further contact. "I wish I could erase all the ugly memories you have of this day."

"When Hollington touched me, it made me realize how very different such things could be. When he touched me I felt anger and revulsion. It was not at all the same as when you . . ." Emma sucked in her breath as though someone had just come up behind her and pinched her. She stared at him, a look of horror on her features.

Chapter Twenty-one

The words left unspoken teased him. Sebastian knew he should leave the subject alone. Yet he could not. "Not the same as what?"

"Nothing." Emma set her glass on the table and rose from her chair. "It is getting late, and I should be going."

He grabbed her wrist when she started to leave. "I think you should stay."

She moistened her lips, a quick slide of the tip of her tongue that left seductive sheen. "If you are concerned about Hollington, I can leave the pistol for you."

"I am not concerned about Hollington." He released her wrist and rose to his feet. "I should be. Yet when you are near I cannot seem to think of anything except how very much I want to make love to you."

She backed away from him. "You regret the day you met me, you said as much."

"I regret few things in my life. One of them is saying that. I was angry when I said it." He glanced away from her, afraid he might lose control of the beast raging inside him. "From the time I was a child I learned to control my emotions. I have always thought a man must keep a clear head. Emotions simply get in the way. Yet when I am with you, it is impossible to rein in my emotions. You have the most infuriating way of shutting down my intellect."

"I realize you find that annoying, but I assure you, it is not intentional."

"I know." He turned to face her. "I realize you might find this difficult to believe, but there are more than a few women of my acquaintance who would do just about anything to gain my attention. Women have stepped in front of my carriage with the hope of meeting me. Women have swooned in front of me with the hope I might catch them. I thought I had solved the mystery of women and what they wanted from me, until you came along."

She lifted her chin at a militant angle. "I would never sink to such foolish tricks to win the regard of any man. I assure you I am not so desperate to marry."

"I am well aware of your thoughts on marriage." He plowed his hand through his hair. "You made it quite clear just how repugnant you found the thought of marriage to me."

"I do not find marriage to you repugnant. It is marriage without affection that I find offensive."

He curled his hands into tight balls at his sides to keep from touching her. If he took her into his arms now, he could make love to her; he saw the truth of her desire in her eyes. But he did not want to trap her into marriage. "I want you more than I have ever wanted another woman. I want you as my wife."

"You want me in your bed. If you cared for me,

honestly cared for me . . ." She waved her hands as though to dismiss the words she had yet to speak. "But you do not. And since you do not, I have been torturing myself with doubts. I am left wondering if I should try to make you fall in love me, which seems foolish beyond reason since you do not believe in the emotion. Or at least you do not believe you are capable of it. But how in the world do you expect me to marry you, when I feel so much and you so little?"

"I have never wanted another woman the way I want you."

She shook her head. "Lust."

"I cannot put a name to the way I feel for you. If it is lust, it is not like any I have felt before. It burns hotter and sinks deeper."

Her lips formed a little O, with nothing more than a whisper of sound escaping. The look in her eyes sealed his fate and hers. The look in her eyes mirrored the need and longing swelling within him. "I have wanted you from the first moment I saw you. I want you now. I shall want you until the day I take my last breath."

She caught her breath in a soft inhalation. Her eyes reflected candlelight and something more luminous, a light that could only be hope. "I have never wanted another man. Only you."

Her soft confession drizzled through him, warm as brandy held over a flame, more intoxicating than any drug. All the reasons he should not kiss her succumbed to that sweet elixir. He watched the expression in her eyes, saw the need for him reflected in the blue depths. "Marry me."

"You are the most infuriating man. One moment I want to strangle you, and the next . . ." She slid her arms around his neck. She held him, as though she would still be holding him when the last star burned from the sky. She held him as though she felt all the longing and need that burned inside him and wanted to ease them. She held him in a way that made him realize he had been waiting for this embrace all his life. "How in the world could I ever hope to resist you?"

"You cannot." He slipped his hand into her hair and spread his fingers against the back of her head, warm strands of silk sliding upon his skin. "I will not allow it."

"Arrogant brute," she whispered.

"Bothersome termagant." He urged her toward him, and she came, like a feather guided by the breeze. Her breath brushed his cheek, warm and damp. Her lips touched his, soft and tasting of brandy. Her lips fluttered softly at the first touch of his mouth upon her, as if she were catching her breath and holding it. His own breath hovered in his throat. Never in his life had he tasted anything more potent than Emma's surrender.

Marriage to Andover. The thought both excited and frightened her. Was it worse to live with him, to risk the depth of his feelings? Or was it worse to live without him, to never know the joy of lying in his arms?

"Tell me your answer, Emma." He pulled back and looked down at her. "Will you marry me?"

The look in his eyes startled her. She saw need in those dark eyes, and an uncertainty that touched her deep inside. The man she had thought always confident looked endearingly uncertain. All the doubts plaguing her responded to the answer rising within her. She could not imagine living without this man. He was a challenge she could not and would not resist. "It would be my honor to become your wife."

He closed his eyes as if in silent prayer. When he

looked at her again, pure undiluted joy shimmered in his gaze. "Emma," he whispered, lifting her in his arms.

She threw her arms around his neck, holding him close while he spun her around and around. The dark rumble of his laughter mingled with the higher notes of her own, a release of joy and relief that reached into the shadows, chasing away fear and doubt. He set her down beside the bed, in a pool of flickering light cast by the lamp on the bedside table.

"In my dreams I have held you a hundred times. I have kissed you and made love to you. Yet each morning I have awakened with a need so deep and fierce I thought it might cripple me."

The truth of his words was reflected in his eyes. This was a man of honor, a man who believed in the impossibility of his own surrender to emotion. Yet he had succumbed to the power of desire and more. Passion and need, longing and desire, smoldered in his eyes with something far more wonderful and unexpected— a genuine affection he did not try to disguise. She stared up at him, amazed and stunned by his wondrous confession. "In my dreams you have held me a hundred times. You have kissed me and made love to me. Yet every morning I have awakened in despair, certain my dreams would never come true."

"It would seem we share a great many things." He touched the embroidery at the top of her gown. "I want you, Emma, so much that I ache. If you want to wait until after we are married, tell me now. And I promise not to touch you until after our vows are spoken."

"Strange. I feel we have already spoken the most profound of vows that could be pledged." She slid her hands over his shoulders, then down his chest. Soft cotton brushed her palms, yet it was the feel of his skin she sought. Cotton warm from his skin parted beneath her touch. She slipped her hands inside his shirt, her fingers sliding into crisp masculine curls. Sleek muscles shifted beneath her touch. His lips parted. She felt the low growl rumble against her hands before it escaped his control and vibrated upon her ears. She pressed her lips to the inviting hollow beneath his neck. The scent of the rain clung to his skin. Beneath that smoldered the spicy scent she would forever know as his alone. "I love you, Andover."

He winked at her. "I think under the circumstances, you might call me by my given name. In fact, I would very much like to hear you say it."

"Sebastian." She flexed her fingers upon his skin. "I think in some impossible way, I have loved you all my life."

He pressed his lips against her temple. "Destiny," he whispered, his breath warm and damp upon her skin.

"I did not think you believed in destiny."

"I did not. Until a beautiful virago stormed into my life." He pulled open the top of her gown. "Since then I have come to believe in a great many things I once thought impossible. I never imagined I could feel like this, as if I have been torn apart and put back together in a completely different way. If this is not love, I cannot imagine surviving anything more powerful."

His words slipped around her, as warm and wonderful and unexpected as a spear of sunlight on a dark and gloomy day. She slid the shirt from his shoulders. "I want nothing more than to be with you, all my life."

He smiled, warm and genuine and filled with boyish pleasure. "The words you hurled at me that night in my coach, they have taunted me. I thought you were a hopeless romantic. Yet now I know the truth. I will feel that each sunrise is brighter because you are sharing it with me. I know I want to share all my life with you. I want to look into the faces of my children and see you there. You were right, Emma. Love is more precious than anything in the world."

Tears rose in her eyes; she could not prevent them. Yet they did not sting so much as they cleansed the fear and pain that had tortured her for so long. "You are my one and only love."

"I want you, Emma."

"Then take me, my darling."

He slid his lips over her cheek and nipped the curve of her jaw, sending sensation rippling down her neck. How she loved the many textures of him, the differences between man and woman. His cheeks had altered with the ebb of the day, smooth skin growing rough and dark with the stubble of his emerging beard.

They undressed each other slowly, peeling away the trappings of society until nothing could hamper the touch of skin to skin. Candlelight flickered over him, as though shaping him from shadow and mystery. The soft flickering light spread across the wide breadth of his shoulders, turning skin to satin. The yellow light tangled in the hair upon his chest, the smooth skin of his hips.

He was more beautiful than she'd imagined he could be, a beauty shaped by power and grace. When he reached for her she hesitated, wanting instead to gaze upon him for a moment longer. She wanted to remember every detail of this night, to write it upon her memory, to have and to cherish all the rest of her days. Finally, when she could not stand the waiting a moment longer, she stepped into the sheltering embrace of his arms.

The heat of his skin radiated against her like the

welcoming heat of a warm brick on a cold December night. He slid his hands over her skin, as though she were the finest silk velvet and he could not get enough of her texture. She explored him as well, reveling in the power of sleek muscles, testing the texture of smooth skin and rough hair.

He caressed her, everywhere, with his hands and his lips and his tongue, touching her in ways she had never dreamed a man might touch a woman. She felt like clay beneath the hands of a master. He shaped her with his gentle touch, blew life into her with each warm exhale upon her skin, until she came alive with need, until her breath came in ragged gasps and her blood pumped so swift and hot she felt she might expire of the need he summoned within her. When the pleasure rose and crested within her, he lifted her in his arms and laid her down upon the soft mattress.

She welcomed him into her arms, eager for the completion that could only come with this joining of man and woman. And he came to her, holding her as though she were more precious than anything in the world. The ample moisture conjured from need eased the slow plunge of his body into hers. She clung to him in wonder, while he eased past her maiden barrier. She sighed against his lips while he coaxed her body to stretch and expand the way her soul expanded to welcome his love.

Under his patient guidance, she learned the rhythm of this ancient dance. In time she moved in counterpoint to him, rising to meet his every downward plunge. Pleasure rose with the gentle friction, tingling and swirling through her. The pleasure gathered, like bubbles growing ever more fervent in a boiling kettle, until it filled her, until it grew too great to remain contained within her. She felt herself coming apart, splintering into a thousand shimmering pieces. In time all the pieces settled back inside her. Yet she had changed. The pieces did not fit as they had before she had met him. Somehow he had taken the pieces of her life and added to them.

His chest expanded against her breasts with a deep inhalation. The scent of his skin teased her nostrils. He lifted himself far enough to look down into her eyes. Her own breath stilled in awe of the expression she saw on his face. He looked at her as though she were not merely the woman he intended to marry. He looked at her as though she were the only woman on the face of the earth he would ever want.

"You are the most confounded woman I have ever met." He brushed his fingers over her cheek. "I had a feeling the first night I met you that my entire world would be tipped on its side by my beautiful, reckless Pandora."

The name came as a endearment this time, an affirmation of the impact she had made upon his life. A thick lock of hair curled above his ear. Emma twisted those silky strands in her fingers. "Have I spoiled your nice orderly life?"

"You have blown it to perdition. And the very strange thing is, I like it this way." Sebastian kissed the tip of his nose. "I appreciate your beauty. I respect your courage. And I admire your honesty. You are the most remarkable woman I have ever met, and I am so very happy that you have decided to live your life with me."

His words curled around her, as warm and loving as the physical embrace of his body with hers. Yet those words sparked a fear within. He admired her honesty. What would he say when he learned the truth about her? She had deceived him. In a certain respect she had betrayed him. Could he forgive her for what she had done to him?

"What is it, my darling?" He cupped her cheek in his hand. "Is something wrong?"

She should tell him the truth. Right here and now. Yet the words would not come. She could not bare to taint this moment with the ugliness of the truth. "Nothing is wrong. Nothing could ever be wrong as long as you love me."

He studied her a moment while she held her breath and prayed he would not press her for the truth. Finally, he smiled. "It has taken me a long time to realize the simple truth in what Mama has been trying to beat into my skull for years. Destiny shall not be denied, my love. And you are my destiny."

Emma crushed the fear crawling upward along her spine. She would not think of disaster. She plunged her hand into his thick hair and pulled him down until she could kiss him. For now she would simply enjoy the blinding pleasure of being in his arms. Tomorrow she would face reality. Tonight she would live her dreams.

Chapter Twenty-two

"From this point on you wish to have all future monies sent to Marjorie Usherwood. At Andover House?" John Knightly looked at Emma through his glasses, the round lenses distorting his brown eyes, lending him a wide-eyed innocence that belied the intellect she knew he possessed. "Your aunt has gone to live with the Marquess of Andover?"

"Yes. Only recently." Emma twisted the strings of her reticule. The pistol she carried within the green bag rested heavily upon her thigh. Yet she did not care to go about without a weapon. Not while Hollington was on the loose. Although they had arrived back in London nearly a week ago without incident, she kept thinking they had not seen the last of Hollington.

Andover had insisted she take two footmen with her this afternoon. Since he had insisted both she and Marjorie move into Andover House for their own protection, she had found it necessary to bend the truth a

Debra Dier

little today. She had not precisely lied to Andover when she had told him she wanted to return to her home to take care of some personal matters. She simply had not told him the entire truth. After leaving Andover's two footmen sitting in her drawing room, she had slipped out and made her way to Knightly's. Still, the entire situation made her feel a jade. "Actually, I am also going to live at Andover House. You see, I am to marry Lord Andover tomorrow."

Knightly's lips parted without a word escaping. Stacks of manuscripts sat on either side of his large desk, making it seem as though he sat in a bowl peering out at her. The combination of his open mouth and the distorted eyes made her think of a goldfish. He pushed the glasses against the bridge of his nose. "I must wish you happy."

"Thank you." She needed every wish for happiness, considering the obstacle that still lay in her path. Through the closed door to her left, she could hear the sound of printing presses churning out the pages of books. The heavy scent of ink and damp paper lingered in the air, a scent that could still excite her.

Five years ago she had walked into this office for the first time, with nothing more than a manuscript and a wild hope that she might find someone who would publish it. John Knightly had seen merit in that first novel, enough to publish *The Country Miss*.

Knightly cleared his throat. "Does this mean we shall no longer have the privilege of publishing your novels? Or dare I hope that his lordship has given you leave to continue?"

"Actually, I cannot say for certain. Not yet."

"Not yet?"

"No." Emma twisted the strings of her reticule around her hand. "You see, I have not yet told Lord Andover that I dabble a bit in writing."

"Dabble a bit?" Knightly folded his hands atop the green pad on his cluttered desk. "Emma, I need not tell you how popular your novels have been. They are far and away the most profitable novels we publish. I would be lying if I said I would not miss them should you stop writing."

Emma's chest ached when she thought of abandoning her writing. "I would also miss writing."

Knightly drummed his fingertips on the desk pad. "I suppose you feel you must discuss the matter with Lord Andover? It might be entirely possible to continue writing without telling him."

"No. I could not." Emma knew it was only a matter of finding the right time to tell him the truth. "I feel honesty is important. Particularly in a marriage."

"Honesty. Yes, it is important. I know I expect it in my marriage." Knightly lifted his chin, his lips turning in slightly. "Has he read your latest novel?"

Emma bit her lower lip. "He has read enough of it to know Sylvester was modeled after him."

Knightly's eyes grew larger behind the thick round glasses. "And you still intend to tell him the truth?"

"I am waiting for the right moment. And then I am going to tell him."

"The right moment." Again, Knightly pressed his glasses against the bridge of his nose. "Yes, I should think you would want to wait for the right moment. Perhaps after a few months of wedded bliss. And in that time you could write another novel. Perhaps one with a dashing marquess as the hero."

Emma gave him a stern look tempered by a smile. "And you would have another novel to publish."

"Well yes." He laughed softly. "Really, Emma, if I were you, I would be very careful how I approach this matter."

"Yes. It must be handled with great delicacy." A

sudden thought stabbed her. "Is there any way Andover could discover the true identity of E. W. Austen?"

Knightly looked surprised. "Do you think he will try?"

"I cannot say for certain. I was simply wondering if he could, should he take a notion to try."

"There are only a few people who know the truth." Knightly folded his hands and rested his chin on his knuckles. "And those people know they must maintain the integrity of our authors. You can rest assured, Andover will not learn the true identity of E. W. Austen from anyone here."

Sebastian sat on the edge of the desk in his library, listening to the progress Roger Tunnicliffe had made since their last meeting. A former officer in Wellington's army, Mr. Tunnicliffe now made his living by handling discreet inquiries for members of the *ton*. If a husband wanted to learn the name of his wife's lover, Tunnicliffe was the man to hire. Should a woman like to know the true nature of the gentlemen who were paying her court, Tunnicliffe would learn everything about them, right down to the blend of snuff each gentleman used. He was of average height, slim, with light brown hair and blue eyes. No one looking at him would imagine he had once worked as a spy in Paris. That was one of his assets. The man could blend into a crowd.

"I have insinuated myself into Knightly's establishment." Roger sipped from his coffee cup before continuing. "From what I have been able to gather, only a handful of people truly know the identity of E. W. Austen. I believe I am close to gaining the confidence of at least one of them."

Sebastian rolled his porcelain mug between his

hands. "I have every confidence you shall succeed."

Roger smiled, his blue eyes alight with pride. "I suspect we shall have the information very soon."

Sebastian remained in his library after Tunnicliffe left. He looked at the dog lying near his feet. "Now that I am close to learning the identity of E. W. Austen, I should decide what to do with the man. Or the woman."

Ulysses lifted his head, attentive to Sebastian's voice. He tilted his head, regarding him in a way that made Sebastian wonder if the animal truly could understand his every word.

"I am not usually a vengeful man. Revenge often leads to some type of nastiness. Still, E. W. Austen deserves some sort of punishment for the crime he or she has committed."

Ulysses cocked his head toward the door leading to the terrace. Sebastian glanced in that direction, but saw nothing of interest. The terrace was empty. He could see no one in the gardens beyond. Still, the dog rose and trotted across the room as though something had caught his attention. Ulysses paused in the doorway, sniffed the air, then dashed across the terrace and disappeared into the gardens.

Sebastian supposed a rabbit had lured him out. He lifted his coffee cup. Steam bathed his nose and lips while a sweet creamy taste flooded his tongue. What was the proper retribution for the trouble E. W. Austen had caused him?

A sound intruded upon his thoughts—a soft click as the French door leading to the terrace closed. Sebastian turned and found Martin Hollington standing near the door.

"You look surprised to see me, Andover." Hollington strolled toward him, keeping the pistol he held pointed directly at Sebastian's chest. "Did you honestly believe I would allow you to walk away unscathed after the trouble you caused me?"

"You have an interesting perspective, Hollington." Sebastian toyed with the cup in his hands. "As I recall, you were the one who kidnapped me."

"Oh that." Hollington paused a few feet away from Sebastian. "But that was simply to pay you back for the way you turned Genevieve against me."

"My sister made her own choice, Hollington."

"You discouraged the match."

"I told you I would not support your cause with my sister." Sebastian held Hollington's gaze while he considered his next move. Emma would return soon. His mother, Marjorie, and her daughters were shopping. They would soon return. He could not allow Hollington to leave this room. "I did not tell Genevieve what she should do."

"I do not believe you, Andover." Hollington's eyes narrowed. "Genevieve would never have chosen Wainwright over me."

"But she did." Sebastian gripped his mug. "She told me there was a coldness in you, a look that entered your eyes at times that frightened her."

"You are lying." Hollington stiffened, the pistol bobbing in his hand. "You filled her with poison. You caused her to turn away from me. And now I intend to make certain you pay the price. From what I read in *The Gazette*, you are about to be married. Tomorrow is the happy day, is it not? You and Miss Emma Wakefield. Where is the little hellcat? I am eager to—"

Sebastian tossed the contents of his cup at Hollington. The coffee hit Hollington's face. He gasped and staggered back while Sebastian surged forward. Before he could reach his adversary, the sound of gunfire cracked against his ears. A bullet plowed into his side, searing his flesh. Sebastian staggered at the sudden flash of pain.

"Damn you!" Hollington shouted.

Sebastian clutched his hand against his side, his palm sliding against the damp warmth of blood. Out of the corner of his eye he caught sight of Hollington's raised fist. He lifted his arm in time to block Hollington's blow. Pain flared from the ragged slash across his ribs. He sucked in his breath, then slammed his fist into Hollington's jaw. Hollington stumbled backward straight into the arm of a chair. Sebastian staggered forward. Hollington scrambled to his feet and grabbed a poker from the brass holder on the fireplace. He raised it as if to smash Sebastian's head.

Sebastian lifted his hand to shield his head from the blow. Gunfire slashed the air. Hollington gasped, a look of surprise crossing his features. The poker fell from his hand. He staggered back, his gaze darting behind Sebastian.

"Bloody hell," Hollington whispered, before his knees crumpled beneath him. He hit the carpet, clutching his right shoulder, his eyes wide with shock.

Sebastian glanced over his shoulder. Emma stood a few feet away, a stunned expression on her features. A thin stream of bluish smoke coiled upward from the pistol she held. "Have I killed him?"

Sebastian glanced at Hollington, then back at Emma's stricken face. "No. You hit his shoulder."

Emma nodded, her eyes wide. After a moment she flinched as though someone had just poked a finger into her side. "Oh my goodness. You are hurt. And I am standing here like a complete dolt."

"It is a scratch." Sebastian staggered toward her, his strength ebbing with each step. "I think we should . . ."

"Sebastian!" Emma threw her arms around him.

"I am all right. Still, I think I would like to sit." Pinpoints of light danced in the darkness filling Sebastian's vision. He sat down hard on the carpet. "I seem to be a little light-headed."

Emma knelt on the floor beside him. "How badly are you hurt?"

"The bullet merely grazed my side." Sebastian looked at the man lying nearby. Hollington was holding his shoulder, whimpering like a puppy in pain. "What of you, Hollington? How badly are you injured?"

"Get me a surgeon!"

"Yes. I think we could both use a surgeon." Sebastian smiled at Emma, hoping to relieve some of the tension he saw in her face. "Do be an angel and send someone for a surgeon."

"Yes. Of course." Emma fluttered her hand over the hand he held against his side. "Is there anything I should do before I fetch a footman?"

Ulysses leapt at the terrace door, barking as though he had just treed a fox. Sebastian glanced toward the door. "You might let Ulysses in."

Emma hurried across the room and opened the door. The large dog charged to Sebastian, then commenced growling at the man lying beside his master.

"It is too late, boy. You cannot play the hero this time. My lady has managed to save me."

Ulysses plopped down beside Sebastian and nuzzled his cheek. His nose was cold and wet, his tongue warm against his skin, and his breath was soaked with the scent of kippers from breakfast. Still, Sebastian appreciated the affection behind the gesture.

"It is all right." Sebastian rubbed the dog's neck. "I am fine."

"I will be right back, as soon as I send someone for a surgeon." Emma rushed out of the room, pale green muslin floating around her.

When Emma had gone, Sebastian turned to Hollington. After glancing at Hollington's wound, he sat beside his adversary. "I am afraid you are going to survive, Hollington."

"That bitch tried to murder me."

Sebastian smiled. "You may wish she had succeeded when you hear what I intend to do with you."

Tears leaked from the corners of Hollington's eyes. Still, he glared at Sebastian. "What do you think you can do with me, Andover? Do you imagine to set me before a magistrate? If you do, I shall make certain everyone hears of how I plowed your future wife."

Anger flared within Sebastian, as intense as the pain throbbing in his side. Only years of discipline allowed him to keep his expression composed, his voice low. "If you had harmed her in any way, there would be no question as to what I would do with you, Hollington. You would soon be standing before your maker, explaining the choices you have made in your life."

Hollington's slim nostrils flared. "I may not have touched her, Andover, but everyone would believe I had."

"Where you are going, it will not matter what you decide to say or do." He leaned toward Hollington and allowed his lips to curve into a smile. "When you learn what I have in mind for you, you may regret the fact that my lady merely wounded you."

Emma sat in a chair beside Sebastian's bed, watching him sip the chocolate she had brought for him. Since he had refused to take the laudanum the surgeon had left, she hoped the chocolate would help soothe him. It usually calmed her tattered nerves at the end of a day. Yet tonight all the chocolate in London would not ease the tension inside her. "Hollington did this all for revenge?"

"He imagined I was the reason my sister had refused his offer of marriage."

"Revenge. It is a useless emotion." Emma sipped her chocolate. Yet the sweet creamy liquid might have been barley water for all she noticed. The weight of her crime against her future husband pressed upon her, like the fine white marble of the stone that might as well grace her grave, should he turn away from her. "You certainly are above taking revenge on someone who has injured your pride. Especially if it was unintentional. Only a weak man lashes out at someone for making a mistake."

Sebastian lifted his brows, a measure of surprise entering his dark gaze. "Are you thinking I was too harsh on Hollington?"

"No. That man deserves to be hung up by his thumbs for what he no doubt did with the women he acquired from Radbyrne." Emma could not prevent a shudder from gripping her when she thought of how close she had come to becoming one of his victims. "I only hope they treat him with the kindness he deserves in New South Wales."

"I am acquainted with the man who will be deciding his punishment. After he reads my letter, I am sure Hollington will get everything he deserves." He turned and gripped one of the pillows piled up behind him.

Emma quickly moved to adjust the pillow for him, her fingers sliding upon the smooth white silk still warm from his skin. "Is that better?"

"Yes." He winked at her. "My darling Emma, you need not treat me as though I were an invalid. It is merely a scratch. If it had not been for Mama's absolute horror at the thought, I would have joined you all for dinner in the dining room, instead of eating in my bed like some palsied old man."

"Jacqueline was right in insisting you rest tonight." Emma smoothed her hand through his hair, the thick ebony strands sliding like satin upon her skin. "If you are not careful you will become terribly ill."

He took her hand and pressed his lips against the sensitive skin at the inside of her wrist. The soft brush of his warm lips whispered through her, arousing her need for him. The sigh rising up within her escaped before she even knew it was there. "It seems an eternity since I last held you in my arms."

It had been an eternity since she had felt the thrill of lying in his arms. After she'd accepted his proposal, Emma had asked Sebastian to bow to propriety. She did not wish to risk the chance of having her aunt or his mother or one of her young cousins see him creeping in or out of her bedchamber. She slipped her hand out of his grasp. "You might as well get those thoughts out of your head."

He gave her an innocent look. "What thoughts, my darling?"

"You can end this innocent act of yours. It does not suit you. You are far too worldly looking to accomplish it. You know perfectly well what I mean." She sat back in her chair, well aware of the power he wielded over her. She never thought very clearly when he was near. When he touched her, she abandoned all hope of coherent thought. "I certainly do not intend to take any risks with your health, even if I were willing to take the chance of someone coming in to see how you are faring. What a sight that would be."

He ran his fingertips over her knee. "It is but a scratch. And if we lock the door, no one will come in."

"I will not explain a locked door to my aunt." She slapped his hand. "You need rest. You are certainly not in any condition to be heaving about on top of me."

"And here I thought you rather enjoyed the way I heaved about on top of you."

"That is not fair." She narrowed her eyes, giving him a stern look, a difficult task considering the way her blood was racing through her veins. "You know very well how much I enjoy being with you in that way. But I do not intend to be the death of you. I prefer to forgo a moment's pleasure for the possibility of having you around for the next forty years."

"But, my love, I am . . ." He grimaced when he reached for her.

"There, you see." She stood and backed away from the bed before he could talk her into anything. "I shall not allow you to have your wicked way, Sebastian. Not tonight. You need rest."

"All right." He leaned back against the pillows. "But if you imagine I shall allow this scratch to ruin tomorrow night, you are mistaken. I have no intention of missing my wedding night."

Tomorrow was their wedding day. He deserved to know the truth about her before they spoke the vows. Of course, if he knew the truth, he might become so angry he would never speak his vows. He could turn away from her, and she would never have a chance to prove to him how very much she loved him.

"Is something wrong, sweetheart?"

Emma looked into his eyes, those beautiful dark eyes. They held such warmth, such affection. What would she see after she told him the truth. "There is something I need to tell you."

Chapter Twenty-three

"My head is still in a whirl." Marjorie smoothed her hand over the ears of a topiary rabbit growing beside a bench in Andover's garden, the privet bush swaying with her movement. "My little Emma, the Marchioness of Andover. It is quite a dream come true."

Emma sat beside her aunt, staring at the wide stone terrace that stretched along the back of the huge mansion. This afternoon she had been married by special license to Sebastian George Jean Luc St. Clair, Marquess of Andover, Earl of Sheffield, Baron of Staplehurst. Because of Charlotte's absence, it had been a small wedding, with only family and a few friends attending the service and the wedding breakfast that followed. Still, Emma had wandered through the day as if in a dream. She squeezed her hands tightly in her lap. "If things were different, it would be a fairy tale come true."

"I know, dear. I keep thinking of her too." Marjorie

patted Emma's hands. "I am certain Charlotte would want you to enjoy this day, to treasure the memories. I only wish she were here to share your happiness."

Emma looked down at her tightly clenched hands, appalled at her own selfishness. Her agitation had little to do with Charlotte and much to do with her own foolishness. "Andover will find her. If anyone can, he can."

"I know he will. I have faith in him."

"He is so very capable. And extremely brave. I have never known anyone who is more honorable than Andover."

"And generous. The girls are astonished by this house. To think Andover wishes for us all to live here, as part of his family. It is an answer to my prayers." Marjorie dabbed at her eyes with a lace-trimmed handkerchief. "I knew he was a kind man when I first met him."

"He is the most remarkable man I have ever met." Emma's chest tightened with equal measures of love and guilt. "He is a hero in every sense of the word. And when I think of what I have done to him, I want to scream."

Marjorie patted her hand. "I am certain he has quite forgiven you for tossing him into the cellar."

"Yes. He has forgiven me for that particular piece of mischief." Lily of the valley grew in curving beds at the base of each topiary figure, making the menagerie seem to rise from a bed a snow. The white bells of the flowers nodded in the breeze that swept across the garden. The sweet perfume of the lilies brushed Emma's face, while the chill in the air penetrated her blood. She drew her white cashmere shawl close around her shoulders. Still, she could not warm the dread sitting like ice in the pit of her stomach. "It is a far greater crime that concerns me."

"What is it, dear?" Marjorie grasped her own shawl close beneath her neck. "What is troubling you so?"

Emma glanced around, making certain there was no one near to hear the truth. The topiary bushes in this part of the garden grew no higher than five feet tall. Beyond the sculpted green figures of rabbits and turtles and other creatures stretched perennial beds. Aside from a few people standing on the terrace, still enjoying Andover's hospitality, no one was in sight. Nonetheless, she leaned toward Marjorie and whispered, "I have not told him the truth about me."

Marjorie's eyes grew wide. "Do you mean to say you never told him about the books?"

Emma shook her head. "I was going to tell him last night. But then my courage deserted me. And now he shall think I kept it from him because I was afraid he would not marry me, which is true. I was afraid if I told him the truth, he would become so angry he would not listen to my explanation."

"Now dear, I am certain you are painting the picture a bit too black."

"He despises E. W. Austen. With good reason. *The Wicked Duke* has caused him all manner of discomfort. Radbyrne actually left that button in Charlotte's chamber because of the stir the book had caused. I am afraid Andover will despise me when I tell him I am responsible for his misery."

"Oh dear." Marjorie fiddled with the fringe of her shawl. "Yes, I can see how he might be dreadfully unhappy about discovering he has married E. W. Austen."

Emma glared at her aunt. "You are supposed to make me feel better about this."

"Yes. Of course." Marjorie studied the fringe of her shawl. "Now let me see. He loves you very much. That is obvious when he looks at you."

Emma's chest constricted when she thought of how much she had to lose. Sebastian had given her his heart. She had no doubt he truly did care for her, deeply. "One of the things he admires about me is my honesty. What will he say when he learns I have betrayed him?"

"Oh dear. It is a bit of a tangle. I suppose he would want all of us to leave the house, should he decide to seek an annulment."

Emma groaned. "If you are trying to make me feel better, you are not succeeding."

Marjorie pursed her lips. "I doubt he would want the scandal of an annulment. And they are rather difficult to obtain. Unless, of course, he can prove that you are insane, and with all that has been happening, he might. Of course he would probably still turn us out of his house. Unless he took pity upon us, which he might."

"Aunt Marjorie, I am not insane."

"Of course not. Not really. I know that. And he could not prove you were insane. At least I do not believe he could. You must rest easy, I doubt he would seek an annulment. And of course a divorce is terribly scandalous. I am certain he would merely exile you to the country." Marjorie's lips curved into what Emma suspected was meant to be an encouraging smile. Unfortunately she looked as though she were having a sudden spasm of stomach cramps. "Which means we would have a very nice place to stay."

Emma twisted her shawl beneath her neck. "There must be a way to make him see how very sorry I am about what happened. I need to find the proper time to tell him the truth."

"Are you so very certain it is wise to tell him at all?"

"Not tell him?" The idea appealed to the coward lurking deep within her. Still, she had enough integrity to banish that seductive thought. "It would not be right of me. He deserves to know the truth. I simply need to find the proper time."

"I do not suppose you could wait until after both Lydia and Mary have had at least one Season. It would be better, of course, if you waited until they were both married."

"Aunt Marjorie, Lydia is fifteen."

Marjorie shrugged. "Would a few years truly signify?"

"Yes. I am afraid they would." As much as Emma would like to avoid the truth, she could not. "I have to tell him. And I will. When the time is right."

"You certainly did not waste any time getting her to a church." Jourdan sat on the arm of a chair in Sebastian's library. He grinned at his cousin over the rim of his champagne glass. "Were you afraid someone might steal her away from you?"

"They spent a night alone together at an inn. The girl has been staying here for the past week." With the tip of his shoe, Montgomery poked at the footstool in front of his chair, a glint of mischief lighting his blue eyes. "My guess is, he wanted to make certain the babe was born within a reasonable time of the wedding."

"I actually did all of London a favor. Emma is far too dangerous running about on her own. At least now I shall have some idea of what lunacy she is about to try." Sebastian shifted on the hard cushion of his chair and turned his attention from his friends to the ladies sitting in the garden. Emma sat on a stone bench in the topiary garden with her aunt. He sipped his champagne, barely noticing the sparkling sensation upon his tongue. Even from a distance he could see how unhappy his new bride looked. She looked as though she had just been sentenced to hang. It was hardly an expression he expected on the woman he had married.

Ulysses poked his hand with his cold nose. He tilted his head and regarded Sebastian, as though to ask what was troubling him. Sebastian smoothed his hand over the dog's head and whispered, "It is all right."

"Pity we do not have an idea of what your nephew will try next. He actually sold you to Hollington." Montgomery shook his head, as though he still found it hard to believe. "At least Hollington will receive justice."

"I watched his ship set sail this morning." Sebastian sipped his wine. "From what I understand they are fairly harsh on men such as Hollington in New South Wales."

Montgomery held his glass up to the sunlight streaming through the windows. "I hate to imagine what Radbyrne may plan next. He has to be stopped before he causes any more trouble."

"How do we find him?" Jourdan asked.

"He needs funds. I have taken steps to control them." Sebastian twisted the stem of his glass between his fingers. Last night Emma had confessed her love for him. This morning she had said those precious words again. He had not realized how important her affection for him could be until she had given it. Yet there was something bothering her. He had sensed it last night. And he could see it this afternoon while she sat with her aunt. The sadness he saw on Emma's face must come from something other than the fact she was his wife, he assured himself. Emma and Marjorie were no doubt speaking of Charlotte. "I will find Radbyrne. And when I do, I will make him regret the day he was born."

"He knows who Gaetan truly is," Jourdan said. "We must find a way to convince him to tell us how to find this monster."

"I suspect it will not take a great deal of effort." Sebastian smiled at the thought of getting his hands on Radbyrne. "My nephew does not possess a strong will. And as I recall, he has a rather weak jaw. I will soon have the true identity of Gaetan as well as the whereabouts of Miss Usherwood."

"I have no doubt he will betray his partner." Montgomery drained his glass. "All we need do is find him."

"Something Woolgrove said keeps bothering me." Sebastian rubbed his fingertip along a beveled edge in the cut crystal of his glass. "He said Gaetan was slumbering directly beneath my nose. Apparently I am well acquainted with the blackguard."

"Woolgrove said you knew Gaetan?" Montgomery twisted his glass in the sunlight. "Do you have any idea who he might be?"

"I have given it a great deal of thought." Sebastian sipped his champagne. "What would push someone into a business as vile as Gaetan's?"

"Money. And perhaps a natural affinity for such debauchery," Jourdan said. "If someone found himself in debt, a business such as Gaetan's would soon fill his pockets."

"Money. Debauchery." Sebastian rubbed the thick fur behind Ulysses's ear. "Aside from Radbyrne, I cannot think of anyone close to me who might be involved in such a vile business. At least no one who is still alive."

"Here you all are." Dora swept in from the terrace through the open French door. She strolled to Sebastian's chair and smiled down at him. "Come, dear. You still have guests who wish to visit with you. And it is not at all fair to deprive the ladies of the company of such handsome men." She looked from Jourdan to Montgomery. "Now off with you."

Both Jourdan and Montgomery obeyed her command. They crossed the room and left by the door leading to the hall, while Dora remained where she stood. She took his arm when Sebastian rose. When they were alone she looked up at him, a troubled expression on her face. "How are you feeling, dear? Is the wound troubling you?"

"Aside from an occasional twinge, I scarcely notice it. Fortunately it was merely a scratch."

"Thank goodness." Dora patted his arm, then glanced down at Ulysses, who had plopped a paw on Sebastian's leg. "You know, dear, if you keep taking in strays, you will have to turn one of your homes over to them."

Sebastian patted the dog's head. "I cannot seem to resist."

"That is because you have a kind heart." She looked up at him, a serious expression crossing her features. "First I want to say how very pleased and proud I am of you. You have always been as dear to me as one of my own sons. I am delighted to see you so happy with your bride."

"Thank you." He lifted her hand and kissed the back of her fingers. "I know you have succeeded in helping to make her feel welcome."

"Emma is a treasure. And since we are speaking of weddings, I have to admit I have made no progress at all with your friend the Earl of Worth."

Sebastian laughed softly. "I would set your sights on another target."

"Yes." Dora sighed, as though she were weary. "I suppose it is for the best. From what I have learned of him, he likes tarts as well as he enjoys deep play. I would not want Arabella to be shackled to a man who would squander her inheritance."

Sebastian stared at his aunt a moment. "That is

strange, I have never known Worth to sink into debt."

Dora waved her hand to dismiss his words. "At times the ones closest to a man are the very last to know of his weaknesses. I speak from experience."

Sebastian did not like to place Montgomery Trent in the same category as his worthless uncle. "I have to believe you have been listening to the wrong people when it comes to Worth. Rumors are easily passed around London. Most have no relation to reality. I have learned that from experience."

Dora shrugged, her plump shoulders lifting the bright yellow satin of her gown. "Perhaps. At any rate, I have decided the man will not do for my Arabella."

"I think you are right on that score." Sebastian glanced out the window to where Emma still sat with Marjorie. Although he did not care to interrupt their tête-à-tête, he was eager for some time alone with his wife.

"I did not mean to eavesdrop, but you and the other gentlemen were deep in conversation when I came looking for you. And I could not help hearing you speak about Bernard. What will you do when you find him?"

Sebastian dragged his gaze from Emma. When he met his aunt's gaze, he saw how troubled she was. "After I find out what he did with Miss Usherwood, I will make certain he and his partner are never able to harm anyone again."

"Do you know who this Gaetan is?"

"Not yet." Sebastian smiled when he thought of how much he would enjoy getting his hands on his nephew. "But I am certain my nephew will be only too glad to tell me."

Dora considered this a moment. "Yes, I suspect he will. Bernard would hardly remain loyal if it meant any discomfort on his part. And I would suppose you intend to make him uncomfortable should you find him."

"I will find him."

"Yes. He is not wise enough to hide for long." Dora stared at a square of sunlight spilling through the windows near her feet. "He has caused a great deal of trouble for so many people. Still, one does not like to have such matters thrown into the light. It would be better to deal with him inside the family."

"His crimes deserve more than a slap on the wrist."

"Yes. He certainly deserves a great deal more." Dora patted his arm. "I am certain you can think of adequate punishment for him, without plunging the family into another scandal."

Sebastian thought of his mother and sisters and their families, as well as his bride and her family. He knew from experience how much pain could be caused when the *ton* grabbed hold of a particularly nasty rumor. He was not eager to expose his family once again to that vicious pack of wolves. "Perhaps you are right. Perhaps it would be best to deal with Radbyrne inside the family."

Dora smiled up at him. "I know you shall do what is right."

It was the most deliciously wicked looking negligee she had ever seen. Of course, it was the first silk negligee she had ever seen. It had been waiting for her when she returned to her room this evening, lying on the counterpane of her bed beside a heavy white silk dressing gown and a note from Jacqueline.

I knew it would take a special young woman to kindle a fire in my son. Thank you for saving Sebastian from his ennui.

Emma glanced at her reflection in the mirror above her dressing table. The woman staring back at her

from the silvered glass looked as though she were
standing in the midst of a filmy white cloud. Embroidered lace edged the round neckline that dipped just
below the hollow of her neck. A pink satin ribbon
wound through delicate eyelet, cinching the material
just below her breasts. She swayed back forth, enjoying
the sensual slide of silk upon her belly, her legs. Her
husband was waiting for her in his bedchamber. The
mere thought of what would pass between them tonight kindled an excitement that tingled through her.
If only she did not have the burden of the truth hanging over her head, tonight would be the most glorious
night of her life.

"Coward," she whispered.

There was nothing else to be said for her. She was
a coward. A fraud. A miserable excuse for a human
being. She drew a brush through her unbound hair.
Sebastian was waiting for her in the adjoining chamber. Waiting for his wife. A woman he imagined was
honest and courageous and . . . what would he say
when she told him the truth?

She pulled on the heavy silk dressing gown, tied the
sash, and prepared to face her fate. It might not be
fair, but she intended to use every possible feminine
wile to distract him from the anger that would come
with the truth.

Although the wall sconces had not been lit in the
large withdrawing room connecting her chamber with
Sebastian's, light from his chamber spilled into the
room, illuminating her path. When she reached the
door to his chamber, she paused. Sebastian was sitting
on the edge of his large four-poster bed, rubbing his
hand gingerly over his side. Although he wore a dressing gown, she knew what lay beneath that heavy black
silk—a white linen bandage cinched around a nasty
gash in his side. For a moment he did not notice her

standing there, and in that space of time the grimace that crossed his features betrayed the discomfort caused by the wound, a discomfort he had hidden throughout the day. The look of pain vanished when he saw her.

He smiled, the warmth of his affection for her kindling flame deep in his eyes. He stood when she entered the room. "I was beginning to wonder if you had turned up shy, my darling."

"And I am beginning to think this might be a poor idea."

"A poor idea?" He lifted his brows. "This is not what I had hoped to hear from my bride on our wedding night. It is a bit late for second thoughts."

"You know very well what I mean. The only second thoughts I am having are those concerning your well-being." She crossed the distance between them and took his arm. "Sit."

He stroked the back of his fingers over her cheek. "Emma, my darling, I assure you, I am well enough."

She tried to ignore the heat swirling through her at his touch. "Sit."

He obeyed, sitting upon the edge of the bed. The covers had been pulled down, revealing white silk sheets. Although it had only been a week since the night they had spent together at the Green Turtle Inn, it seemed an eternity since he had last held her in his arms. "You really should rest," she said, resisting his lure. "You will only tear open your wound if you exert yourself."

"Perhaps you are right."

The glint of mischief in his eyes certainly did not harmonize with his words. "Of course I am right."

"Perhaps I should just lie here and allow you to exert yourself." He leaned back upon the pillows.

His words teased her. The look in his eyes tempted her. "It is too dangerous."

"You can be in complete control, my love." Although he wore a dressing gown, the soft black silk could not conceal the rising proof of his desire for her.

The images rising in her mind teased her. Heat simmered low in her nether region, where a pulse had come to life, beating with her need for this man. "We should not."

"Emma, my love, I could die for wanting you." Sebastian ran his fingertip down her arm. "Come to me, Emma."

Need pounded through her, ambushing her every attempt to resist him. "The wound?"

"Does not trouble me. Believe me my love. I would not jeopardize my chances of living a very long life with you." The warmth of his smile conspired with the heat flaring inside her.

"I would never forgive myself should I harm you in any way."

"Undress for me, Emma."

She could not resist him and the need pounding through her. As if she were under a spell, she obeyed his soft command. She untied the sash of her dressing gown and shrugged out of the garment, the heavy silk falling with a sigh of surrender around her ankles. His hand twitched upon his thigh.

Sebastian's eyes narrowed, like a tiger eyeing his prey. He lowered his eyes, his gaze slowly sweeping down the length of her. Although he did not touch her, heat shimmered across her, as though he stroked her bare skin with his hands. "I do not believe I have ever seen anything more beautiful."

"It feels like heaven." Emma lifted the full skirt of the gown and swished the silk back and forth. "It is a present from your mama."

"The negligee is nice." He met her gaze, and the hunger in his eyes stole the breath from her lungs. "But I am speaking of the beauty who is wearing it."

The look in his eyes spoke of need and more; it betrayed a desire for her that rose above the primitive instincts which drew man to woman. The look in his eyes made her feel as though she were not merely beautiful. The way he looked at her made her feel as though she were a siren of legend, so compelling he had no choice but to want her.

He offered her his hand. "Come to me, Emma."

Chapter Twenty-four

"I have heard tales of how a being could be enslaved by passion." Emma's voice washed over Sebastian, a silken caress upon senses made acute with the need for her. "Yet I never truly realized how potent it could be. Until I met you."

She knelt on the bed beside him. The soft mattress dipped beneath her weight. His body shifted with the movement, drawing him toward her. Her lips parted on a soft sigh at the touch of his hip upon her thigh. Deep within, need tightened upon his vitals, like a bow being drawn back by the hand of an archer. "Passion," he replied. "A desire so powerful it devours every rational thought. I never believed I could feel such things until I met you, my beautiful termagant."

"I shall make you pay for calling me such names," she said, smiling in a way that made him wonder what she meant to do with him.

She lifted the sash of his dressing gown and slipped

one end over the other, unfastening the robe. Slowly she peeled it open, dragging the cool silk over his heated flesh, exposing him fully to her gaze. If he had wanted to hide his need from her, he could not. Not when his member rose in silent adoration, heeding her siren's call. He drew his fingertip over her nipple. The little bud was hard as a pebble beneath the warm silk of her nightgown. Her lips parted on a soft sigh. "Touch me, Emma."

"With pleasure, my lord." She leaned forward. The dark silk of her hair spilled over his skin in a slow sinuous slide. The silk of her negligee teased him. She ran her fingertips down his chest, lightly grazing his nipples above the white linen cinched around his wound. "When I think of how close I came to losing you, I . . ." She closed her eyes. "I cannot imagine my life without you."

"You need not worry." He smoothed his fingers over her cheek. "I plan to stay around for a long time."

"No matter what happens, you must know I love you more than anything in this world." She looked at him. "You mean everything to me."

The desperation in her eyes tugged at his heart. "We are together, and nothing on earth will tear us apart."

"Nothing on earth." She lowered her lips to his and kissed him, as though she took her very sustenance from him.

Sebastian abandoned himself to the desire pounding through him with each beat of his heart. He caressed her, rubbing his hands over the warm silk veiling her skin, stroking her back, her sides, cupping her breasts, sliding his thumbs over the taut nipples. He drank the soft sighs from her lips, desire licking at his loins like hungry flames. When he started to turn with her in his arms, she pulled back.

"And what have you in mind, my lord?"

Sebastian brushed his lips against her chin. "I thought that was obvious, my darling."

"And I thought we agreed you were not to take any chances with your health." She pressed her hands against his shoulders and pushed him down onto the pillows. "Tonight I shall do the heaving about, and you will lie there."

Blood pumped fast and hot, thumping like a fist in his loins. "Do with me as you wish, my love."

She grinned in a manner that made him think of a cat that has just tipped over a pitcher of cream. "You must tell me if I hurt you."

"You must not worry. You could never harm me." He caught a flicker of uneasiness on her features, a look that made him wonder what demon haunted her. Yet before he could question her, she opened her mouth over his nipple and drew the tiny nub inside. All thought fled with the sensation stabbing through him.

After torturing the other nipple, she slid down his body, kissing him, flicking her tongue against his skin, as though she were a hungry flame and he a piece of kindling, igniting beneath her touch. The warm silk of her negligee stroked his skin, teasing him with the femininity hidden beneath. He had made love to more women than he cared to remember at this moment in time. Yet never had he experienced anything more exciting than this—the innocent exploration of a woman in love.

No woman had ever given him pleasure in this manner before Emma. He had always assumed he knew the meaning of desire. Yet now, he realized he had underestimated the power of desire in the same manner he had dismissed the true potency of passion. Desire was not merely an emotion. It was a force of nature, akin to a hurricane. It swept over you, lifted you, dragged you away from reason and logic.

"I love you, Sebastian," she whispered, as she straddled his hips.

The exotic brush of damp femininity teased the tip
of his arousal. It took all his will to keep from surging
upward. Yet he remained still beneath her, allowing
her to control this joining. "And I love you, my beautiful, beguiling Pandora."

Slowly she sank upon him, taking him into the
warm haven of her body. "I shall always love you."

All the lectures his mother had given him about love
and passion and destiny spun in his head. He had
thought himself above the touch of true affection. Yet
now he knew the arrogance of his beliefs. He tugged
open the ribbon that cinched her negligee beneath her
breasts. "I want your skin against mine, Emma."

"I want that too," she whispered.

Sebastian watched, enchanted by his beautiful sor-
ceress, while Emma drew the negligee over her head
and dropped it on the floor by the bed. She leaned
toward him, brushing her bare breasts against his
chest. A soft sigh escaped her lips, mingling with the
deep primitive groan rising from his throat. Pain
throbbed from the wound in his side, a dull ache easily
ignored in the pleasure pumping through him.

He slipped his arms around her and drew her upward until he could nuzzle his face against the lush
warmth of her breasts. The delicate scent of roses after
rain spilled through his senses. Soft sobs of pleasure
spilled from her lips. She was his revelation. Without
her he might have wandered his entire life without
truly knowing the pleasure that could be found between a man and a woman. He licked the valley between her breasts, then slid his tongue upward along
one soft slope until he could take the pink tip into his
mouth. He suckled her while she arched her hips

gainst him, riding him, controlling him as no woman ver had done in his life.

The first delicate contractions of feminine release ugged on his flesh, nearly sending him over the edge. 'et he resisted the pull, wanting something more than is own pleasure. Emma grasped his shoulders. She ode him, arching her hips, until the pleasure crested nside her, until the tiny spasms expanded, grasping is member, dragging him with her. A low growl huddered from his chest, dark and primal, joining the weet sob slipping from Emma's lips, as they plunged ogether into that realm of pleasure.

Emma sagged against him. She slipped her arms beneath his neck and pressed her lips to the hollow below his ear. The innocent fragrance of roses after rain ningled with the lush scent of their lovemaking, swirling through his senses. He tightened his arms around er, holding her close against his heart. He realized ow he had been a fool ever to have attempted to resist the tug of destiny.

"Are you all right?" she asked, her lips moving gainst his neck.

Laughter welled up inside him. "Better than I have een in a very long time."

"I would never knowingly do anything to harm ou." Emma pulled back and looked down at him, her yes troubled. "Remember that and know it for the ruth."

Sebastian smoothed the hair back from her cheek nd dropped the heavy mass over her shoulder. Candlelight flickered upon the tears in her eyes. "What is , love?"

For a long moment she said nothing, and in that nterlude he held his breath, waiting for a blow he ould sense coming. Finally she shook her head.

"Nothing is wrong. It is just . . . the way I feel for you is overwhelming."

He drew his fingertip over the plump curve of her lower lip, her breath warm upon his skin. "Are you certain that is all?"

She rested her head on his shoulder, hiding the expression in her eyes. "Nothing can be wrong as long as I am in your arms."

Sebastian held her close. Still, he could not shake the anxiety twisting in the pit of his stomach. Although she was his wife, he still had an odd prickly feeling that he could lose her in some way. He supposed it was from knowing Radbyrne was still out there, ready to strike again.

Perhaps in time, when all the trouble had been put to rest, when his nephew had been dealt with and Charlotte found, the fear of losing Emma would disappear. Until then, he intended to make certain nothing threatened the joy he had found with his beautiful wife.

As Bernard Radbyrne entered the drawing room of Gaetan's, he was surrounded by a heady blend of opium and spicy perfume. The fragrance lingered like a specter, taunting him with memories of past glory. Two wall sconces burned in the large room, casting flickering shadows over the plush burgundy silk velvet covering the sofas and chairs, empty now except for the shadowy figure of his partner.

"It has a ghostlike quality about it, does it not?" Gaetan sat on a large gilt-trimmed chair near the lifeless hearth, looking like royalty after the fall. "One can almost hear the voices, see the figures of all those girls drifting by in the shadows."

The soft quality of his partner's voice scraped along Radbyrne's spine. "I shall rebuild."

"It is ended."

"Perhaps it has ended here, but there are men will-
g to pay for this kind of entertainment everywhere.
thought I might go to New York," Radbyrne said.

"I had hoped you might realize the true evil of this
usiness. And yet you wish to continue to spread your
oison."

"Such noble sentiments. I did not see you refuse the
oney this place brought you."

"At the time I felt I had no choice." Gaetan looked
own at the floor. "I detest my own weakness. After
discovered the truth, I never should have allowed
is to continue."

"You could not stop me. I allowed you to remain
y partner to prevent the trouble you might cause.
ou might like to think you had some control over me,
ut you never did." Radbyrne turned slowly, his arms
ide. "This was my empire. The old fool might have
arted this place but he had no true concept of how
owerful we could be. I am the one who brought Gae-
n's to greatness. And I shall rule again."

"I fear you are a little mad, Bernard."

"I think you are a fool."

"Where is Charlotte Usherwood?"

Bernard shrugged. "I sold her to a Scotsman named
acLeod. He left town soon after. And I did not
other to ask where he was taking her."

Gaetan was quiet a long moment. "Andover will not
low you to continue."

"Andover will not be alive much longer. I made a
istake in thinking Hollington could dispatch my un-
e." Radbyrne pulled a pistol from his pocket. "Now
see I must do it myself."

"Do put that away."

Radbyrne glanced down at the pistol, then slipped
back into his pocket. "There is nothing you can say

325

to make me change my mind. I will dispense with him."

"It is a pity you did not attend the wedding today. It was a small affair, just family and a few of their closest friends. One could not expect a grand celebration while the bride's family is so deeply troubled. Because of you."

"I simply took a penniless girl and put her to good use." Radbyrne sat on the arm of a chair across from Gaetan. "I would say it was quite clever of me."

"And now you plan to murder your uncle."

Radbyrne curled his hand into a fist on his thigh. "I would not expect you to understand, considering how fond of him you are."

"I had hoped you might feel some remorse, some small twinge of guilt, a stirring of conscience. Now I see you are beyond hope of redemption." Gaetan shifted in the shadows. Light from the wall sconce glittered on the barrel of a pistol pointed directly at Radbyrne's chest. "I regret what must be done."

"Do you think to frighten me with that?"

"I think I shall end your reign with this."

"You do not frighten me. You have not the stomach for it." Radbyrne laughed, the sound echoing oddly in the stillness of the empty house. "If you think I shall fall to my knees and beg forgiveness, you are mistaken."

"I think you will die. May God have mercy on your soul."

Radbyrne reached into his pocket. He pulled out his own pistol just as the crack of gunfire shattered the stillness of the evening. The sound struck his ears on a quick heartbeat before the bullet slammed into his chest. The impact knocked him back, off the arm of the chair. Pain splintered through him, sucking the air from his lungs. A shadow drifted into his line of sight

"I do regret this, Bernard. But you left me no choice."

Bernard dragged air past his tight throat. "I shall kill you for this," he said, reaching for the pistol that had fallen from his hand.

"No, Bernard, you will not." Gaetan stepped on his hand.

Tears of pain clouded his sight. Yet Radbyrne could see Gaetan lift the pistol from the carpet.

"I can see you are in a great deal of pain." Gaetan pointed the pistol at Radbyrne's head. A loud click cracked the air, the sound of the pistol being cocked. "This should end it."

"No!"

"I am sorry," Gaetan whispered.

It was the last sound Radbyrne heard.

Chapter Twenty-five

The next morning Sebastian sat in his library with Felix Dunbarton of Bow Street, listening in detail to the manner in which his nephew had been found this morning. Short and stout, with shaggy dark hair, Felix reminded him of a small bear. He spoke with a slow deliberation that made Sebastian want to reach down into the man's throat and drag the words from him. Instead he pressed his fingertips together and kept his impatience under close rein. The man might be slow, but he was thorough. When he was done with his recitation, Sebastian had a clear image of Radbyrne lying upon the drawing room floor of Gaetan's.

"You say he was shot twice."

"Yes, my lord." Felix flipped open a small brown notebook. "One time in the chest. Another straight between the eyes. I am thinkin' 'twere the last shot that done him in. Being as the first shot looked to have just hit a lung, and a fellow can survive with a shot to the lung. If he is treated well enough and soon enough. We found one pistol beside him. The other was gone. No doubt taken by the one who put the shots into yer nephew. And would you be havin' any idea who might have wanted to see yer nephew dead?"

Sebastian had thought of killing his nephew several times over the past few days. Since he had not pulled the trigger, he surmised the murderer was one of his other enemies. A man like Radbyrne had many. "I am afraid I do not have an answer for you. I was not familiar with my nephew's companions."

Felix tapped the notebook against his chin. "These days the lads of his age are gettin' involved in all manner of mischief. Opium, cards, and who can say what else. It is hard to be sayin' what quarrel came to pass. From what I have been able to gather, the place he was found was once a gaming hall."

Sebastian saw no reason to further enlighten the man. His own involvement in Gaetan's demise was best left unknown. "I would like to see the note you received telling you where to find the body."

"I have it right 'ere." Felix rummaged in the pocket of his wrinkled brown coat a moment before he withdrew a scrap of parchment. "It is fancy paper. If you are thinkin' you might tell the writin', 'twould be hard. The words are all printed."

Someone had left a note similar to this one under Sebastian's front door sometime during the night. The paper and manner of lettering were the same. The messages varied. Instead of informing Bow Street of the whereabouts of the body of Bernard Radbyrne, the note he had received had told of Charlotte Usherwood's fate. That note had been signed *G*. Although this note had no signature, there was no doubt they had been penned by the same hand. Gaetan had murdered Radbyrne.

After Dunbarton left, Sebastian joined Emma and his mother in the blue drawing room. Both ladies rose when he entered the room.

Jacqueline pressed her hand to the base of her neck. "Something dreadful has happened."

Sebastian slipped his arm around his mother's slender shoulders. "Bernard was found murdered this morning."

Jacqueline lifted her eyes to heaven, her lips moving in a silent prayer. When she met Sebastian's gaze, there was a trace of tears in her dark eyes. "I can only feel for my daughter. For the son she bore was not worth the pain he has caused. I must go to her."

Sebastian squeezed her arm. "Do you want us to accompany you to Hampshire?"

"No. There is a great deal to do here. And I leave it all in your hands." Jacqueline took Emma's hand. "I am so sorry for all the terrible pain my grandson has caused you and your family. I only pray you are able to find your cousin."

Although Emma smiled, her eyes remained haunted by sadness. "If anyone can find her, Sebastian will."

"Have faith, my child." Jacqueline kissed her cheek, then turned and hurried from the room.

When they were alone, Emma drew a folded piece of ivory parchment out of her pocket. Sebastian did not need to see the words to know it was the note they had received from Gaetan that morning. "Without Radbyrne, what chance do we have of finding Charlotte?"

"Gaetan has supplied us with the name of the man who paid Radbyrne to kidnap her."

"A Scotsman by the name of MacLeod." Emma moistened her lips, her gaze fixed upon the paper she held clenched in her fingers. "We do not even have a first name. I cannot imagine how we are to find him."

"I will keep looking until we do find him. If I have to hunt down every MacLeod who ever set foot in London."

She looked up at him, her turmoil visible in her eyes. "Do you honestly think we shall find her?"

"I cannot say for certain. I only know that I shall do everything possible to find her." Sebastian took her into his arms. She wrapped her arms around his waist and buried her face against his chest. He felt the fine trembling in her limbs and understood the effort she was making to contain her emotions. "You must not give up hope, my love. This MacLeod must have been connected in some way with Radbyrne. Someone must know him."

"What of Gaetan?" Emma looked up at him. "Do you think he might know more than he told us in this note?"

"I suspect he told us all he knew." Sebastian took the note from her trembling fingers and read it once more.

Radbyrne sold Miss Usherwood to a Scotsman by the name of MacLeod. I know nothing more of the business. Believe me when I say I had nothing to do with it. For my own part in this business, I am filled with regret. I should have ended it when I first learned of Gaetan's a little more than a year ago. My sin is that I did not. For me it is ended.

"I keep thinking of what Woolgrove said to me. He implied I knew Gaetan. That he was close to me."

"That he was close to you?"

"Yes." Something about this note teased him. Yet the possibility taking shape in his mind could not possibly be true. "Still, I cannot imagine who it might be."

The question and the note kept bothering him

throughout the day. His trip to the hospital to make certain the body identified as Bernard Radbyrne truly was his nephew did nothing to improve his spirits. He gazed upon the ravaged face of his nephew and pondered the question over and over in his mind: Who was Gaetan? The person behind the name. What had caused him to become involved in Gaetan's? What connection did he have to Radbyrne?

I should have ended it when I first learned of Gaetan's a little more than a year ago.

What had happened at that time to cause someone to assume the identity of Gaetan? The answers that rose in his mind were more disturbing than the questions. He returned from the hospital and entered his library to face the task of writing to his relatives to inform them of Bernard's unfortunate passing. As far as Bow Street was concerned, Radbyrne's death had been the result of a quarrel with an unknown acquaintance. That was what the newspapers would print the following morning. Sebastian saw no reason to inform anyone of the true nature of Radbyrne's violent death. Soon after Sebastian returned from the hospital, Dora swept into his library.

"I only just received Jacqueline's note." Dora sank into a leather armchair near the fireplace, as though all the strength had drained from her legs. She looked pale, her cheeks drawn, and dark smudges marred the skin under her eyes. He suspected she had not slept well the night before. "I was out shopping with Arabella. I could scarcely believe my eyes. And here I have arrived too late to comfort Jacqueline."

"Mama took the news well enough. She was more concerned about Aveline."

"Yes. Poor dear Aveline. She shall be devastated. I can only imagine what she must feel at the loss of a son." Dora flicked her handkerchief back and forth beneath her chin. "Still, it was clear the boy was on the path to destruction."

"Yes. He was." Sebastian rose from his desk. He opened the liquor cabinet and poured two glasses of brandy. He handed Dora a glass, then sat on the arm of the chair across from her. He studied her a long moment, hoping he might dismiss the suspicions that ragged at him. "It was a familiar path, was it not? Rodenhurst favored many of the same vices."

"Yes." Dora glanced down into her glass. "It is not kind of me to say, but his death was truly a blessing to our family. I give thanks every day that my sons did not follow in their sire's footsteps."

Sebastian glanced at the dog lying near the hearth. Ulysses had his eyes partially open, as though he wanted to keep on eye on the humans nearby. "As I recall, Bernard and Rodenhurst were very close."

"I am afraid they were." Dora sipped her brandy. "This is excellent."

"I acquired a cask of it while I was at a little inn called the Green Turtle." Sebastian sipped from his glass, allowing the brandy to ease the tightness in his throat. "I have been sitting here writing notes to those relatives who have not yet heard the news of Bernard's death. If not for the fact we have no real way of finding Charlotte Usherwood, I can honestly say the person who killed him did us a service. Relieved me of the question of what to do with him once I found him."

"Yes. It is a shame about the poor girl. Still, I wonder if Bernard would have been much help in retrieving her. From what I gather, he sold her to someone, the way he sold you to Hollington." Dora leaned toward the fireplace, reaching a pale hand toward the coals burning in the hearth, as if she were cold. "It was fitting, the way he died. There in the drawing room of the place where he had tortured so many girls."

The words struck with a certainty he could not ignore, just as he could not ignore the horrible weight pressing against his chest. "How did you know where he had been found, Aunt Dora?"

She flinched as though he had come up behind her and surprised her. "What do you mean, how did I know? Jacqueline told me about it, of course. In her note."

He wished he could believe her. Yet all the annoying pieces to this puzzle snapped into place, shaping a picture he loathed. "She could not have told you because she did not know. I simply told Mama that Bernard had been murdered. She did not ask for details, and I saw no reason to burden her with them."

Dora stared at him, her eyes wide, her lips parted. "You must be mistaken."

"I wish I were. But I am not." Sebastian rested his glass against his thigh. "Rodenhurst was Gaetan, was he not? He and Bernard began the business. And you discovered it soon after your husband died."

Dora's lips parted, then closed. She looked away from him, her attention fixed on the glowing red coals in the hearth. "Strange, I have gone over and over in my head what I should do if you discovered the truth about me. Yet I had not expected to feel such relief. It is as if a weight has been lifted from my chest."

And placed upon his, Sebastian thought. "Why did you continue with Gaetan's? You must have known what type of place it was?"

"Yes. I knew." Dora closed her eyes. "I wanted to end it. But Rodenhurst had drained us dry. I had Arabella to think of. We would have lost everything."

"You could have come to me."

"Yes." Light from the hearth flickered upon the tears leaking from beneath the dark fringe of her lashes. "I had thought to do just that. But there was Bernard, assuring me I need not get my hands dirty. That he would continue as before. And there was so much money. And I was so frightened of what would happen should anyone discover the truth of what my blasted husband had done. I could only imagine what Bernard would do should I betray him. The simple truth is that I took the easy path instead of doing what was right."

"The easy path." Sebastian rubbed his brow, wishing he could find an easy solution now. "You shot Bernard."

"Yes. He was intent on murdering you. I could not allow him to cause any more trouble. I decided it was the best course of action." Dora sat back in her chair and smiled at him. "And now, my poor lad, you are faced with the problem of how to deal with me."

Sebastian looked her straight in the eye. He had known this woman all his life. Until this horrible business she had never harmed a soul. "What do you imagine I should do, Dora?"

"That is a terrible question." Dora stared at him, looking as vulnerable as a girl at her first ball. "I would like to forget I ever learned about Gaetan's. But I suppose you would not see fit to allow me to walk away from this unscathed."

"I do not believe you will walk away from this unscathed." Sebastian leaned forward and took her hand. "All my life you have been there, telling me how very important it is to be a good man. You are a good woman, Aunt Dora. And now you must live with the knowledge that you allowed Gaetan's to continue. If you had stopped Bernard when you first learned of Gaetan's, Charlotte Usherwood and many other girls would be home now, safe with their families."

"I know." Dora lowered her eyes. "I did all I could to find out where Miss Usherwood was being kept.

But Bernard did not know. Or, at least, he would not tell me." She looked up at him. "I had nothing to do with her kidnapping. You do believe me?"

"Yes. I believe you."

Although Dora smiled, her eyes reflected the ugliness that had been scrawled upon her soul. "What happens now? What shall you do with me?"

"I have no intention of doing anything with you." Sebastian patted her hand. "Your part in this is ended."

Emma sat in the blue drawing room of Andover House, listening to her husband. Although she understood the words he spoke, it took several moments for his meaning to sink past her disbelief. "Dora was Gaetan?"

"Her husband was the original Gaetan. He and Radbyrne started the business." Sebastian crossed the room and sat on the footstool before her chair. "I told my aunt her part in this was ended."

Emma stared at him. "You intend to do nothing?"

"I think she has been punished enough, knowing her silence allowed Radbyrne to continue his ugly business." Sebastian took her hand. "She had nothing to do with Charlotte's kidnapping."

"She could tell you nothing more about what happened to my cousin?"

"Dora questioned my nephew on several occasions. Each time he assured her he did not know what had happened to Charlotte after he delivered her to MacLeod. I was hoping you might understand my reasons for not trying to impose further punishment upon her."

Emma stared at the hand he held close around her own. Although a part of her wanted some revenge for Dora's part in this tragedy, another part understood the mercy Sebastian had shown to his aunt. "I believe you are right. She has already suffered for her crime."

Emma thought of her own sins. "It is important to understand how a person may come to make a terrible mistake. I suppose each of us has done something in the past to hurt someone unintentionally. It does not necessarily mean that person is bad."

Sebastian lifted her hand and pressed his lips to the place above the engraved gold ring he had placed upon her finger. "Dora is a good person, Emma."

"And you are a fine man, Sebastian St. Clair." Emma slipped her hand from his grasp and threw her arms around his neck. The aroma of leather and spices and man teased her senses. "The ability to forgive and to show mercy, is a fine, decent quality."

He held her close. "Is there something wrong, my darling?"

Emma closed her eyes and sought for the courage to tell him the truth. It evaded her, kept at bay by her fear of what he might do when he heard what she had done. "No, my love. Nothing is wrong as long as you love me."

Chapter Twenty-six

Emma ran her fingertip over the gold letters tooled upon the dark blue leather of her latest book. A quiver of excitement always passed through her whenever she held one of her books for the first time. Yet this one just might hold the key to her future happiness.

"I am still amazed by how quickly you managed to write it." John Knightly folded his hands atop his desk. "It is astonishing."

Emma had commenced writing the book soon after her wedding. She had finished it a month after retiring to Sebastian's country home in Hampshire for the summer. They had returned to London for the autumn a few days earlier. "I was inspired."

"It is very likely your finest book yet." Knightly pushed his glasses against the bridge of his nose. "Full of adventure and romance. And, of course, it has a very satisfying ending."

"Thank you." Emma folded her hands upon the

cover of her book. She only wished things had worked out so well in real life. Although they had searched for months, they were still no closer to finding Charlotte than they had been the day she had been kidnapped. "The story was very close to my heart."

"I could tell. The character of Lord Amesbury is obviously patterned after your husband." Knightly cleared his throat. "I would think Lord Andover would be quite pleased with the way he is portrayed in this book."

Emma cringed inside when she thought of what Sebastian would think when she finally presented him with the truth. Perhaps it had been cowardly, but she had kept her secret for the past six months. "I hope he does."

"Will you continue to write?"

"I would like to." Emma thought of what her husband might say and do about the knowledge that his lady wife was actually an authoress. "After today I may need to continue writing. We shall see how my husband reacts to the knowledge that he has married E. W. Austen."

In the coach on the way back to Andover House, Emma hugged her book to her chest and rehearsed the speech she had prepared for this day. A speech that included another little surprise too. He would understand, she assured herself. He was a very compassionate man. A kind man. A reasonable man. He certainly would forgive her for this one little sin.

When she entered the house, Foster informed her His Lordship would like to see her in the drawing room. She handed him her pelisse, gloves, and hat, trying to appear calm while butterflies fluttered in her stomach. She gripped her book and proceeded to the drawing room, her mind wrestling with the task that lay ahead. She opened the door, stepped inside, and froze. The book fell from her stunned grasp with a soft thump upon the carpet. Yet she did not notice. The sight before her seized her attention.

Sebastian stood near the white marble fireplace in conversation with a tall, dark-haired man. Although he was a handsome man, the stranger held her attention for only a moment. Her aunt Marjorie was sitting on the sofa near the fireplace, beside an elegantly dressed lady, a woman who looked a great deal like Charlotte.

"Emma." The lady rose and rushed across the room. She threw her arms around Emma and held her close. "It is so good to see you."

Emma remained frozen, as if turned to stone, her poor abused brain afraid to believe the miracle hugging her so close. Her heart pounded fast and hard, sending a wave of dizziness over her. She clung to the specter, and whispered, "Charlotte?"

"Yes, dearest." Charlotte pulled back and gripped Emma's arms. "My poor dear Emma. Mama has told me the horrible ordeal you have been through trying to find me."

Charlotte did not look at all as though she had been through an ordeal of any kind. Her golden hair was swept back from her face in an elegant fashion, with wispy curls about her temples. Delicate embroidered lace trimmed the high neck of her pale blue cambric gown. The same lace formed twin flounces at the hemline. It was a costly gown, obviously made to fit Charlotte's slender figure perfectly.

"Oh Emma, our prayers have been answered," Marjorie said, from her place on the sofa.

"Charlotte," Emma whispered. "You look wonderful. What has happened? Where have you been? How did you come to be here?"

"It is a little complicated." Charlotte glanced toward

Sebastian and the handsome stranger near the fire-place. "First, I must introduce you to my husband."

"Husband?" Emma forced her numb legs to move while Charlotte ushered her toward the men. Charlotte was married. She was alive and well and married. Thought chased thought through the turmoil in her brain. Charlotte's voice buzzed in her ears while she was introduced to the dark stranger. She barely heard his deep voice when he told her how happy he was to meet her.

Emma looked at Charlotte. "Did you say his name was Maxwell MacLeod?"

"I would watch myself if I were you, MacLeod." Sebastian took Emma's arm. "When that look appears in her eyes, someone usually gets hit with something."

"You need not stand there grinning at me." Emma turned her attention from her husband back to Charlotte. "How in the world did you end up married to the blackguard who had you kidnapped?"

"Lord Andover told us all about your attempts to find the MacLeod who paid that dreadful Bernard Radbyrne to kidnap me." Charlotte slipped her arm through MacLeod's. "But let me assure you, Maxwell had nothing to do with my kidnapping. The truth is, we were both merely pawns in a demented scheme that his brother devised to put an end to Max's engagement."

Emma fixed MacLeod in a steady stare. "Your brother had my cousin kidnapped."

Maxwell smiled, faint lines flaring at the corners of his pale blue eyes. "I am afraid he did," he said, his deep voice colored with a soft Scottish burr.

"He dragged me all the way to New York." Charlotte patted her husband's arm. "And Max was perfectly dreadful at first. You see, he thought I was working right along with his brother. I had to literally hit him over the head to make him see reason."

Sebastian laughed softly. "I see it runs in the family."

Emma resisted the urge to poke him in the ribs. "I cannot imagine how in the world your brother might think he could use Charlotte to end your engagement. Yet it would appear he succeeded."

"My brother met Radbyrne when he was in London visiting my Uncle Angus. Apparently Radbyrne was boasting one night of how easy it was to acquire any woman a man might want, even a lady of quality. That gave my foolish brother an idea, an idea that required an innocent lady of quality and a few doses of sleeping powder."

"A few doses of sleeping powder?" Emma asked.

"Yes." Charlotte glanced up at her husband, in a way that spoke of secrets shared. "The first time I met Max we were both awakening from a deep slumber. You see, after I fell asleep, his brother John placed me in Max's bed. It was a most astonishing position in which to find myself."

Max wiggled his brows at his wife. "Not to mention revealing."

Charlotte swatted her husband's arm playfully. "Max was a perfect brute. But somehow he has grown on me."

Emma stared at Charlotte, amazed at the story unfolding. "John did not harm you?"

Charlotte shook her head. "John was very polite. He is actually a pleasant young man, though a bit spoiled. But he did not harm me in any way. Unless one considers the mean fashion in which he used me to gain what he wanted."

"I was engaged to marry, and John thought the woman better suited him. On that score he was right." MacLeod covered the hand Charlotte held upon his arm with his own. "Although he caused a great deal of trouble, and for that I am deeply sorry, I can say with all honesty that I am grateful for the chance he gave me to meet Charlotte."

When MacLeod looked down at Charlotte, any doubt about his role in this crime vanished. Emma knew that look; she often saw it in her own husband's eyes. It was the look of a man deeply in love with his wife. Charlotte had that same enchanted air about her.

Emma took her cousin's arm. "You shall have to tell me everything."

"I have been thinking that it will make a splendid story," Charlotte said. "It could quite surpass *The Valiant Viscount.* Or perhaps even *The Wicked Duke.* I am certain there is very little you need change."

Emma's stomach clenched. She glanced at Sebastian, hoping the reference to E. W. Austen was lost on the sharp intellect of her husband. Sebastian looked completely unconcerned while he strolled toward the door. He bent to retrieve the book she had dropped, then examined the cover. "*The Magnificent Marquess.* This must be the latest E. W. Austen."

Emma's heart stopped, then surged into a headlong gallop. "Yes, I just . . ."

"You were very quick about this one," Charlotte said. "I saw copies of *The Wicked Duke* in New York. It is very popular there as well."

A muscle flashed in Sebastian's cheek. "Apparently there is no end to E. W. Austen's accomplishments."

Emma wished the floor would simply open up and swallow her. Yet floors seldom did what one wanted. "Charlotte, you . . ."

"No end at all. I always knew cousin Emma would manage to . . ."

Emma threw her arms around Charlotte, before her well-meaning cousin could say something that might destroy any chance she had for dealing with this problem on her own. "It is a miracle. To have you back," she said, loudly enough for everyone to hear. Then she lowered her voice to a whisper for Charlotte alone. "Please, not another word about the books."

When Emma drew back, she saw a hundred questions in Charlotte's blue eyes. Fortunately her cousin refrained from finishing her thoughts on the topic of E. W. Austen.

Although Emma was eager to finally unburden herself of the truth, she decided to wait until they had retired for the evening before facing her demon. She did not wish to spoil Charlotte's homecoming with the unpleasant sight of the Marquess of Andover tossing his deceitful wife out of the house.

During the day, the excitement of having Charlotte back home—safe and sound and happy—had been tempered by the very real fear Emma could not dismiss. When she had the chance to tell Charlotte what had happened during her absence, her cousin had been horrified to learn she had very nearly exposed Emma. Although Charlotte had assured her that Sebastian must forgive her for writing *The Wicked Duke*, Emma did not have the same confidence. What would Sebastian say when he learned the truth?

After preparing for bed, she joined Sebastian in his chamber, as was her habit each night. This night she found her husband lying in bed, pillows propped beneath his back while he read a book. A book with a dark blue leather cover. He glanced up when he noticed her. "I am beginning to understand what you like about this E. W. Austen."

The breath in her lungs turned to lead. She could feel it pressing upon her heart. "Are you enjoying it?"

"E. W. has quite a flare for the dramatic." Sebastian looked down at the page. "This is the description of the hero, Simon Sinclair: 'He was the most compelling man she had ever seen. Too bold in appearance to be dubbed handsome by the conventions of current fashion. He was instead truly magnificent in a purely masculine sense of the word. Tall and broad shouldered, his physique conjured to mind statues carved of white marble. His was a beauty born of power and grace. A beauty enhanced rather than spoiled by the scar that sliced through one black brow.' "

Emma paused beside the bed. Light from the lamp on the bedside table poured over his broad bare shoulders. His black hair was tousled as if he had just combed his fingers through the silky mane. The contrast of dark masculinity against a background of plump pillows encased in white silk would have added a beat to her heart, if that organ were not already beating wildly. "Simon sounds quite appealing."

Sebastian continued looking at the page. "It would seem E. W. Austen has some type of obsession for creating characters with scars through their brows. Since this man is tall and dark and a marquess, I suspect I shall have people assuming this Simon is actually patterned after me."

"At least Simon is a true hero. Loyal and honest and honorable." Emma tried to moisten her lips, but her mouth had turned to parchment. "A man who understands the quality of mercy. Simon is a true knight errant."

Although Sebastian kept his gaze upon the book, she could see his lips curve into a smile. "I find this book a trifle strange. Simon was falsely accused of murdering his fiancée. There is even something in here about a book being published that painted him as a scoundrel. Why do you suppose E. W. Austen would write such a book when it clearly comments on *The Wicked Duke?*"

"I suppose E. W. Austen regrets very deeply the harm she caused you. No doubt she wishes she had never written that horrible book."

He looked up at her, his expression unreadable. Yet she sensed an expectancy in him. "Why do you suppose she would regret writing a book that has become so very profitable?"

"Because she loves you more than anything in the world." Emma forced air past the anxiety threatening to strangle her. "Because she hopes you can forgive her for writing it in the first place. And for not telling you about her occupation in the second place. Can you?"

Sebastian allowed her to hang a moment before he took her hand and tugged her toward him. She sat on the bed beside him, still uncertain what he meant to do with her. "I was wondering when you were going to get around to telling me about your literary endeavors."

She stared at him, his words taking a moment to pierce the veil of fear clouding her mind. "You knew?"

He smiled, a little grin that held just a glimmer of triumph. "I have known for about four months now."

"Four months! And you never said a word about it?"

He shrugged. "I thought it was better to allow you the chance to tell me."

"You thought it was . . ." She leaped up and glared down at the grinning rogue. "Do you have any idea the torment I have been through? Wondering if you would despise me when you discovered the truth. Of all the despicable things to do, that is one of the most odious I have ever heard of."

He drummed his fingers upon the book. "And what

do you call convicting a man before you even met him? What do you call writing a book that blackens a man's name?"

"I thought you were guilty, so I never thought I was blackening your name. The rumors about you were all so . . . so . . ."

"False."

"Compelling." She folded her arms across her chest and glared at him. "You should have told me that you knew."

"I was waiting for my honest wife to tell me."

She flinched at the direct assault on her honor. "I would have told you. I wanted to tell you. I just . . . I was so afraid you would despise me if you knew what I had done."

"Despise you? How could I ever despise you?" His deep voice wrapped around her, lush with a vibrant need for her he did not try to disguise.

He offered her his hand. Emma did not hesitate; she knew a chance for redemption when she saw it and she intended to take it. When she rested her hand in his, he closed his fingers around hers and drew her down upon the bed. "You forgive me?"

"You managed to drag your family out of poverty with your talent and your perseverance. Although I am not fond of *The Wicked Duke*, I am more than a little fond of the brave lady who wrote it." He tucked a lock of her hair behind her ear. "I love you. Now and always."

"I love you, so much it frightens me at times." She lifted his hand and kissed his palm. After a moment she lowered his hand to her belly. "There is something else I need to tell you."

He winked at her. "I suspect the babe shall be born near Easter."

She released her breath in a quick huff. "You knew about the babe as well?"

He flexed his fingers against the pale blue silk of her dressing gown. "We have been married for a little more than six months, my love. Any man who is not aware of the times his wife is indisposed is a man who does not frequently make love to the lady he married. Since I do not fall into that category, I am well aware of the fact that you have not been indisposed these past two months, and I was quite certain of the reason."

She pushed against his shoulders. "Arrogant brute!"

"Infuriating termagant." He cinched his arms around her waist and dragged her down on top of him.

She struggled a moment, then settled upon the hard plane of his chest, her cheek nestled against his shoulder. She nuzzled her nose against his skin and drew in the warm masculine scent of him. Perhaps it was reckless to try for more happiness than she already possessed, yet she could not resist. "I suppose you will frown upon any further books."

He stroked her hair. "If it makes you happy, then I see no reason why you should end your days as E. W. Austen."

"You truly do not mind?"

Sebastian pressed his lips to the tip of her nose. "As long as I am always your hero."

Emma slipped her arms around his neck. "Always."

DECEPTIONS & DREAMS

DEBRA DIER

Sarah Van Horne can outwit any scoundrel who tries to cheat her in business. But she is no match for the dangerously handsome burglar she catches in her New York City town house. Although she knows she ought to send the suave rogue to the rock pile for life, she can't help being disappointed that his is after a golden trinket—and not her virtue. Confident, crafty, and devilishly charming, Lord Austin Sinclair always gets what he wants. He won't let a locked door prevent him from obtaining the medallion he has long sought, nor the pistol Sarah aims at his head. But the master seducer never expects to be tempted by an untouched beauty. If he isn't careful, he'll lose a lot more than his heart before Sarah is done with him.

___4582-6 $5.99 US/$6.99 CAN

MacLaren's Bride
Debra Dier

BESTSELLING AUTHOR OF *LORD SAVAGE*

She is a challenge to the gentlemen of the ton, for they say she can freeze a man with a single glance of her green eyes. Meg Drummond wants nothing to do with love—not when she has seen her own parents' marriage fall apart. And though she promises to marry an Englishman to spite her father, she has to find someone to win her stubborn heart. Then Alec MacLaren charges back into her life, unexpectedly awakening her deep-seated passions with his wicked Highland ways. He kidnaps and marries her out of loyalty to her father, but once he feels her tantalizing body against his, he aches to savor all of her. He knows he needs to break through the wall of ice around her heart, gain her trust, and awaken her desire to truly make her...MacLaren's Bride.

___4302-5 $5.50 US/$6.50 CAN

Dorchester Publishing Co., Inc.
P.O. Box 6640
Wayne, PA 19087-8640

Please add $1.75 for shipping and handling for the first book and $.50 for each book thereafter. NY, NYC, and PA residents, please add appropriate sales tax. No cash, stamps, or C.O.D.s. All orders shipped within 6 weeks via postal service book rate. Canadian orders require $2.00 extra postage and must be paid in U.S. dollars through a U.S. banking facility.

Name_____
Address_____
City_____ State_____ Zip_____
I have enclosed $_____ in payment for the checked book(s).
Payment <u>must</u> accompany all orders. ❑ Please send a free catalog.

The Rogue and the Hellion
CONNIE MASON

When an audacious highwayman holds up his coach and points a pistol at a rather crucial part of his anatomy, the Marquis of Bathurst has a critical choice to make—give up his dead brother's ring or lose the family jewels. Gabriel decides to part with the memento, but he will track down the green-eyed thief if it is the last thing he does.

When the most infamous member of the Rogues of London takes her in his arms, Olivia Fairfax knows his intentions are far from honorable. Gabriel's hot pursuit makes her pulse race, but is he after a lover or the hellion who dared to rob him at gunpoint? Either way, Olivia knows it is her turn to hand over the goods, and she is ready to give him both her body and her heart.

A Rogue's Promise
PEGGY WAIDE

Eighteen years ago, deep in the mountains of China, Lady Joanna Fenton's father found a sacred statuette. The two-headed dragon is reputed to beget prosperity, but for Joanna, it brought nothing but heartache. Her father was obsessed with the piece until his death. Now, the artifact itself has disappeared.

Her search takes her to the darkest establishments of London, and from those rat holes steps a friend. He is a smuggler, a man who has forsaken his noble heritage for the shadows. A man who sees that she does not belong. And when MacDonald Archer swears to aid her, Joanna realizes the secret to true happiness is not in Oriental charms or spells, but in love.

Belle

Melanie Jackson

With the letter breaking his engagement, Stephan Kirton's hopes for respectability go up in smoke. Inevitably, his "interaction with the lower classes" and the fact that he is a bastard have put him beyond the scope of polite society. He finds consolation at Ormstead Park; a place for dancing, drinking and gambling . . . a place where he can find a woman for the night.

He doesn't recognize her at first; ladies don't come to Lord Duncan's masked balls. This beauty's descent into the netherworld has brought her within reach, yet she is no girl of the day. Annabelle Winston is sublime. And if he has to trick her, bribe her, protect her, whatever—one way or another he will make her an honest woman. And she will make him a happy man.

___4975-9 $5.99 US/$7.99 CAN

WANTON ANGEL
SHIRL HENKE

A devoted artist, Elizabeth Blackthorne has earned a scandalous reputation with her free-spirited ways—she's been known to run about unchaperoned and even pose nude. But Englishman Derrick Jamison is uncharted territory. He acts like a foppish dandy, yet his disarming smile and intoxicating touch inspire feelings more extraordinary than her reputation.

Beth Blackthorne bowled him over the day they met. True, the fire-haired American didn't mean to topple him, but the fit of her lush body against his completely distracts Derrick from his mission of spying against Napoleon. From the United States to Italy to England, her siren call beckons until he knows the only safe harbor he will find is in her arms.

Major Wyclyff's Campaign

KATHERINE GREYLE

Pity, plain and simple, makes Sophia accept the offer of marriage from the dying Major Anthony Wyclyff. He is wildly handsome, but nothing will overcome her happiness at being "shelved." Then the blasted man recovers! Not that she wishes anyone ill, but Sophia expected to bury the earl's son along with all her childish hopes and dreams—not tumble with him in the dirt. He is resolved to claim his bride, though, and he forces her into a strategic retreat, to act in ways she never dreamed. His flanking attack brings him closer than ever—into her manor, her parlor, her bedroom—and the infuriating officer wagers he'll have terms of surrender within the month! Yet when his fiery kiss saps her defenses, Sophia swears the only terms she'll hear are those of love.

FOR THE LOVE OF LILA
JENNIFER MALIN

Tristan Wyndam envisions his late mentor's daughter as a bespectacled spinster, not a youthful beauty. He anticipates helping to secure her inheritance, not escorting her—unchaperoned—to Paris. But Lila Covington defies all his expectations—and society's conventions. She does, however, promise to protect his reputation on their illicit journey, striking the Englishman speechless. Then she dons britches to play the part of a boy and her enticing legs render him breathless. But it is her performance as his wife that leaves him senseless with desire and longing for all the trappings of a real marriage. Luckily the befuddled barrister suspects he possesses the only lure strong enough to snare a liberated lady: true love.

LYNN McKAY

SWEET DECEIT

Diana Rainville would do anything for her aging, beloved spouse. Even the unthinkable: To protect the family legacy, he beseeches her to produce an heir with another man. Diana trembles in her innocence, but agrees to receive Lord Baldwin—for her husband, for a baby of her own. But how can she accept the passion she finds in Gavin Winslow's arms? Nothing more than duty can lie between them. Bound by honor, they part ways. Diana tends her ailing husband; Gavin serves his country. Those tempestuous nights have not only created a child, however—a union has formed. And when disaster strikes, Diana and Gavin prove that the ties binding a man and a woman, ties that promise to last a lifetime, are sanctioned first and foremost by the heart.